The Shadow of a King

The Shadow of a King

C.M. Gray

Published 2016 by Creativia
Paperback design by Creativia (www.creativia.org)
ISBN: 978-1534655485
Cover art by Adriana Hanganu from http://www.adipixdesign.com/
Visit C.M.Gray's blog at http://www.author-cmgray.com/
Twitter: @cgray129

Please note that I use British spelling throughout. You will see doubled letters (e.g. focussed), ou's (e.g. colour) and 're' (centre) as well as a few other differences from American spelling. It's also typical for British writers to use single quotes for speech rather than the double quotes familiar to American writers. I hope this will not spoil this story for any American readers.

Dedicated to my children
Dylan & Yasmin

Contents

Introduction

Thanks so much for choosing to read The Shadow of a King, I do hope you enjoy reading it as much as I have enjoyed writing it.

I think I should point out to readers of Shadowland, the first Uther story, that, The Shadow of a King, is not a direct sequel, but is a 'standalone' tale incorporating some of the later events in the life of Uther Pendragon. Although it isn't strictly necessary to have read Shadowland before this, I would, of course, recommend that you do!

The Shadow of a King is a work of historical fantasy, not historical fiction, so being fantasy, I get to throw in a few strange and fantastical things to entertain myself as I'm writing and for you as a reader; I hope that's going to work for you.

As it is historical, I try to use as many of the known 'facts' of the time as I can, but this is the time known as the Dark Ages, because there are very few facts and written accounts with which to work. These were the years, roughly speaking, between 476–800 AD when there was no Roman emperor in the West and their empire was ending. However, before they left, the Romans, and especially Caesar, wrote much about the British tribes, how they lived and how they fought.

Within the tribes, their history was mostly of the oral tradition with stories and legends told by travelling bards around crackling fires on dark nights. Much of what I draw upon to form the basis of my book comes from the old stories and legends of Uther, stories that these bards may well have told. Eventually, they were passed on and then written down hundreds of years later in books like the Mabinogion, a collection of eleven ancient Welsh tales that were transcribed around the year 1400 AD from tribal folklore.

We know that the bards were Druid trained for twelve years to recite stories, histories, poetry and songs upon the Isle of Mona, which was known as Ynys Mon in the old British tongue as well as current Welsh or better known these days as Anglesey Island. It lays a little way off the north-west coast of Wales. The bards in the tribal days would travel among the villages and settlements reciting their stories, singing their songs and telling the news of the time. They were the town criers or newspapers of the age bringing news and information to people who had little or no contact with the bigger world beyond the horizon.

I have written The Shadow of a King after researching and reading some of the legends handed down by the Bards. It is worth noting that a legend is not a myth, but a folk tale with some historical grounding that has been retold over the years. The historical grounding within The Shadow of a King is that Uther Pendragon did exist. His name was first mentioned in the Historia Regum Britanniae (History of the Kings of Britain) compiled by Geoffrey of Monmouth, a Welsh cleric who lived between 1100 and 1155 AD. Geoffrey claimed he was merely translating into Latin a far more ancient text, which makes it legend. Whatever the case, it is from this book that most of the poems and stories regarding the exploits of Uther and Merlyn and even Uther's more mythical son, Arthur, have come. Certainly it is where I have based a lot of my story, with a very tongue in cheek offering of what might have taken place if these legends had indeed taken place, for who is to say what actually did happen, these after all were the Dark Ages and the Druids were... well, ask Uther about Druids...

Oh that I could see to the Other Realm –
that I could learn the magic of the Ancients.
Oh that the secrets of the Druids
could be whispered in my ears
that I might know their beauty and their power –
that I might love again this land
and hear the voices of the Goddess and the God
in the trees and in the rivers.

Damh the Bard

Chapter 1

Glastening Abbey - AD 472

'No… please, do not move him. The King is not to be moved… I beg of you.' The nun stepped in front of the advancing warrior and pushed her hands against his chest, hindering his passage further into the dimly lit cell. 'There must be some mistake… the King is gravely ill.' She was flustered, almost beside herself in her wish to turn these intruders around and see them gone. 'The Abbess is not here, she sleeps now, but she left instructions that he cannot be disturbed… you may kill him.'

The warrior looked down at the small figure blocking his path. Her gown, as with all of these nuns, was a covering from head to foot of coarse black wool, stained and showing signs of many repairs. This nun was gazing up from beneath her cowl with a look of abject horror at his intrusion. Her pale white hands fluttered ineffectually against his stained and dented breastplate; then she glanced towards her charge, the lone figure that lay upon the cot within the damp, dark cell. Beside the cot, a single stub of candle was set upon a small table, its light reflecting from a thick torc of twisted gold, the dull metal gleaming in the candlelight; the candle guttered in the invasive draught sending shadows dancing along the rough, stone walls.

'Spirits preserve us, what a piss-hole,' the warrior whispered under his breath. Rats were moving close by, he could hear them, squeaking and rustling amongst the floor rushes in the darkness; the whole place reeked of vermin. This was a godforsaken place, even if it was an Abbey. Rank with the smell of rat piss, burning herbs and rotting flesh, but it was still an improvement on smells around the gathering of tribes he had so recently left. The Abbey was deathly cold, but at least it was out of the incessant, drizzling rain. The warrior raised a hand and rubbed absently at the knot of wires, shaped into the form of an intricate cross that hung between the ends of his own, somewhat thinner, gold torc at his throat. The cross was not a Christian emblem, but something far older, a connection to the ancient spirits of the land. For like many of his ilk, the warrior was still a follower of the old ways. He had not yet been won over by the honeyed words or threats of certain damnation delivered by the priests, should they not turn their backs upon their ancient Gods and follow the one nailed God. He didn't like nor trust them. Touching the cross had been an unconscious reflex to ward off the evil that he felt dwelt within the Abbey. He had not wanted to come here this night, but then fool's errand or not; he would do the Druid's work and so be it.

With a sigh, he removed his helm and brushed his fingers back through long, greying hair. It was thinning badly as the gesture rudely reminded him. He was tired, weary to the bone, truth be told, and his arms felt heavy from a clash with a Saxon raiding party during the dark hours of their riding to the Abbey.

They had met upon the wooded road, both groups startled to come upon the other, neither wishing to tarry yet both needing to pass the other. After a brief period of both parties shouting and taunting each other, each attempting to force the other to turn and run, they had fought, which of course had been inevitable. The clash had been brief and violent, but on this particular occasion, they had not taken any losses and sustained only one small wound to a member of their party. The Saxons, once past the Britons and heavy with raided goods, had fled towards their own border; it wasn't deemed prudent to pursue them considering the mission the Druid had tasked them with.

Drawing a deep breath, the warrior calmed himself. 'My name is Sir Ector, and I am sorry, lady, I surely am, but there is no mistake. My orders were spoken by the lips of the Druid Merlyn himself; our King must rise.' Turning, he threw his helm back into the hands of one of his men, gently brushed the sobbing nun to the side and approached the low sleeping pallet.

While he dropped to one knee beside his King, his two companions entered fully into the cell, bringing with them dampness and the sharp smell of the rainy dawn that had settled on the metal of their mail and armour.

'Sire.' In the inadequate light from the flickering candle, Uther Pendragon, High King of the Britons, appeared for all the world as if he may already be dead. Sir Ector studied the dying man and felt the small light of hope that he had been desperately holding onto, begin to dim, this surely could not be a man who within days would be leading a mass of warriors into battle. It would be some kind of Christian miracle if the King ever rose from this pallet again unless it was to be taken to his funeral pyre.

'Sire.' Sir Ector studied his King for some sign of life, some indication that he was hearing him. Yet there was nothing. The King's skin was white and mottled, hanging upon his bones as if it were made up of gossamer layers of autumn leaves, dry and yellow in the candlelight. The closed eyes of Uther Pendragon, eyes that were once so fierce and full of pride, were sunken back into their sockets, seemingly lost within the shadows of his soul.

'Uther, can you hear me, or is it that you are already walking in the Shadowland?' The room was silent as all within watched anxiously for something. Reaching out, the leather and metal of his armour creaking, Sir Ector placed the back of his hand close to Uther's mouth, holding it still for a few moments as he felt for breath. As he moved his hand up to the King's brow, the eyes fluttered open, and Sir Ector drew back sharply.

'Forgive me, Sire. I would not have disturbed you, but...'

The eyes blinked several times as the King returned from wherever it was that his soul had travelled, possibly to the gates of the Shadowland itself? Turning his head, he cast about the dim cell and finally found the features of the kneeling warrior. 'Ector?' The voice was weak, brittle, yet more than just the whisper Sir Ector had been hoping for, Uther Pendragon still lived.

'Sire, forgive me... the Druid has summoned you to the battlefield. He tells that the spirits have spoken to him, and it is time for you to lead us once more.' Sir Ector turned and gestured. One of his men stepped forward, and together they went about the task of gently raising the King to his feet.

It was a shock to find that Uther Pendragon weighed no more than a child. The King was pulled upright to hang limply between the two warriors. His head lolling down against his chest, the dirty white tunic he wore coming to just above bony knees, the heavy woollen leg wraps falling untucked about his ankles. Sir Ector began to wonder anew if these pitiful remains were just some hollow shell, an empty husk of the man who had once united the tribes of Britain, his former King, his friend. Had he witnessed life in the dying body, or had the King's soul merely turned back one last time before finally moving on? Despair returned to fill him once again, a fear that both the spirits and the old Druid might be wrong.

They dressed him quickly in warm woollen clothing and then placed a heavy cloak about his shoulders, then shuffled out of the cell with the nun's shrieking protests following them into the rush-strewn corridor.

More nuns arrived, drawn by the commotion, and it immediately became more difficult to manoeuvre with their charge as now several holy sisters began to wail and protest at seeing their King being moved.

The Abbey had originally been built as a fortified home by a Roman governor and was one of the only stone-built buildings in the area. A former chieftain had moved in when the Romans had left and then finally it had been gifted to the nuns by Uther when its previous owner had lost both favour, and then his life, in the King's court, but that had been some time ago. It was a narrow, dark labyrinth of halls, rooms, and passageways, with much wooden construction added to the former building over the years. Old and in a state of advanced neglect, it was damp, the thatch of the roof green and black with mould and mildew, the rooms and passages teeming with mice and rats. As they pushed past the nuns and moved through the confines in search of the main passage, the mixture of aromas became even stronger, mould and decay, vermin and unwashed bodies, concoctions of herbal medicines and communal cooking.

The spluttering torches that the warriors held sent a confusion of shadows ahead of them making it difficult to find their way out to where they had left their horses.

It was Sir Ector who led them, still pushing aside nuns who wept and implored him to take the King back to his rest. They sought to bar his way and confuse his direction, but he pushed on. And so, after much confusion and no little time, it was he who was first to emerge into the damp, but thankfully, sweeter chill air of the new morning.

Towards the east, he could see that the dawn sky was growing lighter low on the horizon, and it was just beginning to chase away the clinging darkness within the small enclosed square of the Abbey where they had left their horses.

He stopped; the rain pattering against his armour. Lit by the light of flickering torches that spluttered in the drizzling rain, twenty or so nuns sheltered beneath the eaves to the sides of the courtyard. However, it wasn't the nuns that had caught his attention and brought him to a halt, it was the tall figure dressed in black who stood alone in the middle of the open area, hood raised against the rain. As soon as they had emerged carrying the slumped body of Uther, the figure had raised its arms, palms out to bar their way. Somewhat startled, Sir Ector held up his torch aware of others coming out of the Abbey behind him. He was relieved to see the figure was no spirit, but as evidenced by the slim white wrists, that it was a woman, almost certainly the Abbess herself.

'What madness do you bring to our Lord's house?' she hissed. 'The King is dying. Does he not warrant your respect in these, his final days? Has he not done enough for his people that you must steal him away in the dark of the night? In the name of our Lord God, I tell you that he cannot be taken, he is the King. You will return him to his rest and leave him here to pass in peace.'

The Abbess stood unwavering, defying the heavily-armoured group to depart carrying their burden. Behind her, horses skittered and moved nervously, alarmed at the sudden raised voice and flickering torches. Eyes wide and staring, their warm breath clouded in the chill air, they continued to shuffle, the sound of their hooves clattering on the stone cobbles echoing strangely about the enclosed place, which only brought them more distress. They were big horses, bred for battle in open fields, not confined spaces such as the Abbey's courtyard and they were unusually skittish. The tribesman holding their reins in both hands, whispered soft promises and affections to them, pressing his face into the muzzle of the biggest, a mottled roan, as he tried to reassure them. The horse tapped the ground with its hoof and snorted, but his efforts seemed to calm them.

The Abbess was a tall woman and, as her position dictated, she was accustomed to being obeyed, yet after a moment's hesitation, whatever spell she had woven broke and Sir Ector and his men pushed past ignoring her and headed towards their mounts. The Abbess watched, her arms slowly returning to her sides as the King was hoisted unceremoniously up upon the back of one of the horses. He swayed in the saddle, yet somehow managed to keep his seat as his feet were thrust into the stirrups and then lashed into place. His eyes were closed as the warriors moved around him. As he began to slump forward, Sir Ector and one of his men quickly moved in to pull him back upright and then held him while an oak plank was set against his back and a length of flax linen wrapped tightly around both the King and the board, securing him erect and in place. The Abbess walked forward, dropping the hood of her cloak as she did so, and placed a hand upon the King's leg in a strangely familiar gesture. Long hair as black as her robes framed a striking face that appeared ghostly in the predawn light. Reaching up, she thrust an object into his hands, just as they were being tied to the pommel of the saddle. She felt him grip the object as the rough hemp of the rope dug into the flesh of his thin wrists.

'Go with God, Uther Pendragon, and I pray that the spirits may also be with you through this day. It seems your tasks among us may never be complete. I fear your people ask too much of you.' With a hand covering her mouth to stifle a sob, the Abbess stepped back into the company of the weeping nuns.

Armour was attached to the King; greaves for his legs and a breast-plate to cover his chest. Over this was placed the heavy wool cloak that was tied in place around his body to protect him from the rain and also to shield the ropes that held him in place. The tribesmen all mounted, and in a final gesture, Sir Ector produced a golden crown from a bag set behind his saddle and tugged it firmly into place upon his King's lolling head. Preparations complete, he finally looked across to the Abbess.

'I am truly sorry, Morgana, but you know this is Merlyn's doing and not mine. I would let him die with dignity, here with you, but Merlyn says that he has communed with the spirits, and they call for the King to lead us in battle one final time. You know I cannot argue with either the spirits or the Druid.' Without waiting for a reply, he kicked his horse into motion, and the five mounted men clattered out into a cold grey dawn, the sound of their departure disturbing a host of crows into flight, the birds rising like winged smoke from an old dead elm to circle raucously above them.

The Abbess walked to the gateway and watched the riders go, four men moving at a trot, whilst the fifth bounced from side to side, appearing stiff and ungainly as they rounded the Tor and passed the muddy track that led up to holy Avalon.

'Close the gates.' She waved impatiently, and two nuns rushed to do her bidding, dragging the large, heavy gates closed with an echoing boom, shutting out the world of man.

One of the nuns stepped forward. 'Mother, we must pray for the King. Our Lord God shall cast his light of protection over…' The Abbess held up a hand as the rest of the nuns gathered around her expectantly.

'Sisters, you must indeed pray for our King, assemble in the chapel. However, I shall make my own preparations and then retire to my chambers and pray alone.' She clapped her hands, and the nuns moved off into the dark Abbey while the Abbess headed towards a separate doorway, intent upon devotions of her own.

His body did not feel his own. Shapes and sounds drifted to him as if through a fog. It felt as if he were constantly falling, turning around and around, yet never landing nor coming into contact with the ground, just a never-ending drop where he spun and spun yet felt no need to scream, it was as if he were watching from afar. The consciousness of Uther Pendragon sat well behind the clouded eyes letting the sounds of cheering, calling and crying wash around him; it was all a dream that he would either awake from and laugh at, the absurdity of it all… or, perhaps, he may never wake again, it mattered not to him.

'Is he dead?'
'No, he is not dead.' Sir Ector glared around, spat with distaste and then raised his voice above the murmuring of the gathering crowd. 'Uther Pendragon lives and has come to lead us to victory against the Saxons.' Standing up in his saddle, he shouted out above the heads of the gathered tribesmen, *Step aside and make way for your King.* The growing huddle of battered warriors moved reluctantly to either side as Sir Ector, and his men led the horse carrying Uther Pendragon through their ranks and towards the cluster of pavilions set at the highest point on the hill. Wiping a sheen of wetness from his face, Sir Ector glanced up at the blue and white encampment on the hill above them, the wet pennons upon the pavilions as limp and lifeless as the gathered tribes.

There was less mud on the higher ground, but a direct route up the slope would mean more chance that the King might fall, and that could not be allowed to happen. He guided his charge towards a gentler, more winding path upward and they plodded on, trailing warriors that were keen to see the return of their King. Sir Ector looked back at the men traipsing after them through the mud. They were filthy and wore a ragtag assortment of armour, crests, and colours. Each man carried either a bow, a sword, or the majority, a spear; none walked unarmed. They were tired and disheartened, but not yet defeated. He realised that the sight of their King had already sent an energy amongst them that he had not seen for many long days. Glancing up he saw that even more men and women were running in from the outer shelters as news that the King had returned reached them and still more from the far woodland where those less fortunate had been sheltering. He glanced across at the white, unconscious Uther Pendragon as he swayed and rocked with the movement of the horse and wondered, not for the first time, what magic the Druid was about to unleash.

It was a terrible thing to be doing to a King, to the man he had stood beside, fought beside, eaten and laughed beside as he had risen from being a snotty kid with a big sword to the unifier of the tribes after his brother had died. The fact that Uther had been raised in an Iceni village was also a point of honour of course. As leader of the now landless Iceni, since the Saxons had forced the tribe to leave their ancestral lands, Ector knew his place was beside the King. He had known it was his place to bring him back if anyone was going to do it, but it hurt him to see the man, his friend, his King dying like this. To see him struck down, so close to death and yet not crossing into the Shadowland to be with those who had passed before him, it was not right, it was beyond his understanding, but he knew it was not right.

At the top of the hill, men had begun emerging from the pavilions, drawn by the commotion that the King's entrance had caused. As yet, he couldn't see the Druid, but he knew he would be there. They moved on.

It didn't take long to get to the top and more level ground, and as soon as they reached it, Sir Ector let out a sigh of relief that his King hadn't fallen backwards into the mud on the climb up. He tugged on the reins of Uther's horse so that it drew alongside him.

'Sire,' he hissed, trying to keep his voice from carrying. 'Uther... wake. Spirits help you, but wake Sire.' The King continued to sway in his saddle either asleep or dead; it was hard to tell which. Sir Ector muttered an oath and tugged on the reins again as his horse stepped forward. Three men had moved away from the group at the pavilions. They were walking towards them; the youngest already several strides in front of the others. Sir Ector saw the smile of joy turn to a frown of worry. The young man broke into a run and took the bridle of Uther's horse as soon as he reached them.

'Father? Oh, God, what have they done to you, Father?' He glared across at Sir Ector.

'My Lord, you were instructed to...' But the words died on his lips as the other two men arrived. Releasing the reins, Sir Ector sat taller in the saddle, fearing that he may now have displeased both the future King and also the Druid. Yet as he approached, the Druid was smiling, nodding at him.

'Well met, Sir Ector. Fear not, you have done well.' The old Druid moved forward, still smiling at them all warmly as if Uther were fit and well and strong enough to lead a horde of warriors against the whole Saxon nation. Sir Ector glanced at the King, just to be sure he was still the same dying man he had dragged from his death bed, and indeed, with eyes closed and lolling in the saddle, Uther still appeared to be far more dead than alive. The horse shifted, and Uther's head rolled alarmingly.

'Father! You... help me get him down.' The young man, aided by two warriors began to disentangle the King from his mount, while around them, several hundred tribesmen watched in silence. The only man who appeared delighted by the whole spectacle was Merlyn.

'Did you have any trouble at the Abbey, Sir Ector?' enquired Merlyn as Uther's hands were being untied. The King swayed backwards, but Sir Ector quickly reached across and held him upright again.

'No, Merlyn. All was as you said it would be.'

'And Morgana… the Abbess, how is she, did she delay you?'

'She was most vexed at us for retrieving the King,' Sir Ector stared into Merlyn's blue eyes – 'Most vexed indeed, but that was the whole of it.' Warriors were untying Uther's feet from the stirrups, and it was all Sir Ector could do to hold onto the King until he could be lowered gently to the ground.

'No, the King must stand.' Merlyn moved forward as the horses were led away and Sir Ector dismounted.

'My Lord Druid. The King, my father, cannot stand. Indeed, we still pray for some sign that he still lives. I shall want the reason and truth behind this or…'

'Patience Arthur. Have a little faith and find some patience. Believe in your father because he needs you now as much or possibly more than he has never needed you before.' The old Druid, white robes flapping in the breeze and long, grey hair wet and plastered to his scalp, approached the sad King as he slumped between the two tribesmen. Passing his staff to Arthur, he reached out, cupped the King's head between his two palms and then studied the King's face closely. He pressed his forehead against the King's.

'Wake up, Uther. It is time to come back and live in the world of man one last time; I'm sorry, old friend, but you must… awaken.'

As the Druid stepped back, Uther Pendragon opened his eyes, shook the two guards away groggily as if unsure how they came to be holding him and gazed about at the gathered men. A wave of murmurs and cries travelled back amongst the crowd until after just moments, cries of *'the King, the King'*, almost became deafening.

Merlyn stepped forward, took Uther's shoulders, and stared into the King's eyes once again. 'Welcome back Sire. I think it may be best if we had a little talk.'

Chapter 2

Alone Amongst Friends

Uther sat hunched over a bowl of steaming broth, slowly spooning the rich mixture into his mouth, a look of tired contentment upon his face. He was listening with studied interest to Arthur as his son spoke of the months he had been away, of all the raids and skirmishes, and of the preparations they were making before meeting the main Saxon force in the coming days. Uther appeared not to notice, or was perhaps merely unconcerned as much of the broth spilt and soaked through his beard and onto the rough wood of the table in front of him. Around the pavilion, several others, including Merlyn, were content just to observe and witness their King's improving condition.

'The Saxons have been pushing us father. Our forces number less than half that they were a year ago, and yet the Saxon forces continue to grow. Angles are now crossing the water to join them, and the Saxons, under Octa, begin to scorn us as they have never done before.'

Arthur was a serious and earnest young man of just fourteen summers and big for his age. Training with weapons since he was a child had given him broad shoulders and a well-muscled physique. He had the strong jaw and serious nature of his father, but also the soft eyes and understanding nature of his mother, he would make a good King. As he spoke, he frequently glanced across to Merlyn or Sir Ector to confirm his words.

'Octa?' Uther lowered the wooden spoon and glanced from Arthur to the old Druid.

'Octa leads the Saxons here and is the son of a man you once knew upon the battlefield, a certain Hengist.' Merlyn motioned for Arthur to continue his explanation, which the boy seemed eager to do.

'Sir Ector has told me of the day you killed Hengist's brother, Horsa; maybe it will be me that kills Octa?' Uther looked at his son, shrugged and returned to his broth. He and Arthur weren't close, a situation that nobody could comprehend and everyone, including his son, blamed entirely upon Uther. From the moment of his birth, Arthur had lived within the household of Sir Ector, primarily to learn his martial skills, but within Sir Ector's household, he had also been under the direct control and tutelage of Merlyn in preparation for the demanding burden of becoming High King of all the tribes, the Pendragon.

Among the Britons, the placing of a son within another household at an early age was common practice. It was thought it would help to unite the tribes, however, to send a child away at birth was totally unheard of. Little reason had been given for this arrangement, yet Uther had apparently handed the squalling infant into Merlyn's care the very same day Arthur drew his first breath. Because of this distance, Uther had missed much in his son's development, and he was now enjoying the young man's company as he explained a few of the changes in relations with the Saxons that had taken place since Uther had fallen ill, a little more than a year before.

Arthur continued. 'Octa and his forces await us at Valerum, just two days march from where we gather the tribes here. Soon we will march and, God willing, we will finally push them back to the eastern coast.'

'God willing, my son, God willing indeed.' Joseph, the chubby priest who was Arthur's adviser, and very much his shadow, leant forward and patted the boy's shoulder beaming around at everyone. Uther glared at him, and the priest sat back, the smile dropping from his face. Arthur didn't notice the exchange; he was too flushed and excited. 'More men join us daily and now that you have returned to lead us, even more shall come. I am even more assured that we shall treat the Saxons to a stinging defeat.' Arthur smiled around at the assembled warriors, chiefs and elders seeking confirmation of his words. Uther could see that the men were all fond of his son, Sir Ector clapped the boy on the shoulder and calls of agreement came from several others including the simpering priest.

'Our King must rest,' announced Merlyn, using his staff to pull himself up onto his feet.

But Uther shook his head. 'I think I have rested long enough; it is time for me to talk to our men and women.' He stood and then reached out for support as he swayed on his feet.

'There will be time for that tomorrow, Sire,' said Merlyn, looking from Uther to the men, who were all showing signs of concern for their so recently returned King. 'Please, I would ask you all to leave us. I will talk with our King and then he will, indeed, rest.' Before Uther could say anything, Sir Ector took hold of Arthur's arm and led him from the pavilion talking quietly to him, with the priest skipping quickly behind them trying to keep up. The others followed mutely, several offering tidings and reassurances to Uther as they left.

When they had all gone, Merlyn turned once more to Uther. 'Sit down, Uther. You are newly awoken from what I can only imagine has been a long and weary sleep and of course, you are eager to catch up. However, your body is still weak. Let me explain a few things to you... sit, sit.' He gestured to the bench and Uther sank down, pushing the remains of his meal aside and leaned heavily on the table.

'Uther, you have been deathly sick, this I do not need to explain to you. You took a bad wound just after Beltane of last year. You were hunting for boar as I recall.' Merlyn shook his head at the absurdity of the incident. 'As you convalesced, the fevers took you and death almost claimed you, however, because of the agreement that was reached with the spirits when you fought and killed Horsa, we have a little...' - he waved his hands absently in the air and his eyes flared a little as he sought the correct words - '... we had a little opportunity to bend the rules.'

'Bend the rules... bend which rules?'

'Bend the rules of life and death, my friend.' The old Druid waved his hands for Uther to sit still and listen.

'Your son is very nearly ready to take the crown and an extremely fine leader he will become, of this I have no doubt. But this Octa has become somewhat of a problem and Arthur is not yet ready for him. Sir Ector and the others have done their best, but...' - he raised his hands gave a small look of despair - 'we have been losing too many men Uther. We are being pushed back towards the western coast. The Saxons and now the Angles take our lands and our people and make them their own, the tribes of Britain are a dying people.'

'What rules have been bent, Merlyn, what have you done to me?'

'Done to you? Uther, you walk, talk and breathe, whatever it is that I have... done to you, you might be a little grateful, hmm, don't you think?'

Uther slowly shook his head. 'I am never sure when I should be grateful to you, old man. You have played with me all of my life, and I'm sure that any agreements reached with the spirits were not done with my interests at heart, and they were certainly done without any approval from me. Do I not have any say in matters?' Uther rubbed at his eyes and cast a glance at the sleeping pallet. 'I am, after all, the King.' Then a thought struck him, and he turned back to the Druid.

'If I am so badly needed at this time, should I not reclaim Excalibur? If I carry that blade, then surely I would stand an even greater chance of leading our men in victory.' He watched Merlyn intently, his hopes of seeing the blade once more rising as he thought the Druid was in truth contemplating its return. However, Merlyn's face broke into a grin, and he shook a finger at Uther.

'You have carried the sword Excalibur, now it waits for another to wield it, perhaps it shall be your son, Arthur, perhaps another, we have yet to see. But you, Uther, you will never carry that blade again. I shall leave you to rest in a moment but understand this; I sent for you only because your people need to see you riding at the front of our ranks, at the head of our warriors as they go out to fight. If you lead your men in this last battle, I have foreseen that the Saxons will be beaten so badly, that it may take years for them to recover. Arthur needs that time, Uther.' Merlyn stood. 'Your people need that time. We need you to be our King in one final, glorious battle. Welcome back old friend, it is truly good to see you.'

Uther arose slowly, with no little difficulty, as the first light of dawn announced itself by gradually revealing details of the draped cloth that hung over his sleeping cot. Although stiff and still drained of energy, he was, nevertheless, glad that the night was finally behind him. Exhausting, fitful visions had plagued his dreams, wolves, Picts, Merlyn wielding his staff... Arthur and, of course, Excalibur, while all the time he had felt the need to run, to get away, but then, as he turned to flee, he always fell, tripping and falling through the trees of the forest, bleeding, crying and feeling helplessly lost as in desperation he sought for escape.

It took a little time to rise and force his body upright and sitting, and then finally to stand up on unsteady feet. Pushing through the untied flaps of his pavilion, he was met by a brightening day that was, thankfully, free of rain. There was a stiff breeze blowing in from the east, and thick clouds were passing at speed above them, appearing like so many small boats chasing across a river as Uther stared up at them content for a moment to be awake and alive. It felt cool and clean, and there was a palpable air of relief that the rain had finally ceased. As he looked out over the thousands of men, women, children and animals that made up the gathered masses below him, he could feel it; a growing optimism. It showed in the smiles on people's faces that he could see moving further down the hill and despite his bad night of sleep, Uther felt so alive, more so than he had in a long, long time.

'Good morning, Your Grace.'

Uther glanced around and saw a young Iceni warrior standing to the side of the pavilion's entrance, tussled blonde hair and a large hawkish nose that didn't make her unattractive; she was grinning in obvious delight at being in the presence of her King.

Uther smiled, 'Oh, good morning...?'

'Maude, Your Grace. My father was with you at Mount Badon.' She drew herself to order, holding her spear more upright, obviously proud to be guarding her King.

'Maude... good morning Maude. Would you be so good as to aid your King? I am still a little weak from my illness and your support would be most welcome.'

'Of course, Lord.' Maude moved to Uther's side and held out her arm tattooed in swirling blue for him to take, which he did, shuffling forward on unsteady feet.

'The rain has stopped, Sire. I don't know if that was your doing, but it's the first time it's stopped in.... well, it feels like weeks!'

'I assure you, Maude, that stopping the rain most certainly wasn't my doing. It might be something Merlyn could accomplish, I wouldn't put that past him, but I am merely a very frail and mortal King.' He smiled as Maude frowned, and then said, 'I would need to be in far better health to stop the rain and stronger still to make the sun come out.' He laughed as Maude glanced at him with an astonished look on her face.

'Uther, you're awake!' Coming up the hill towards them with his robes hitched up as he walked carefully over the long, wet grass, was Merlyn, beaming happily through his scraggy white beard. 'And I see you are already bringing joy and...' - he glanced up at the scudding clouds - '... and possibly a little sunshine, or is that too much to hope for?'

Uther smiled. 'I've just been explaining to my new friend Maude, that I am not capable of much at all at the moment. I believe that if we are once again about to fight a decisive battle, as you have indicated, Merlyn, then I would like some information so we might turn things to our advantage. Perhaps we can meet Octa a little more prepared than he expects us to be.

Although daylight had long since broken the hold of darkness, the chamber was dim, the shutters still closed, and only the smallest chinks of light were able to enter. The thin, bright shafts speared through the darkness, made whole as they reflected on the floating motes of dust and the smoke that lazily escaped from the small dying fire. The hearth was set in the middle of the room, and its fire had burnt fiercely for most of the night, but the bright flickering flames had long fled along with the supply of wood, leaving just a few glowing embers and a steady trickle of smoke.

The lone figure kneeling before it stared into the last glowing embers oblivious to the lack of light and the cloying, dense atmosphere.

Hers had been a long day and then an even longer night. She had spent most of the daylight hours, scouring the woods and countryside, gathering ash bark, mugwort, henbane and after visiting the hanging tree at the base of Glastening Tor, she had finally located a healthy mandrake plant, a rare find that only the most knowledgeable knew of, probably escaped from some ancient Roman herb garden.

Tradition dictated that the mandrake only grew upon ground that has been touched by fluids released by a hanging man. She knew it to grow in other locations as well, and that it was a rare non-native root growing from original plants brought in by the Romans during their occupation. She had already searched several abandoned old Roman villa sites, but finally, she had found her plant away from the villa, ten paces to the north of the hanging tree and had thought at the time that it was a good omen.

The extracting of the mandrake root took a little more precaution than had been necessary for the other items. After carefully digging all around to loosen the root, she had tied a rope, firstly to the base of the plant and then to her horse, and she had pulled it from a distance, chanting and covering her ears lest the sound of it being drawn should strike her down and kill her. The root once extracted was big and healthy, and resembled a dirty, stunted fat man. Once back at the Abbey, the kitchen garden had provided the final ingredients necessary. She had then eaten a sparse meal and then locked herself away, feeding the fire with the wood and a mixture of the roots, plants and herbs that she had gathered, both to banish the cold and, of course, to bring on the visions that she craved.

Now it was over, at the end of her night. The sweet pungency of the earlier blaze still hung heavy, and her thoughts and mind remained beyond the smouldering residues of the fire, they were currently many leagues away watching the dying King.

Her knuckles whitened as she gripped the last small branch of scented rosemary, twisting and worrying at the green sticks, the pointed, fragrant leaves long lost to the detritus and dust before her.

'He lives, yet remains a broken wretch of a man,' her mumbling voice signalled that she was close to her return. She began to sway, back and forth in time with her words. 'Uther Pendragon, you will... not... escape... your... penance. I shall not allow the Druid... to claim you again.' After a few moments, her eyes fluttered open, and Morgana Le Fay began to weep. Her body shook, and then her frustration erupted, and she pounded her thighs with her fists. The sobbing slowly began to subside, she stopped hitting herself and became still. Opening her eyes, she drew a hand across them to wipe away her tears and noticed the small, broken twigs she was holding. She lay them gently where she judged the fire still held enough heat to make them burn and then sniffed as they began to smoke and watched, her mind drifting a little, recalling her visions.

The King walked, he lived and was, by some strange miracle or Druidic trick, somewhat healthy, assuredly a whole lot more healthy than when she had last seen him, strapped to the back of a cantering horse.

'He still dies and, once he is returned, he shall surely die once more; slowly, in remorse... and alone. There must be cause for him to be returned and for that, he must return, close to death.' Gathering what was left of her energy, she rose from the floor, wincing at the cramping stiffness in her bones, and brushed the dirt and bits of twig from her robes.

The nuns would be finished with morning prayers and already about the many tasks it took to run the small Abbey. Crossing to the window, she threw open the shutter allowing the fresh air to enter and the smoke to depart and leant upon the sill. Gazing out, she brightened a little. One particular task that she kept for herself was the care of the Abbey's small flock of chickens. The prospect of being in the open and collecting some eggs lifted her spirits. With a sigh and a shake of her head at the strangeness of life, be it by the will of God or the eccentricities of the spirits, she walked from her chamber and headed down the dark corridor towards the gardens and waiting chickens. Uther Pendragon would return soon enough; it was inevitable, and when he did, she could get back to the unravelling of his soul once more. Mayhap there was a way that his return could be assured. She became lost in thought, and then her pace became brisker with her decision taken. A journey must be made, and a contract struck.

* * *

Within the central pavilion upon the hill, it was hot, uncomfortable and crowded with Druids, elders and warriors. The air was ripe with a heady aroma of stale exhaled breath, unclean bodies sweating in leather and plate armour and the ever present odour of horses. In the midst of the throng, Uther was starting to feel weak. He had been around men like these and Councils such as this for most of his life, yet this day the atmosphere offended him as it had never done before. His head ached, his back hurt, and he was longing for the release of his pallet, a little silence and the chance to be alone. It felt as if everyone in the pavilion was crowding him, looking for him to provide answers, expecting him to bring about some glorious victory after all their recent defeats. He shifted his position on the rough wooden bench and then pushed back hard against whomever it was that constantly leaned over him.

He glanced back into the bearded, surprised features of Sir Gareth, one of the most eager warriors and he knew, a good friend to Arthur.

Drawing a breath he swallowed the rebuke he had been about to make and offered a smile and a little courtesy. 'Please, Sir Gareth, would you give me a little room.' The young warrior blushed and offered a mumbled apology before stepping back a little. Uther wiped the back of his sleeve across his brow, turned back to the business at hand and tried to make some sense from the information he had been hearing.

'I don't understand why we are just gathering our forces and then marching up to Valerum like so many cattle being driven to market? Explain to me again whose idea was it to fight a battle there?'

'It was Octa, Sire,' muttered Sir Ector.

'In that case, I certainly don't like the idea,' said Uther. 'Why are we doing what he wants?'

Sir Ector cleared his throat and sat a little straighter. 'The Saxon made a challenge for us to meet him upon the battlefield to settle our… differences once and for all. There has been no real battle with the Saxons since you became ill. We clash with them daily in some form or other as they mount raids against our holdings and attempt to force our border and we push them back, but this is the first time we have called to gather the tribes and are ready to form a shield wall.' Sir Ector kept his gaze upon the table where a rough plan of the country had been chalked. It was preferable to raising his eyes and looking into what he knew would be the piercing, blue-eyed gaze from his King.

'Settle our differences? What differences are we settling, Sir Ector? That they steal our land and, once conquered, force our people to bend under their Saxon rule. We strike them back, as we have always done, blood is spilt and on and on and on… This, I trust, has been our main complaint against our eastern neighbours, and theirs against us? You make it sound as if they are inviting us to dance at the Beltane cele-brations rather than enter into battle.' Uther drew a breath and rubbed his eyes. 'We shall continue to clash with the Saxons regardless of the outcome of this battle. Throughout my reign we have made countless truces, fought scores of battles, reset our boundaries and, for a while, they have always honoured those agreements. But then more of their cursed longships arrive, and they seek to force the borders again. What we need is a decisive victory to gain some time so we can make our land our own once again under a new King as Merlyn suggests.' Uther looked towards Arthur, who sat opposite him. The young prince appeared, for a moment, as if he were about to object to the implication of Uther ever giving way to him, but Uther raised his hand to still him and spoke on.

'The land you indicated, the area chosen for the battle... here.' Uther placed a finger upon the chalked table. 'Have our scouts made any assessment?' I assume it favours Octa and his forces?'

'Yes, Sire. They already gather, however, it is on our border, which means neither side should be favoured.'

'I propose we gather our troops in the woodland, here,' - Uther's finger moved - 'to the south. 'How many men, chariots and horsemen do we have to make up our numbers? And what do we know of the Saxon strengths, how do they prepare for our upcoming dance? We need information, Sir Ector. I sorely miss Cal and his wolves right now, but perhaps we can find out a little more before our shield walls clash. Send out the scouts and get us information. It is knowledge that shall gain us our victory over Octa, not just a wall of hacking, thrusting steel, although we will need plenty of that. Let us talk of our forces.'

The Council continued throughout the day, calculating troops, reckoning supplies, comparing strengths and discussing the merits of the terrain around Valerum, until the light began to bleed from the day and bellies in the pavilion started to growl, bemoaning the lateness of a meal. The table was cleared, and those of a lesser rank sent to pass word amongst the men that plans were forming and that their King was preparing to lead them to a great and decisive victory.

For those that remained seated around the long uneven table, mead and ale were brought along with pallets of boar, pheasant and venison. The meal was eaten in the Roman style, from trenchers of thick, substantial platters of bread that were placed in front of each man and the food piled up and eaten from the top of it. The fat, grease and the rich gravy that accompanied the meats, all soaked into the bread, which was torn to shreds and enthusiastically and noisily devoured.

Five days later the tribes began to depart. The camp was dismantled, and the scouts led each tribe to the woodland south of Valerum.

Chapter 3

Gift from a Crow

'His foot. Spirits man, tie it off... hold the horse still or for the life of me...' Uther heard the exchange although couldn't see Sir Ector and the other men as they continued the task of binding him to his horse, tugging him to and fro so he felt as if his head might burst. Humiliating it may be, but with his energies still much reduced, he was most certainly unable to keep his seat for any length of time without the aid of wood and hemp to hold him in place. He gasped as the horse took fright. It skittered and danced beneath him, and he was thrown somewhat violently to the side. It was all he could do to stay upright even though he had already been tied quite securely to the saddle. Thankfully, the beast settled, and he silently gave thanks to the spirits that it hadn't broken away and galloped off and that he had managed to keep his seat. The wooden board was once more in position, holding him stiffly offering a mixture of support and torment in equal measure. It was so tight and unyielding that when the horse moved it pressed into his back and despite the layers of padding, it constricted his breathing, but at least, it kept him in place.

With little else to do but endure, Uther gazed out from under the leather and steel helm that they had put on his head and tried to focus on the constantly shifting images as they spun past in front of him. His fever had returned, his vision was hampered, and it was hard to move his head. After a while, he was aware that he was slipping in and out of consciousness and that his condition, once again, was declining quite quickly, yet he was also mindful that this was a madness that he must endure.

They managed to bring his horse under control once more, and he swallowed the feelings of nausea, forcing his eyes to focus as his view stopped spinning and things began to come into focus. His breathing was rasping, echoing loud in his ears because of the helmet, and he felt a wave of panic that he tried to quell by drawing in slow deep breathes. The men finished with their knots and as they stepped away, the horse calmed now that it wasn't being pushed and pulled about.

'You are secure, Sire.' It was Sir Ector's voice, 'Are you well, King Uther?'

Well... how could he be well? But he knew Sir Ector enough to know that the warrior would require an answer.

'I live, Sir Ector, I live and endure,' he murmured. 'However, you should get us moving before I stop living and simply die of boredom.' He heard Sir Ector laugh, and then he must have moved away to find his own horse.

Uther returned to his own small world, still trying to swallow back nausea; the smell of dung, both horse and human that filled the damp air wasn't helping. He endeavoured to focus on some riders ahead and a rumbling chariot, and felt a bead of sweat trickle down from his brow, tickling him in a most irritating way. He couldn't get to it because his hands were tied quite securely to the saddle. Setting his mind to ignoring it, he concentrated his attention instead past the narrow nose guard of the helm, once again watching the churning throng of tribesmen as they readied for war around him. He drew in a breath, feeling the rope constraints around his chest tighten. The rope was a necessity; he knew that, but the helm wasn't. He hated the helm more than anything else. Merlyn had been smiling as he'd buckled it on, reminding Uther of when it had been passed to him by a crazy old Druid munching acorns so many years ago.

It had been the day after they had experienced a dreaming at the bottom of the Druid's well, Uther had been a boy then, a boy named Usher.

'He gave it to me, and I wore it at the battle of Aegelsthorpe, but I am now sure it was meant to be passed to you, Uther,' Merlyn had said. 'Truth be told I had quite forgotten that I had it, but it made itself known to me and now calls to be worn by its King in battle.' Uther had stared at the Druid, watching the white whiskered face as the buckle was fastened, rocking his head to the side as it was tightened and wondered what he still had planned for him, this man he had once called friend.

Oh, spirits, he was tired, so thoroughly exhausted.

Without warning, the horse broke to the side once again, dancing around in a circle as one of the men struggled to hold onto the reins whilst talking to the horse, to calm it. It was a jittery beast and no mistake, thought Uther. He heard others move in, trying to control his frightened animal and Uther resumed his own private misery, gazing out over the heads of warriors, chariots and horses as they spun past his visor.

The rain had eased at first light following a night where it had fallen relentlessly, drumming on the fabric of the pavilion above Uther's head, lending him dreams of charging horses and thundering chariots, but now it had all but stopped. As the mass of humanity had grudgingly roused themselves, the sun had risen somewhere behind the cloak of clouds to offer a weak and feeble light that barely pushed aside the darkness to welcome this new winter morn.

Uther sighed again, the sound loud in his ears. It was not a cold day, in fact in his layers of armour and cloaks, Uther Pendragon, High King of the Britons, was uncomfortably hot. He glanced up as best he could beneath the helm and watched as clouds in various shades of grey passed leaden and low above them. Uther felt his stomach gurgle. *Oh spirits, allow me to keep my dignity today, don't let me shit myself.* Casting his eyes past the closest horsemen to the encampment, he noticed that the same stiff breeze that was driving the clouds was tugging at the smoke as it rose from the countless fires being abandoned by the moving tribesmen. However, while the air was undoubtedly being purged, he reflected that it still remained somewhat pungent. Uther could smell the horses, the men and the mud, in fact, he realised that his sense of smell felt much sharper than he could ever remember it being before and right now he wasn't sure if this was such a good thing.

The horse moved beneath him, and he realised they were finally setting off. His attention returned to the warriors that he could see in front of him as they formed into ranks and joined the day's march. Men and women who had gathered here, drawn together in his name.

Riders had been sent out days before Uther's arrival. The fighting men and women of the Britons had been summoned from every tribe that remained at war and were still regularly raiding and clashing with the Saxon invaders. Even now, twenty-five years after the battle at Mount Badon, the different tribes could easily be distinguished by the way they dressed, or if their hair was worn long or cut short, how a group all wore beards grown long while another, calling and joking with them, were all clean shaven. Pennons and banners flew in the breeze, and he noticed that more warriors held identical shields that were decorated with the mark or sign of their clan, tribe or lord. The majority still carried an assortment of mismatched weapons and shields, with most still favouring the spear. Uther could see the horses, chariots and warriors daubed with white or blue handprints, swirls and spirals as the tribes had always done to set them apart.

His chin dropped to his chest and he snapped it back up, was he already dead, or was he somehow still alive? It all seemed like a dream he felt so removed from everything, so remote; Uther Pendragon lost this one battle, this time with consciousness, and slept.

* * *

'A woman demands to see you, we found her, riding alone... a woman, she...' The Saxon warrior who had just burst through the wooden door and ducked beneath the thatch of the entrance, now stood shuffling uncertainly upon the reed-strewn floor. He had left his spear and shield outside and was rubbing his hands together absently to dispel the cold. A simple round helmet was clamped down over his head and beneath his thick wool cloak, he wore the green tunic edged in red that marked him as from one of the northern Germanic tribes. Tearing his eyes away from his lord and protector, he glanced about at the other occupants of the large wooden hall.

As a newcomer to these shores, he had never had reason to enter this structure before. It was of far bigger construction and of a more ornate design than any of the other thirty or so huts that surrounded it in the centre of the village and was, therefore, quite a distraction. Glancing to his side, he confirmed the presence on the doorframe of brightly painted carvings. His eyes followed the twisting, moving shapes up the doorpost and then along beams, following them where they were most plentiful on the heavy beam that fronted the upper sleeping platform. Patterns and rune carvings painted in bright, vivid colours that seemed to jump and dance in the flickering firelight forcing his eyes to follow the scene. He could see bears prowling through vines and trees, wolves and deer running, battles raging and twisting and turning, and throughout, were intricate patterns and swirls.

He became vaguely aware of children's laughter, but as he looked to see where they were his eyes were stopped once more by the sight of several impressive shields leaning against the wall. The laughter sounded again, and his exploring eyes finally made it to the far corner of the hut where three small boys were watching him, distracted from their play with an old dog, its muzzle grey with age, its flapping ears were shredded in testament to its years of faithful service as a hound of war. He swallowed and tried to gather his wits, looking now for the familiar figure of his lord.

Close to the boys, two women were working a handloom; they had ignored his entrance, their heads still bent low to their tasks. Tending a large cooking pot that was suspended by a chain over the central cooking fire was another woman. She was staring at him, still frowning at the unwelcome draught that he had admitted into the hall just moments before, the waft of air having released a flurry of sparks in front of her.

The warrior realised with a sense of alarm that his mouth was hanging open and he quickly closed it with an audible click, which made the boys laugh again, they were still watching him, waiting expectantly for the exchange that was about to take place with their father. Feeling a flush of shame, he quickly turned back to his lord, who sat on a bench on the other side of the fire, watching him, waiting for an answer to a question he hadn't heard.

'I said, you found who riding alone? What are you spluttering about? What woman makes demands upon me at any time, especially now at the end of my day?' Octa scowled at the intrusion, but he was warm and content, and truth be told, he was intrigued by a woman who could so unsettle one of his men, even if it was one who still had his feet wet from the crossing. He tried to remember the warrior's name. He was one of the newcomers, come to find his place in this green land so rich in soil and plunder. He watched as the warrior fidgeted with his single, dull metal armband, after finally returning his wandering gaze.

'A woman has ridden in, Lord. She wears the black robes of the Christians and stands like a crow waiting to pluck the eyes from my face. Lord… she has no escort and rides past our guards demanding to speak with you. We turned her away, yet she will not leave and insists upon an audience without delay. She contends that you will speak with her. She talks of aiding you with a wergild, a debt of blood for which she knows you seek payment.'

Octa smiled, now even more intrigued by the distraction of this visitor. 'A woman that dresses like a crow and speaks of wergild? I shall keep my eyes covered, to be sure. However, if she is one of the Christians, I doubt she carries weapons, and if she does, then I'm sure my boys will defend their father.' He laughed, opened his arms and the boys came charging over and leapt into their father's lap. 'Bid her enter.'

The warrior ducked out, pulling the wooden door closed behind him with a bang. Octa hugged his boys and then sent them to play back in their corner, the dog wagging its tail enthusiastically at their boisterous return to its company. He smiled, watching them as they giggled happily, the dog trying to lick at their faces, its huge tattered head, nuzzling them affectionately.

The doorway creaked open again, and a slim figure, covered from head to foot in folds of black cloth ducked low to enter. *This truly is a crow that has come to visit me,* thought Octa as he made the sign of protection, the description was not unwarranted; a shiver of superstitious fear ran through him at the simile. He studied her as the crow-woman slowly stood straight, squinting slightly as her sight became accustomed to the light within the hall, quickly scanning the space about her as she threw back the hood of her cloak.

The woman's skin was pale, made almost white by the contrast of her long black hair and lips shown red from the cold of the early winter evening even in the gloom, she was quite beautiful he realised, but in an unsettling way. Before either she or Octa could say anything, the old war-hound stood and took a pace towards her, hackles rising as it gave a low, threatening growl, the ageing pet once more the hound of war as it readied to protect its charges from the intruder. For a moment the people in the hall became silent, and then the animal took another step towards her, its growl growing louder. She cast a quick glance in his direction, before raising a hand towards the dog; the index and little fingers extended while the rest of her hand clenched into a fist. Her head tipped forward and, as she stared at the dog, she made a small keening sound and slowly lowered her hand. The dog responded immediately, tail dropping, it slowly sank to the ground and lowered its head between its paws and then whimpering, it shuffled back to the protective embrace of the three boys.

One of the women working the loom hissed and made a sign of protection while her companion picked up a knife and made to rise, but Octa was already on his feet.

'Witchcraft? You bring dark magic to my hearth?' He advanced towards the visitor, the long blade of his seax held before him, but as he got closer, he saw she was smiling.

'I bring no magic into your home, Lord Octa. A simple trick to confound an old dog. I apologise, I do not wish you, nor your kin, any insult or injury; I am at your mercy.' She bowed her head and spread her arms wide in formal supplicancy. 'The fact of the matter is that this evening, after travelling almost all of the day, I come to you tired and unprotected, seeking only to bring honour and victory to you and your people.' Octa lowered his blade and, after a moment, waved towards the fire, indicating that his visitor should sit, which she did with obvious relief, plainly exhausted from her journey.

'You are a guest in my village and in my home, and as such I welcome you, we were about to begin our meal, you will join us.' It was said as a statement of fact rather than an invitation. He signalled to the woman tending the fire and watched silently as first a bowl of steaming meal stew was offered and then a smaller bowl of warm apple wine was poured and set before his guest.

'I thank you for your hospitality, Lord Octa.' The woman sipped some of the fragrant brew and then placed the bowl in front of her. 'I am the Abbess Morgana. I lead a small group of sisters in the worship of our Lord at the Abbey at Holy Glastening. Are you familiar with our Abbey my Lord?'

Octa accepted his own bowl of stew and then nodded. 'Although I have not yet been there, we know of the Abbey, because...' - he waved his hands as he thought of the correct words - 'our... contacts... have told us that your King Uther is there dying, yes?' He fished out a piece of eel from the bowl and gnawed the meat from the central bone before tossing it towards the dog. The old hound lifted its head to glance towards the offering, but then went back to sleep, giving a low whining sigh, Octa shook his head.

'Until recently, King Uther was indeed a guest at our Abbey, in fact, he was under my personal care.' Morgana took another sip of the wine and then set her bowl down and smoothed her robe. 'Now, however, the King has risen. He was summoned by the Druids and has now returned to his warriors. As we sit here enjoying the heat of your hearth, he is preparing to lead the tribes against you and your men when you meet at Valerum.'

'How can a dying man lead troops? The reports that I received claimed that he was standing at the gates of the Shadowland, that his light was almost gone from this world... were those reports incorrect?'

'Your informant did not lie. The King has been gravely ill and had almost passed. I did not think there was anything else that could be done for him. His spirit had faded, he had not taken sustenance for many days, his body was weak and he was more than halfway towards death.'

'Yet he now walks and leads men to battle, this half dead King? Something is not right with this; your Druids have enchanted him with their spells.' Octa gazed into the flames of the fire. 'And why do you, a Briton, come to me with this news? Do you seek to profit some favour or plead with me? To perhaps gain some kind of promise that we will not raid your Abbey for its gold and silver or turn me from my task of making this a Saxon land?'

'There is no gold or silver at Glastening and I seek no favour from you, Lord Octa, I come offering you information and ask nothing from you in return. I know you have wergild, a debt of blood to collect from King Uther, he killed your uncle, Lord Horsa, when you were still a child and I have heard it said that you have long wished this debt paid. I bring you information, but I have my own reasons for doing this. I will have the King returned to my care before you kill him and you will help me accomplish this.' Taking a small clay bottle from her cloak, Morgana leant forward and held it out. Octa sat back and stared down at the flask for a moment before glancing up questioningly at his guest.

'There is a grove to the west of Valerum that is sacred to the Druids; your raiding parties will no doubt know of it. The King will rest there before he meets with you in battle, or perhaps after. I do not know which, but I have seen that he will be there.' Morgana waved a hand dismissively. 'Anyway, there is a pool in the grove into which you must tip this potion. It will only bring an affect upon King Uther.'

'You say you have seen he will be there? You have the gift?' Octa glanced across to the women working the loom; they had both stopped and were listening to the exchange. The elder of the two gave a barely perceptible nod, and Octa returned his attention to Morgana. He stared into her eyes for a moment and then, reaching out, he took the bottle. 'Let us hope he visits before the battle commences, this half dead King of yours is a bad omen... an evil omen. I care not for your motives in this, but we will treat him to your potion and may Loki choose to cast him down.' He smiled, studying his guest. 'You didn't start fluttering and crossing yourself at the mention of one of my Gods, yet you wear the black of the Christian priests and you have that,' he pointed to the simple wooden cross hanging from a cord around her neck. 'You are a strange one; you are not like the Christians who come to preach amongst my people.' He smiled and gestured towards the cross again. 'You are not a real follower of this nailed god are you? You, I sense are something more.'

Morgana's hand touched the cross and drew in a breath. 'I follow many teachings, Lord Octa. I find truths and messages come to those who will take the time to listen. Truth passes through many lips, through countless ears and are attributed to many Gods. Yes, I listen and pray to the one God of the Christians, I find it prudent in many ways, but I also listen and speak with the old Gods, for, more often than not, it is they who speak to me the loudest.' She drew back her sleeve to show an intricately inked design that covered her forearm, a serpent that wrapped around and around her arm in writhing coils, only to reappear again to bite its own tail.

Octa studied the serpent, admiring the artistry as Morgana twisted her arm, the snake seeming to move in the flickering firelight. 'I evoked the name of Loki earlier, and it seems that was not just some idle twist of my tongue, for is not your serpent the image of Midgardsormr, which is the seed of Loki? So, you follow the old Gods of my people too?'

Morgana nodded and covered her arm.

Octa smiled. 'Sometimes the Gods put things in our path as some kind of test, they play with us and make for us challenges, and then they drink their mead and ale while they wager against each other, laughing at us as we try to determine what they would have us do. You have brought me such a challenge and I feel their eyes upon us at this very moment seeing which way this game shall be played. You know that I cannot disappoint my Gods.'

Chapter 4

The Half Dead King

'The King has been wounded, he bleeds. Bear him from the battlefield lest this day of victory is wrought with the sorrow of his death.'

Uther heard the words amongst the screams and cries of battle, felt the pain, which was a sudden, bright, stabbing light through the fog of his understanding and could feel his lifeblood as it pumped wetly from his wounded neck in thick, sticky, throbbing beats.

Unable to move from still being strapped to his horse, and incapable of seeing properly thanks to the limitations of the helm that had, ultimately, saved him from a mortal blow, Uther Pendragon allowed others to guide him from the field. If anything, it was a release from a day where he had felt little more than a garlanded piece of meat, displayed like a stuffed swan on the Samhain feasting table. A day spent as a painted figurehead paraded up and down the battlefield as ranks of screaming warriors shouted and screeched their encouragement, which had almost, but not quite, covered the taunts and insults being hurled from the Saxon ranks just beyond, as they writhed and howled behind their own bristling wall of shields.

'Half-dead King,' those Saxons had called him, and he had felt it, half-dead and little more than half-alive. With his breath rasping loud in his ears, echoing and bouncing around his helm along with the jolting motion of his horse, he had wobbled and bounced behind the fluttering pennons and screaming figures of Sir Ector and the other senior tribesmen as they drove the men and women under their commands into a frenzy ready for battle. He had tried to focus on the warriors through the narrow field of vision offered by the helm, but his head was moving so much that it was hard to focus properly, so eventually he had closed his eyes and tried to find a better place.

He could imagine what was playing out around him amid the noise and chaos. He was aware that the warrior, Maude, rode to his right side, protecting him as best she could, shield raised; while Arthur and his priest, Joseph, had ridden behind them and Sir Ector and his men to the fore. Stones, mud, and fouler things had been the first objects to be hurled from the Saxon ranks to his right, banging and bouncing from the protective shield of Maude, while behind him he could hear the priest whimpering and wailing, complaining incessantly at the futility and injustice of a priest being upon the field of battle.

'I cannot preach to the heathen, nor can I call down the fire of God's justice upon them while we parade like this. It is a mockery of my station to be here; I am a man of God, not a fighter.' The wheedling voice had receded from Uther's hearing as the ranks of spearmen began to swarm forward, taunting both the Saxons and each other as the mead and ale continued to flow, and courage and daring rose to its peak level.

As the procession had turned at the end of the line and yet again made its way forward, the missiles rained upon them once more, along with laughter and mocking insults, which, in reality, Uther knew to be fact rather than insult, for he was indeed a half-dead King. If Uther Pendragon had still possessed just the smallest shred of his former dignity, then surely, it would have withered and died right there without the need for blade or arrow, upon the meadow outside the town of Valerum. Yet he did not die, and he felt no concern for the taunts, for any shred of dignity that he had once possessed had long since been flayed from his soul.

The day had been drawn-out and tiring as the shield walls had finally surged forward to meet and then clashed again and again men and women, faces contorted, screaming and howling at each other. Shields met with a clattering crash that shook the ground and then locked together as the straining warriors on both sides pushed and heaved against one another. Spears and swords stabbed between shields seeking an unprotected arm or leg, a wound that might break apart the opposing wall while axes arced over the top, to hack down upon shield and helm and skull. Blood had spilled and sprayed as warriors drove into a state of invincibility fought in a bloodlust until their humanity returned in a rush and both men and women felt the cold, hot kiss of metal then screamed and dropped away, finally alone in their agony. Many died quickly, while countless others, the less fortunate, continued to live. Their screams and cries of their distress and suffering added to the noise of battle as they collapsed to the cold mud and grass of the field, victims of the most terrible of wounds, trampled into the muck and blood beneath the feet of the battling horde.

Horsemen and chariots joined the throng, the shrieks and cries of both men and now horses filling the air until Uther had at once become deaf to it all, concentrating instead on the steady gasping of his own laboured breathing as he continued his desperate internal struggle to endure.

Given its freedom, his mind stepped back from the world of man and journeyed back to a time in his youth, to a time where he rode on the battlefield of Mount Badon, upon a war chariot with Samel, a friend now long since dead. It was while he was trying to remember where the little warrior had fallen, that a Saxon arrow had glanced across the cheek guard of his helm knocking his head to the side before slicing deeply across his neck. The searing pain had shocked him from his musing, to be enveloped once more in the stench and roar of battle. His horse was turning wildly in circles beneath him as he cried out, but the sound was lost amongst the cacophony of noise and madness around him.

'The King has been wounded.' His attention snapped back. He could now tell that the voice giving instruction was that of Maude, the warrior who had attached herself to him back at the camp. He felt her horse bounce against his, steadying it, and her face, creased with concern, loomed into his vision as she assessed the damage that the arrow had caused, pulling his head to the side to expose the wound. A cloth of some kind was pushed against him and held while Maude, and now another warrior tried to direct Uther's horse away from the battle.

'We have all but defeated the Saxons, King Uther.' Maude rode beside him, holding the cloth to his neck. 'It was as the Druids proclaimed, your presence has brought us a great victory, the Saxons are drawing back, they are leaving.'

The wound was a deep heavy throbbing that all but consumed him. He wondered if each beat of his heart was forcing more of his lifeblood to the surface to ooze from his body yet it mattered not a whit to him, he realised. His task had been completed; they could lay him down to die in peace now, and Arthur could reign in his stead without the imminent threat of a Saxon invasion. As the sounds of battle receded, Uther Pendragon tried to surrender his life and instead, sought a path to the Shadowland.

When next he became conscious, it wasn't the sounds of battle that greeted him, nor, to his immediate regret was it to the sights and sounds of the Shadowland, although it was only the realisation that he was still feeling some considerable pain that finally convinced him of this. His neck burned where the arrow had sliced him, but this he only added to the multitude of various pains and discomforts that were his to suffer. The light was hurting his eyes, so he closed them and drew a deep breath, it was rich, damp and earthy and felt good to his aching lungs. He drew another and listened to the sounds of rustling leaves, soft birdsong, and dripping water and slowly opened his eyes again. At first, his vision was blurred, and he could only register that it was overwhelmingly green in this place. Others were here; he could hear them moving softly only a few steps away.

'Drink.' His head was lifted and a cup placed to his lips. He gazed up into the face of Maude as she tended him and he tried to drink, but couldn't. He studied her, seeing her face dirty and blood splattered, still reflecting an overwhelming concern for him.

'What have we done to you, my Lord? Yet, still you endure.' He watched as a tear trickled down her cheek, carving a track through the blood and grime. 'Please Lord, you must try to drink. We are at

the holy well, close to Prae Tor. You must drink, this is holy water...
it will help to heal you.' She glanced up and began to back away as
another figure bent down beside them.

'She is right, Uther, drink deeply, and all will be as it should be.' It
was Merlyn, smiling happily as if his King was not laying amongst
the fallen leaves of the forest, dying. 'It was as I foresaw, Uther. You
brought us a great victory today. You gave our warriors courage when
they saw you and the Saxon ranks were eventually broken. Even now
they are running back towards the coast, and though I doubt they
will leave our shores, they will, at least, remain within the East while
Arthur is allowed time to mature and take the crown. You have won,
Uther. You have done all we could ever ask of you... drink.'

And so Uther Pendragon drank the water.

'Come to me and gather around my sons.' Octa gestured for the boys
to come, and they leapt up from where they had been busy playing in
their corner. 'I shall tell you this night the story of the Sceadugenga,
the ones they call the shadow-walkers and perhaps also find a story
for you before you sleep.'

The boys ran to their father's fire and sat at his feet, always eager
when he found time to speak to them and truly excited at the promise
of a story. The old war hound, the boys' constant companion, also rose
stiffly to its feet and moved hesitantly to join them, wagging its tail,
aware that it was intruding on a forbidden part of the hall, yet brave
enough to approach because its young masters were already there.

Octa opened his arms in invitation, and the youngest clambered up,
beaming happily at the honour.

'You have heard of them before, and perhaps' – Octa's voice lowered to a whisper – 'perhaps, you have even been close to one yet
never knew it.' The fire crackled, drawing the boys' attention, and the
oldest placed another log on top of the embers before glancing up to
his father to hear more.

'When a warrior has the ability to draw the shadows of the night about him like a cloak and walk unseen through the darkness, he is known amongst us as a Sceadugenga or shadow-walker. Among the Saxon people, the deeds of the shadow-walkers are legendary, for although every boy, and many of the girls too, are trained, almost from the moment they can walk, to hold a sword and spear, few amongst our people are ever chosen to become shadow-walkers.'

'I wish to train as a Sceadugenga, father, teach me,' said the oldest jumping to his feet.

'And me, and me, father, please,' came the chorus of requests from the others.

Octa smiled and motioned the boys to return to their places. 'It is not for me to call you, to train you in their ways. I promise you that I will make warriors of each of you. I will train you with the spear and with the sword, and when the time is right, I will stand proudly beside you in the shield wall, but it is only the shadow-walkers themselves who can take you to the side, if they see that you are worthy, and then train you in their ways.'

The boys exchanged glances, and silent pacts and oaths were exchanged to become Sceadugenga at any cost.

'When the volk, our people, gather around their hearths and fires to bask in the heat and watch the flames devour the logs, we listen to the tales of our poets and scops as they tell their stories of heroic adventure, mighty battles, and the games that the Gods play with us, but boys, we all know it is the tales of the Sceadugenga that we love to hear the most. So train with your spears, fight well with your swords, but if you wish to be a Sceadugenga, move with the softness of the breeze, the silence of smoke, for then you may be chosen to train with the Sceadugenga and become a walker within the shadows.'

Four shadow-walkers had set out from Octa's village. Slipping silently and unseen through the forest and fields with the darkness of the night wrapped tightly around them. They had travelled through three nights towards the tribal lands of the Britons, easily slipping past their own patrols and sentries and passing like mist through tribal villages and sleeping communities. On towards the West and the disputed border with the native Britons they travelled, always by night, faces blackened, their clothing no more than a collection of rags. They rested by day, tucked away unseen amongst the roots and leaves of the forest. Only once they reasoned they must be close to the end of their journey did they emerge from the darkness, to locate their final destination.

Several hours before dawn on the third day of their travels, they abducted a young woman from her path as she walked between two large communal longhouses. They swarmed from between the trees like spreading smoke to envelop her and then silently drew her back into the shadows. She fought because that was her nature, and it troubled the shadow-walkers, fearing the small sounds of the scuffling would be heard and bring others to her aid.

'Hold her,' the hissing voice was urgent with the need to remain unfound. The girl was bucking and kicking in the arms of one of the walkers like a snatched pig and would probably be squealing as much as a pig if their leader didn't have his hand firmly clasped over her mouth. Grasping her head to stop it jerking, he bent down to whisper in her ear.

'Silence child, we are the spirits of the night, we are the ones that fill your darkest dreams, but we will not harm you if you hold still.' She continued to struggle, and he gripped her head even tighter, then lifted it and pounded it on the forest floor three times. 'I... said... hold... still... or I will hurt you. I will cut your throat, we will drink your blood, and you will die this night and never reach the Shadowland.' She stopped her struggles and gazed up past his hand that was still held across her face. Her tear-filled eyes reflected her distress, and he could feel the wet of tears and slimy snot on the palm of his hand.

'We seek the holy well that must be close to here. The place where your Druids gather.' He was aware that his speech would be strange and accented to her, the words these Britons used felt cumbersome and uncomfortable in his mouth, so he spoke slowly. 'Do you know the place I speak of? Is it near?'

The girl let out a small mewling sound and then nodded. She screwed her eyes shut, gathering her resolve and then stared up at him once more. 'We will not harm you girl, not if you place us onto the right path. How far is this place? How might we find it?' The hand slowly relaxed and lowered from the girl's face, and she drew in a breath before snorting back a sob.

'It is close, this place,' her voice was high pitched and shaking, the words spat out quickly in her haste. Her head turned from side to side looking for the others she couldn't see but knew were there in the darkness. 'Don't hurt me... please.'

'The direction, where do we go from here... quickly.'

'Take the northern road, towards Prae Tor. That's the big hill you can see in the distance. The Druids' grove is upon the western slope... please, please don't hurt me.'

The Sceadugenga slowly stepped back from the girl, holding her frightened gaze until the shadows set their cloak around him and he was swallowed by the darkness of the forest.

For a few beats of her heart, the girl lay unmoving, still straining to see the man, not quite sure if he was still there or not and still expecting the stinging slice of a knife at any moment - yet none came. Cautiously, she moved her head from one side, and then to the other, searching the darkness for the men, or spirits or whatever they were, but it was only the shadows and gloom that stared back. A breeze moved through the trees rattling the branches above her and from far off she heard the remote, hooting call of an owl. Fear and relief overwhelmed her, and she collapsed back in a fit of sobbing, finally able to believe that she was still to live.

Some short time later, when she had blundered through the darkness scratching herself badly on branches and bushes, and she had made it back out onto the path, she looked but there was no sign of her mysterious captors, they had disappeared completely. Wrapping her thin shawl about herself to ward off the shivers of superstitious fear as well as the cold, she set off towards the few clustered huts that made up the settlement she had been taken from, not quite sure how she was going to explain her experience.

They came across the pool just as the sky was beginning to lighten to the east. It was as the girl had said, on the western slope of the large hill, set within a small copse of trees. Approaching cautiously, as was their nature, they identified a small hut that was home to the few Druids who tended the pool and, believing that the occupants still slept they made their way towards their journey's end guided by the sound of trickling water.

As they entered the open glade between the trees, they were greeted by an abrupt drop in temperature, and a thin mist that was covering everything, grass, rocks, and water. It swirled about their legs and lapped against the rocky foot of the hill like water in a bowl, twisting and turning languidly, driven by unseen forces that they couldn't begin to comprehend. This was an ancient place.

Cautiously, their leader, a man named Coenwulf, took a few steps forward, probing out with his foot in search of the water's surface. It was hard to distinguish where the water began, and the grass of the glade ended. Even to their night trained eyes, everything was shrouded in near complete darkness, the mist obscuring any features they might have been able to see. The approaching dawn was delayed in this holy place by the surrounding trees, trees which the more they looked seemed to be reaching out across the mist-shrouded surface of the pool as if trying to protect the deep and sacred waters beneath.

'Get this done brother,' muttered the walker closest to Coenwulf. 'Let us leave this place for something sits wrongly with me here. It may be that we offend the Gods with this task, I...' The man shivered and glanced about him. 'I don't like being here. Just throw the potion. Throw the whole bottle in and we can leave.' He watched the shadowed figure of Coenwulf unwrap the small bottle that he had been carrying ever since being entrusted with it by Octa. As he drew back his arm to throw, a noise caused both men to hiss and crouch. Their two companions who had stayed on the approach path to guard against being disturbed dashed in looking for the source of the sound. It had been a low reverberating tone as if a large bell had been softly struck. For a few moments they said nothing, waiting for the bell-like sound to return or something to happen, but nothing did.

'What was that?'

'Shhhh.' Coenwulf held up a hand for his men to be silent, then crouched down to pat the ground around him.

'What are you... you dropped it?'

'I dropped it, yes.' Locating the bottle he held it up to the night sky, moving it around trying to see the liquid inside. He shook it by his ear. 'The top fell out, but most of the liquid remains.' Turning, he threw the bottle out into the centre of the mist and was rewarded with a 'plop' as it hit the surface.

'Most of the liquid remained? Little dropped out? If the top wasn't in there then...'

Another tone filled the glade, and without another word, the four shadow-walkers backed towards the edge of the trees and melted into the gloom of the forest.

Moments later, three Druids rose from the mist and walked to where the bottle had been dropped. They were older men, bearded with long untidy hair and dressed in long faded robes. They moved with an un-hurried ease, the mist parting with a wave of a hand to reveal the stop-per from the glass bottle, a bunched piece of leather still wet from its former contents. Popping the leather into his mouth, one of the Druid chewed it, washing it around making his cheeks bulge as he tried to identify what had been the contents of the bottle and then spat it out. The three huddled together and after a few moments talking in low murmurs they began to chant. The deep chime sounded once more, just as the first rays of sunlight lit the topmost branches of the trees above them.

Chapter 5

A Return to Glastening

'The King returns... the King is coming back... the King, the King, the King!' A flock of nuns ran in, to gather around the gates at Glastening Abbey, eager for a glimpse of the small procession as it approached across the rolling hills. There appeared to be almost a hundred horsemen in the assemblage, along with several carts, chariots, and fluttering pennons. The larger part of the group was stopping to gather some way off while a smaller contingent and one of the carts continued on up towards the Abbey and were just passing the sentinel elm and its cloud of angry crows. The day was grey and cold, a stiff wind causing the riders to hunch in their saddles.

'Do you see him? Does he ride or is he stricken?' The nuns craned their necks, seeking for some further detail to brighten an otherwise dreary day and a dull, monotonous life.

The lead riders carried banners, which could now be seen as white dragons on a dark red background that, as they got closer, appeared to be spitting their flames with each snap of the breeze. The intrusion of the riders as they passed by the sentinel tree sent the crows up in a flurry of feathers to circle above them cawing and complaining.

A bell began tolling its dirge from high in the wooden bell tower, and the sound of annoyed shouting could be heard from inside the Abbey and, as more nuns came out to run across the yard, chickens flapped and squawked to get out of their way. The nuns, as they gathered about the gate, were doing a good imitation of the clucking chickens as they gossiped, chattered and called to each other; the approaching visitors a very welcome respite from the tedious regulation of Abbey life. Morgana, Abbess of Glastening, arrived, hushing and shushing them as she also tried to see some detail of what was approaching.

'Sisters, calm yourselves. Kindly recall that you are daughters in the service of our Lord, not maidens seeking ribbons at the Samhain festival.' She clapped her hands, and the nuns gathered around her appearing suitably chastened and even more like chicks surrounding a mother hen. 'Prepare the King's chamber, and we must be ready lest he has been struck down by some injury upon the field of battle.' Several nuns dashed back inside the Abbey while the rest scuttled behind Morgana, to await their guests.

The first of the horses came through the great wooden arch and entered the old Roman courtyard, the sound of their hooves clattering and echoing around the stone enclosure. Sir Ector was third in line, he pulled his horse to the side and dismounted with no little difficulty and stood swaying before Morgana. He appeared to be stiff and even wearier than the last time she had seen him. Blood splattered the front of his tunic, and he had a dirty rag tied about a wound on his forearm which he favoured, cradling it protectively with his other arm.

'Morgana, a good day to you.' He glanced at her then around the Abbey, clearly unhappy about being back so soon. Stretching his back he gestured towards the open cart that was still creaking and struggling up the small incline towards them.

'Our King is not well again; we know not what afflicts him. He took a small wound on the field of battle, a gash to his neck, lots of blood, but it did not sever his lifeline. If that had been cut, we would never have stopped the bleeding.' He rubbed at his sore arm, then drew a breath and looked her in the eyes. 'The battle was long and especially tiring for him, but whatever it is that ails him now, it is more than just fatigue and a scratch to the neck.' Sir Ector turned at the sound of skittering hooves, but it was nothing, one of his men was calming his horse, the huge animal was highly stressed after the recent battle and obviously unhappy to be within the enclosed courtyard once again; he turned back to Morgana.

'We are both now aware that Merlyn had him under some sort of enchantment, but whatever it was, it has evidently deserted him. The Druid told us to bring him back here and place him directly into your care.' Sir Ector leaned closer: 'Morgana... Uther is dying again. I don't know if you can save him this time. I believe it may indeed be more of a kindness to allow him to pass in some comfort and peace.' The cart finally arrived, and the two stepped to the side and watched as Uther was unloaded and taken into the Abbey under the guidance of several nuns and the grim, sad figure of Maude, the King's protector. Morgana noticed that Uther's armour had already been removed, but that he still wore the dirty stained clothing that he had dressed in prior to battle. His eyes were closed, and he looked as white as the thin shroud with which one of the nuns was trying to cover him, he looked, very much, as if he may already be dead. Laid out on a simple wooden plank, his arms had fallen to the sides and were swaying with the movement of the board; he made a pitiful sight.

'Hurry sisters. Place the King in his former chamber; I shall attend him shortly.' Morgana turned back to Sir Ector. 'You may leave here now, your duty has been done. The King has now been returned into our hands, and we shall care for him. Take your men, your battles, and your blood and leave this holy place.'

Sir Ector took a deep breath, and after a moment smiled and shook his head slightly as if deciding against a parting remark of his own. He and Morgana had never seen eye to eye, and that was not about to change now. He turned and accepted his horse's reins from one of his men, and taking a firm hold of the saddle's pommel, heaved himself back up whilst shouting, *'Mount!'* The sound echoed around the confined space as Sir Ector, followed by his men, turned his horse around towards the gate and spurred it into motion, out into the cold afternoon air to be mocked once again by the crows.

'Lay him upon the cot... carefully sisters, carefully. He has taken enough knocks and offences to his person. We shall care for him now as befits our King.' Morgana watched as the two nuns began to remove the King's soiled garments, being careful to treat their King with the care and reverence he was due. Sir Ector's men had already removed the heavy mail vest, they cut his tunic and surcoat away revealing his linen camisia, the thin undergarment was soaked with dried blood and stuck to his skin. A bowl of water was called for and then placed on the floor beside the cot; a cloth was used to dribble water onto the camisia until it gradually relinquished its hold upon the King's body. The wound itself had stopped bleeding some time past, yet it still appeared red and angry, and when probed it was seen to be leaking a clear, slightly cloudy fluid.

Morgana inspected it, touching and prodding the livid flesh before sniffing at both the wound and then the King's breathe, taking notice of his white complexion and slow breathing as she did. 'We must cleanse the wounded flesh, and if it continues to weep so, then we may be required to cauterise it with a hot iron. For now, use fresh urine to bathe it and then apply a honey salve. We must keep the evil humours at bay.'

'Yes, Abbess.' The nuns continued, gently removing the soiled linen, cleaning the thin, lifeless body with the wet cloth. Morgana noticed Maude standing by the side of the door. The female warrior appeared lost and uncertain of what she was doing there in the cell.

'You do not have to be here, we can care for the King, he is in the hands of God; you have done all you can for him.' For a few moments the girl didn't move, but then she turned towards Morgana and shook her head.

'He was in my care. The battle was finished, he... he did not seem to be so badly hurt.' She shook her head as if to clear it. 'I was assigned to him, and I shall not leave his side. Do what you will to make him well, I will not get in your way, but I am not leaving.'

Morgana frowned. 'As you wish.' She turned back to the nuns. 'I shall prepare a hot infusion; we shall attempt to improve the King's vigour and rekindle the flame of his health. Let us give our King the very best care, sisters. And pray for him as you work, our King now needs our prayers to guide him through this terrible time.' Morgana ignored the King's protector and watched as the nuns worked, and as she did, she smiled, it had taken a little time and no little manipulation, but Uther Pendragon was now back in her care.

The first few weeks of the King's return to Glastening Abbey passed with Uther seemingly unaware of the world about him. His battered and weakened body lay in the damp cell and was cared for by the nuns who cleaned, fed and prayed over him day and night. However, while his body lay still, his mind wasn't bound by the tortures of his flesh. Memories and dreams plagued his spirit, transporting him through a bewildering series of events and improbable dialogues. Some of his past experiences returned to be lived once more, such as his first contact with the sword Excalibur, handed to him wrapped in a dirty cloth by Merlyn and then thrust once more deep into a block of stone to await another. The incredible jolt of bonding with the weapon was relived once again and evoked such a strong emotion that his body had jumped and twitched, scaring the nuns who had been praying at his side. Of course, he was unaware of the distress he had caused his carers and his body had calmed quickly as the dreams moved on so that once again, he was holding his newborn son up to the first light of dawn knowing he must give him up; the still body of Uther Pendragon wept.

Laughter, tears, and screams of anger filled his mind. Flashes of colour, looming faces and flocks of crows, always there were crows. Sorrow and loss overwhelmed him as he learned of the death of his closest friend. How could it have happened? Once again he agonised over the mystery of his friend's death. Oh, Cal... He had found him lying on the pile of sleeping furs, Cal's body slick with blood, so much blood. It looked as if someone had entered the sleeping shelter and speared him where he lay, yet the guards at the door had not let anyone pass, and there was no way an enemy who was set upon murder could have entered unseen. It was one of the greatest mysteries of his time. Yet, only Uther had known of his friend's nocturnal life, when

Cal's mind and spirit had travelled in the body of a wolf. It was the wolf that had been killed, Uther knew that, but somehow the blow had also killed the body of Cal. Uther had never managed to get over Cal's death, even though it was just one death amongst so many that he had witnessed over the years.

Strange hallucinations began to plague him. Evil spirits that laughed and teased him as they tried to pull him towards dark and forbidding places. Fear and panic overwhelmed him as he struggled desperately attempting to break free, and when he did and made to run it felt as if his legs were soft and weak and he found it impossible to place one foot in front of the other. This dream, of course, faded as all dreams eventually did, yet this was sleep not easy to awaken from, and another quickly replaced each wondrous, terrible or delirious dream.

Once, he felt himself completely awake, high in the wooden watch tower of Tintagel fortress. Waves were pounding on the cliffs far below, and a breeze was strong and salty as he gazed out over the great expanse of the sea towards the distant land of Erin. He knew it was there, beyond where the moon shimmered and the clouds gathered low on the horizon. He could tell that Igraine wasn't here, knew she wasn't in Tintagel anymore, for some reason the remembrance of her passing came as a renewed shock, overwhelming him as the grief hit him like a solid hit to his chest and he felt himself fall, out of the window, down through the cold, dark, wet air towards rocks that rushed up to greet him. Yet before he met the ground, his mind turned itself inwards once more, and a Druid was squatting on a rock staring at him, cackling and pointing as Uther swayed upon weak, uncertain legs.

'Thou art the Pendragon.' As the Druid spoke, Uther's gaze was drawn to his lips, wet and red, drawn back in a toothless mocking grin. Small flecks of spittle and acorns erupted with each word, and Uther felt himself step back, 'Thou art the Pendragon, tis true, yet for now, thou art but a half-dead King.' Cackling laughter faded into an uncertain distance as Uther sank away to be embraced once more by his sorrow and his grief.

It was the rain that finally woke him. The soft sounds of it splashing and splattering onto the stones below the small window and echoing up into his cell. Once his mind had identified water, then it was the nagging thought of it, a drink of water so incredibly precious, because his neglected body was so, so thirsty that he was dragged up and out of his dreams.

Returning, surfacing back into the world of man demanded that he had to claw and pull himself upwards as if from a deep, dark well. He struggled through thick veils of consciousness that needed to be parted and pushed away as dreams and distractions sought to hold on to him, to lure him back into their deep, warm, languid embrace. But the thought of sweet, cool water drew him on, each effort to reach the surface taking him closer and closer until…

'Water… water…' He heard voices, he couldn't tell what they were saying, and his eyes remained stubbornly closed so he couldn't see who was close to him. He felt his head lifted gently, and a rough, cold object touched against his lips. Water spilled, dribbling down his cheeks into his beard and he opened his mouth, desperate to feel it enter, and then he felt the cold bite of it pass his teeth, flow over his parched tongue and then trickle down into his throat. Which of course made him cough and splutter, and sent his head spinning.

Once he had recovered, he drank again, this time managing to swallow some without coughing it back up. All too soon it was taken away, and his head gently laid back down. He was exhausted. There were still voices, but he couldn't tell what was being said. His head hurt, it was pounding, and his eyes seemed to be glued shut, he couldn't open them. He reached up with trembling fingers and teased first one and then the other open. Light exploded in his head, and he snapped his eyes shut again, rubbing at them with clenched fists, a low moan escaping his cracked lips. As his head was lifted a second time, he managed to open his eyes, just a little, to see the proffered cup.

'Drink my Lord… please.'

Uther sipped a little more and glanced up into the face of Maude. He stared at her mouth, which was a thin hard line of concern; it was strangely fascinating.

'I shall tell the Abbess that you have awoken, my Lord. They have been praying for you; there always seems to be a few here,' - she glanced about her at the empty cell - 'they must have stepped out. I prayed to the old Gods,' she whispered, 'I knew you would return.' She smiled down at him and lowered his head once more. Uther closed his eyes, the efforts of drinking having already taxed his strength.

As his mind sought rest, his head filled with images of battle and the memories of his humiliating final days, riding tied to his horse as a figurehead for his warriors, and of Maude ever at his side. That his life had come to this, a life that at one time had felt so blessed and charmed as he undertook to bring the tribes together under the single Pendragon banner. Tribes that for years had existed in peace yet had been held apart under their separate identities and subject to the rule of Rome. And then one day, the Romans had departed, just packed up their carts and gone, but Saxons from the continent had been quick to recognise the opportunity. Firstly they had raided, attacking the small settlements close to the coast, killing, raping and burning before taking to their boats and the safety of the sea. But then, once they found so little resistance, they began to arrive in greater numbers upon the shores of what the Romans had called Britain, what Uther and his friends had simply called home, and the Saxons, and then the Jutes, and Angles, began to settle in greater numbers.

Uther had just been a boy, leading a happy, easy childhood in an Iceni village, until through a series of events that still seemed somewhat of a blur, he had found himself rising to become leader of the united tribes. He had gone on to spend many years clashing with the Saxons, trying to force them back towards the eastern coast while the Saxons sought to push the Celts back towards the west while they took full control and settled the fertile lands, first of the Iceni and then the Trinovantes and Catuvellauni. To the frustration of the tribes, more and more boats had arrived every year after the winter storms, each longboat carrying more Saxons, Jutes and Angles from across the sea, - desperate, aggressive people that not only made war but were greedy for the tribal lands. Yet, for the most part during Uther's reign, the tribes had managed to slow and often halt the spread of Saxon rule. They had managed to keep the western part of their lands free of settlers and Arthur still had a Kingdom.

'You are smiling. When I was called to attend you, I thought I might arrive to find you dying, not smiling. You look as though you just kissed the Beltane Queen.'

Uther surfaced from his thoughts and slowly managed to part his eyelids. Morgana was sitting close to his side, wringing out a wet cloth. She must have just wiped his face, but he hadn't felt it.

'Welcome back to the land of man, you have slept for quite some time. I have sent your puppy, Maude, out on an errand. She fusses over you while you sleep and has been spending far too much time in here getting in the way of my nuns, but she will be upset that she was not here when you finally awoke. Where have you been, where have your dreams taken you while you have been away from us, Uther?'

Uther's head was swimming, and his head was pounding. 'I was...' his voice felt weak in his raw, dry throat. 'I was... thinking about Arthur. Thinking... thinking how, despite everything, that he might still have a Kingdom after all this is done. That maybe it wasn't just another battle that will mean nothing, the same as so many of the others seem to have been for nothing when we cast our minds back. I was daring to think that this time, we might possibly have done as Merlyn proclaimed and stopped the spread of Saxon rule, stopped their settlers long enough to...' a fit of coughing took him and pain lanced up his side and pounded in his head as his wounds came back to remind him of their presence.'

'Rest Uther. I have faith that you will heal with our help, but I am a great believer in sleep to aid in that healing. If your body tells you to rest, then do as it asks and sleep. Here, drink this.' She gently lifted his head and held a clay cup against his lips. It was warm and aromatic with the smell of summer pastures and warm, soft hay. He looked up at her as he sipped feeling the warmth spread through his body as it slipped down his throat.

'This is a herbal infusion of my own making,' said Morgana smiling down at him. 'It is a blend of camomile and feverfew to bring you rest, some mint and yarrow to aid in the healing of your wounds and the essence of a few other plants to help loosen the secrets from your mind. Rest and sleep will assist in your body's recovery. However, we must also place no little concern for the healing of your mind and of your soul, and for this we must talk. You will tell me the truth of your life so that we can unravel the mysteries and make you whole, both within this life and also in the eyes of our Lord. You are going to say of how you first met my mother, the truth of what transpired and why she would never tell me what truly happened to my father. This shall be your real healing, Uther, and I shall be your confessor so that you may heal without any guilt upon your soul... are you, perhaps, ready to bear your testimony?'

Uther Pendragon gazed up into the stern black eyes of Morgana and tried to order his thoughts. It felt strange that he would tell all to Morgana le Fey, yet strangely he also felt somewhat compelled. She tilted his head, and he drank a little more of the brew. It continued to warm him, seeping down inside him to send a glow out through his body, and felt good. He glanced up into her kindly face and felt a growing urge to explain everything, all his thoughts and dreams, his schemes and confidences. It suddenly felt that it would be such a relief to purge his mind and body of all the secrets that he carried... and so he drank more.

'What should I tell you? What would I say? You know I do not follow your nailed God. I am a Pagan in the eyes of many.'

'You are the son of God and a good man, Uther. I want to know more of you. You knew my mother of course, but you also knew my father, and I still do not truly know what happened to him, except I am told that he was one of your staunchest allies and was with you when you all took ship to the Isle of Erin. I was very young then, but I remember a warm sunny day, waving and shouting as part of the crowd of onlookers as the ships made ready to sail. It was late in the year, so although the sun was warm, there was a cold breeze tugging at my hair and making all the pennons and banners flutter and flap as the people and warriors gathered on the beaches. I remember you there too. Walking through the crowds talking to people, smiling and making jokes so they wouldn't worry about the journey you were going to make.' She smiled and closed her eyes as she remembered that day so long ago. 'Do you remember seeing me? I was just a little girl back then, of about eight summers. You ruffled my hair and said I was as pretty as the day. All around us sacks and provisions were being taken out to the boats through the surf, it was a wonderful day that I remember so well.' She stopped smiling, her face becoming stern again as she gazed down into Uther's face. 'Yet something terrible happened on that voyage, I know that. You must tell me everything; you will tell me, Uther Pendragon. I need to know, and you need to tell. We have as long a time as is necessary to bleed the poison from your soul, and you will begin by answering an extremely simple question, why was it that you all sailed to the Isle of Erin?'

Chapter 6

A Cleansing of the Soul

'It was Merlyn who called for the voyage to Erin, the quest, and I too
remember it well.' Uther sipped the last of the infusion and let his head
be lowered to the sleeping cot. He was tired, but his mind was also
back at the seashore on a sunny day with his feet crunching through
the stones of the beach, watching as weapons and the last supplies
were being carried through the surf and placed into small skiffs so
they could be paddled out to the larger boats that were waiting some
distance off shore. He could remember the high feeling of excitement,
the people as they laughed, sang and danced. There had been drums
beating and the reedy tones of horns and pipes; it had been more like a
festival rather than the beginning of a dangerous raid against a hostile
people.

'It was all at Merlyn's insistence,' muttered Uther, 'it was all to en-
able a healing, a healing for the land and for the spirits that were lost.
Years before my brother Ambrosius began to gather the tribes, when
the King called Vortigern ruled, the Saxons committed a terrible mas-
sacre upon a group of our people. The story as it has been handed
down and told around the fires during the cold nights of winter, has
been named by the bards as *The Night of the Long Knives*. It carries
this name because all that those few who survived could remember
were the long Saxon knives slashing and stabbing, murdering all, men,
women and children, all as they sat and feasted with the Saxons as
friends. Those Saxon warriors were led by Hengist with his brother

Horsa by his side. Horsa was the same Saxon that led the Picts as they destroyed my village and killed my parents when I was a boy.'

Morgana nodded and sighed. 'I've heard both the story of your village being attacked and, of course, the telling of, *The Night of the Long Knives*, it has been told many times over the years. Also, the story of how you killed Horsa after the battle of Agelsthorpe, they are all well told and often repeated. What I want to hear, is the story that is not well told, I need to hear this, and you need to tell it. Your soul is troubled, Uther, you need to open up to our Lord and me and say what happened, why you went across to the Isle of Erin as the winter season was closing in and on what many thought to be a perilous journey with no hope of success, and I want to know what really happened to my father. I will make another infusion for you, and then you will impart your story, a story in which I might play some small part.'

Uther nodded and watched as she retreated to brew her herbs. Perhaps it was indeed time to lighten the load that burdened his soul, Morgana might not like the story he would tell her, but the Druid could not demand his silence forever, surely. He would begin by explaining of Pendragon Tor, the fortress upon the hill and how the idea of questing was first conceived by Merlyn...

In its seventh season back then, in the year that the priests now tell us has been given a number of four hundred and forty-three, because it is that many years after the death of their nailed God, the hill fort was already becoming quite a formidable construction, although still a shadow of what it would eventually become. Built high upon a previously unnamed hill, it overlooked a great bend of the river Eden on its eastern boundary, while to the west far below was the expanding village of Outhgill.

Uther gazed out, the fresh wind carrying with it the sharp smell of rain of which there had been a lot at that time. He looked up and saw the clouds were still running fast over the high mount that they had named *Wild Boar Fell*. It was named that amongst the warriors because just two summers past, Uther and his men had killed a huge wild boar upon the summit.

The animal had led them a spirited chase, firstly flushed out by the dogs from the lower forested southern slopes, they had run their horses through the trees driving it towards open ground. As the slope had become too steep for the horses, they had dropped down and moved higher on foot, driving the beast on ahead of them until they emerged from the trees onto the higher, open ground and saw their quarry approaching the summit. At the crest of the hill, it turned and regarded them with its small beady eyes. They walked towards it, circling around the huge beast while it fought for breath, its enormous chest heaving to draw in air after the exertion of its run. Its head was tossing angrily from side to side as it turned in a circle trying to see all of the danger around it, slashing its sharp tusks in warning as they approached.

The animal had ended its life high up on the Tor with Uther's spear through its chest moments after it had turned and ran straight at him seeking to break the circle and return to the protection of the trees. For Uther, it had been terrifying and exhilarating all at once. As the memory came back to him, he could still hear the jubilant screaming of his men and the smell of the huge boar's dying breath while it snorted its anger and blood into his face, the spear still twitching and jumping in his hands.

Uther dropped his gaze to the lower part of the wooden palisade that he was standing on, then to the thatch of the long meeting house which was just below him. Pendragon Tor had been constructed in the northern tribal lands of the Brigantes; the site had been chosen shortly after the decisive battle of Mount Badon. Uther had needed somewhere to base himself and this site was far enough away from the newly settling Saxons and was conceived to be neutral ground for the stronger southern tribes, who, he knew, would be quick to anger should their new High King show any sign of favouritism. It was also just a few days travel from Ynys Mon, or Mona as it was known to most, the island home of the Druids, which of course made Merlyn happy.

The construction of the fortress had been made from wood, and wood had been the main material used in its construction as it continued to evolve and grow. Three formidable palisade rings surrounded the central huts and halls; each pieced together out of huge tree trunks that had been sunk into the earth, their tops sharpened to points. It had been cold and muddy in the first few winters, as Beryn and his men had begun the construction of the first defensive ring, and then eventually, the first of the halls. Improvements had continued and as more room was needed, a second and then third palisade ring were constructed. It now made a comfortable dwelling for several hundred members of Uther's court. As he stood high atop the inner wall, Uther was considering the newest addition to the fortifications. Beryn, he could see, was taking the expansion to a whole new phase, a high wall of stone was being built much lower down the slope on the top of a newly dug line of steep earthworks.

'Do we plan on remaking the whole of Pendragon Tor in stone, Master Beryn? Will we ever finish? I must say that this new line of defence is very impressive, yet I fear there is no end to your designs.' Uther watched as Beryn blushed red through his thin straggly beard. The little man had been waiting patiently for Uther as his King studied the landscape of his Kingdom and was visibly relieved to be talking about his new project rather than having to trade pleasantries.

'I merely wish to offer protection, my King. Wooden walls serve well, they have done so for many hundreds of years, yet a wall of stone is surely a better line of defence, worthy of a King and one that can surely never be burnt or broken.' He indicated towards the wall and the masons as they heaved the massive stones up and into position. 'The wall will be two strides thick and will have a gatehouse there, at the road crossing, and two small towers at either end.' He indicated the selected positions with a sweep of his hand. 'No Saxon raiders will ever pass; they will fall against this strong wall and be beaten before we loosen one single arrow, just as the Picts and Scots fell against the great wall the Romans built in the north. This method of building is not, in fact, new, rather it is something the Romans brought to our land and then took their secrets of construction with them when they left, but we have been studying how they cut the stones and how they lay them together and bind them; we have learned much.'

'It is a fine wall, Beryn,' said Uther smiling, 'I shall sleep inside its confines secure in the knowledge that your construction is protecting us and that no Saxon will come to disturb my dreams.'

'Thank you, Lord. With your leave, I shall go to assist the men in selecting the main beams for the gateway and instruct how best to shape them, please excuse me.'

Uther waved him away and then turned at the sound of a shout.

'Uther!'

Merlyn was clambering up the grassy slope of the earthwork towards him, smiling as always as if the world had just made him privy to the best kept of secrets. The old man's hair and beard were both long and now almost entirely white, the breeze blowing them into a cloud of wispy abandon about the Druid's head, which didn't seem to be bothering him in the least. Uther could see him grinning through it, the shine of his blue eyes catching in the morning sun as he strode along, lifting his dark robes up to give his bony knees ease of movement. In his left hand, the old Druid clutched his staff, which was adorned with shells, bones and all manner of animal and bird parts, he thumped it, rattling it down, planting it heavily with every step.

'Uther, I've been looking for you everywhere, what are you doing staring out at honest men working when there is a Council meeting taking place that you are meant to be attending.' He started up the wooden ladder to the walkway, the staff now landing with a *clonk, clonk, clonk*, as he climbed, he was still talking. 'We have plans to make and decisions to take and...' He finally arrived standing beside Uther to look out at the view and had glanced down to see what had been drawing Uther's attention. 'Oh, and why is Beryn building that new wall, is that your idea?'

'Are you telling me you hadn't seen all the work being done down there? I thought you Druids were supposed to be incredibly observant.' Uther grinned at Merlyn's obvious discomfort.

'We see much of what needs to be noticed. Possibly some of the smaller, unnecessary details get past us. Are you so worried about a Saxon attack that you thought a big stone wall was necessary? Though probably not a bad idea, I suppose.'

'It wasn't my idea. Beryn is mostly left to his own devices; he conceived this all on his own. He had some notion to build with stone and so he is, to protect us. We live in dangerous times, and I for one am glad that he is constructing this new wall. A wall that we might live behind in safety, or that we can retreat behind should it ever become necessary. Our people must have a heart that they can focus upon and protect, Pendragon Tor is the heart of our people, and so Beryn is making it a heart that no enemy can strike and kill. Now, tell me, what of this great Council meeting. I don't think I am late... it does seem rather important to you, which gives me cause for worry. What plans are you making now Merlyn? You are not normally so distracted by the meetings of us mere men, what surprises are you going to spring upon us, will you not give me some warning? I am your King after all.'

Merlyn waved his hands about as if swatting at troublesome flies. 'I have no surprises, Uther, fear not. There are, you are right, one or two points that I would like to discuss at some length. This is the first meeting in some time that representatives have joined us from nearly all of the twenty-seven tribes. We even have Gerlois from the Cornovii, a rather troublesome man, so I understand, calls himself Duc of the Cornovii, though in truth, he rules both the Cornovii and the larger Dumnonii tribe to their north. Duc... just as they call their Lords in the tribes across the water... anyway, he arrived at first light. I have been waiting for this Council for some time, and I know you have as well.'

'Of course, I have, it has always been so difficult to bring all the leaders together for Council meetings. However, I wonder if both you and I are seeking the same outcomes and agreements. When we move into the new raiding season after the winter storms, we must be prepared for the Saxon's attacking and prepared as a unified people. They will be in even greater force this year; we know that longboats have been arriving since the winter storms of last year finished, swelling their numbers. I want our people prepared to throw them back and send them running to the sea.' Uther laid a hand on the old man's shoulder and looked deeply into his eyes, a practice he had copied from Merlyn in order to gain another's undivided attention. 'You know that I shall be proposing the structure of our Council as we sit at my new table, we have spoken of it many times, and I hope you will present no surprises for me, Merlyn?'

'Your plan is sound, Uther. I shall support your codes of honour in every way that I can. The Druids are with you, you know that. However, I have a small embellishment that I think will have your blessing.'

Uther frowned, uncertain where this Druidic embellishment might take him and was about to object, but Merlyn waved his concern away and smiled. 'Fear not, Uther. All is as it is meant to be. You speak for the minds and hearts of our people while I shall speak for the spirit of the land and for the Druids. I am merely seeking to weave together all that is important to everyone here, along with all that is necessary to the spirits in the Shadowland. To bring everything together... all so that the wheel may keep on turning as it is meant to turn.' Merlyn started down the ladder, catching and hitching up his blowing robes, so they didn't trip him. Halfway down he stopped and glanced back up at Uther.

'Upon Ynys Mon, we recently completed the rites of oak and mistletoe and have discovered a great necessity, one that can benefit our people and also the spirits. It is this to which I shall address the gathering, so fear not.' He grinned up at Uther.

'As you usually do, you speak in riddles, Merlyn. Yet, I trust you like I trust no other. Let us join with our Council. It should, at the very least, be an interesting meeting.'

'It should indeed, Uther, It should indeed.'

The meeting hall of Pendragon Tor was large as befitted a King. At its centre blazed a huge fire, while shields, lances, and a large boar's head decorated the walls. Flickering torches had been set at regular intervals about the hall so that it was well lit, but also smoky. As Uther entered with Merlyn by his side, his attention was immediately drawn to the far side of the hall where twenty-six men, each dressed in very different styles that ranged from animal skins and coarse wool to oddments of both old Roman armour and newly fashioned plate and leather made by the tribes themselves. They were talking, arguing, shouting and laughing. Uther approached the table where they were all gathered, and they stood and called their welcomes. Uther smiled, and greeted each, in turn, moving about the table until he was face to face with a man he had only met briefly on two separate occasions.

'Duc Gerlois, welcome.'

'My Lord King.' Gerlois brought his fist to his chest in a Roman style salute, and then gestured to the table. Why is it round?'

Uther smiled and walked around the huge circular table to where his own place had been marked with a chair slightly larger than the others. He sat and then ran his hand over the smooth grained surface, delighting in the rich, solid feel of the wood beneath his fingers. 'You don't like my new table, Duc Gerlois?'

The others took their places as the Duc answered.

'I did not say that I didn't like it, King Uther, I merely ask why it is round?' He also stroked his hands over the shining surface, as polished as a pool of winter ice. 'I have seen many fine tables, and indeed, I have one at Tintagel that will easily sit twenty people. This, however, is the first I have seen that is round. Indeed, if we were to sit here and feast then it might be somewhat difficult to reach the platters at the centre.' He smiled at the others seated about him, and there was laughter and several similar comments.

The assembled tribal leaders, or Lords as was the more common title these days, were an extremely colourful and diversified group of people. Gerlois, the newcomer in the group, as he had rarely attended meetings, was a man in his late forties. Once a warrior of some renown, he was somewhat overweight in these his later years. His deep, ruddy complexion was brought about by his love of the strong red wine from across the sea and was covered by a full dark beard that spilt down across a broad chest and rotund belly, he had a habit, Uther noted, of carrying a constant scowl.

Uther banged on the table with the flat of his hand to bring the group to order. 'This, my Lords, is no ordinary feasting table, it was built for a far weightier task than merely displaying food. No, I instructed my craftsmen to construct this table, not for meals, but so that we, the leaders of this land, may sit as equals to discuss the weighty business of building and defending our Kingdom.' Uther gazed about at the twenty-seven men seated around the huge table. 'Each of you represents one of the great tribes of the Celtic nation of Britain. You are the tribal lords, and you have placed me as the high lord, the Pendragon.' There were murmurs of agreement from around the table.

'As you well know, I was raised amongst the Iceni, was placed in their care by my father, King Constantine, so that I would be hidden from his enemies, while my brother, Ambrosius was raised across the water amongst the Romans. As the Pendragon, the Lord of Lords, I now have no one tribe of my own, other than you, the representatives of all the tribes who sit at this table.' He stood up and adjusted his sword, Excalibur, which hung at his side, and walked slowly around the gathered lords.

My wish, when we sit here at this Council table, is that we sit as close to being equals as is possible. I am no Caesar and nor do I desire to be. I have no wish to rule this land alone without your unbiased council. My Lords, you each bring many years of experience as tribal leaders, and so I ask that when we, the leaders of the tribes, gather here... ' - he slowly turned, looking each man in the eye - '... that when this Council is assembled, no single person is placed at its head, for this table... has none. Here we each must be able to speak with equal status without fear of creating offence. Here, at this round table, no one man can be better, no greater status will be given to any one of us for holding larger lands, or leading a stronger or richer tribe, here there shall be no precedence, not even for me, your King. Each of us must be able to speak as an equal without fear of retribution.'

Uther stopped pacing once he had returned back to his own chair, but remained standing, his hand resting on the hilt of Excalibur. He noticed Sir Ector, leader of the now landless Iceni since the Saxons robbed them of their domains, was sitting a little straighter in the chair beside him to his right, while Merlyn, as representative of Ynys Mon and the Druid Council, was smiling and nodding happily in the chair to his left.

'It is my wish that at this great table, the path of our peoples can be planned using free thought and free speech, with honour, with courage, and with dignity.' Once again he took a moment to look around the table and placed a hand on Sir Ector's shoulder.

'Now I know that is possibly asking a lot of you all… considering that according to the Romans we have a history of being a somewhat callous, vicious and warmongering people.' This brought some laughter and noise as the table was banged with hands and fists. 'Yet this is my wish as your King, and I hope that you can all see the wisdom in this action. We must act as one people in our common fight against the invaders with each of us playing his part if we are to survive. We must think as one people and become one force. We are many tribes, yet we are all one people, we are Britons, and these other people who have arrived from across the sea are attempting to overrun and conquer us. Let us work together and see how this might be stopped. Let us find a way for our people to be strong and able to reclaim our lands once more.'

There were renewed calls of support and agreement from all around the great table as Uther retook his seat.

'And so to our first order of business, my Lords, let us each report on what is greatest in our hearts and most eager upon our lips. Let us start with you, Duc Gerlois.'

'The first Council of the Lords is spoken about often,' said Morgana, interrupting Uther's thoughts. 'I know it was where the tribes resolutely became one nation and spoke with one voice. It must have been extremely problematic before that meeting.'

Uther looked up at Morgana as she held the bowl out for him. He noticed Maude sitting in the shadows behind her; the girl must have slipped in while he was talking, he hadn't noticed her, his mind so distant as it travelled the misty roads of his past. She seemed happy to see him awake, and he tried to smile at her. Leaning forward, he sipped from the rough earthen bowl Morgana was holding and felt the warm liquid ease a path down his dry throat, the fragrant steam tickling his nose.

'It was almost impossible before these meetings. Every Lord, who had called himself a King, before we drew the tribes together had his own ideas about how things should be done; there were so many differences and feuds between the tribes. Our warriors couldn't mount any meaningful defence; we couldn't gather a significant number of warriors from different tribes together to meet a strong enemy. I was their King, the Pendragon, yet at that time, I was still trying to persuade a group of different tribes to come together. That table... it was simply a large round table, yet it made our people one.' Uther coughed, and it was a few moments before he could speak again.

'It was Merlyn that really gave that Council a purpose at that meeting. All because of an event that had taken place several years before; *The Night of the Long Knives*, as it was known.' Uther coughed and felt a wave of dizziness flow through him. He closed his eyes and felt himself drift back into a sleep filled with memories of the past. Once again he was a boy sitting by the flickering flames of the huge central fire in the meeting house back in his village, surrounded by his family and friends. Calvador was beside him, and he could feel the rise of excitement and awe as the bard who had arrived at the village earlier that day began the telling of his story, arms waving sending his shadow climbing the wall like a great, dark spirit, his eyes flashing around to include everyone in his tale. This bard was good, better maybe than most that had visited the village, but any bard, good or bad, was cause for the villagers to congregate and be entertained, but this one, Uther remembered, was an exceptionally good one...

Chapter 7

Night of the Long Knives

Night of the Long Knives

He was an older man with streaks of grey in his long beard, which he wore twisted together in a thick plait. To the amusement of the children and many of the others in the room it was decorated with any number of sticks, bones, and shiny things. A mass of wild, unkempt hair sprouted from his head, giving the appearance that it had a life of its own. It floated and flowed in waves and clumps and through the flickering light of the fire, it seemed as if a cloud had been attached to his head.

A Druid trained upon Ynys Mon through twelve long years of study; this bard had served his time and some. He had travelled through the tribal lands for more than twenty years since leaving the island, practising and perfecting his craft.

Jumping and spinning to gather their attention, he had called his introductions and given news and greetings from the tribes and villages through which he had travelled, and now he was promising to tell a tale to entertain all those who had assembled and were now suitably hushed, save for the passing of ale and mead and a few nervous whispers. As the bard stood and raised his arms all became even quieter. He turned a slow, full circle to view his gathered audience and to signal that he was ready to begin.

'Tonight my friends, I bring you a story that you may think that you know well, but it is a tale that needs repeating lest we all forget.

For tonight I shall tell you an account that truly took place, I offer no invention. I shall tell you a story of trust broken, of the hope for a peace destroyed. This is a story of black-hearted murder and slaughter. Tonight… I shall recall… the Night of the Long Knives.

You may well remember from other telling's, for this is a well told story, that the party of King Vortigern had travelled long and hard for many days through forest and tribal lands to reach the agreed meeting place. An assignation with the Saxons to end the fighting between our peoples, to talk of truce and friendship. But as our people neared the end of their journey, they began to walk more slowly as if their feet had become heavy. Their heads were bent low against the constant wind and rain that drove across the wet, open, desolate moors of the middle-land, this was the final stage of the journey before they would arrive at their destination.

King Vortigern and the Britons had awoken early from their overnight camp on that last morning before the sun had risen and given light to their path. They set out across the moors and now their horses and the carts laboured hard across the hilly ground of the middle-land. Forty carts filled with all the materials necessary to build a hall and with food enough for a great feast to celebrate the new union. Yet, as they neared, each man and cart were moving no faster than they had to, for they marched carrying dread and anxiety, for it was a meeting few in the party wished for or had faith in, yet still they followed their King.'

The bard shrunk in on himself and plodded slowly around the floor; his face creased in agony and despair, his back bent as if crippled by the heavy burden he carried. After two circuits of the room he straightened.

'The negotiations had long been discussed, riders from both sides had travelled back and forth between King Vortigern and the Saxon Lord, Hengist, many times over several cycles of the moon, discussing the details of the peace, the location for the meeting on neutral ground and the Saxons' demands for metals, food and land. For Vortigern, these final negotiations would take place with a desperate hope that a meeting of our two peoples would bring a final peace to our troubled land, yet it was a meeting that many had cautioned against, and so the King's party travelled slowly, carrying heavy hearts.'

The bard turned and pointed his finger around at his captivated audience, the grimy digit ending close to Calvador Craen's nose. Cal leant back into Usher, and they both fell back into several other boys of the village, people laughed, and the old bard cackled before leaping up and spinning around, his long grey robe flapping.

'Four hundred and twenty-eight warriors made that journey with their King, walking with hope in their hearts, but fear squirming in their bellies. The King and the warriors of the tribes had fought the Saxons for many years, yet that summer the battles with the Saxons had been especially fierce, and many warriors had been slain on both sides of the shield wall. Since the summer sun had cooled and the chill of winter was first felt, the Saxons had been sending emissaries who talked of a time of peace, they wanted a meeting so that a border could be drawn, a border that would be honoured and never crossed by either side.'

The bard halted his tale and once again looked around at the gathered tribesmen, a look of disgust finally contorting his features as his voice rose. 'But, those cunning and conniving Saxons should never have been trusted, he was warned by so many, yet King Vortigern believed he had to trust them, that there was no other way to save his people. He had already taken Hrotwyn, daughter of Hengist, to be his second wife, hoping that the union would bring an end to the hostilities, yet even that had not been enough for the two peoples to find a reconciliation or cool the Saxon's hunger for land. The fighting and raids had barely paused long enough for the wedding celebration. Some say that, in the end, it was the loss of his son, Vortimer, that finally brought the King on this journey and this desperate attempt for peace. His son's death had robbed him of all appetite for war or even for revenge; there had been so much blood spilt and he knew that somehow... it had to stop.'

Once again the bard paused in his tale. The central fire crackled and spluttered as it shifted, embers rolling and logs settling. It gave a good heat to the hall as the cold night whispered at the walls and the birds and animals nestled, rustling overhead in the thatch. The bard slowly began to stride around the fire, dragging his feet, head dipped low as if he too were walking with the exhausted, doomed warriors.

'On... and on... they trudged, as the wind tugged at them and the rain left them sodden. Across the moors, over the paths in the high hills and on through the bogs towards the chosen place that had been deemed agreeable to both sides, to the old flint mines of the ancients at Stanenges.'

Once more the bard slowly walked around the fire, his head bowed low as if he were carrying the weight of the travellers' fears, then he paused and glanced up, then stood straight, took a stick from beside the fire and flourished it in the air. 'Now remember if you will, the Saxons had first come to our land at King Vortigern's invitation, can you believe that?' He stared around at the children in the front row of kneeling figures.

'Three longboats full of fierce fighting men were paid to help King Vortigern, charged to aid his warriors in pushing back the raiding Picts. To send them running, back up into the cold north, for those Picts had stolen our crops and cattle and raided our villages bringing fire and death, too many times. For their help in ridding us of the Picts, the Saxons were gifted an Island that lays off the eastern coast of the Trinovantes lands and it was theirs to call their own. Thanet it was named, which means fire in the old tongue, and there they feasted well and enjoyed the generosity of King Vortigern for several years. But once the Picts had been stung and the fighting was past, our Saxon allies became restless. More of their longboats were arriving after each winter season, and soon Thanet was found to be too small, and they began to spill across to farm on the mainland. There were now Saxon settlements where there had once been Iceni and Trinovantes villages, and so our allies became our enemies, the shield walls clashed, we fought and have been fighting ever since.'

The bard sprang around the fire swishing his wooden sword over the heads of small boys, fighting imaginary foes, he yelled and screamed his war cries until others in the hall also jumped up and called, shouted, and fought invisible Saxons. Finally, the bard sank to the floor, where he waited until the villagers had crouched back down and a calm had settled upon the hall.

'But the fighting had gone on for season after season without an end, the Saxon wasn't leaving, and peace had become all but a desperate hope as the numbers of the dead rose on each side, and so when the Saxons came suggesting peace, a meeting had been negotiated.

Once the King and his people arrived at Stanenges, the carts were unloaded, and a meeting hall was constructed on the open grassland. It was surrounded by the burial mounds of the ancients, close to their old flint mines, and there our people waited to talk peace with their despised Saxon enemies.'

The bard halted his tale once more, his bushy grey eyebrows rising as he held a finger high. 'Another curious thing,' his voice rose to a high, questioning tone, 'the assurance had long been agreed by both sides that no blade would be worn by any person at the talks, lest uncalled violence should break this chance of peace for both our people. And so it was that King Vortigern, his senior warriors, his advisors, and all of his men and women warriors... carried... no... blade. I ask you, can you imagine how it must have felt? To be walking almost naked amongst your enemy, the men and women you had so recently faced across the shield wall... with no blade in your hand? This was no ordinary courage.' There were murmurs of disbelief and fear from among the listeners, but the bard held up his hand calling for quiet.

'It was of course an uneasy meeting as the two sides first came together and approached each other cautiously like two packs of angry wolves. However, to begin with, all went well, words of greeting were spoken by both. Good words. Words of promises and regret at the blood that had been spilled, words of hope and trust and of new beginnings.'

Once again his face contorted in hatred, and he shook his fist, then looked up to the thatch, dropped to his knees and howled, 'Yet these words from Hengist… leader of the Saxons, were all just like the bleating of a sheep, for Hengist was really a wolf, and he had trapped our people; the Saxons had lied.' Cries of anger, shouts of outrage and the long drawn out wails of the old women filled the hall.

'As the warriors entered the hall they were called by the Elders of both sides to draw together, to mingle as new friends should, so they could share the great platters of prepared food and forge new bonds. Saxon sat with Trinovantes; Iceni drank ale with the same Saxon warriors who had driven him from his land and for a short time, filled with hope and promise, and the two peoples became one. Yet all this hope and trust was for nothing, for as the sun began to set over the burial mounds of the ancients, Hengist rose from his seat at the side of King Vortigern and called for his warriors to draw their *seax*, their long fighting blades that they had each hidden, strapped to the inside of their legs, and he called upon them to slaughter the men and women of the tribes who sat by their sides.'

Within the great hall, the wailing of the old women rose, and the shouting anger from everyone was getting louder and louder. The bard began to slash and stab at imagined warriors, leaping and dancing, thrusting and stabbing, and the villagers joined in, whooping and screaming their hatred, calling their oaths of revenge… until fighting for breath, with the stick thrust beneath his arm as if he had been stabbed, the bard slumped to the rushes of the floor and waited for the noise in the hall to lessen so he might continue.

'Listen to me everyone, listen while I tell you of how the blood flowed, and our people suffered. Even though the warriors of the tribes tried to defend themselves and their kin, they could do nothing… nothing, for they had honoured the treaty and carried… no… blades,' the bard was sobbing as the noise around him rose once again, he had to shout now to be heard as anger and despair matched each other in volume, 'long knives stabbed and slashed as every Saxon warrior rose to confront the man or woman who sat beside him, the person with whom he had just shared meat and ale and stabbed and cut, and the blood sprayed and flowed. The Saxon killed our people… all of them, with their long, bright knives. Many tried to escape; they ran from the hall in search of their weapons, but the Saxon fell upon them and slaughtered them all. And when it was done, almost all the four hundred and twenty-eight of our people were dead… save King Vortigern and his few closest aids, who were held back, unable to do anything to help the people as they were butchered.' The noise in the hall dulled to sobbing and wailing as quiet was called and the people hushed so the bard could go on.

'In the first light of dawn, as the crows descended to begin their feast upon the dead who had been dragged from the building and now decorated the burial mounds, the Saxons torched the feasting hall and led our King away in chains as he wept for those slaughtered and the future of his people. Spared because he had taken Hrotwyn as his wife, but also so that he could be whipped into obedience and become the Saxon's dog.' The noise in the hall was just a murmur now as the bard rose to his feet and stared solemnly around at his angry, weeping audience.

'We tell and repeat this story to remind us all, do not trust these Saxons. Do not listen to their honeyed words. We are the people of this land and them… they are the curse that we must one day turn back towards the sea and send back to the land from where they came. We must never trust them. We must always remember the lesson that our people paid for so dearly, at the Night of the Long Knives…

Chapter 8

The Druid's Quest

'*Remember well, that Night of the Long Knives,*' cried Merlyn, and then gathering his emotions and with more control he continued; 'We must continue to tell our children and repeat it often around the fires until it has become deeply imprinted upon our minds and the shadows of our souls. That event was a terrible curse brought upon our people, and it was the beginning of the end for King Vortigern.'

Merlyn had risen to his feet during his telling of the tale. The others had reported on the business within their tribes and their own raids and clashes with the Saxons, but when Merlyn's turn had come to speak, he had chosen to begin with a tale from the past. Wasting little time on anything else to do with Ynys Mon and the Druids, he had just stood up and told his story.

'After the Night of the Long Knives, well before the sons of King Clarens, the old King, had risen to unite the tribes against the Saxon invaders, King Vortigern had lost all hope and any heart for the fight. Already bowed low by our enemy before that terrible night at Staneges, he was a broken man who thereafter was instructed daily by his Saxon overlords upon which decisions he might make. He had given up on any hope of opposition to them; he was our King, but he was their man to control as they wished.

As this Council now sits, we are once again in charge of our own destiny. This is our home without Saxon rule. We beat them at the Battle of Mount Badon and we beat them at the Battle of Aegelsthorpe.

Under King Uther, we can one day hope to reclaim all of our tribal lands and send the Saxons running back to their longboats.'

The chiefs and lords announced their support and banged upon the table, several calling and swearing their allegiance to Uther once again. Merlyn held his hands out, palms raised, and waited until once again there was hush.

'The truth, my Lords, is that the spirit of the land we call our home and also the spirits of our slain people at Stanenges need to be healed if we are ever to succeed and expel the invaders from our shores. The Druids have long discussed this, and all the proper rites and ceremonies have taken place to understand the problem of our land and see what actions must be taken. Knowing our path; it was agreed by all of the Druids, that it should be I who represent them here in attendance at this great Council and that I should explain the necessity for your aiding us in bringing about a great healing. It is the wish of the Druids that I call upon this Council, this meeting of alliance and strength amongst the tribes of Britain, this gathering of good men,' Merlyn's voice rose, and he raised his hands in the air to invoke the gravity of his words, 'to truly unite and perform a great and worthy quest for the betterment of our peoples and of our nation. My Lords, it is imperative that we heal the land at Stanenges, for it suffers, that we free the spirits of our people, for if we do not, then the earth at Stanenges will become a weeping sore that will grow and infect us all. It will continue to expand throughout the land and weaken us until we are finally overthrown by our enemies until we are pushed back into the sea, and become all but a lost and distant memory in this country that was once ours and ours alone.'

Merlyn stopped, leant upon his staff as if weary of the telling and drew breath, considering the atmosphere of those gathered. 'The spirits of our people still roam the old quarries and burial mounds upon the grassland at Stanenges. They are unable to rest or pass into the Shadowland. Their suffering continues and does not end. They are in torment and feel a great and terrible anguish at being so tricked and betrayed by the cursed Saxons. We must help them, those who were so betrayed, to find their peace and a clear path so they may take their final journey and walk through the great gates into the Shadowland beyond to join their ancestors. The land at Stanenges must be cleansed, and the spirit of the earth returned. It must become a place of light, not of darkness. In the name of our people, in the name of the spirits of those that died there, I call upon you at this gathering to embark upon a quest, a journey and an undertaking for our people, to fully unite and to make right... what we all know was a terrible wrong brought upon our people and our land.'

The response to Merlyn's speech was immediate and enthusiastic as the lords and chiefs around the table rose to their feet and shouted both their support and words of outrage at the atrocity, with many oaths of revenge, the tumult of which echoed about the hall, yet Merlyn could see there were many still questioning, with no little concern, to the thought of what such a quest might entail.

'A quest is what I ask of you, my Lords,' he continued, 'a gathering of some of your bravest warriors to set out for that land across the water to our west, to the Isle of Erin.' There was a disturbance as a chair was thrown back, Merlyn stopped and glanced up.

'You would have us gather boats and voyage over the seas while the Saxon laugh and enter our lands unhindered?' Gerlois, Duc of the Cornovii stood, hands on his hips staring around at his fellows, a look of disbelief and incredulity upon his scowling face. 'Is this not the basis of what we have been discussing here today? As the Saxon nip and bite at us, raiding our villages, taking more and more of our land. That we need to increase our defences, to continue holding them back and bring them to account. Surely, if we take half our warriors and abandon our lands for your quest... well, then there will be nothing left but a Saxon homeland upon our return.' Murmurs of agreement followed this as Duc Gerlois resumed his seat.

'I do not propose that we send every last warrior,' replied Merlyn. 'It is you, not I, my Lords, who are best to judge how many warriors can be spared. I propose that we take some small amount of boats, cross the sea, and then move quickly through the lands of the Coriondi tribe to a place long known in Druidic lore. To a mountain named as Killaraus by the people who dwell there. Once upon this Mount Killaraus, we will find an ancient ring of stones that was set upon the mountain in times long past. It was constructed in a time before the ancients walked the earth, placed there, so legend tells by a race of giants who called themselves the Fir Bolg. This wisdom that has been spoken and passed through the generations by our bards was first given to us by a people named the Tuatha De Danann, the people who came after the giants left their land.' Merlyn stopped speaking and gazed about at the somewhat amazed, but silent lords. He decided to continue before the questions and protests could begin once more.

'We will gather the stones, return them to our shores and then erect them at Stanenges. The Druids will see to it that they are correctly placed and that their healing powers calm the spirits of the slain and return order to the land and, therefore, aid us in our fight against the Saxon invaders.'

Duc Gerlois cleared his throat loudly, interrupting Merlyn yet again. 'This voyage across the seas in search of stones cannot be wise, my Lords,' Gerlois appealed to the others at the table and then turned to Uther, who had been sitting in silence, listening. 'I mean no disrespect to Merlyn nor the Druid Council. In the lands of the Cornovii, and also, the Dumnonii where I hold sway, we have many sacred sites and our Druids keep us true to the old ways, even as the followers of the nailed God walk amongst us seeking their disciples, we still follow the ways of the old Gods... I would support this quest charged to us by the Druids, of course, but we cannot weaken our hold upon our borders, can you not see that?'

Before Uther or Merlyn was able to answer, one of the other Lords stood and raised his hands high, indicating that he wished to speak. Merlyn glanced over and saw that it was Cunobelin, one of the younger lords in attendance. He recalled that the young Lord was named after one of his famous forebears, a warrior ancestor who had risen to lead his tribe against the Romans when the legions had first entered the land and defeated them in the time of the warrior Queen

Boudicca. Being so named must have been a burden for the young man to carry, yet he bore it well. Cunobelin had been quiet for most of the time that he had been sitting at the table, and Merlyn had all but dismissed him, thinking him possibly cowed by the presence of so many other great tribal leaders. He studied the young Lord, his thick, black hair, long and uncut in the old style of the tribes was tied back in a warrior knot. Heavily tattooed arms showed the blue swirling symbols of his tribe. His features were darkly tanned boasting a myriad of scars as testament to his years fighting with a blade. It was obvious that he worked hard to honour his ancestor's name. A particularly vicious scar ran from the top of his left brow, across his face, and down the length of his cheek to his chin, it pulled slightly at his lips giving the impression that the young Lord was always offering a cynical smile. The others at the table hushed to give him room to speak. Throwing back the yellow cloak that marked him of the Trinovantes, Cunobelin leaned forward onto the table and stared at Merlyn. The patterns of his tattoos seemed to move as his muscles flexed, he was choosing his words carefully.

'The Trinovantes… will be honoured to join your quest, Merlyn,' he coughed and cleared his throat before glancing around at the others. 'Many of our people were at Stanenges, at the Night of the Long Knives, we know that their spirits still walk the grassland. As you are all aware, the Trinovantes, my people, have been forced from our lands and will not be missed upon the borders. Therefore, in the name of the Trinovantes, I commit three thousand warriors to this quest.' There was much whispered talking as Cunobelin resumed his seat, but before Merlyn could respond, Sir Ector rose and smiled across at the old Druid.

'The Iceni will also support your quest, Merlyn. Our lands have also been stolen from us by the Saxons, and we have no villages to protect. It is true that we have the honour of forming King Uther's personal guard, but with his permission I would like to commit a thousand of our best warriors and also, with my King's permission, I would like to lead them.' He sat and Merlyn saw that Uther was rising to speak, he gestured for him to continue.

Uther stood and walked over to a small wooden chest at the side of the hall.

'Within one cycle of the moon, we shall be celebrating the festival of Samhain.' He lifted the lid, removed a rolled scroll of vellum and brought it back to the table where he spread it out, placing a cup on one side and a knife on the other to keep it from curling. Upon the vellum, the inked pattern showed the outline of the tribal lands of Britain, and to one side amidst a sea of blue was the Isle of Erin.

'As we begin our celebrations for Samhain, the lands will be cooling as the Goddess Cailleach makes ready to draw her cloak of winter across the earth. The seas at this time will become angry, making it difficult for us to make the crossing to Erin, however...' - he tapped his finger on the cured animal skin map - '... past years have shown that it will also be difficult for the Saxon's to bring their longboats from their land across the seas here.' He moved his hand towards the other side of the map while the lords craned their heads to see what he was pointing at, several of them had still not seen the concept of their land depicted like this, and there were many whispered questions exchanged. Others, including Gerlois, Duc of the Cornovii, walked around to take a closer look.

'This will be the time to make your quest, Merlyn, within the lunar cycle before we celebrate the Samhain festival if this Council decides we are to embark upon it,' Uther continued. 'After Samhain, much of the raiding will have finished until winter is over and our borders will require fewer of our warriors to be used in defence. In the lunar cycle before Samhain, a small band of us could make the crossing and complete this quest.'

Gerlois threw up his arms, clearly exasperated. 'But you ask us to send our warriors out across the water while the storms blow and the Gods toy with our attempts to make a crossing?' He feigned astonishment that anyone would be so foolish in attempting such a thing. 'We of the Cornovii know the sea. There is good reason that both we and also the Saxons bring our ships into the rivers during the winter season and do not raid or cross the seas until the thaw. Do you not, my King…' Gerlois bowed his head and opened his arms in a gesture of appeal, '… do you not think this quest just a little, ill-advised, perhaps reckless when we should be more concerned with strengthening our borders?'

Uther rose from his study of the vellum and turned to face the smiling Gerlois. 'I do agree that a quest across the sea to the Isle of Erin is reckless in many, many, ways, my Lord. Not only will we have the weather and the Gods to contend with, but if we manage to survive the crossing, then it will be the tribe of the Coriondi and probably more Saxons that have been settling in Erin that we may have to either fight or evade; they may not be too pleased to see us. Merlyn, you do indeed set us a daunting challenge, yet I find the concept of a quest to be a good thing. It will not only test us in many ways, but it will help to unite this Council and also further unite the tribes as Britons. If we can accomplish this feat, then we shall indeed become stronger, more united and also, we might heal the land at Stanenges.' He turned to Sir Ector and Cunobelin. 'My Lords, I thank you for your support, but I feel this should be a smaller group of warriors if we are to succeed.' Uther turned to Merlyn. 'How many ships would be necessary to transport these stones?'

'There are a large number of stones, yet the quest can be accomplished with just twenty-two boats,' - Merlyn smiled at Duc Gerlois - 'and do not fear for the weather, my Lord. We shall arrive safely; some will probably be a little sick from the motion of the sea, but the Gods will preserve us.' Gerlois features clouded at the rebuke, but he held his tongue and stepped back offering just a curt nod.

'Twenty-two boats will make us a force of almost fifteen hundred,' Uther thought for a moment, 'we shall take warriors from as many tribes as wish to accompany us, but the Iceni and Trinovantes will have the honour of sending, at least, two hundred warriors from each tribe so our borders will not be left weakened.' He turned to Sir Ector and rested a hand upon his shoulder. 'You and I will both accompany this quest, old friend, and Duc Gerlois…' Uther turned to the Duc of the Cornovii, '… as you have no border under threat from our Saxon invaders and because you have been so helpful during our discussion here, perhaps you would also like to join us… as Merlyn said, it may help to bring us all together.' Several other lords began to speak and push forward, eager to offer their support with warriors who could make the journey, yet Uther and Gerlois just stared at each other, until Gerlois nodded, turned and walked away.

Eventually, Gerlois offered twelve of the ships that would make the crossing. The Cornovii had long been a tribe that traded by sea, their boats hugging the coast to exchange goods with neighbouring tribes and also making the crossing to the mainland, visiting and trading with tribes there with whom they shared a common heritage. Their boats traded Cornovii tin, copper, and, when in season, the shining bounty of the pilchard, for when the vast schools of fish visited their coastline every year the pilchard were easy to catch and arrived in such large numbers there were too many for their own villages and so they were traded far and wide. In turn, the Cornovii boats would return with wine, ceramics, precious Roman glass goods and produce from far distant lands that were much prized by the tribes of Britain.

It took a little more than one full lunar cycle for all arrangements for the quest to be made, so that twenty-two boats were tethered just off the western coast of the Briganti tribal lands. The weather was good the day they gathered to voyage; it was sunny and small white clouds were blowing down the coast above them like so many passing sheep upon a hill of deepest blue, promising good voyaging weather.

The boats lay anchored by large stones some way off from the shore and were lifting and falling with the rising waves, the sound of the hulls as they slapped down upon the water carrying across to those amassing upon the beach. Gulls circled, calling and screeching above the small skiffs as they made their way back and forth between beach and boats loaded with provisions while groups of warriors waiting on the beach hunkered down together waiting their turn to be taken out, the different tribal groups laughing and calling to each other.

'A good day to you, King Uther.' Glancing about to see who had called, Uther saw Duc Gerlois walking down the beach towards him. Beside him, he was guiding a young girl, her long hair black as night blowing in the breeze. Uther judged her to be of about eight summers; she was very pretty and obviously very excited to be on the beach with so much going on around her. She had a huge grin on her face and was glancing from one side to the other distracted by the milling confusion of boats and people. The crunching sound their feet made on the loose pebbles was also a distraction; she was happily lifting her legs and stamping to make even more noise. He watched as she stopped and then dropped her father's hand so she could pick up an especially unusual stone.

'Oh, get up girl. King Uther, may I present to you my daughter, Morgana.' Gerlois turned and waved the girl forward; she glanced up before rising to make a small bow and gesturing with her hand in imitation of the way the Romans once had.

'I am delighted to meet you, Morgana... Duc Gerlois.' Uther smiled and gave his own version of the bow. 'Have you come to see us leave upon our quest, Morgana?'

'I have, King Uther. My father brought us all to wish him well upon his travels, but I didn't realise that it would be as nice as this!' She smiled and gestured as a group of warriors laden with spears and shields jogged past and down into the surf. The three of them watched as all the warriors began to clamber into the small skiff at the same time, some laughing, others shouting advice or frowning in confusion, but all eager to get in the skiff and be on their way. They were clearly unused to boats and how to enter them, which was causing more laughter and curses in equal measure, then a bigger wave came in and rocked the boat sending several of them falling into the surf while the others tried to hold on and keep the boat with them as the tide tried to pull it away. Morgana giggled at their predicament, and then dropped to her knees again, to pick up another stone which she examined closely.

'Here is a token for each of you, she held the stones out, one for her father and the other she offered to Uther. Uther took his and inspected it earnestly, turning it in his fingers, it was an unusual thing indeed, eggshell white with a swirling blue pattern much like a tribal tattoo.

'I do believe this is the nicest thing I have ever been given, thank you, Morgana. This is the perfect talisman. It will travel close to my heart and protect my every step on this perilous quest.'

Morgana smiled, and then her face became more serious: 'If I ever need it to protect me, King Uther, then you will return it, won't you?'

'Of course. It will be a bond between us. A talisman to protect us both through all of our journeys.' Uther smiled again and turned to Gerlois. 'Is your wife, and I believe you also have two other daughters, are they here with you as well?'

'They are,' muttered the Duc, 'but I seem to have misplaced them in all the excitement of being here. I shall be sure to present them just as soon as I can find them.' With a last smile, Gerlois tossed his stone to the side and allowed himself to be drawn down the beach by Morgana, who appeared more eager to take a closer look at the skiffs bouncing about in the waves close to the shore.

Uther opened his eyes. 'You gave me back the stone, our stone, didn't you... the last time I was here before they took me away to battle? I remember holding it; you pressed it into my hand. I didn't know what it was at the time, but now I do, it was the stone taken from the beach as we left for the Isle of Erin. So the stone has been passed once more, and I suppose it did its job, as it always seems to do. I still live after all.' He coughed and closed his eyes as pain ripped his chest, and then weariness flowed over him trying to draw him down into sleep. After a moment, he smelt the warm flowery steam of the hot brew and then Morgana was holding his head as he sipped her special infusion... and then he slept.

Chapter 9

The Curse of the Sea

The twenty-two boats were readied, loaded with warriors and supplies and then they took to sea. The majority of those aboard were making their first ever voyage in such a vessel and for many, it was the first time they had even seen the sea, which was evident from the many warriors sitting on the beach staring in awe.

Each boat was made from oak and carried a single sail. For the most part, they had both high prows and sterns and were crafted for coastal waters, not to survive long voyages and heavy seas. A middle section was lower to accommodate rows of oarsmen, which was necessary to give the boats more power and allowed them to be more manoeuvrable within strong tides and river systems. The sails were heavy, made of flax and hemp fibre and it was necessary to keep them as dry as possible lest they lose shape and become saturated and unmanageable.

As soon as the signal had been given that all boats were loaded and ready to leave, the sails were heaved aloft by thick ropes, the wind snatched at them and they were suddenly moving. To those first time seafarers on board, it appeared as if the wind was eager to catch at the cloth, impatient to drag them out into the fury of the sea. It was a time of excitement and also no small amount of fear with many a curse and appeal to the Gods made as the deck pitched and rolled beneath them. As the wind took hold and turned the boats towards open water, frantic activity ensued. The short anchor ropes were hauled in and the anchor stones stowed safely away below the plank deck. There was then much manoeuvring, confusion and shouting as every boat tried to find its own patch of sea to head into whilst trying not to collide with any of the others.

Eventually, they were clear, and with enough distance between the boats to sail and be comfortable. The oars were lowered and the first shift of warriors began to heave upon the huge, solid rowing oars, twelve oars to a side and two rowers to each oar. There were between sixty and eighty warriors aboard each boat and when not rowing, there was enough deck space between the rowers to allow those not rowing to rest. There was also space in the dark, damp confines of the hold below the plank decking, but while the weather was fair, below the deck was not going to be a popular choice, the cramped confines stank to begin with, and once underway it would quickly worsen.

As his boat took to the sea, Uther was enjoying the feeling of freedom that setting out on a new adventure gave him. He was smiling as he stood by the two steersmen and even helped as they leant hard on the long steering oar that trailed down to the waves behind them. They strained against the might of the sea attempting to turn the vessel onto a new course while the steering oar struggled mightily to evade their grasp. He enjoyed the battle between man and ship, fascinated as the great wooden beast was slowly tamed and responded, the boat's prow coming around as if it were some great sea monster sniffing for its path amongst the waves. Finally, when the steersmen judged the boat was heading in the right direction and the sail set to catch the best of the wind, they were able to lash the great steering oar in place. They were now hitting the waves almost head on, meeting each with a heavy slap against the hull that blew a fine spray of salt water back over the craft, covering the tribesmen who sat, rowed or lay upon the open deck. Uther knew that with good weather it would take the flotilla of boats little more than a day to make the crossing, but then of course once there, it would take some time for Merlyn to locate the right piece of coastline they were looking for. It meant that at least one or possibly two nights would have to be spent at sea, which when planning the quest hadn't seemed too much of a hardship, however, now as they approached the main channel, with the open sea laid out vast and empty before him, he was beginning to appreciate what two days aboard a ship might really mean.

The deck rose abruptly and beneath him as they met a particularly big wave, and a little alarmed, he staggered to the side of the boat to hold on. There were worried cries and exclamations from tribesmen unaccustomed to being at sea when it then dropped away and slammed down into the trough of the next wave sending up an even bigger wash of water back over them.

'It will calm a little once we get out into deeper water. We are feeling the effects of two great seas coming together at the moment as we round the cliffs.' Merlyn came up beside Uther and gestured towards the headland. He looked to be thoroughly enjoying himself, moving easily with the movements of the deck beneath his feet, seemingly without need to hold onto the side. Uther noticed the old Druid was eating something. Pulling meat off a bone with his teeth with little concern for the amount of his hair and beard that he seemed to be chewing on. Uther watched in fascination as the wind sent both hair and beard floating about the old Druid's head in a swirling cloud.

'*This is wonderful, I love to be at sea like this,*' shouted Merlyn as he waved the bone about, pointing at the waves, the land and then the milling ranks of warriors before them. '*I feel much closer to the spirits when the wind is gusting and the water, so deep, is sliding past beneath us.*'

'What are you eating?' Uther touched his hand to his lips as a sudden wave of nausea threatened to overwhelm him. He tried to swallow, but his mouth was suddenly dry. After just a short time under sail, he was already feeling quite ill, he burped and put his hand to his mouth. 'And how can you possibly want to eat anything?' Studying the Druid, Uther shook his head and dragged his eyes back to the rolling waves. He tried to ignore Merlyn, and not think of the meat grease he had noticed caught in the Druid's beard. Truth be told, watching Merlyn eat, coupled with the motion of the boat, was beginning to make him feel more than a little sick, his stomach gurgled, and he felt an urgent need to hang over the side of the boat and empty it.

Walking two steps to the side, he stared out at the other ships around them. He tried to choke down the nausea, drew a deep breath and watched as the oars dipped into the water before lifting clear with a rush of spray. The tribesmen in the closest boat were laughing and shouting as they heaved on the oars to send the vessel surging forward. His own boat lurched beneath him and he felt the timbers tremble, flex and shudder as if the craft were alive. Holding out a hand, Uther steadied himself and decided he needed to move about, maybe that would help. He staggered past a grinning Merlyn and jumped down to the central walkway between the rowers, trying his best on the moving surface to step between the warriors who were covering the deck without stepping on them. Several attempted to rise, either to let him pass or in deference to him being their King and leader, but he motioned for them to remain where they were as he picked his way through.

'Please, I can get past, stay there.' He took several steps making his way around the closest, but then a few strides in front of him a warrior rolled onto his side and puked noisily down onto the feet of one of the rowers.

'*Ahhhh!*' The oarsmen screamed his disgust and punched out at the vomiting man hitting him heavily on the shoulder, but it had little effect, the one being sick ignored the blow and just kept retching, trying to throw up more.

'You dirty, disgusting pig… go away, get away with you.' The oarsman kicked out but then leant back quickly as a boy darted in with a leather bucket of sea water and emptied it down over both the sick man and the mess he had made. Uther watched as the puke washed away to disappear between the floorboards, unfortunately, the awful smell remained. Uther clamped a hand over his nose and mouth.

'E's all right, e'll live. I was sick lots when I first got on the boats. E's just the first; there'll be plenty more of them sick afor long.' The boy shook the last few drops of water from the bucket and then skipped back across the crowded deck easily navigating his way amongst the sprawling warriors and then, holding tight to the hemp rope, he launched the bucket from the back of the boat to fill it again.

Uther watched, glanced back at the groaning man then spun around, back towards Merlyn, and for a moment was at a loss as his own stomach threatened to make itself known. The smell of vomit was being blown away by the wind, but it was too late for Uther, he managed to make it just past Merlyn, and then the contents of his stomach erupted over the side of the boat. The last thing he heard before losing all interest in anything but his own suffering, was the cackling cry of the gulls as they swooped and Merlyn laughing and commenting on how the Gods of the sea could so easily bring a King to his knees.

During the hours of darkness the rowers took their rest, and the boats continued on under sail. Uther awoke to the strange sounds of the boat around him as it moved steadily on towards Erin. He could feel it rising and falling beneath his prostrate form, pushing the rough, wet wood of the deck against his cheek as it rose and then he could feel it dropping away beneath him, the slap of it meeting the water, juddering back up in a most alarming way that made his head spin and stomach gurgle. He groaned and made a half-hearted attempt to rise, but found even that simple act impossible. He gave up and tried to ignore the movement and pungent smells that assaulted him, and just listened, allowing his mind to calm and explore his surroundings. Ropes were creaking, the low murmur of people talking came from somewhere close, and there was a flapping sound that, after a few puzzled moments, he reasoned to be the pennon that flew at the top of the mast. Oh spirits, he felt awful. It was cold, yet there was a sheen of sweat and spray upon his face, his head was pounding with a rhythm all of its own and his throat was sore. He swallowed and groaned again.

'Uther...? Uther are you back from the edge of the Shadowland?'

Uther ignored the voice. He knew it was Merlyn, and right now wanted nothing to do with the Druid or his stupid quest. Truth be told he would be happy just to die right now and be done with it all.

'Uther, suck on this.'

A bit of wet wood… or something foul was pushed past his lips and he tried to push it out with his tongue. 'Ahhh, nnooo…' But it was pushed back in and he felt his arm lifted. Something was being pressed painfully into his inner arm and Uther tried to struggle, confused by what was happening.

'Be still Uther. The root is called gingiber. It is from a little plant that the Romans brought with them, and one for which the Druids upon Ynys Mon have found many uses. I was told it might be a great relief should we encounter sickness from the rolling of the boat, but I hadn't realised the afflicted would be you.'

Uther sucked on the slice of root and although it had a most alarming taste, he did actually feel his stomach began to calm. 'And why are you hurting my arm?' He managed to sit upright against the side of the boat, which at first was a mistake as his stomach began to gurgle once more, but then he sucked down the strange tasting juices from the root and after a moment his stomach settled again.

'Oh, this? You have a point on your arm right here,' - Merlyn pushed even harder - 'that also drains the sickness from you. It's quite clever really isn't it… feeling any better?'

'But you let me suffer all this time…I feel awful. Why now? Why did you just leave me to…?'

'It would not have been wise to give you something untried, would it, Uther? When I was sure of the calming effects of the root upon myself, I merely waited for you to awaken so that I could give it to you.'

Uther pulled himself to his feet, stared out over the rolling waves and took a deep breath. He could see the dark outlines of several other boats that weren't too distant, and a half-moon was casting its light between scudding clouds. In the far distance, lightning flashed.

'Are we in for a storm?' The idea of being at sea in this boat with a storm tossing them about conjured the most alarming images.

'I think not. By daybreak, we should have sight of Erin and if the storm has reached us by then, well, we can shelter in one of its many bays or rivers. Enjoy this journey, Uther, and chew your gingiber, for tomorrow you must lead us as we seek to land and you may find that hard if you are still weak at the knees and taken with the sickness.'

Although he couldn't really see Merlyn's face other than the white of his teeth and his luminescent cloud of hair, Uther knew that the old Druid was grinning at him, once again mocking the King of the Britons.

The first watery light of dawn found that they were indeed in sight of land. A dark and choppy sea surrounded them and a stiff breeze was pushing the boats along the coast at a fine pace. Nobody spoke as the distant land slipped past, gradually revealing itself as it shed its cover of darkness. The coastline appeared bare of trees with rocky cliffs and high barren hills that rolled off into the distance. Seabirds were spiralling and calling from cliffs stained white by countless generations of their kind that had painted the rock face with their faeces. Waves were breaking with pounding savagery that echoed back to those on the boats. There seemed to be numerous bays and inlets where they might have found shelter, yet Merlyn guided them on, keeping them a good distance from the coast. After some time, it began to rain. Not a great, torrential downpour, but more a drizzling sky that brought with it a feeling of misery and painted everything and everyone in different shades of grey.

'Where is it, Merlyn?' mumbled Uther as they stood leaning on the side watching the coast pass them.

'Patience, Uther. We will arrive very soon, I think. We are watching for a peak, some way inland from the coast that rises high above the rest and has a peculiar shape. I thought it resembled a ram's horn the last time I observed it from the sea.' Merlyn rubbed a hand over his face to wipe the accumulation of rain and spray from his beard and then screwed up his eyes, peering out at the distant hills. 'I have seen it on two past occasions. There will be no confusion for us when we arrive, but we are not there as yet.'

Behind Uther, the tribesmen took up the oars and began rowing to the songs of the oar master whose job it was to keep the rowers in pace with each other. His singing of familiar rhythmic songs that the rowers joined in with had quickly become a natural part of the boat, with favourites called for and often repeated. Uther saw that Sir Ector had taken a seat at the oar-bench. He was aware that the old warrior and also Cunobelin had spent much of the voyage either sitting their turn at the oars, encouraging others as they rowed or aiding those that had just sat back from their turn, nursing sore muscles and strained backs. Throughout his period of sickness, Uther had given little regard to anyone else on the vessel and he was suddenly glad that not everyone had suffered as he had and especially pleased that Sir Ector had been able to take command in his place. He spat the remains of his gingiber over the side and watched it float back to be swallowed by the sea. Then he took another small strip from inside his tunic and put it under his tongue, hoping that Merlyn had a good supply for the return trip.

'It works well, does it not?' Uther turned to see Merlyn grinning at him again.

'It has returned me to life, old friend,' said Uther breathing deeply. 'I trust that the casket I saw brought on board for you, contains a goodly supply?'

'It does, but your sickness is now past, Uther. You are well enough to begin preparing for when we land.'

'Preparing in what way? What are we likely to encounter, Merlyn? Do you know something of what awaits us? Will the tribes attack us as soon as we land… or are you taking us into Saxon territory?'

Merlyn leant on the ship's side and stared into the water for a moment, apparently choosing his words with care before replying. 'It is not the Saxon we need fear on this quest, Uther, nor the local tribes, not really, although they may not be too happy that we plan to remove their sacred stones. No, the true danger of our quest will be borne by just one of us and we have no idea who that man might be.'

'Riddles, Druid. You always speak in riddles. Will you not tell me something of the nature of this danger? Must we fight some terrible monster? Or scale an impossible cliff? I will gladly take this challenge myself if needs be, yet I would dearly like to know the challenge to which I must submit.'

'It may be you, Uther, but then it may not, we shall see. For when we make camp at the base of Mount Killaraus, we shall meet with the Druids who dwell there, and if they are to allow us to remove the stones, they will undoubtedly have a task for us to perform to show that we are worthy. It is not a task that I have foreknowledge of, so it makes it a bit difficult to be ready... doesn't it?'

'More Druids? Why is it you Druids make things so complicated? I would rather just fight, get the stones, and move on.'

Merlyn smiled. 'Oh, but Uther, when was life ever easy and uncomplicated? Whatever it is, I am sure we shall prevail. Anyway, it does make life a bit more interesting, doesn't it... and I know you like a challenge.' Merlyn looked up and pointed before Uther could reply. 'Our journey by sea is almost over. I believe we are getting close now. Look, just beyond that headland... there,' - Merlyn pointed - 'I think that may well be Mount Killaraus peeking out of the clouds there. Does that look like a mountain to you?'

Uther stared ahead through the thin misty cloud to where Merlyn was waving his hand and saw what appeared to be a tall cloud formation amongst the wispy grey layers, but then the more he stared, it did start to look more solid, and he realised that Merlyn was right, it was indeed a mountain.

It was late in the day when the first warriors jumped down from the silent boats onto the marshy land that bordered the river estuary and quickly formed up into a shield wall. They marched steadily towards the encroaching woodland while others jumped down behind them and drove huge stakes into the soft earth to tether the boats. A short while later runners returned to report that nobody native to Erin was waiting to meet them, neither in friendship nor in ambush. Uther had them set up watches and patrols while small trees were cut and a simple stockade erected for those being left to guard the boats.

'Most strange, Uther.' Merlyn was staring towards the trees and then up along the wide estuary towards the distant mountain that now stood tall and foreboding, just a short way distant. 'I am sure that our landing must have been noted. I would have expected a delegation of some kind to have approached us by now. I'm sure they will arrive soon. The settlement of Difelyn is just a short walk along the banks of this river, and I know that there are Druids here, both up on the mountain and also close to the village. If we remain without contact until morning, then I would suggest that we approach with a just a small group, no more than one hundred warriors would be correct until we know how we are to be received.'

'We shall do as you suggest, Merlyn.' Uther was about to turn away when he noticed several men leave the forest some distance away to stand watching, leaning on long spears. A few, large shaggy dogs ran about them sniffing at the ground, tails wagging.

'I think our presence has been noticed,' said Uther.

After a few moments and several words exchanged, one of the spearmen began walking towards them through the long grass. Others in Uther's party had noticed them then, and several came up to stand beside him, including Sir Ector and Duc Gerlois. Merlyn took a step forward and raised a hand in welcome, yet the walking man continued to stride on and did not respond.

'He doesn't look too pleased to see us,' said Sir Ector as he fingered the sword belted at his waist. 'He's not one of your Druids then, Merlyn?'

'No, Sir Ector, he is no Druid. He is a warrior from Difelyn, and I am sure he comes to find out why we have visited their shores. Imagine if you were close to your settlement and you came across several hundred armed warriors, what would you be thinking? What would you do?' Merlyn turned his attention back to the new arrivals. 'His friends are still watching, let us see how welcoming our hosts wish to be.'

'Whatever his intentions, he is somewhat courageous to be walking alone towards the likes of us,' rumbled Gerlois, 'very brave, or possibly he could simply be incredibly foolish?'

The man was getting closer now, wading through the long grass. The way he swung his spear, planting it in front of himself with every stride made it seem that he was propelling himself forward upon a boat pushing through the waves of a lush green sea. His short robe was flapping about bare knees, and as he got closer, they could see that upon his head he wore a flat hat of some kind and upon his face was set a grim scowl. As he neared, he called out in a strange guttural tongue and waved his arms in the air to emphasise some point or other as he pointed across towards the river and the boats clustered there.

Everyone looked at Merlyn. 'What, by the spirits, is he saying?' asked Uther. 'Do you speak whatever tongue that is?' The man halted some twenty paces from them, hands on his hips, the breeze blowing the fringe of hair about his face. He still showed an absence of fear at being so close to so many armed and warlike strangers.

'You speak our tongue, do you not, my friend?' Merlyn smiled at the man, then took a step towards him, made a sign in the air, and bowed deeply. 'We come to your land in peace. We are visitors from across the sea, and this man is our leader, King Uther Pendragon of the Britons.'

The man glanced from Merlyn to Uther and then copied the sign Merlyn had made before bowing. 'I speak yer tongue, right well. You may call me Dara. Will it be this man, yer King, who shall make the challenge of me?'

'Challenge? Must we challenge you to gain passage through this land?' Uther glanced across at Merlyn and then back to Dara.

'We have exchanged names, and now it is only fitting that your champion should cross blades or staff with me,' Dara tilted his head as if questioning the concept of a challenge. 'It is our way.'

'And you are the champion of your people?' asked Uther. He glanced across to the other warriors who still waited, far back, close to the woodland. 'We have no need to fight with anyone. We have said, we come with only peaceful intentions.'

'Well, yer still have a need to fight with me,' Dara grinned and turned his spear in the air, spinning it around and swooping it from side to side, it disappeared around his back, and then came back in front to a juddering halt, the end vibrating with the shock of it and the point aimed squarely at Uther's face. 'I stand in your path, and I am indeed a ...a... champion of my people, one of them anyway, we have many.' He raised the spear, leant on it, then standing upon one leg he lifted his foot and rested it on the calf of the other; he was still grinning.

Several of Uther's men started to speak at the same time, each either begging or demanding the opportunity to wipe the smile off the spearman's face. Uther placed a hand upon Sir Ector's shoulder but then pointed at Cunobelin.

'Very well. I name the warrior, Cunobelin, as our champion.'

The Trinovantes warrior unclasped his cloak, allowed it to fall from his shoulders and reached out to take the spear one of his men was offering. Scowling, and with his eyes firmly clasped upon his opponent's, Cunobelin walked forward, whirling the spear in his own display of proficiency.

There were calls of encouragement from many as warriors gathered around, others coming from near the ships, laughing and shouting to one another, excited by the diversion. They moved to form a large ring around the two men leaving them plenty of room to fight.

Dara was grinning still, dancing around the edge of the circle, spinning and jumping as if in great delight like some maiden at her first Beltane dance. Uther glanced across to the trees, but the spearman's companions seemed unconcerned by what was happening, but now there were only two. They were just watching, standing as Dara had, each upon one leg, leaning on their spears.

The fighters circled each other, Cunobelin side stepping while Dara continued to dance as if it were all just so much fun. A few exploratory thrusts and slashes were made by each man, but for some time there was little real contact as each took the measure of the other. The crowd of warriors began to weary of the wait for blood.

'Get him, Cunobelin.'

'Knock that silly smile from his face.'

'Stop playing with him and…'

Cunobelin struck. The two men had been circling, oblivious to the noise and distractions about them, but now, after a lifetime of fighting the warlike Saxon, Cunobelin had already taken the measure of his opponent and made his attack. The spearman, Dara, was dancing and hopping all over the place, but there was a rhythm to it, and Cunobelin had obviously measured it. Feinting with the top of his spear as if about to strike Dara's head, Cunobelin reversed and swept the bottom of the spear around to take out the man's legs. Shock registered on Dara's face as he fell heavily. The watching warriors became silent, before roaring their approval.

Walking to the far side of the circle, Cunobelin waited for his opponent to rise, which he did, quickly. The smile was gone, as was the hat, it now lay crumpled on the grass. The spear twisted in the air again, and Dara nodded to Cunobelin, possibly in acknowledgement of a worthy opponent. Then the two combatants took a moment to assess one another again, and then the fight was back on.

The two men rushed to the centre, and the clash of wood meeting wood rang loud again and again. Dara was definitely more focused now, and Cunobelin took several hits to his body. The dancing had stopped, and he was altering the blows that he threw, quickly pressing Cunobelin hard, but the Trinovante had spent too much time on the battlefield to trade blows for long. On the field of battle, when the world turned to madness, the life of a fight was measured in heartbeats. There was no time for style or technique, no time to wait around and see what the murderous whoreson that was trying to kill you might do. It was kill or be killed and be on to the next enemy, the other one, two, or more bastards who were running towards you, screaming out their hatred as they brought blood-splattered blades and spears down to cleave and stab into your flesh and bone.

The two fighters traded a flurry of heavy blows as they circled, and then Cunobelin, launched a wicked overhand thrust that almost struck home, forcing Dara to duck low and step backwards, almost tripping as he did. Cunobelin leapt after him and knocked his opponent's spear upward, kicking out at the exposed knee as he did. He felt his blow strike true, and the man cried out and fell.

For the briefest moment, Cunobelin stood over the fallen man with the point of his spear at the other's throat, and then he stepped back and allowed Merlyn to move in and tend him.

After a few moments probing, Merlyn looked up. 'The leg is not broken.' He looked relieved. He glanced back at Cunobelin, and then at Uther, as he crouched down beside the fallen spearman.

'You fought well, friend Dara,' said Uther, 'but we have come to your land in the spirit of peace. You gave your friends back there enough time to get away and warn the settlement that we had landed. That's why you made your challenge to us, isn't it?'

Dara looked up at him, the grin now back on his face despite the pain he must be feeling.

'Aye, I looked to delay yer for sure. We thought you, Saxon when first we took sight of yer, and we find the Saxon to be a most disagreeable people.'

'We are no friend of the Saxon, and we wish no ill upon your people.' Uther glanced across at Merlyn and then continued. 'We journey upon a quest, charged to us by the Druids upon the Isle of Mona, Ynys Mon. We are looking to correct a great wrong that was brought upon our people by the Saxons. The same invaders have also entered our lands. We came here seeking the stones that stand upon the great mountain.'

'Well,' Dara made to rise, and Uther and Merlyn took an arm each and helped him to his feet. Cunobelin handed him his spear and Dara leant heavily upon it, testing his leg. 'If it is the stones yer seek, the ones we call The Giant's Dance, then yer have but a day of travel ahead of yer. But first yer must visit the Druids who care for the stones before you can set yer feet upon the mountain. You will find the Druids at the cave, close to where the path leaves the forest. One of our people will guide yer.'

'We would be grateful for this,' said Uther, while Merlyn beamed happily at the man, but then Dara's smile dropped. He looked from Uther to the men immediately around them, and then back to the many armed men who had resumed the work of erecting the stronghold close to the boats.

'Of course, if yer planning on staying, and it is more than just visiting the stones that yer after, then you will have to meet the Stranger.'

'The Stranger?' asked Uther. 'Who is this Stranger?'

'If yer seek to move the stones, as legend has said that men will try to do, then yer must convince Uath the Stranger, that you are worthy.'

'And where will we find this Uath, so that we might convince him?

'The Druids know,' Dara glanced at Merlyn, 'this Druid knows as well, yer can be sure of it. This, after all, is the way with Druids, is it not? Tricky buggers all of them.' He grinned. 'Follow me.'

Dara turned and strode off back across the field as if he had not just taken a heavy blow to his leg. Uther and his men began to follow. One of the dogs ran across to greet Dara as they approached, it barked savagely at those that followed, but Dara hushed it with a word and a gesture, and it fell into step by his side.

Uther turned to Merlyn. 'Uath the Stranger? Do you know what this is about Merlyn? But then, why do I ask, of course you do. This is just one more time when I find that all is not as I thought, and that you are just playing with us as if we were runes made of bone being cast down upon the dirt by your feet, rather than living breathing men.'

'Oh, come, Uther, do you really think I would bring you into a situation where I thought you could not triumph?'

'I think, Druid, that you would do whatever you thought necessary to accomplish your needs and wishes, and that I am merely one of your runes.' He moved away to walk with Sir Ector and Cunobelin. Uther put his hand upon Cunobelin's shoulder and congratulated him; then the three men started to discuss the fight, talking in low voices.

'When the lives of men and Druids meet there is often confusion,' said Duc Gerlois coming up to Merlyn's side. 'I think we are in for some interesting days. I wonder who shall survive and who shall fall and be left behind upon this far shore?'

Chapter 10

Morgana Le Fey

'Abbess, are you well? Can we aid you? Are you ill?'

Morgana felt a jolt and opened her eyes. She realised she was kneeling, in the herbage garden, between soft waving fennel to one side and the pretty yellow and white flowers of feverfew to the other.

'Oh, my…' She must have closed her eyes for just one moment… and then fallen asleep. Picking up her stick, she heaved herself up to standing. How long had it been? Her legs had become cramped and protested the need to straighten, so some time then. Oh, and there was an ache in her lower back helping persuade her that she really must have dozed off whilst filling her basket. She clearly needed proper sleep, but there was too much to do, and the King was talking at last, finally, after so many years of silence, she was learning the truth of what happened so many years ago.

'I am well, Sisters.' She glanced across at the two nuns. They were obviously uncertain of what to do, their faces betraying their worry at finding their devoted mother collapsed among the plants.

'I am well, truly, worry not. I was gathering a few leaves and roots to make the King's herbal infusion; he is still weak, and I see that it does him good. I merely dozed off amongst God's creations; our Lord has been watching over me, fear not.'

'Yes, Abbess, but you should sleep. Please, allow us to take over and care for the King, only while you recover your strength.' The young nun, a wisp of a girl, reached out a freckled hand and took hold of the basket, but Morgana refused to let it go. The two looked at one another for a moment until the nun dropped her hand and lowered her eyes.

'I am sorry, Abbess; I presume too much. How might we help you?'

Morgana sighed and straightened, then glanced down into the basket, calculating for a moment what ingredients were needed and what was still missing.

'You can take this basket back and leave it outside my chambers. Also, collect camomile… and I think you will find some verbenae if you look close to the water trough on your way back… go on, go!' She passed the basket and flapped her hands at the two nuns, and they scuttled off, eager to do her bidding.

Morgana watched them go and then, gathering her robes, she sighed and walked on among the plants and flowers of the herbage towards the small broken gate that was set in the back wall. She was indeed tired and could feel every one of her forty-two years, but walking was helping to ease the cramp that had set in, and she was now feeling awake and eager to find the remaining ingredients and return to her chambers.

Nudging the gate to the side, she had to push through where the brambles had overgrown, unpicking the thorns from where they reached out and snagged at her cloak, and then she was past and could walk on up towards the hill. She knew that close to the path, further up towards the tor where the sheep grazed in the summer months, would be the small brown mushrooms that were vital for the infusion. Once combined with a little of the mandrake root, she knew they could influence and bring forth the stories from the King. As a whole, the broth would indeed soothe his parched throat, reduce his fever, and with the addition of honey, lend him strength. However, it would be the little mushrooms that finally let loose his tongue, and the mandrake would give him need to tell, to unload the burdens from his soul… and then she would know the truth of things, and he would pay for a childhood lost, a mother stolen from her and a father surely murdered in cold blood.

The path meandered on and upward for some time, until high above the Abbey, she stopped for breath and gazed back to be certain she was not being observed. A cold wind tugged at her cloak, but the rain clouds were still absent, and it was now a brighter, more pleasant day. There was no sign that any of the nuns that she could see working in the gardens or walking around the Abbey far below were watching. Drawing a determined breath, she turned back to the path, and being careful of her footing on the slippiest parts, continued to climb.

Just below where one of the last clumps of old apple trees were still left upon the tor, she saw what she was looking for, small brown mushrooms growing in groups, wavering in the breeze upon long slender stems. Making a pouch in her robes ready to hold them, she crossed and began to pick. Once she had about twenty, she forced herself to standing, and then waited for a few moments as the expected wave of dizziness passed over her. It slipped slowly away, the brightness of her vision faded, and she soon felt well enough to start back. Perhaps this next infusion should be brewed just a little stronger? She thought about the story Uther had been telling. Whatever took place when the quest arrived on the Isle of Erin was surely a reason for the troubles that had flared upon their return. Stepping carefully, Morgana made her way back down the path and returned to the Abbey.

'Uther… King Uther… please, my Lord… wake.'

Uther could hear his name being called as if it was from a far distant room. It echoed through the passageways of his mind, and he grasped and reached for it, seeking to pull himself out of the dreams that had troubled him. Dreams of giants and blood, Druids and a distant land that had caused such distress and confusion for so many people.

'Uther… awake my Lord. It is a pleasant day, and I have brought you warm broth. You are still weak; the broth will lend you the strength that you need to recover.'

Uther opened his eyes. It was Maude, his protector who sat at the foot of his bed, while beside him, his eyes turned, it was Morgana le Fay, or Morgana the Witch as many had called her, yet now she was Abbess, yes... he knew that. Uther felt a wave of confusion for Morgana, why was she here, did she care for him, was that it? She was the child born by his own wife, Igraine... that was true, but she was no child to him... his mind was whirling, it was difficult to make sense of anything, where was he?

'Uther, sit up a little. Here, let me help you.' Morgana reached down, looming into his vision and lifted him so that Maude could place a bolster behind him allowing him to sit up straighter. His head floated for a little as the two women fussed beside him, and then a bowl and spoon appeared in front of his face, and a little broth ladled into his mouth... it felt good, and then he remembered that he was at the Abbey and that Morgana was caring for him, how had he forgotten that?

'You were telling me about the voyage to Erin,' Morgana was saying, 'it sounds as if you were not a born sailor, my Lord.'

'I... at first, I did not enjoy being at sea this is true.' Uther slurped upon the proffered spoon and then coughed as the warm broth caught in his throat. After a moment he was able to take another spoonful and then he put his head back and stared at the dark beams around the small window, his mind wandering. He still felt the need to talk, despite being so tired, and to explain about the voyage to the Isle of Erin, so many years ago, so strange.

'Once the sickness had passed, I began to enjoy being on the boat, the fresh air and vast expanse of the sea. I remember it smelt good.' He looked up at Morgana and frowned, 'Why am I telling you this? It was so long ago... so long.' Morgana brought the spoon to his lips one more, and he drank the liquid down, the spoon returning several times as he gazed up at her trying to make some sense of his situation.

'Why don't you tell me of you, Morgana? I have spoken plenty; I am still tired, and it is now your turn to tell me of your life. I remember so little about you as a young child. When I... when I took Igraine, your mother, for my wife… you would have been some thirteen summers I think.'

Morgana spooned another measure of broth into the King's mouth and looked at him for a moment before speaking. He couldn't tell what she was thinking, but something was going on behind those dark eyes.

'Very well. I had had fourteen summers when my father was… when my father died. He had sent me south of Tintagel hill fort to live in the nunnery at Laherne,' the words seemed to spill out as if they had been shut up for years and were only now being given wing, he saw her lip tremble at the released memory. 'It was not an easy transition as you may imagine, from cherished daughter of a royal court to fresh novice with a religious order with which I held no affinity nor understanding. My father had tolerated the new religion, allowing the monks and nuns to preach and gather converts, but I had no understanding of them or their faith until I was forced to leave one cold winter morning, placed upon a horse and taken to Laherne.'

Setting the bowl upon the low stool, Morgana uncovered a small pot and held it to her nose. Uther could smell the familiar fragrance of the infusion she had been giving him. She poured a small bowl and then placed it close to his lips, but he ignored it. Instead, he looked up at her and tried to see the girl she had once been that day on the beach.

'Forgive me, Morgana, and that is for many things, I know. But please, tell me how you came by the name Le Fey… I have heard many stories, not all of them kind and surely not true, yet you carry the name and have never tried to spurn it, at least, as far as I am aware.'

She ignored him, tipping the bowl to his lips until it spilt and ran down his chin and onto his chest. Then she frowned at him as if about to rebuke him like a small child.

'Drink, my Lord, and I will tell you. I will tell you a most uninteresting tale of a lost and confused young girl who was so desperate for friendship and comfort, for there was none to be found at Laherne, that she took to the woodland and danced with the wild Fey of the trees and learned their ways… or so the whispering tells… is this the story you would hear?' She tipped the bowl once more, and Uther drank deeply, content to listen to her words...

Life with the nuns was hard beyond anything that anyone could think possible. Woken at various times during the night, the twenty or so young girls that were in training there were ushered into the small chapel and then made to kneel on the cold stone floor where they were led in prayer. They were forced to learn the responses that the priest would call without every fully understanding the meaning or reason behind them. That is, beyond enduring long enough to be allowed to return to the small cells that they shared, three to each cell, and there to steal a few hours of sleep on a rough straw-filled pallet. It was a long way from the rooms she had occupied in the fortress at Tintagel, or at one of her father's other strongholds.

After a little more sleep, they were woken to follow the candlelight procession of sleepy girls back to the chapel for more prayers until daylight. Then the nuns would share a meagre communal meal before chores, followed by more periods where they were encouraged to pray alone.

It was only after being at Laherne for two full years that Morgana discovered both route and opportunity to leave the nunnery between nightly prayers and make some time for herself.

Once outside the main building she would flee across the fields, or walk the lonely path along the cliff tops, a favourite destination when the nights was clear and she could gaze at the moon as it reflected upon the vast expanse of the sea.

Often, when it was too windy, cloudy or raining on the cliff top, she would walk to the edge of the forest, at first, to peer into its dark, soulless depths enjoying the smells of rich earth and decay and then on later visits to lose herself in its emptiness. She listened for the sounds of the night where the hunters of the animal kingdom prowled and life and death were just fleeting moments. As her courage and curiosity grew, she began to enter, to walk the paths when lit by moonlight and to leave the world of man behind.

The night she met the Fey was one that found her at her lowest ebb. She had developed a sore upon her knee that was becoming worse with every passing day. When she had shown the nuns, their answer was that she must have sinned in the eyes of God and that she should drop down and pray for forgiveness and healing, they forced her to her knees and stood over her while the pain flared, and she prayed in a loud sobbing voice, but the sore became worse, and her prayers went unanswered.

After several days, one of the friendlier sisters brought her a poultice made up of leaves, wet straw and mashed onion that had been steeped in vinegar. It was applied to her leg, bound in sackcloth and her hopes rose, but it was soon apparent that the poultice only made it worse. The sore became even larger and swollen, making her leg stiff, difficult to bend and therefore to kneel. A yellow puss oozed behind the poultice causing her great pain, and now she had the added worry that she might now lose her life.

Although she was greatly in need of as much rest and sleep as she could find, Morgana continued to escape the confines of Laherne. After prayers late one night with tears still drying on her face, Morgana opened the shutter in the storeroom window that she knew to be unobserved, and slipped carefully down into the darkness and limped across the fields towards the forest beyond. Beneath her bare feet the grass was cold and wet, yet this brought her no discomfort, only joy; it was such a blessing to be free and away. She shivered and wished she had thought to bring her shawl as it was a cold night, but knowing it would be more sheltered by the trees, she hobbled on, looking back from time to time in fear she might be seen from the Abbey.

Once at the treeline she relaxed and took a deep breath. There was no moon visible, yet its light from behind the clouds was enough to find the fallen tree that she knew made a comfortable seat. She fussed with the poultice for a moment making sure it had not come loose in her haste to be away. And then she stopped, looked up towards the forest as she felt the eyes of something... or someone was upon her.

'You are hurt, child.' The voice came out from the darkness. It was accompanied by a soft fluttering. Morgana tried to locate the sound, her hand coming up to her mouth to stifle a scream.

'Fear not, we are not here to hurt you... although we would be quite capable of doing so should we wish.' The voice was dry, like a whispered breeze dancing through the branches of the trees. 'We have watched you here before and have come to know you, but now you come to us in pain, this draws us.'

'Yes, my leg is hurting... who... who are you?' Morgana rose from her seat and took a step back as the sound of wings flapping came once again from the dark depths of the trees. Her heart was beating loudly in her ears, but she managed to restrain the impulse to turn and run. Instead, she strained her eyes, trying to see into the blackness of the forest, but it was hopeless, there was nothing to be seen.

'I am the one they call the Morrigan in the tales and stories told upon cold and moonless nights. I am one of the Fey, and I have watched you and know you well. You and I shall come to know each other well, Morgana, very well, but first, we must attend to the wounds of your flesh before we might feed the needs of your mind. Enter the forest my dear; I would have you meet my kin.'

Small dim lights appeared floating close by and Morgana felt herself step forward into the forest and the world of the Fey.

As she entered, the lights seemed to gather her up. Her mind filled with light, and she could see the trees and branches around her glowing with a rainbow of colours, pulsing with the energy of their life force. What she had at first perceived to be but dim lights, were now golden. They spun her round, and she smiled and felt the joy of her being. As they moved through the trees, the Fey, for that is what they were, whispered with their voices high and musical. They talked to her and instructed her in the nature of all things, constantly moving, dancing and spinning, twisting and turning, around and around until, with a start, Morgana was back at the edge of the forest, dawn was breaking, and a bell was tolling calling the faithful to prayer.

The bell... oh heavens, the bell....she was late... as she ran across the fields she didn't notice that her knee was now healed, nor did she see the black crow that flew over her having now claimed her as one of its own, a child of the Morrigan and the Fey.

'I visited the Morrigan and the Fey for many years, learning their ways. She still talks to me, teaches me, and helps me with the needs of my life, Uther. You cannot understand the knowledge and gifts that were bestowed upon me.' Morgana tipped more of the infusion into the King's slack lips; his face lost to the story and the power of the brew.

'And now once more it is your turn to speak. Earlier, you mentioned someone called, the Stranger. Uther, did the Druids make you meet with him? Tell me more of what took place before you were able to visit the stones? Was this Stranger one of the Druids?'

Uther's face split into a huge grin, and his eyes focused for a moment. His hand came up and pushed the bowl that Morgana had been pushing to his lips, to the side.

'The Stranger, when we met him, was no Druid, Morgana, no, not a Druid... not really.' His face was now a huge smile that slowly crumpled until a tear rolled down his cheek. 'The Stranger was not a Druid nor an ordinary man; when we met him he was a monster, a terrible, terrible monster that caused such awful pain... much the same as your Morrigan, he was not something of this world.

Chapter 11

Uath The Stranger

'The people of Difelyn made us very welcome.' Uther took a few laboured breaths and licked his lips before continuing. 'I had feared that once they knew we were in their lands to take the stones, to take away what must surely have been a holy place to them, to remove it… that they would become hostile. But at that time, of course, we had not even seen the stones, nor considered what a task it might be, so they were welcoming.' Uther leant forward and sucked the infusion noisily from the proffered bowl. It felt good as it slipped down his throat. It was sweet with honey and had a flowery taste edged with a strange mustiness that was not unpleasant, after another breath he continued.

'The people of Difelyn were not angry that we had arrived, they were intrigued. Their stories told that one day men would come and attempt to take the stones. I suppose they didn't really believe it because the stones were so huge, massive, and they didn't see how it could be accomplished. The very idea of us picking them up and leaving must have sounded so ridiculously absurd, so of course they weren't worried we were going to run off with them. I think they were just interested to see what we might try and do. They allowed a hundred of us to rest in Difelyn, they fed us, shared their fires with us and gave us enough of their ale and clear spirit drink that we all lost our heads in the celebration. We awoke late, all feeling the ill effects of the Erin brew, and the next day they took us to see the Druids.

'What type of drink hits so hard that it makes a man wish he was dead?' Uther staggered over the loose stones of the path and rubbed at his head as he walked.

'I think we may already be dead and all this is just an evil dream. There is a taste in my mouth that even my dog would spit out... and my head is still pounding with the sound of those infernal drums.' Duc Gerlois hawked up a gob of phlegm to emphasise his point and then stopped to clasp his temples. 'Ohhh... where are we going and why could I not stay sleeping?'

At that moment, Merlyn strode past the two men, swinging his staff and smiling happily. He gave them a little wave. 'We go to visit the Druid camp upon the mountain, my Lords. Isn't it a beautiful morning? Breathe deeply, enjoy the experience of being close to this land.'

'That Druid is infuriating,' growled Gerlois as he watched Merlyn stride ahead. 'It was he who kept pouring the little bowls for us, and I am sure he was drinking as much of it as we did.'

'No doubt he has some potion or other, some root or herb he is sucking on that clears his head and stops his stomach from churning so.' Uther stopped and watched as the Druid passed Cunobelin, slapping him on the back as he went. It appeared as if the young Trinovantes lord was suffering as much as Uther and Gerlois because he staggered under the Druid's blow as if he had been struck by a Saxon battleaxe. As they reached him, Uther gathered the young lord under his arm and the three helped each other along, still complaining irritably.

By mid-morning, the warriors of Difelyn had brought them through the foothills and up onto the lower slope of Mount Killaraus. For those that could summon the effort to look about them, the path had taken them from the settlement, up through woodland and past numerous smallholdings where family groups gathered to scratch an existence from small tilled fields. They passed through some cool, dark woods and then emerged from the low treeline to the sight of sheep scattering, leaping and calling in fright at the unexpected appearance of the long line of warriors. The low clouds that had covered the earlier part of their trek with layers of mist had all but disappeared; the sun was now making an appearance and the day was warming. The view out across the land towards the shimmering sea was enough to bring many of the warriors to a halt. They stopped to rest and skins of weak ale were passed back and forth.

'*Are we close now, Merlyn?*' shouted Uther. '*Is there much further to walk, because I for one am about to lay right here on this soft green grass and fall asleep.*' There were many calls of agreement as others lay back delighting in the fact that it was the King himself who had called the halt. Uther shaded his eyes and watched as the Druid strode back towards him.

'You choose a good spot to break your journey, because we are close, worry not.' Merlyn squatted down leaning on his staff. 'You can rest here for some time should you wish. The caves are just a short walk further through the trees,' - he pointed further along the path - 'and I am told they have a hall being prepared for our arrival.'

'Our arrival, how do they know we are coming?'

'They are Druids, Uther; they know we are coming.' Merlyn stood and turned at the sound of a horn being blown, floating as it was carried to them on the wind. It was deep and seemed to make the whole mountain and everything around them vibrate. Every head turned to the distant trees where their guides had just disappeared.

'This seems a little ominous, my King,' rumbled Duc Gerlois. 'Should we perhaps form a shield wall or maybe be ready for an attack of some kind?'

'They are Druids, Duc Gerlois; there will be no attack. They seek to welcome us, nothing more.' Merlyn turned to Uther. 'I shall go ahead and prepare the way. Remember that we are here to be tested, it shall go well, I have no fear of that but do be ready, may the spirits be with you, King Uther.' Merlyn rose and walked away towards the trees without waiting for Uther to reply, and Uther lay back content for a while to allow the sun to warm his face.

Unfortunately, Uther didn't get a chance to fall asleep, though he was close. His mind was drifting, just imagining that he was back near his village, at the lake with his friend Cal. They were talking about going for a swim… which seemed like a good idea, but then he was brought out of his reverie by a shout from down the line that someone was approaching.

Uther sat up and rubbed at his eyes, blinking them and shielding them from the sun's glare as he tried to see who it might be. A figure had stopped by a group of warriors further down the path and he could see them pointing back towards him.

Wearily he rolled to his side and heaved himself up. 'To your feet, my Lords. I believe we are about to meet our first Erin Druid.' The others roused themselves and after a few moments, they were all waiting in some sort of readiness as the Druid came walking towards them.

He wore the usual long robes of a Druid, his were a dirty grey, had his hands clasped before him as he walked and a smile set firmly upon his face, but he was young, Uther noted. He had started to think that all Druids were old with long grey hair and even longer beards, but this one appeared to be not much older than Arthur, and his beard was dark brown and cut short to his chin, but he still wore the same, idiotic Druid smile.

'I bid you welcome to Erin, King Uther, my Lords. My name is Finis and I shall be your guide as we enter the cave.'

'Thank you for your welcome, Finis,' said Uther. 'You didn't happen to see a Druid by the name of Merlyn, did you? He was travelling with us and went ahead.'

'The Druid Merlyn is well and has already left us to visit with the Council as they meet upon the high fell. You are to be our guests here for a few days until he returns. Please, let us walk. It would be my pleasure to see you settled and bring you food and ale.' Finis bowed his head and swept his hand in the direction of the trees.

'No more strong ale, at least for the time being, friend Finis,' rumbled Duc Gerlois. 'However, a place to rest and a little food would be most welcome. I am quite ready to finish our little walk today.'

'A hall has been prepared for you. Please, follow me.' Finis turned and walked back in the direction that he had come and Uther and his men gathered their things and followed in a ragged line.

When they passed through the small curtain of trees through which the Druid had disappeared, they emerged into a large open clearing, dominated by an enormous cave that towered over their heads. The Britons began to bunch up as they passed through the barrier of trees, stopping to gaze in awe at what appeared to be the huge mouth of the mountain gaping open above them. It looked as if the mountain was taking a huge bite out of the land and had paused, for just one moment, to contemplate its task.

High above, the ragged edge of the overhanging cliff had the appearance of jagged teeth set into terrible jaws. Smoke drifted between the teeth and birds circled and called, swooping between the points apparently indifferent to any risk that the jaws might close.

'Oh, I know why the Druids like this place,' muttered Uther. Looking about him he realised that his men had all halted, yet Finis was still striding on towards the cluster of halls and roundhouses erected further on within the cavern. Smoke rose from several and he estimated that the Druids must number near a hundred, even when one of the larger halls had been prepared for visitors. Finis had turned and was gesturing for them to follow.

'Come on, let us enter the mouth of the mountain and hope it doesn't decide to taste us,' called Uther, leading his men forward past strange rocks piled one upon another and even stranger totems, branches tied with cloth, feathers, bones and the skulls of animals, birds and rodents.

As they stepped from the light, passing under the rock canopy far above, they entered the Druid settlement and began to hear the echoes of their own footsteps, and then other strange sounds began to float about them. Chanting and the soft sound of drums filled the air, along with a dry whispering, as if a soft chant were coming from countless voices. Druids began emerging from all around to watch the sight of so many warriors walking amongst them. One Druid, dressed in dirty black robes, walked forward, pointed at the group and started shouting and spitting angrily, but another quickly came and quieted him, leading him away.

'Truth be told, King Uther, I am not too comfortable in places like this.' Duc Gerlois was indeed looking a little distressed as he tripped along, picking his way over the rock-strewn floor of the cave. 'I find Druids to be a little... well a little confusing and unpredictable to say the least. We have a small grove just a short way from my fortress at Tintagel. Nice enough people I am sure. I have little to do with them, but whenever I pass by, they flap branches at me and make the strangest noises, rattling bones and blowing horns... I don't mind telling you; I find them all just a little... well, just a little disturbing.'

'You are not alone, Duc Gerlois. I don't think anyone who is not a Druid could ever understand them or some of the things they consider to be normal. The trouble is that the lives of Druids rarely come into contact with many of us. We have little opportunity to become accustomed to their ways.' Uther glanced back and saw that the Duc wasn't alone in his unease. Many of the warriors were wide-eyed and obviously just as agitated as Duc Gerlois to be walking in the company of Druids. Usually, if a band of warriors should chance upon a Druid grove, they would carefully retrace their steps, find a different route, and leave the Druids undisturbed to continue their ramblings and rites alone. Sending them back to the boats wasn't an answer, they would have to hold strong until they were in the hall and then there would be opportunity for rest.

The crowd of dirty Druids parted as they neared the largest hall. There was much muttering and swaying, but none other approached. Uther found himself touching the dragon shaped pommel of Excalibur and drew his hand away. He led his men through the Druids and then on towards the smiling Finis.

The hall was large. As they entered through the sturdy plank doors, Uther could see at least eight different areas with fires already burning, with seating and pallets set about each of them promising solace and comfort to his men. The hall was at least fifty paces long and almost as many wide. A high thatched roof rose above them and was open at both ends to help disperse the smoke. Supporting the roof was a framework of heavy beams intricately carved with Druidic runes and knots. It was warm and welcoming, and Uther felt his apprehension fall away as he entered and was welcomed once more by Finis and two older Druids, their long grey beards plaited and laced with an assortment of sticks, bones and shiny things that caught the flickering light of the fires. One of the old Druids stepped forward and raised his staff, the bones sticks and shells rattling as he did so.

'Welcome, Uther Pendragon, King of the Britons. Welcome, Lords and warriors. We have eagerly awaited your coming,' - he leaned forward, smiling, and lowered his voice as he spoke to Uther - 'we have watched you from afar,' he nodded happily to himself. 'You are most welcome here amongst us. Rest with us here while you await the return of the Druid Merlyn, we shall care for you while the Stranger sees things right.'

'The Stranger? We have heard much talk about this Stranger. Who or what is he?' asked Uther, as behind him the warriors spread out towards the different fires and platters of food that were being brought in and laid upon the low benches.

'Worry not about the Stranger. He is who he is, and all is right and part of the story of life.' The old Druid smiled, but Uther felt a rising of frustration at the familiar sound of Druidic nonsense.

'You are not going to tell me who he is or what he would have of us, are you? Very well, we shall meet whatever takes place with honour in our hearts and if need be, blades in our hands.'

'That is how the story tells, for without honour and blade to balance, how can each turn of our path to the Shadowland possibly be bright. Especially of you who walks the earth with so little understanding of days and nights beyond the reach of your fellows, is that not so?'

Uther glared at him and decided it was a worthless undertaking to trade words with a Druid It was all utter nonsense. As the Druid smiled and nodded his head as if he had just received an answer to his cryptic question, Uther turned his back to him and went to sit beside Sir Ector and Duc Gerlois.

Where at least the fire was hot, and the food was good.

Nobody saw or noticed as the great doors swung in, inaudible upon well-greased hinges, but the colossal crash of the doors slamming home silenced the warriors who had spent the last few spans until darkness, eating, drinking, and resting around the fires. At once alert, every warrior sat up to look towards the entrance, setting their cups to the side, hands moving towards weapons, they stared at the figure who had entered.

There, stood a true giant of a man. Eyes glowing like the coals of a fire, the stranger towered higher than any of the warriors present. His head as he walked almost touched the beams of the roof and his brow and nose, set above a thick and bristly beard, cast shadows across the hall, this was no mortal man, this was a giant from tales of old.

As the giant passed the warriors to either side, waves of body heat and a rich, pungent odour passed over them and they shrank back, but every eye returned to follow his progress. About his waist, he wore the skin of a cow tied with rope and grass while across his shoulders he wore a cloak of greasy, matted wool. Silence filled the room save for the heavy tread and the sound of the oaken log that he dragged behind him, held in one massive fist as easily as most men would drag a club. In the other hand rested an axe.

Dogs that had been moving about amongst the warriors, begging treats or stealing from the tables whenever they could, slunk to the back of the hall, tails touching their bellies, and whimpered in fear at the giant's coming.

Slowly, each footstep reverberating against the roof beams so that they shook and dust dropped to fill the air, the figure strode towards the hearth where Uther sat waiting with his most trusted warriors seated about him.

As he reached the centre, the Stranger planted himself dominantly, legs apart, threw down his log in front of the fire and stood, silently challenging anyone to speak, but with the shock of his entrance nobody did. His shoulders sagged in resignation and he addressed the hall.

'My name is Uath, and I am known to all who will hear me, as Uath the Stranger,' his voice was deep and slow, the gravel of it felt within the belly of all those that were present.

'I roam this sorry world seeking one man amongst the multitude who might hold fast to his word.' He turned a full circle, dragging the axe as he surveyed the faces turned towards him, finally completing his turn he stared at Uther as he sat amongst his men. 'A simple task, an easy thing to find you may think, but you would be wrong.' Again, all stayed silent in shocked disbelief as they waited for the huge giant to go on.

'I have spent an eternity walking this earth searching for a man who would hold a contract with me, a man who will keep to an agreement that we make. That tonight...' - he turned a circle once more, staring into the soul of every warrior present before continuing - 'that tonight this one brave man should step forward... take this axe,' - he held the huge axe up high - 'that the man I seek should take this axe and strike my head from my shoulders... while tomorrow as the sun sets I may return and then strike a similar blow to him,' - he looked deeply into the eyes of Uther Pendragon - 'do I ask so much? Surely there is one here tonight, a champion filled with warrior's blood, who will meet these simple terms?'

The answer he received was silence because it smelled so badly of Druids and magic it was impossible to comprehend or make any sense out of.

Uath turned again, taking in all those present. The hall remained silent save for the crackling of the fires. A smile crept over the giant's face and he spat into the fire in scorn, the phlegm hissing as it hit hot embers.

'Silence? You answer me with silence, and so I say there is no champion here, there is no man of honour amongst you.'

Uther leapt to his feet, as did many others each calling their contempt and outrage at the Stranger's words. But it was Duc Gerlois who strode to the centre of the hall and looked up into the giant's face as it towered above him.

'You have no right to call this gathering dishonourable,' he bellowed. 'I will hold fast to my word. I will cut your evil head from your shoulders; I... will answer your challenge.'

'Duc Gerlois, no.' Uther walked around the fire and took the Duc's shoulder. 'This is a trick. This is Druid magic; this is not...'

Gerlois leant forward and spoke in a low voice into Uther's ear. 'This is just Druid tricks, I agree, King Uther, but this is a mortal man, a big one I grant you, but this man can and will be killed. He expects that no man will walk forward and take his challenge.' He turned without waiting for Uther to say anything in reply.

'Kneel then, Uath, the Stranger. Kneel at my feet and I give you my word, I will cut off your head this night, and tomorrow night, if you return, you may take mine.' He smirked as he said these last words and looked around at the gathered warriors. Smiles and no small amount of laughter greeted him as all realised the absurdity of his words. Yet, beside him, Uath the Stranger fell to his knees, placed his huge head upon the oaken log, and waited for the blow to fall.

The hall returned to quiet as the warriors stared at Duc Gerlois, waiting to see if he would pick up the giant's axe. It took a few moments for Gerlois to realise that the giant did indeed expect him to cut his head off, but realise he did, and with no small effort, the Duc lifted the huge axe, tested it's weight in his hands for a moment, and then swung it high.

Firelight caught the blade as it flashed down, whistling its death song as it cut through the air. With a meaty *thwack*, it struck the creature's neck, cleanly cutting through to embed itself in the log beneath. For a moment the head held, and then slowly it lolled forward to thump onto the flagstone floor. Instants later, it was followed by great gouts of blood pumping and spurting past the axe blade from the severed neck splattering those closest with scarlet droplets and hissing where they landed in the fire.

Gerlois stood for a moment gazing down at the bloody mess and then gestured with his hands as if showing all present what he had accomplished. An uncertain smile crept across his features, and then it slowly dropped as the massive body stirred, and then rose to its feet, the lack of its head affecting neither its composure nor poise.

The hall was silent as all stared in awe as the giant, headless body bent down, reached for the axe and rocked it back and forth to lever it from the log. The blade squeaked loud in protest at each effort to rock it free, and then once accomplished, the giant crouched back down to claim its head. Rising, it hugged the shaggy, bloody head against its expansive chest, the face staring outward while blood ran in glistening rivers down from the stump of the severed neck and gore dripped from where its life's essence had so recently flowed. The creature turned and marched through the silent hall towards the great doors, carrying its blood-soaked baggage, the eyes turning within their sockets from side to side offering a look of glowering disdain for all present who had borne witness to this terrible event.

'My father... he would never have...'

Uther's attention was snapped back to the present, and he looked across to Morgana, who had her hand against her mouth. She looked ill. Never one to have much colour, she still appeared whiter than usual, even in the gloomy light of the cell her skin was in stark contrast to the black of her hair and robes.

'Was this all real, or a dream?'

Uther's glanced up to see Maude staring down at him.

'The Druids, they could have placed a spell, poisoned the food... they could have tricked...' Maude's words trailed off.

'Did he come back?' Morgana reached out and clutched at Uther's arm. 'This Stranger... did he return? I don't understand. My father arrived with the boats, with you, didn't he? This awful Stranger must not have returned.' She offered a hopeful smile, her grip upon his arm tightening.

Uther sighed, once again feeling the burdens of his life and the need to sleep. He closed his eyes and as he did he heard liquid being poured and caught the familiar smell of the infusion. The bowl was pressed to his lips, and he sipped, it lent him strength, enough at least to answer.

'He came back.' Uther glanced from Morgana to Maude, who was now crouching beside the Abbess. 'He came back as he promised he would, and he was no illusion or figment of our imaginations, Uath the Stranger was very, very real.'

Chapter 12

An Oath of Blood

The door to the great hall opened and Duc Gerlois forced his way in past groups of animated warriors fighting, laughing and fooling. As he pushed through towards Uther, the crowd began to quieten and part as they realised it was he who had entered. Every eye turning upon him, every warrior in the hall glad that they were not walking in Gerlois' boots, dead man's boots at the hands of a giant arrived from the deepest of nightmares.

Every man and woman there had witnessed the spectacle of the night before, yet few could still believe what their eyes claimed to have seen. For most, the night had been sleepless and most of the day had been spent talking about and recalling the events that had possibly taken place. Possibly, because how could it have happened? How could a man lose his head and then pick it up and walk away? Yet, it must have taken place because, as was constantly being pointed out, there was a very large log and a huge sticky pool of blood in the centre of the hall. They had thrown down dirt and swept it as best they could, yet the evidence remained as proof that the giant had entered and issued his challenge. Proof that the incredible drama of his decapitation had taken place, and if that was to be believed then it was also proof they had seen the giant pick up his head and walk from the hall. A bridge between worlds had been crossed and it was Gerlois who stood alone upon the other side peering into the Shadowland, and so they stared.

'I walked to the path,' Gerlois hissed as he rounded the great central fire and sank down beside Uther. 'The Druids did not stop me; we can leave.' He glanced up, saw that every tribesman in the hall was still watching him, and then he put his face in his hands. 'He will be back, he will return and he will take my head,' he mumbled, and then he turned to face Uther. 'He will take my head, what do I do?'

Uther reached out and took the Duc's arm. 'What about the Druid trickery? You said it yourself and I agree, this is just a trial, Duc Gerlois. To take the stones, the Druids want to know that they are going to a people who are worthy, who have honour. I do not believe that when the giant returns, that he will cut your head off,' - he shook his own head - 'you started this because you are brave, and so you have to go through with it. You have to play this Druid game. When he walks through that door, you...'

'All so easy for you to say, my King,' hissed Gerlois through clenched teeth, he was sweating, his eyes darting about. He fumbled with a knife and stabbed it into the table angrily. 'You are not the one who is going to have to put his head on that stump and... I know that I was the one, but...' he left the sentence unfinished.

'You will prove we have both honour and courage in abundance, my friend. I do not believe the Druids would hold with this for long, allowing this Stranger to enter their sacred place and murder their guests, it is too incredible to be believed. I say again, you were right when you said that this was just a Druid trick, they are playing with us once more. Hold to this Gerlois, and you will get through this and we will return triumphantly with the stones.' Uther clasped him by the shoulder and after a moment, the Duc, somewhat reluctantly, nodded.

By late morning, the warriors were restless at being so confined and several fights had already broken out. Uther knew that being restrained in the hall like this was going to end in further disagreements and before long, bloodshed. When asked about them leaving, Finis had no problem other than suggesting that they should stay low on the mountain and not try to take the path up towards the stones.

'The Druid Council is meeting there with Merlyn and others. They will have completed their business and the rituals that are necessary within just a few days.' He smiled, looking deeply into Uther's eyes and nodded his head as if hearing something. 'Might I guide you to see the waterfalls, we could be there and back before nightfall?'

Despite finding the Druid infuriating, the idea of walking his men for most of the day appealed to Uther and so he agreed and they trailed out behind Finis, following him through the cave past the community of Druids. Each Druid paused as they went by, halting whatever intricate complexity of Druidic life that they were involved in to watch them pass, before going back to mumbling, swaying, chanting or sitting as still as stone staring off into the darkness, as was their way.

Once they arrived outside and into the comfort of a drizzling rain, the warriors were visibly relieved to be away from the Druids and once more under a leaden sky that was, at least, familiar and something they could understand.

They followed after Finis as he led them on the trail. At first, it twisted and turned back the same way that they had first arrived, through the meadows and woodland, but where the path they had followed dropped down towards the settlement of Difelyn, they instead turned upwards over a small hill and on towards the next valley. By midday, they had again risen to new heights and were walking through lush green woodland dripping with the rain that was falling above them through a high canopy of leaves, and when they finally emerged, it was to see a huge waterfall splashing a torrent of water down into a pool at its base.

It was impressive, a true wonder of nature, and Uther could see why it was favoured by the Druids. A hawthorn tree, covered with small pieces of cloth torn from the cloaks and clothes of visitors grew close to the pool and beside it, an enormous upright stone stood towering over the visiting warriors – runes, cut crisp and clearly, showed upon its surface. While the warriors spread out, avoiding the stone, Finis walked to it and started a small fire at its base using a piece of glowing ember that he had carried from the Druid cave in a small clay pot that was hung from his neck on a cord and some dry twigs pulled from his robe. The blackened rocks around the base of the stone showed that this was a regular ritual. When he had a small blaze going, he smothered it with green leaves and smoke billowed up and drifted around the edge of the pool.

'This is a ritual practiced here,' said Finis as Uther looked on. 'Rituals are important to the way of things.' Behind Uther the warriors were spreading around the clearing, some laughing and joking as they hunted the few deer that had been seen, scattering when they first came out of the woods, while others were content to sharpen blades or rest. It was too cold to swim.

'By doing this, we call upon the three worlds of land, water, and sky,' - he gestured towards the smoke as it drifted around the pool - 'the smoke is our pathway touching each of the worlds and it is through this that we are able to talk with the spirits of the ancestors who abide here.'

'You speak with those that have died? With people who have walked this land in times before? Would they know the history of the stones?' Uther asked, but wasn't sure how much he wanted to know. He had spoken with Merlyn many times but never felt much the wiser for the conversations.

'Perhaps they do... we shall see. I am able to speak with the dead as we all are if we would but listen. For they are in the wind which touches us, in the air that we breathe and within our words spoken and the songs that we sing.' Finis smiled and wafted smoke towards his face and then out towards the pond. 'They are all around us; they are in the waters of our land, in the rivers and within this pool, which holds so much memory. They are in the earth that nourished them with food and which their bodies nourished in turn when they died. Our ancestors are in our blood and in the stories told, in the mistakes we make, and in the lessons we have learned. They are also in each child's smile, in every ploughed field and in each glimpse of hope. Our ancestors are all around, but also, within us, it just takes a little effort and understanding to call upon them and ask for their guidance.' He smiled, sank to his knees and began to speak in soft tones as the smoke continued to swirl about him.

Uther stepped back, glanced about in case an ancestor should show himself, and then decided to leave the Druid to his ritual. It was always better not to try and understand what Druids were doing. He looked for Duc Gerlois, but could not see him, so he joined Sir Ector.

The old warrior was talking with several others, discussing the imminent return of Uath the Stranger. One voice was raised suggesting that they should all bring the giant to battle as soon as he entered the hall. Uther was about to interject, but stopped and listened as Sir Ector tried patiently to explain that if they all fought him, then there was no way that the Druids would see they had any honour, and they would not be able to take the stones; a point that Uther had already come to.

As he approached, they all stood. 'Do not fret. We are merely pieces within these Druid games, nothing more,' said Uther as he crouched down beside them. 'It pleases them to taunt and play with us like this. Duc Gerlois will be spared at the last moment, and we shall all be celebrated as worthy and honourable men.'

'But the Duc is not here, Uther. We were just discussing when he was last seen. I am not sure he even joined us on this small journey today.' Sir Ector shrugged.

Uther shook his head. 'He would not leave. He will be waiting back in the hall when we return, or he will join us shortly. I have faith in him.' He stared around at the warriors, saw the looks in their eyes, and began to feel his faith slip slowly away. If the Duc was a coward, then he was jeopardising the whole quest, betraying them all.

When they returned to the hall within the mouth of the mountain, the Duc was not there.

Druids, both male and female brought in platters of food, ale and mead and the warriors, hungry from their day's walk, were happy to be so entertained. Wrestling matches were pitched between warriors of different tribes and there were contests with axe and spear.

It was late and the mood somewhat more sombre when the heavy doors were thrown back with a great crash that echoed about both the hall and the cave outside. The sound was accompanied by a gust of cold wind and the smell of falling rain and the giant figure of Uath the Stranger stooping low to enter. Whole once more, without a single mark on his great thick neck, Uath strode into the hall cradling the heavy axe in his hands. He slowed his pace and walked unhurriedly towards the central fire, glowering at the warriors who were once again struck dumb with awe. When at last he reached the hearth and the oaken log set before it, he stood silent and unmoving, his thumb rubbing against the axe blade, the rasping noise that it made the only sound beyond the crackling of the fires. After some moments of contemplation, he turned a slow complete circle, and seeing that Duc Gerlois was not in attendance, he hung his head, shook it slowly in sadness and then spat upon the stones of the floor, but as he did, a voice rose from the back of the hall.

'I am ready to honour your challenge, giant... I am ready to strike your head from your shoulders, and when you return tomorrow, I shall not fear to offer you the same pact.' Cunobelin walked from the ranks of warriors and, standing in front of the towering figure, accepted the proffered axe amid a cacophony of noise, calls of encouragement and lament, anger and fear, slowly the sounds died.

The giant met the warrior's gaze for one long moment, then shrugged and knelt beside the oaken log, placing his head so that it might be cleanly struck.

Wasting no time, Cunobelin cried out as, with all his strength, he lifted and swung the huge axe, and with all the force he could muster, struck.

'*Ahhhh yuhhhh!*' The axe met the log with a solid '*thunk*,' cutting cleanly through the neck, parting the head from the shoulders with such force, that it bounced across the flagstones with great gouts of blood pumping after it, spraying across every warrior seated within five paces. Cunobelin let go of the axe and stepped back.

A moment later, the giant's body rose, walked around the log and with blood still pumping from the ruined stump of its neck, levered the axe free from the wood, and then crossed to where his head had rolled to lay beside one of the great carved beams that supported the roof of the hall. As before, he picked it up and held it with the face staring outwards. The eyes rolled around in their sockets for a moment, and then settled and glared from side to side at the warriors who had witnessed its torment, and then the giant slowly walked to the door and left.

As the massive door boomed shut, the hall erupted into pandemonium as all began talking, shouting and arguing with one another.

'I had to do it.' Cunobelin wiped away a stray spot of blood that had landed upon his cheek and sat down next to Uther. 'Someone here needs to meet the giant's demands and it seems it wasn't destined to be Gerlois.'

'You have a great heart, Cunobelin. Your ancestors are proud of you, as am I, your King. This act will not go unrewarded, and I am certain... that you will not lose your head when that monster returns. I have lived around Druids from an early age and I know the games they play and the riddles they mutter.' Uther smiled and clapped the warrior on the shoulder. 'For now, my friend. Let us drink and celebrate the bravery of the Trinovantes and their Lord.'

Uther stood and raised his drinking horn. Ale slopped over the side and there was laughter from some who saw this, he smiled and saluted them with the horn.

'Warriors of Briton, I call upon you to drink, something I know you do well.' There was a cheer and many calls of agreement. 'We honour the Trinovante tonight and the bravery of their Lord, Cunobelin. For he is the one amongst us who accepted their challenge and struck the head from their monster. It is he who shall laugh in the face of the Druids and regain their respect for all of us when he shows that they should never throw dice with a Trinovante!'

A roar of approval filled the hall and ale and mead flowed as the latest developments to their quest were discussed and bantered over. Uther sat down again and smiled into the stern young face of Cunobelin. They touched drinking horns and drank deeply, and then they both turned to look across the fire towards the blood-soaked log and wet, slick flagstones. The blood was as dark as night and reflected the flickering from the flames and they were both thinking the same thing. That tomorrow night, Uath the Stranger, would return.

'Forgive me, King Uther.'

Uther opened his eyes and tried to understand what was happening. It was dark within the hall, save for the soft glow from the burned down fires, but he judged it was some time around daybreak outside. There was a dark shadow hunched beside him. He could hear the ragged sound of breathing and the occasional sniff; it was obviously Duc Gerlois.

'I… I could not return to… to greet that giant, I just… but I see there is blood, fresh blood, what happened? Tell me what I must do to make amends, please… forgive me, King Uther?'

'You can find me water. That would be the first thing you could do. My head is fit for nothing but bursting at the moment.' Uther sat up as Gerlois went off in search of water. By the time the Duc returned, clutching a jug to his chest, Uther had managed to rise from where he had slept and was now sitting up at one of the low tables, gazing out at the sleeping warriors as they snored and passed wind around him.

'Water, I fetched it from the stream, it is good and clean.' Duc Gerlois thrust the jug towards Uther and some slopped out of the top to splatter upon the table. They both stared at it for a moment, and then Uther cleared his throat.

'Where did you go yesterday?' Without waiting for an answer, he picked up the jug and drank. It tasted good and helped to still the thumping tension in his head.

'I was scared, but I did not mean to leave, I... I wasn't running away.' The Duc was silent for a moment, staring at smoking embers of the fire. 'I didn't know what to do, but I couldn't bring myself to return. I've been sitting, freezing on the mountain asking the Gods, the spirits and my ancestors to help me, to give me guidance and help bring back the life I had, which now seems to be in ruins. I have been watching the clouds float past when the moon has shown light and then sat listening to the rain dripping through the trees above me when all around was in darkness. My ancestors did not speak; I heard nothing, no guidance, just the empty echo of my heart.'

'Uath the Stranger returned as he promised.' Uther turned to face Gerlois. 'When you did not step forward, Cunobelin of the Trinovante did. He took the giant's head and tonight, it will be he who must lay his head down to be struck.' They both turned their eyes to the log, still black and glistening with congealing blood. Uther drank more from the jug and then put it down with a thump.

'I don't have advice for you, Gerlois. I don't know what you must do to make amends, but I do know that it will not be easy. Your cowardice is a betrayal of your people. Others will no doubt die because of your weakness and our whole venture might well fail.' He stood and then made his way through the sleeping bodies and out into the cave in search of somewhere to empty his bladder, leaving Gerlois to ponder how he would face the day and the warriors who would soon awaken.

This day's march was down to the sea and the boats they had left there. For much of the time, Duc Gerlois walked towards the back of the line alone, save for a few of his tribesmen who spoke little to him and showed every indication that they would prefer not to be in his company. He endured jibes and a few small insults from warriors around him that at first he felt were almost justified, and so he walked on and bore the shame. But then later, on the return march after they had checked upon the boats and warriors stationed there and gathered a few provisions, the insults had continued and his temper had started to rise.

'Enough!' He spun upon the warrior who had been whispering loudly behind him. Some notion about facing men in battle and excrement soiling the legs. It was nothing, but it was one insult too many and he now found himself confronted with a Trinovante warrior, who, far from backing away because he faced a Lord, was holding his spear as if he meant to stab him.

'Because you could not hold with the challenge that you made... that you...' - the warrior stabbed forward with the spear -' ...made. A great man had to take your place, and King Uther and all of us who quest with him lost any respect that we might have gained from these people.' He spat at Gerlois feet. Several of the other warriors were trying to calm him but he shrugged them off. Others were turning back now to see what was happening. Gerlois glanced about, but Uther, Sir Ector and anyone who might possess a voice of reason were towards the front of the line and had already passed some distance ahead.

The warrior was young and eager for the situation to turn into a fight. Gerlois turned to face him and felt his own men come to stand behind him; he felt a small amount of comfort from their support. He studied the warrior. The boy, for he was not much more than that, was bare-chested above baggy leggings and a length of course wool that had been coloured a deep red, worn slung over one shoulder. His hair was thick and black and tied at the side with a piece of rough hide. A badly painted swirl decorated his face and neck, daubed by a hasty finger with blue woad before they left the hall, was Gerlois guess.

'Do not test me, boy. I may have earned some scorn, but I'm done now and I will not be pushed by the likes of you.' The Duc glanced to his side and seeing that one of his men held a spear, he snatched it and now armed, stood to face the grinning warrior and two of his companions. The main party of warriors were out of sight having passed up into the woodland. Here, they were on open ground with a cliff on one side and a meadow behind; a few sheep ignored them some distance away offering just an occasional bleat. He could hear others running in to see what was happening and knew that this situation had to be finished before it got out of hand.

'Let us step back and we shall say this never happened, what do you say?' He looked questioningly at the warrior but saw what the answer was going to be even before it happened. The warrior's spear snaked out and might have taken him in the shoulder if he had been any less of a fighter himself. Gerlois stepped to the side and knocked the spear away sending a half-hearted response with his own.

'Last chance, and I'm not normally a man given to offering chances, *step away!*' He shouted the last, but the warrior cried out in anger and attacked in earnest, stabbing and then slashing with his spear. The two others did not join in, but looked nervously to one another, and then towards warriors that Gerlois could hear pushing through the crowd behind him. 'Protect my back!' He called to his men and then concentrated solely upon his adversary. The boy was no real match for him, but he was also no child. Gerlois loosed his own combination of stabs and cuts using both ends of the spear, herding the warrior towards the cliff where he knew he would have the advantage and possibly force the young warrior to yield.

They were on the edge of the cliff now, a drop long enough to kill either if they were to fall. *'Back away!'* cried Gerlois, but the Trinovante was in no mood to submit, he stabbed out narrowly missing the Duc then spun the spear to try and catch the Duc on the head. Gerlois ducked feeling the spear pass over his head and realised he should have removed his heavy cloak, he was hot already and it was getting in his way, he was blind on his right side when he raised that arm. Too late now to get rid of it, he just had to go on and finish as best he could.

The air was filled with noise as warriors shouted and screamed in excitement. The blood of battle coursing through their veins as the combatants were urged on, the young warrior becoming even more reckless. Gerlois realised he was tiring. He was the older man and it had been many years since he had trained regularly. His arms were aching, feeling spent and he could hear his own breathing loud in his ears. This needed to end... and then amid the screaming he felt a surge of hope, as he discerned that some were pushing back the crowd, trying to stop the violence. He took an almighty swipe which made the young warrior step back, and he hoped might possibly offer a chance for someone to jump in and halt the fight, but his spear travelled past the warrior and caught one of the men who was trying to enter, hitting him, hard across his chest, sending him stumbling back. For one awful moment, the man stood upon the cliff's edge, staring at them in silent incomprehension, his arms spinning in circles as he sought for balance, and then he fell.

'*Cunobelin!*' The cry went up as warriors moved cautiously to the edge of the cliff and peered over.

Gerlois dropped his spear and sank to the ground. A moment later someone was trying to pull him up, trying to lead him away. 'Oh spirits, I killed …' Panic returned and began to overwhelm him, he looked up into the face of the warrior who was desperately trying to drag him away. 'I killed him; I killed Cunobelin.'

'Yes, Lord, and if we do not leave you may well have killed us all.'

Chapter 13

The Oaken Log

Warriors sat about their fires in restrained silence. There was no drinking or feasting this evening. There were no wrestling bouts nor games of dice being played. One of their greatest champions had fallen, and there was not a man nor a woman present who did not bitterly feel the loss. When the great doors crashed back to shiver the timbers of the hall and Uath the Stranger entered, he stopped and glanced about him. A puzzled expression crossed his face, he hugged the great axe to his body and rasped his thumb across its blade. Slowly, he walked on to the fire across from which Uther sat with his closest warriors. Uath turned a full circle and stared at the silent gathering, his big cold face finally becoming a grin until his laughter bellowed out loud, the sound of it booming throughout the hall sending motes of dust to dance down from the roof and float in the air.

'So… now two of your bravest and best have failed in their promises with me, great warriors of Britain. Their honour and courage turned to piss and whimpers when the time came to lay their heads upon the log.'

'Your contract is a bargain for fools, Uath the Stranger.' Uther rose from beside Sir Ector and pushed aside the hands that urged him to remain seated. 'You may keep your bargain, for it is an agreement only for the simple minded. We have seen the manner of your contract, where through some Druid trickery your head is struck yet you return remade and unharmed. Do you think us of so little wit? We are mortal

137

men. Any one of us would die and not return if our head was removed, and so I repeat myself… your contract is for fools.'

'Scared are you, Uther Pendragon? Lily-livered like your champions?' The giant threw back his head and laughed once more. 'You are like a spineless child.' He lowered his head until it was at the same level as Uther. 'A spineless, gutless child… and a coward, like your men and all these cowardly warriors who watch us now, yet say nothing.'

Uther felt a rage build within him as angry calls and hissing filled the room. Seeing the axe in the giant's hands, he snatched it, wrenching it from the other's grasp. He was vaguely aware of Sir Ector rising and shouting *'Nooooo!'* Then without waiting for the giant to set his head upon the block, Uther swung with all his might and the blade whistled as it sliced through the air, severing the giant's head from his neck in one explosive strike. The head leapt, spinning from the shoulders up towards the rafters above, spraying blood about the hall as it turned. Beneath it, the body slowly buckled and collapsed to the floor with a crash, just as the head hit the stones with a dull crack.

He was aware of hot blood as it splashed across him, yet cared nothing for it as he stepped after the rolling head and smashed it repeatedly with the flat of the axe until it was nothing more than a bloody mess. He stood there, breathing heavily amid an awed silence as his vision swam. A moment later, he turned as the body of Uath the Stranger slowly pushed itself up and stood. Uther staggered back and then watched dispassionately as the giant scooped up the remains of its head in its arms, and then walked slowly from the hall.

The following day was spent preparing weapons. Grim expressions spoke of dissatisfaction with the way they had been treated by their hosts that were far louder than any voices of complaint. The sound of stones rasping against metal as blades were honed and tempers were given an edge, rang loud and continuously about the hall. The Druids had now included their King in their games, which meant that every man and woman there was preparing for war, to die alongside him should the giant take his head. It was never mentioned to leave and walk the hills. There were no games nor contests to test their strengths, nor was there drinking, gaming or feasting. The mood was as sombre as the time before battle when every warrior communed with their innermost thoughts and prepared their path to the gates of the Shadowland. This was the place where their journey would begin should they die and seek to pass the gates into the Shadowland. They would follow their King should he fall, but the giant, Uath the Stranger would also die and then, quite possibly, all and every Druid and native of Erin that could be hunted down, for that would be the way of it.

Uther spent his day in silent contemplation. Seated at the low table set by the biggest fire, he stared into the dancing flames; his eyes lost to the hot coals as he prepared himself to meet the Stranger. In his heart, in his soul, he did not believe that he would lose his head. He still held Excalibur. He had always known that he would somehow pass the sword on or that Merlyn would demand he relinquish it; he simply couldn't die like this. He wasn't afraid to die. However, this wasn't the time; he knew that. But still, the thought of kneeling down and placing his neck upon that sticky log of oak, regardless of his disbelief in the outcome being his death, was not an easy one to envisage. He now knew what Gerlois had gone through, the thoughts and the doubts... and the fear that he could feel trying to rise up from where it shivered in his belly in its attempt to overcome him. Yet stay he must, and face this Druid game he must, there was no possible thought of doing anything else, and so he watched his warriors prepare to die in full knowledge of their intent, for he knew it would not happen.

At the appointed time, the doors crashed back and every warrior silently rose from where they had been sitting and waiting, and stood to glare and finger their blades and spears as the giant, once more whole without any scar nor cut to suggest its head had so recently been separated from its body, took its slow walk towards the fire and their King.

Uath the Stranger walked unhurriedly, regarding the watching men and women, noting the blades and spears levelled towards him with dispassionate interest, and then he turned to see if Uther was there and smiled and said in his deep rumbling voice, 'Uther Pendragon, you have not fled.' His big craggy face split into a mocking grin and he hopped and danced the last few steps to stand beside the log. 'Your fear must be eating you from deep inside like a worm devouring an apple. I am quite sure that your bowels are about to empty upon the floor.' He bent down and peered below the table expectantly.

Three old Druids entered and stood beside the doorway and Uath turned and bowed to them, before returning to sneer at Uther.

'Did you think to flee like your so called champions? Did you not wet your britches at the thought of…?'

'Silence.' Uther stood, placed Excalibur upon the table, and walked around by the fire to stare up into the giant's ugly face which towered above him. 'Save your breath and cease your taunting… for you are not real.' He turned and bowed his head to the Druids, finally acknowledging their presence, and then walked around the fire and knelt beside the log. Trembling only slightly, he placed his neck upon the bloody wood and pulled the cloth of his tunic down, exposing his neck so that the axe might find its mark and cut true. He felt the giant move beside him and saw the shadow of the axe as it was heaved up and raised to the top of its swing. There was not a sound in the room, yet the tension was deafening. Holding his breath; Uther Pendragon's nerves tingling in anticipation. Yet with nostrils filled with the stench of the blood staining the floor around him, he did not feel the bite of the axe nor the welcoming embrace of his ancestors. Hesitantly, he turned his head to glance up at the giant.

Uath grinned. 'You need to stretch out your neck a little better if I am to strike cleanly, King Uther. Your neck is so thin and scrawny, like a little bird, that…'

'Hush, Uath the Stranger,' Uther returned his neck to the log and stared at the floor, 'strike me swiftly, as I struck you, and be done with this game. We are warriors gathered here and we thirst. We will drink the Druid's ale this night and take their stones tomorrow… finish this game, for my knees are pained crouching here. I would like to return to my seat.'

He heard the giant 'humph' as he lifted the blade. Saw the shadow of the axe rise once more and then, as warriors drew breath around him anticipating the execution of their King, he saw the shadow of the blade fall.

It struck with an almighty crash, shattering the stone upon which Uther knelt, just a hand's width from his face. He felt the breath of it passing to kiss his cheek and for a heartbeat, Uther's mind raced to make sense of what had happened. Then he pushed himself up on shaking legs and turned to confront the giant, yet it was not the giant, Uath the Stranger that stood smiling at him happily, it was Merlyn.

The three Druids walked through the ranks of stunned warriors and silently bowed before Uther.

'Uther Pendragon. The Druid Merlyn has long counselled that you are the leader that our people have long foretold would walk the land for time without end. That you are the man who would prevail when others, the bravest, would or could not stand. Two of your champions stood to meet the challenge of, Uath the Stranger, yet it was only you who was able to live and judge and understand within your rage, that all was not as it seemed. You met the challenge of, Uath the Stranger, and survived. We, the Druids of Erin, salute you and condone your movement of the holy stones.' With that, the three Druids left, leaving Uther glaring at Merlyn.

'Did I ever mention to you, old man, that I hate the games you Druids play?'

'I do remember you mentioning that a few times, Uther,' Merlyn laughed and nodded his head happily, 'yes, you said it a few times, but doesn't it make life far more interesting?'

The next morning was a late start.

As soon as the old Druids had left the hall the evening before, other Druids had entered bearing jugs of mead and ale and platters of venison and boar and the warriors had feasted and celebrated. Uther had felt such a weight lift from his shoulders that he had joined in, accepting both the calls of congratulations and support, as well as horns filled to overflowing with frothing ale and strong, dark mead.

Now, as he stumbled along behind Merlyn, the songs and noise of the celebration still pounding his skull, Uther was again regretting the ill effects of drinking too much, and he wasn't the only one. Beside him strode Sir Ector, who wasn't talking, and behind them strung out downhill along the winding path were his sullen, suffering warriors. At least, it wasn't raining, not yet, anyway. Grey cloud once again covered the sky and when Uther raised his head to squint up towards the peak as it rose above the green cloak of grass and trees, he saw it was almost lost in cloud and looked desolate and cold. A strong wind buffeted them, but Uther barely registered it, he was simply forcing himself to climb and hoping that they would soon arrive at the site of the holy stones. With his breath echoing and rasping in his ears and his head feeling fit to burst, it was all he could do to force himself to put one foot in front of the other, and to avoid the tufts of grass and little hillocks left by countless travellers before him that might otherwise send him stumbling. All he could think of was pushing on, get Merlyn's stones, and leaving, but as with most things to do with Druids, and Merlyn in particular, it wasn't quite as simple as that.

Uther finally reached the top part of the path where Merlyn stood waiting for him, a big excited grin upon the Druid's face. As Uther took the final steps and looked up at the Druid, with his robes flapping in the wind and wispy beard floating about his head, he had the strangest notion that if Merlyn were a dog, his tail would be wagging from side to side. Finally, with legs shaking slightly from the climb and his breathing still laboured, Uther gazed past Merlyn and stared at the stones. The tribesmen were arriving, gathering behind him, strangely silent as they also took sight of the stones that they were to remove and bring down to the boats.

The wind was gusting hard. Uther could feel it pushing at him as if invisible hands were trying to turn him and send him walking back down, which, if he weren't so exhausted, he might be tempted to do. After finally seeing the stones that he had heard so much about, and for so long, he now realised that this whole ordeal was just another pointless exercise dreamt up by the Druids so they could laugh at them all. He didn't know whether he should also laugh, although he felt he could certainly weep, or possibly have his men hang Merlyn up by the ankles from one of the impossibly large stones they were all staring at and then head back down to the boats. It was tempting, but he was just too tired.

'Merlyn, what by the spirits are we doing here?' Uther pointed at the stones. 'I suppose you thought that we might each sling one of these upon each shoulder, and then run with them back to the boats?' He slumped down onto grass cropped short by the numerous sheep that were ignoring them, aside from an occasional curious glance while chewing mouthfuls of grass. The sheep were grazing around the really big… in fact, impossibly huge was a better description, grey stones, each of which was taller than if a man were to stand upon another's shoulders, and with surely even more of the stone buried beneath the soil.

'Merlyn, have the spirits robbed you of all your senses? How could you imagine we might move just one of these stones, even just a little bit? This is all nonsense, isn't it? A great Druid game that you have played with us?'

Merlyn shook his head in denial, 'Oh come, Uther. You give up on things far too easily. The stones are what they are, and they are… perfect. Let us look at them, come…' He reached down and pulled on Uther's arm trying to raise him. All around them the warriors were in different attitudes of rest, happy to let their King and his Druid discuss the impossible while they napped or drank from skins of weak ale.

Uther pulled his arm away. 'Leave me alone, Merlyn. This is utter nonsense and I want no more part of it. There is no possible way we could bring these stones down to the boats, and even if, with the greatest stretch of my faith in you, I was to think that we might possibly be able to do it, then the boats would sink. Those stones are very, very big.' He lay back on the grass and closed his eyes. 'We will rest here and then return to the hall. At sunrise we leave for the boats and sail for home, we are done here.' He felt rather than saw Merlyn turn and walk away. The Druid was muttering something, but he didn't care what it was, he smiled. The stones were set in a circle, some upright and others were laying horizontally on top, and they were ridiculously big, vast grey lumps. Mottled with greens, browns, and livid orange growths of moss and lichens; really quite beautiful. They had obviously been there an eternity and they would surely stay there for another eternity. All that talk about a race of giants, the Fir Bolg putting them there thousands of years ago, was obviously true, if he had ever had a doubt about the legend before, then he didn't have one now.

After a short rest, they left, Uther glanced back and saw that Merlyn was still preoccupied with walking around the stones, muttering and pacing; he looked to be measuring them. Uther shook his head and began the walk back down to the hall; it was relatively pleasant now that most of his stress and the hurt in his head had left him. The sun was trying to shine between the clouds and it was all quite agreeable. It was a relief to be past the excitement and tension of the quest; it would soon be over and he would be happy to return to Britain. He wasn't looking forward to sailing again, his brow creased at the thought of it, but he would chew Merlyn's magical gingiber and no doubt it would soon pass.

Warriors were laughing, probably at Merlyn's idea of taking the stones away. Uther smiled again, what was that crazy old Druid thinking? He may as well have suggested plucking the sun from the sky, it was equally impossible.

It was far easier walking downhill rather than uphill, and Uther's mind was soon wandering on its own amongst the bigger questions that faced him, of continuing to unite his people and turning back the Saxons, one thing was for sure, it was time to leave the Isle of Erin.

It was dark, some time before daybreak, when the warriors, led by Uther made their way out of their lodgings and through the Druid's strange cave. Despite the darkness, many of the Druids were awake. As the warriors came from the hall and began to file out, the Druids turned towards them and began a low chant that reverberated throughout the confines of the cave. Firelight flickered, offering just enough light to make their way through the smoky haze until they emerged into the darkness of the early morning, the chanting still faint and haunting behind them. They carried torches and walked in single file, and by the time they had passed the first growth of woodland and were travelling the path across the lower slopes towards the main forest, a bleak dawn was breaking and they no longer needed burning brands to light their way.

'It is good that we are leaving.' Sir Ector was walking at Uther's side. He was rubbing at his naked arms keeping the early morning chill from his flesh. 'I look forward to setting sail and looking back at this mountain, and then I hope we never have to lay eyes upon it again.'

'I feel the same; this was a waste of time, just a Druid game.' Uther looked across at his old friend. 'It is true that the Gods play with us, but it is the Druids who do their bidding. Even with the test of Uath the Stranger, even after we passed it, after Gerlois was humbled, and poor Cunobelin died, there was still no prize, because it was always unattainable. An impossible dream that we could touch, but we could never grasp. I am sure the Druid bards are already putting the verses together for their next epic, and I am almost sure that Merlyn and his friends spent all of the night laughing and congratulating each other about how clever they were. I wonder what next they have in store for us, for we are truly just the rune bones in their great game of life.'

They reached the protective cover of the woods, and as the first drops of rain began to fall they made their way through the dim, still twilight of the interior. It was as if the forest had held its breath it was so still, just the sound of dripping water descending, drop by drop, leaf to leaf, from all around. It was cold amongst the trees, and a thin mist was rising from the rich earth and fallen leaves of the forest floor accompanied by the rich, earthy smell of life and decay. The warriors passed through in silence, aware they were walking close to the veil between this realm and the Shadowland and they were fearful of disturbing the fragile balance.

When they emerged, it was still raining. They quickened their steps, happy to be through the trees, anticipating the shelter by the boats and fires to warm themselves and dry what could be dried. As they came into sight of the camp where the boats were anchored by the bank of the river, they saw the warriors left there to guard the vessels had constructed several small communal huts and shelters. Smoke was rising through the loose thatch. The small community held the promise of warmth and shelter, so they quickened their pace once more, running and laughing towards it through the long grass when cries rang out from the sentries, and a horn was blown announcing that the King had returned.

Unfortunately, the huts quickly became cramped with the return of the King and his party. They were draughty and the thatch let in streams of water in several places, but this was to be a swift halt upon their homeward journey, so for the short time expected they settled in. Woollen and hemp tunics, cloaks and britches were draped close to fires to dry and soon the draughts were beaten back, and each hut became hot, stuffy and noisy. The ground both within the huts and paths outside were churned to a sticky mud as warriors walked between them, and supplies were taken out to the boats to be stored below deck as they made ready to depart.

One of the female warriors pushed through and caught Uther's attention, raising her voice over the noise. 'The Druid, Merlyn, is by the boats, King Uther. He had me come request your presence so that you might prepare with him.' She shrugged her shoulders. 'He has some rafts he wants tied behind the boats, or so he says...'

'He has rafts with him?' Uther stood. 'So I, the King, am to come at the call of the Druid, Merlyn? I think not, not this time. I am still not best pleased with him; he can wait.' Sitting down once more, he returned to the map he was trying to make with the help of Sir Ector and several others. Although he had no intention of ever returning to the Isle of Erin, he had thought it wise to record all the details he and the others could remember should the need some day arise. It may possibly be a wasted effort, but should Arthur or one of his descendants ever have need to come this way, then they might be a little more prepared than this quest had been. They were discussing the coastline that they had sailed past before sighting the high peak of Mount Killaraus, the settlements, cliffs, and estuaries when an extremely wet and bedraggled Druid pushed his way through the crush of warriors and crouched down beside Uther.

'We leave soon?'

'Uther turned around and smiled when he saw how wet the Druid was. Somehow it made him feel better seeing that Merlyn was suffering a little. His beard hung in wet clumps, and his woollen robe lay soaked and heavy upon his skinny frame. However, for some reason, his old friend seemed far too happy for the way he appeared.

'Yes, Merlyn, we are leaving as soon as the boats are loaded.'

'Good, good.' Merlyn used his staff to heave himself up. 'The stones are ready. It will be a quick and simple task to...'

'What do you mean the stones are ready?' Uther rose and put a hand on the Druid's shoulder, turning him around before he could walk away. 'You got the stones? How can you possibly have brought the stones down from the mountain?' But it was Merlyn, so he decided it may be so... 'Are they in the boats? And they haven't sunk yet! This is ridiculous, if you have managed to get them in the boats there won't be any room for us. Merlyn, did you think at all that...?'

Merlyn was giggling, it was annoying, his shoulders were rocking, and his face creased up in delight.

'Uther, I told you we would bring the stones and we are doing just that. It was a simple enough task,' - he winked and held up a bony finger - 'simple enough that is if you are a Druid.' He started to walk off again but turned once more. 'Simple anyway, for a very special Druid.' He pushed back into the throng of warriors cackling in delight.

'Oh, spirits. What has he done?' Uther followed as the old man passed through the hall, out into the cold rain, and then down to where the boats were moored. It was getting darker, despite still being early in the day, and the rain seemed to be falling with even greater determination. Uther glanced up at the greyness above him and shivered; it would be better to stay in the overcrowded hall than risk setting sail in this.

Close to the boats, a few miserable warriors were standing sentry huddled under a temporary thatch, he raised a hand to them and then glanced about for Merlyn. The Druid had clambered up onto the deck of the closest boat and was now peering down into the water to the other side. He turned as Uther approached and pointed down into the water, jabbing his finger in different directions.

'One hundred and sixty-two of them,' he did a little dance, 'one hundred and sixty-two and all brought down by a little old Druid!'

Uther grabbed hold of the wet timbers of the boat, hauled himself up and went to join Merlyn on the other side of the vessel. The river beyond the boats was filled with what appeared to be shallow rafts just breaking the surface. They were tied together with stout rope, the waves of the river breaking gently on their sides with the occasional larger wave rolling over them.

'But... Merlyn, stones don't float. They just don't.'

'Shhh, not so loud. The stones don't know they aren't meant to be floating.'

Uther looked down at Merlyn's smiling face and shook his head.

Morgana's growing exasperation forced her to break her silence. 'But stones really don't float... are you trying to tell us that you just pulled the stones behind you, and they floated across the sea?'

Uther opened his eyes. He hadn't realised he had been speaking. Oh, spirits, he had a headache, and his throat felt dry again.

'There was nothing simple about bringing them back.' He tried to focus. He could see the dark shape of Morgana; she was holding a cup out to him. Craning forward he sipped, then felt the infusion flow into him bringing relief to both his throat and his head. Maude was sitting at the bottom of his sleeping pallet behind Morgana, also wearing a look of confusion, but she didn't appear to be angry, Morgana seemed angry.

'Floating stones… incredible, but I have always maintained that the Druids of old were gifted beyond all our understanding,' said Maude to deflate the tension.

'Amen to that,' said Morgana. She was obviously irritated that she had broken his concentration and had stopped speaking. She was frowning as she offered the cup again, and Uther sipped. His eyes were able to focus now, and the infusion was helping to clear the tension from behind his eyes.

'So my father was branded a coward, you floated the stones by some insane miracle and brought them back here, and then what happened?'

'You make it sound so easy, but our troubles weren't over; Merlyn insisted that we set sail as soon as possible. He refused to see that we should wait until the weather cleared, but we could all see the weather was getting worse. I suppose, looking back on it, that his magic may have had limits and he was worried that if we waited, that the stones would stop listening to his mutterings and persuasions and would begin to sink. Whatever it was, and I am still not sure how he convinced me, but convince me he did, we broke camp that same afternoon and set sail into the storm.'

Chapter 14

The Wrath of Lir

What little daylight there had been as they made ready to leave had turned to near darkness before the boats had lost sight of the land and the storm was upon them. Rain lashed the Britons in stinging torrents driven by a gale that whipped the waves into a frenzy about them. The seafarers had the barest shelter and could do little other than surrender themselves to the torment and try to endure. Beneath the boats, an angry sea rose and fell as mountainous waves pounded the vessels. It flung them around as if one of the Gods was toying with them like a child playing with straw boats, raising them to the heavens and then, with little warning, dropping them back down, the deck falling out from beneath the warriors' feet leaving them floundering, to hold on as they crashed back down into the turbulent sea and icy seawater that washed over them. The planked hulls flexed and buckled, groaning under the stress of the ordeal, water already streaming in through weaker seams as warriors bailed it back out with chains of leather buckets.

Uther's thoughts were constantly with the stones that he was all too aware were trailing behind the boats, unseen somewhere out there in the darkness. He waited, bracing himself each time the boat dropped away, expecting it to land upon a stone and smash itself to bits. And each time when they had fallen to the bottom, between waves, with the next growing over them, he would look up at the angry sea rising like a mountain and expect one of those colossal grey shapes to appear, rearing up over them before dropping out of the sky to crush them. It was worse knowing that if it didn't happen this time, then the chances were it would surely happen the next.

Thunder boomed, and lightning flashed and crackled overhead sending many of the warriors cowering under the rowing benches in superstitious terror while others battled the sea and bailed its waters. For far worse than the threat of the storm and the possibilities of colliding with the huge stones trailing behind them, was the certainty that an angry sea god had risen and was trying to kill them.

'*Tis, Lir,*' shouted Merlyn over the noise of the storm. The wind was whistling and howling through the shortened sail and past the mast sending vibrations shuddering through the boat. '*Lir... the sea God, Lir is angry that we have taken the stones from the Isle of Erin, but don't worry, he is angry, but Lir is an old God, he will tire soon enough.*'

Uther stared at Merlyn; the Druid's face illuminated by lightning as if it were in clear daylight. Rainwater poured down Merlyn's face, but the same silly grin was still in place as he shook his fist in Uther's face.

'*He cannot have the stones; they are ours now!*'

And then as if in answer to Merlyn's words, the boat dropped away once more sending both men stumbling against the side. Uther watched in dismay as he held on, but Merlyn was picked up by the wash of the wave and dragged over the side within an instant to vanish in the inky depths of the storm.

'*Merlyn! Someone get a rope...*' He turned to see that nobody had heard him above the roar of the storm, so he scrambled down under a bench where earlier he had seen a coiled rope. After a few moments groping in the darkness, his fingers closed around it. Struggling to his feet again on unsteady legs, he held onto the end and hurled it overboard, desperately hoping to feel the solid resistance of the old Druid catching hold and clinging on... but there was nothing. He hauled it back in again, bracing himself against the side, hanging on to the slippery wood, nearly falling overboard in the process himself as the boat crashed into another wave, the wash of water soaking him to the skin once more before the deck lurched up into the night.

'*Merlyn!*' As they readied to crash down again, Uther stood and threw the rope, watching in the flickering light as it snaked out across the waves, but he couldn't see the Druid, and again, nothing took hold of the rope. He slumped down against the side and tried to ignore the feeling of loss and desolation that suddenly overwhelmed him. Merlyn was annoying at the best of times and infuriating most of the time, but he had been with Uther every step of his rise from village boy to King of all the Britons. He had to be alive, confound him, he was Merlyn!

Uther stood and gripped onto the side, wiping the spray and rain from his face, he stared out into the darkness waiting for the next flash of lightning. There was a solid boom and then almost immediately a shrieking crack as a jagged streak ripped across the sky. It was so bright that for one long moment, everything stopped as if unmoving, lit in the brilliant flash. The boats, some rising and some falling, the trailing lines, several stones rising, huge waves caught at the instant that they were breaking in sprays of foam, each drop of driven rain momentarily halted. It was all captured in that one brilliant, still moment and within it, Uther saw the grey rags of something floating between the next vessel and his, it had to be Merlyn.

Tying the line about his waist he beckoned the closest warrior to come to him. The man didn't want to leave the protection of the bench he was cowering under; he realised that it was Gerlois, and he was shaking his head.

'Uther screamed at him over the noise of the storm, '*Gerlois, come here... now!*' The Duc glanced about and then with obvious reluctance, crawled out. He got to his feet and slipping awkwardly, his arms held wide for balance, made his way over until he was gripping the side next to Uther, his face a picture of distress.

'*Tie this to the bench and when you see me raise my arm, pull me in.*' Uther grabbed for the side as the boat heaved upwards and looked again for Merlyn. Gerlois was still holding the rope, but not moving, just holding on, staring over the side at the roiling sea.

'*We should cut the line... the stones are holding us.*' The Duc took a knife from his belt.

'*Nooo, leave the stones. The Druid has gone into the water... I need your help...* '

'*He is dead,*' - Gerlois glanced over the side - '*he's gone, and soon we will be too.*' He made to return to the shelter of the bench and Uther grabbed him again.

'*No, he is not dead, and we are not going to die either. Now take this and tie it to the bench or Merlyn really will die... do it!*' Uther handed him the rope and pushed him towards the bench and the Duc finally did as he was told, tripping and then crawling to the bench as the boat rose up beneath them once again.

Turning back to the sea and holding tight to the ship's side, Uther waited for the next flash of lightning, it came moments later; he saw what he had thought was Merlyn once more and leapt head first over the side.

The moment he dived, the boat was pitched up, and the side of the ship caught his ankles a hard blow that tipped him so that he landed in an untidy splash of thrashing limbs. For a moment, he was enveloped in hissing, bubbling confusion, in near silence compared to the roaring madness above. Forcing his arms to move, he did his best to ignore the pain in his ankles and clawed his way upwards in search of the surface. The rope about his waist was both a hindrance with its weight, but also a welcome security helping him find the right direction for the surface. He kicked and swam, dragging himself up through the water until he was finally drawing in a gasping breath of air. All around was howling confusing, but another flash showed the dark shapes of two vessels some way off and then when he glanced back to see the boat he had left, blinding lightning flashed behind it, and he just managed to clamp his eyes shut in time.

'*Aaahhh.*' He turned once more and kicked out in the direction that he hoped Merlyn would be in, it was so confusing, but there was no time to think about it or get any help from the boat. Trying to ignore the howl of the wind and the crashing of the ships as the next flow of waves caught them up, Uther began to swim, dragging himself through the water.

He felt the sea rise as the next wave picked him up and he stopped swimming and tried to see, but his eyes were stinging from the salt-water, and the flashes of light were too brief, so he swam on. Another crack of thunder moments later was followed by a flash of lightning, and once again he was at the top of a wave, he rubbed at his eyes and stared around, then realised he was looking at the bundle of rags he had seen before, it was Merlyn, and quite close, but he was floating face down.

'*Merlyn!*' Uther tugged on the rope trying to get more freedom of movement, it gave, and he swam on, kicking out, swimming hard, but with his head raised, the rope a constant weight trying to draw him down, yet he swam, desperate to catch sight of the Druid again. The boats were passing him, he could feel them, and when the next explosion of lightning hit, it confirmed that they were now a good distance further on through the swells, he began to feel a wave of panic, they were both going to die out here alone, yet the line was still about him, so he kept going and then he saw him again, '*Merlyn!*'

Feeling a renewed surge of hope, he swam hard, then managed to catch hold of the limp body; he struggled to turn him over. The Druid was limp and unmoving. He held Merlyn's chin up with his hand to keep his face out of the water, and tugged hard on the rope, lifting one arm above his head and waving in the hope Gerlois would begin pulling them in, but the line was slack, and the boats were moving on. If there were any close, they were lost in the awful madness of the storm, but surely one of them must be near? He pulled on the rope again, and it still remained slack, if that cowardly bastard, Gerlois had…? His legs kicked as he trod water and then, without warning, something hit him and pushed him along, and he realised it was one of the stones! The top was almost at the same level as the surface of the sea and the line pulling it was right beside him, they were being dragged along, so he pulled Merlyn close and then struggled as he used the last remnants of his energy to haul himself up on top, then dragged at the unconscious weight of his friend, pulling him up beside him.

Sitting high on the rising stone, Uther began shivering violently, he turned Merlyn over and put his face close to the Druid's mouth, but he couldn't tell if he were breathing or not. There was so much noise and movement that it wasn't a surprise, but he hoped he must be living. He needed help; he pulled the rope in, arm over arm until the loose end skittered across the surface towards him. He held it up and felt the end; it had been cut.

Turning back to Merlyn he slapped the old Druid's face. *'Oh, Merlyn... come on, wake up, breathe!'* He slammed his fist down onto Merlyn's chest and then almost fell off the stone when a skinny hand raised and caught his arm before it could impact a second time. The Druid jerked upright and coughed a lungful of seawater into Uther's face.

'Ugh, Merlyn... you're alive.'

Darkness enveloped them once more, the Druid coughed, made some gurgling choking sounds and then Uther heard him throw up before he heard his ragged, gasping attempts at breathing. Lightning flashed, and Merlyn was suddenly staring at him, a frown creasing his face. *'Very observant... why were you were going to hit me?'*

'Well, not really hit you. I thought you were nearly dead; I thought it might help.' Uther was beginning to feel more fool than hero for saving Merlyn. *'I found you and dragged you here. You might have died if...'*

'How are we going to get back on the boats? Why did you drag me here and not onto the boats? Oh, Uther, did you think about...?'

Uther dived over the side and reached for the rope leading forward to the boat it was attached to. *'Stay there; I'll send someone back for you.'* He didn't wait for an answer but started to pull himself along the rope towards the boat that was somewhere ahead in the darkness. If the Druid fell off the stone then so be it. He was such an infuriating and most ungrateful old man.

Two days later, the worst of the storm had passed, and the boats were sailing under a grey, leaden sky with no sight of land, but, at

155

least, it had stopped raining. Every person on board was exhausted, soaked to the skin and extremely cold. Gerlois had claimed that the rope must have become fouled. That he had tied it to the bench and even tried to pull it in when Uther had not come back, but it had been severed. There was little point in Uther pursuing the matter further while at sea, but he vowed to know the truth of it when they returned.

Looking around the boat, Uther saw warriors shivering, their faces white, drawn and tired. He knew it was a matter of urgency to get somewhere that they could dry out, eat and rest, but that didn't appear to be likely anytime soon. The wind was still strong; the sea continued to be rough and controlling the boats was still difficult, but they were underway and being sure to keep some distance apart. With the might of Lir's storm now mostly abated, they could, at least, raise the sails and then man the oars in changing shifts. Uther requested a count be made of the boats, and they discovered several were missing, either lost to the storm or driven so far off course that they could not be seen. He prayed to the Gods that it was the latter and that the stragglers would rejoin the small fleet closer to home.

It was on that second day after the storm, as the light was leaching from the sky and the chill of evening was dropping over them once more that the cry came from one of the other boats that land had finally been sighted. For all they knew, it could be any part of the coast of Britain or even the land of Frankia, or because of the storm they may even be looking at another part of the Isle of Erin, but thankfully it was land. They sailed towards it until darkness claimed them once again and then the fear that they might be driven onto a reef or a rocky coast forced them to hold off. A cold, desperate night was spent waiting for the first signs of daybreak.

The hours of darkness were indeed long and testing, as, unable to sleep, each warrior faced their inner demons listening, ears straining, for the sound of breaking waves in case their boat had ventured too close to the rocks, or they had been drawn back out to sea away from the hope of the voyage ending. Eventually, a weak, wet dawn slowly greeted them, revealing that they had not drifted and, in fact, were just a short distance from the coast. White-crested waves were breaking upon low cliffs and rocks, making them glad they hadn't tried landing at night and wary of approach even during daylight. Heading north, they sailed along the coast until around the middle of the day they sighted a settlement built just a short way above a rough stony beach. A few small boats were drawn up above the tideline. It was shrouded in the smoke of its own fires and appeared at first that the occupants had deserted the place upon seeing the approaching boats. They dropped their anchor stones, and Uther sent a small group ashore. After some time, the warriors came down to the beach and called out that the people were there and were coming out of hiding, and that this was indeed the coast of Britain. It soon became evident that they had arrived on the shores of the wild region of Cymru; just half a day's sail south of Ynys Mon, the Island of Mona, home of the Druids.

The cluster of twelve, small dwellings had been named Llangelynin by its occupants, or that is what the warriors claimed to have heard because the people were speaking a dialect with which they were unfamiliar. They were a poor, suspicious group who had hidden when the boats had arrived and in fear they were being attacked by raiders, which apparently had happened before. They caught fish and farmed small patches of the rocky soil and seldom saw visitors. When they knew there was no danger, a small group of men and women, trailed by a collection of grubby children, emerged to sit on the beach and stare open mouthed at the boats.

Merlyn claimed he would be able to speak with them and so went ashore to negotiate the barter of both fresh and smoked fish. After replenishing their water skins, the men pulled hard upon the oars, rowing into the cold northerly wind in search of Ynys Mon, to deliver the stones that, despite all attempts of the God, Lir to reclaim them, were still floating behind the boats.

At first, Uther thought the Druids would be pleased; or at least they should be he reasoned, but then Uther was never sure with Druids. The boats arrived at a small bay, guided by Merlyn, and the stones were untied and pulled in until they touched the tideline of the beach where they immediately sank. Four old Druids appeared and watched the whole thing from high on the beach without offering any help or sign of welcome. They were all dressed in the familiar grey robes, carried staffs that they leaned upon and had long hair and beards, or three did because the fourth was an old woman. Uther raised a hand in greeting, but they did not respond. Nor did they move to do anything with the stones, they just left them there, which was a little disappointing to all of the warriors who had been waiting to see how they would be lifted or floated up onto the land.

'Are we not welcome here, Merlyn? Those four aren't making much of an effort at greeting us.'

'Uther, you are not a Druid, therefore, you do not see a welcome because you are correct, you are not welcome here, this is sacred soil.'

'That seems just a little ungrateful, don't you think, Merlyn? We did go all the way to the Isle of Erin to bring these stones back for them.' Uther stared at the four, and they stared back at him. 'How are they going to get those stones up to Stanenges?' He glanced at Merlyn and Merlyn merely stared back at him. 'You're not going to tell me are you? You Druids might want to work on that, how people perceive you. With this attitude, let's just say, I'm not so keen on accepting any more Druid quests,' - he poked Merlyn in the ribs and the Druid stepped back, a look of genuine surprise on his face - 'and like it or not, the Druids are in debt to me. In fact, you, Merlyn, are in debt to me.' He turned around and addressed his men, raising his voice so that the Druids on the beach would be able to hear. 'We are leaving. The Druids don't want us to see their tricks, and they don't seem happy with their gifts.' He waved at the stones and stared up at the Druids, but they were obviously unmoved and just continued to watch the boats. Then the old woman squatted down and relieved herself, unconcerned that the three old men were beside her, or the boatloads of warriors on the beach were watching. She just pissed, pulled tufts of grass out of the ground and watched as the wind blew them away.

Uther turned back to his warriors in frustration. 'I thank you all for joining and enduring our quest, it has been a success, and we shall join together for the celebration of Samhain. We have stories to tell our friends and families who wait for us, so let us sail for home and then we shall feast and drink mead and ale!'

And so the boats set their sails for what Uther hoped would be the final time. As they slipped away, he looked back and saw the Druids were now walking down to the stones. He watched them pick up sticks and driftwood and then as the figures became too small to see, he saw a plume of smoke as they lit a fire ready for whatever rituals were necessary to deal with their burden. He turned and shrugged, determining to give neither the Druids nor the stones any more thought.

'Druids,' he spat. 'It is as well that we do not know more of their ways for I am sure it would not sit well with us.'

Sir Ector laughed and walked to the oar bench ready to take a seat. The day was warming, and the sun had somehow found its way through the clouds, it was good to be going home and if Merlyn had calculated correctly, they would be arriving promptly as the Samhain celebrations were getting underway.

Chapter 15

Igraine

The return to the village of Outhgill, at the foot of Pendragon Tor, was a far better experience than their reception upon Ynys Mon. News of the quest's return had run ahead of them and by the time Uther led his warriors into the village the Samhain celebrations were already underway and a large crowd was ready to greet them.

It was a sunny, pleasant day, if a little chill. An autumnal wind blew leaves from the trees and promised colder weather was not far away. Banners and pennons were fluttering from trees, huts and halls, the wailing of pipes and the steady beat of a drum filled the air and people were laughing and dancing. As Uther's party entered, a great cheer went up, and children, friends and families ran to welcome the King and his warriors home. For some time, laughter, tears and shrieks of delight filled the air, drowning out the sounds of the music. Uther greeted a few people and then looked on, happy to be back, happy for his warriors, but also acutely aware that he had nobody close to him to run up and embrace him, to welcome him home. It wasn't the first time he had felt this way.

He stood beside Merlyn and watched with a smile upon his face as Sir Ector held his baby daughter and hugged his plump, blonde wife. His small son was bouncing at his feet and calling plaintively to be picked up, and Uther smiled as Sir Ector reached down and pulled his son close. All around them, similar scenes were taking place.

Uther felt a wave of emotion wash over him. It was at times like this that he felt the loss of his parents and of Cal most keenly. His parents had died when his village had been raided by Picts, and his childhood friend, Cal, who had been the only other survivor of that terrible day, was now nearly eight years dead, killed by a Saxon spear. The only other person he had known as long was Nineve, Cal's younger sister, who was now leader of the Druids, but she hadn't shown herself for several years, and then, of course, there was Merlyn. He glanced at Merlyn, who was beaming happily, dancing oddly to the music the way all elders seemed to have a knack of doing, as he waved to children. Uther sighed and walked on into the crowd, feeling both happy to be home, but also a little sad. He determined to shake the feeling off and celebrate being back from the quest.

He passed a group of jugglers and tumblers who were performing, mostly going unnoticed as the homecoming continued. Two of the jugglers were spinning knives, passing them back and forth while others were tumbling, spinning and turning, shouting loudly and clapping to try and gain people's attention and draw them over.

People from the fortress had seen their arrival and were coming down to welcome the King and his party. Uther instructed some men to go back up to bring ale casks and skins of mead. He accepted some bread and meat from one of the slaves who was carrying a large platter and noticed that she was a pretty girl. She became aware of his appraisal and turned back, smiling before walking away. He smiled in return and felt himself blush self-consciously, but continued to watch her. She had blonde hair, similar to Aethelflaed, wife to Sir Ector, Uther mused. He lost sight of her in the crowd and sighed. Aethelflaed was Saxon, so perhaps the girl had been captured on a raid; there were a number of Saxon slaves working at the fortress, he would seek her out later.

'You need a wife.'

Uther glanced over to his side to see who had spoken and saw Merlyn grinning at him.

161

'Oh, I'm sure you would like to arrange me a match that the Druids would approve of, Merlyn, but I shall choose my own wife, thank you very much.'

Merlyn gave a little laugh, shook his head and walked away.

As Uther passed a small group of chatting villagers, two warriors pushed past and quickly apologised when they realised whom they had jostled.

'Begging your leave, King Uther, there is a dog fight being organised down by the river and we're told one of the bulls will be baited there before it is taken up to the fortress to be slaughtered.' The man was grinning in anticipation of seeing the entertainment: 'You should come.' A female warrior pulled on his arm and dragged him away, laughing. 'Sorry, King Uther,' she called back to him, then turned to her companion and Uther heard her hiss, 'The King doesn't want to come see the dogs with the likes of you!' He watched them as they ran down towards the river hand in hand, laughing together, he sighed and walked on.

Outhgill was filling with more people all the time as servants and slaves continued to arrive from the fortress carrying food and ale, and word of the celebrations reached smaller communities in the outlying areas. There was no point in feeling depressed, there would be time for a family, and for Saxons and Druids later, for now, it was just good to be back amongst his people.

The sound of shouting caught his attention and he looked over to see people gathering around a man standing high up, on a tree stump. Behind him was the familiar crude wooden cross. He was calling out urgently for people to gather around to hear his message. Uther realised it was one of the travelling Christian priests, attempting to gain converts no doubt. He decided to listen but to stay some distance away to hear what the man was saying.

'… follow the Lord Jesus, for forgiveness can be granted for all of your sins. By the grace of God and his Son, our Lord, who suffered for you upon the cross, cast aside your wickedness, your evil ways and…'

It confounded Uther that anyone would listen, he glanced about, but people were. Just a small group but they were listening, and he could see that the priest already had a following, a sad looking collection of people mostly dressed in rags, showing colours of different tribes. They stood behind the priest and were hanging upon every word that he said with strange smiles and nods of understanding.

'...born to the Blessed Virgin, our Lord healed the afflicted and brought forth miracles in the name of God our Father. I say to you, turn away from your life of sin, do not worship pagan Gods for there is only one true God. Follow the Lord's path with us...' Uther decided to move away. He was still not sure why, but he didn't much like these priests and their nailed God. He didn't trust them, and part of him wanted to go so far as to have them thrown out of Britain to spread their faith elsewhere. He knew that the Saxons had little use for them, but like here they were still tolerated for the most part. There were enough Gods here already he reasoned, especially with the ones the Saxon's had brought with them, one more wouldn't count for much, but he knew the nailed God of whom the priest spoke was jealous of other Gods. He knew these priests claimed that theirs was the one and only God and that all the others, that everyone in the tribes had grown up so closely with, simply didn't exist, which was absurd.

Merlyn walked over and took his arm, guiding him away from the priest and his audience.

'You don't want to listen to that, Uther. If he gets to the bit where there is a ghost it will only confuse you, it does me. There are so many Gods, ghosts and spirits, but those fools will tell you there is only one, can you imagine that, only one! And even if you are able to limit your imagination to that, then know that he doesn't treat his people very well as far as I can see, except for a few of the fatter priests I've seen that is.' Merlyn drew Uther away towards where a group of Lords and Chiefs were gathering before they would head up towards the fortress to meet before the feast. They were watching a small group of dancers, girls trailing ribbons with flowers in their hair. Uther and Merlyn stood to the side and waited for the dancing to end.

'Now, I will grant you that our Gods can be a little cantankerous at times, just look how upset the God, Lir, became when we took his stones,' - Merlyn's eyebrows were raised as he looked to Uther, sharing the memory of the storm the God had brought forth - 'but we also have Gods who bring us healing, luck and honour. Spirits and sprites inhabit every grove, every pool, pond and meadow. I ask you, how can one God accomplish all those things?'

'Who is that?'

'Who is who?' Merlyn, spun around trying to see who Uther was looking at.

'There… going past the jugglers over there.' Uther pointed and started to walk, with Merlyn doing his best to keep up beside him as they pushed through the crowd searching for whoever Uther had seen.

'A girl… she's wearing a blue cloak with a lighter blue gown beneath…' He glanced around, 'did you see her?'

'With all these people? No, Uther, I did not see her, but I'm sure if you are meant to meet her then…'

'There she is,' interrupted Uther, and pulling the hood of his cloak over his head; he dashed on through the crowd trying to keep the blue gown in sight.

He found her watching some children as they danced and laughed around a small band of players. The musicians, two of whom were blowing upon pipes while another beat a rhythm on a large tabor, seemed quite happy to have the children to entertain. Uther stood some distance back and studied the young woman, being careful not to be seen by any of the group lest he should have to approach and introduce himself before he was ready. And she was, he realised, a young woman and not the young girl he had first thought, but she was beautiful for these few years, not despite them. Indeed, he realised, one or more of the children dancing so gaily may well be hers; he felt a twinge of regret that she may be both a mother and a wife to another. She was smiling and clapping her hands, unaware of his attention.

He was at the point of moving away, unwilling to intrude upon another man's family, yet he felt himself rooted to the spot, something within him was making him stay and continue watching her, just for a few moments more.

Somehow he realised, he had managed to disappear. He knew he had chanced upon a rare moment, the amount of time that he could remain anonymous like this could surely be only moments before he was recognised or called for. He wasn't quite sure how he had done it, or how long it would last, but at this moment, he felt invisible. He pulled his cloak tighter and the hood closer about his face, willing the moments to last as he gazed upon this woman.

He had tried on many occasions to slip away and just be himself, to be Usher again, the name he grew up with when he was in hiding as a boy, rather than Uther Pendragon, the King. These days it was a little more difficult to remain unseen for long, yet from beneath the concealment of his hood, for these few precious moments, he was alone amongst the crowd, just another visitor to the celebrations, and so he continued to stare.

Her hair was covered with a white scarf, held in place by a gold plaited cord, but he could see that her hair was a dark, rich auburn where it escaped in curls and fell upon her shoulders. Her cheeks were flushed with the excitement of the music, and they coloured, even more, when she turned and saw him regarding her so intently.

Embarrassed to be discovered, he bowed his head and then hastily removed the hood that had hidden him so well. He heard the indrawn exclamation of shock when she realised it was the King who had been spying on her. She curtseyed low, keeping her eyes downcast as she waited for him to approach.

He motioned the musicians to return to their playing, for they had also abruptly stopped which was drawing, even more, attention. Oh, how quickly a perfect moment can pass.

'I am sorry to intrude upon you, my Lady.' Uther wasn't sure where the words came from as his heart seemed to be fluttering inside his chest like a fish freshly landed upon the bank. 'It's just that I saw you and I do not believe that we have met before. I felt I must come to introduce myself and beg the honour of knowing your name.' A soon as the words tripped out from his lips he bemoaned his lack of preparation. He sounded like a fool, he realised. Like a bumbling, village boy asking a maid to dance for the very first time. It was hardly the behaviour of a King.

But she had the grace to blush as she smiled, and then she glanced at the children before returning her gaze to him and their eyes seemed to lock together. Something awoke within him and, for one long eternal moment, he felt he was lost within her eyes. Brown eyes, the colour of hazelnuts he reflected, with flecks like pure gold that danced in the light. *Oh, for the sake of the spirits... I sound like a lovelorn fool... but she is so pretty...* Uther wiped a sudden flush of sweat from his brow. The sounds of celebration had all but disappeared and after a moment, he realised that her lips had been moving and that she was saying something. She was pointing to the children, introducing them. Two young girls were walking towards them... the youngest girl was familiar, but he couldn't place her.

'I'm sorry, I didn't hear you, there is so much noise here.' Uther felt himself blush and cursed himself again. *That had also sounded so pitiful.* He forced himself to be calm and think before he smiled at the girls and then spoke... *oh, but she was so beautiful.* 'Your name, what did you say your name...?'

'Uther!'

Uther turned to see Merlyn making his way through the crowd.

'Uther, we need to attend the fortress. There are...'

Uther ignored Merlyn and turned back to the girl. The two children had returned to their dance, but she was still smiling at him.'

'What is your name? I hope we might meet later... at the fortress... the feast?'

'Uther, we really must leave. There is much to prepare before...' Merlyn noticed the girl for the first time and dropped the sleeve of Uther's tunic which he had just taken hold of to gain the King's attention. 'I am sorry, King Uther, my Lady.' Merlyn smiled and stepped back. 'I am sorry, but we do need to be away, Sire.'

Uther cast a despairing look to the girl and took a step backwards to Merlyn, knowing he did indeed need to attend the assembly at the fortress.

'Igraine, my name is Igraine, King Uther, and I am sure we will see each other later.' She called the last of this as Uther was being drawn through the crowd by Merlyn.

'Who is she, do you know her? I haven't seen her before and I'm sure I would have noticed her.'

'Stop grinning like a fish, Uther; it does not become a King. I think you will find she is the wife of one of the visiting lords. Possibly not the ideal choice for you to have desires upon. Possibly the Saxon girl earlier would be a better choice for now... Uther?'

Uther realised Merlyn had been speaking and was staring at him as they walked. He glanced across at the Druid and saw the old Druid was smiling.

'It was you who mentioned I needed a wife,' said Uther a little indignantly.

'Yes my King, but even I did not expect you to act upon my advice quite so quickly.' They were both laughing as they started up the Tor towards the new stone and timber gatehouse to Pendragon fortress. Uther glanced up at the pennons flapping in the breeze and decided he was looking forward to the evening's feast far more than he had been previously. It was indeed, highly probable that the lovely Igraine was wife to one of the tribal leaders, and if that were the case, then so be it. Yet possibly some other explanation for her being here might arise... so why not dream a little...'

As Uther and Merlyn passed through the gates, they could see that the preparations for Samhain were well underway. In the lower level close to the gates, animals were in pens waiting to be slaughtered, eyes wide and agitated. The shrill cries of their agony and distress filling the air to mix with the acrid smell of their blood and piss. Several large fires were already burning so that once the beasts and fowl had been killed, they could be cut apart and the meat cooked.

There would be two main gatherings. Uther, the Lords, tribal leaders and other invited guests would eat in the main hall of the fortress, while those of lesser rank would dine below in the two smaller halls and, with weather permitting, meat, ale and mead would also be served to the villagers who would gather outside within the lower stockade - nobody would go hungry whether they be King, chieftain or warrior, nor even surf or slave on feast days.

At the King's approach, a number of servants came seeking his approval of some arrangement or other. Much had already been completed. Food and drink was being taken care of; musicians would move up from the village later in the afternoon to entertain those within the fortress walls while others would enter the main hall for Uther and his guests. For some time, both Uther and Merlyn were occupied with the chieftains and lords as they passed on reports of what had been happening within the land while they had been away, and so, for a while at least, Uther's mind was distracted from all thoughts of Igraine.

Uther sat in judgement for a number of situations that had taken place during his absence. The Saxons, so it seemed, had been quiet for the most part. However, a hall had been burned close to the border with the former Iceni lands, and this was troubling. The Lord, his family, and retainers had all been slain, and when questioned, those who had escaped had claimed there had been a disagreement between the Lord, a man named Budoc, and his closest neighbour, a Saxon from across the disputed border. It seemed that the son of Budoc had been a little too keen to bridge the divide between Celt and Saxon by bedding the Saxon's daughter, a lovely girl by all accounts by the name of Mildritha.

'But why did this need to end with so much bloodshed?' asked Uther. 'Surely this should have been the prelude to a joyous time bringing the people together?'

'Well, Sire, there had been good relations between our people. The Saxon settlers were fair in their treatment with us until this time.' The man who had come to report the crime was dirty from days of travel. He looked miserable, as well he might considering the place he had called home had been burnt to the ground. Two small children and an old woman sniffled and shuffled a few paces behind him.

'My Lord's son may well have put the girl with child... well he did, we all knew that, and then refused to know her. When the Saxons came, they were in no mood to talk as my Lord wished, for as I have said, they had enjoyed a peaceful existence as neighbours before this day. The Saxons came and were deeply angered. They dragged my Lord's son from the hall and killed him in front of all of us that had been woken so rudely from our sleep. And then they set the hall aflame, refusing to allow my Lord and his family to leave... they all burnt, they died a horrible death, King Uther. It was not necessary. I shall always remember the screaming and crying... the pleading from within. It will live with my children throughout their lives I can assure you of that.' The two children began to sob, and he turned to hush them. They ran to him, and he held them close, casting his eyes low as he waited for his King to respond.

'We shall house you here at the fortress and find you gainful work if you wish.' Uther signalled for Sir Ector to join him and the old warrior came and kneeled at Uther's side.

'Sir Ector, at first light, you will send riders to this hall and learn the truth of what occurred there. Discover what happened and then we shall see how we should respond to this attack upon our people.'

'I shall send fifty mounted warriors at first light.' Sir Ector rose and moved away along with the man and his children who were crying as the man gave thanks to his King.'

'Who next wishes to petition the King?' A murmuring went up from the people crowded into the back part of the great hall as the next in line to speak to the King was sought.

Uther wondered how much longer he had to endure this and knew it would be well into darkness before he could begin to relax and take part in the night's feasting. He had asked Sir Ector to allow only the neediest cases to be brought forward, but it still seemed that there was no end in sight.

It was dark with both fires and fire-braziers lit around the hall when the last small group was brought forward. A dispute regarding the ownership of sheep that had strayed onto another man's land. The owner of the sheep claiming there was no confusion, they were his sheep while the owner of a patch of land growing green vegetables, now claiming ownership as his right, his vegetables after all, were now inside the sheep. Uther leant forward in his chair and held his head in his hands. He was feeling tired and bereft of patience at this point. He cared little for the man's sheep or of the other's vegetables, yet he knew they needed a decision from a third party, from him. A system had to be devised to handle these smaller cases. The Lords and Chiefs dealt with such things within their own lands, but many people sought out their King to give a final decision, but these cases needed to be heard by others, by someone else, possibly Sir Ector. He looked up as the sound of sheep bleating came from the other side of the door.

'The sheep remain the property of their owner, however, you are charged to keep them from your neighbour's land in future and shall give him the next lamb born to your flock in payment for his lost crop.'

'But, King Uther...' began one of the men, but Sir Ector raised his voice above the objection.

'Silence! Your King has spoken and given his decision. Leave, and if this is not agreed and finished, then the King shall take both sheep and land, and you shall have nothing... now leave us. The two men backed away and were hastily ushered out by two warriors.

'Are we done?' Uther looked about the hall. There were still a lot of people milling about. Some bringing drinking jugs, horns and clay cups to the tables, while another group looked to be musicians. They were probably waiting until they were told to start playing.

'There are other complaints and problems that can be brought in front of you, King Uther,' said Sir Ector wearily. 'More lands have been stolen, thefts taken place and a lord has just caused a commotion and beaten his wife in public, the Duc of the Cornovii, I believe, but I think we can safely allow those crimes and problems to await the morrow, we are finished for today.'

'Good, let the feasting begin. Why did Gerlois beat his wife?' Uther rose from his chair and walked down to Sir Ector. Merlyn joined them, and they moved to stand beside one of the large fires. All three accepted horns of ale from a slave and stared at the crackling logs and smoke that rose up towards the thatch high above.

'I am told he beat her because she strays, my Lord. Not to another man's bed, I understand, but she does not stay by his side as he wishes. It seems she is a woman with a mind of her own.' Sir Ector shrugged, 'I think he is still a little upset by what happened upon the quest. He has already asked that he be allowed to leave with his warriors and servants. I explained that it would be deemed an insult if he were to depart before the feasting had finished and he has agreed to stay, but he is not happy, perhaps he took out a little of his frustration upon his wife.'

'I have not met the lady,' muttered Merlyn as he drank from the horn and then lowered it, smacking his lips with relish at the taste of the ale, 'but I am told that the Duc regularly beats his wife, not something that I can personally approve of, a lord beating his wife as if he were some common serf, but we have no law against it.'

'I do not agree with it either, I find it to be cowardly,' muttered Uther, 'but after our experience with him upon the Isle of Erin, I can believe he is the type to do such a thing. To be honest with you, I find it hard to take a measure of the man. One moment he is our friend and staunchest ally, the next he is cutting the rope that was our lifeline back to the boat, I still believe he cut it despite his protests to the contrary. I also dislike him running, trying to slip out the back door as he did at the Druid's hall and like he is trying to do now.' He held a hand out feeling the heat of the fire upon his palm and stared into the flames. 'Despite all of this, I think I would like to be presented to both the Duc, and his wife. We need to move forward, not backwards. Let us see if we cannot mend both the Duc's reputation, so badly broken upon the quest, and also the marriage that he chooses to disapprove of so publically.

It would be best for the tribes if the Duc once more becomes a worthy ally and not a dishonourable outcast.'

Morgana brought the bowl that she had been holding down hard upon the stool, splashing drops onto Uther as he lay prone in his cot.

'An outcast? Dishonourable? And he would not have cut that rope. It is evident that you had already decided my father's fate by this time. You had met and already coveted his wife, my mother.'

Uther looked up to see that Morgana was trembling with rage, and he could see now that she had been weeping while he had been talking.

'It is true that your father and I did not much like each other, even then. But it is also true that as we began the feast, I only wanted to bring both him, the Dumnonii and the Cornovii tribes back into the alliance.'

'Drink this.' Morgana thrust the clay cup towards Uther until it touched his lips. He was thirsty so he drank, his eyes flickering from Morgana to Maude whom he could see back in the shadows, a worried look upon her face. He flexed his toes and fingers trying to loosen the stiffness that seemed to be taking hold of him, then drank more and looked once again into Morgana's angry eyes. She had her father's eyes he noticed, but the determined look and the crease of her brow was that of Igraine. He felt himself drifting back to sleep, his last vision that of Morgana staring at him with a look of pure hatred.

Chapter 16

A Broken Cup

The celebrations continued throughout the afternoon and on until the light began to fade from the day. The weather had remained fair throughout, but there was now a strong breeze and a chill in the air that promised the cold of winter was approaching. Uther decided he was glad the quest was behind them and he was back amongst his people once again.

Within the great hall, it was warm; guests were arriving and the musicians had already begun their playing. Glancing about, he realised this might be the last chance he would get to slip away and get a little fresh air before the feasting began in earnest, and so he discreetly withdrew in search of the cool of the evening and strolled out and through the upper wooden gates. After exchanging greetings with a few guests moving in the other direction, he eventually found a quiet unobserved spot where he could look down into the lower stockade.

He watched as people moved happily between the two smaller, communal halls, milling around the many fires where a variety of meats were being cooked – grouse, ducks, geese and swans all being turned on long spits, whilst on other fires, cuts of boar, deer and mutton were being roasted, the sound of the meat's fat dripping, hissing into the fires, where it wasn't being caught in clay bowls to be eaten later, carried back to him. Uther drew in a breath, rich in the scents of cooking meats and freshly baked breads and smiled. He took it all in, enjoying the moment of being alone and watching the people of the tribes as they celebrated the beginning of Samhain.

The light was almost gone, the darkness of Samhain almost upon them. Uther glanced up, feeling a chill of superstitious dread for this most special of evenings. The breeze had swept the sky clear of any clouds and he could just make out the sparkle of the first stars.

All around the walls of the lower stockade, fire braziers were being lit, both to illuminate the merriments and also to keep the evilest spirits of the night at bay. The Eve of Samhain was the one night of the year when the spirits of the dead, those who had passed into the Shadowland within the last year, would be able to push through the veil between the worlds. The Druids told that the veil between the worlds was at its thinnest during Samhain, so the dead would enter and walk upon the earth for one final time, saying their goodbyes and dealing with any unfinished business. Every tribesman knew they should take great care because, upon the Eve of Samhain, it was not only the spirits of the dead that would be entering the realm of man, but it was also spirits of a more evil and mischievous nature that would be set loose upon this world, all for this one most special of nights.

Warriors were patrolling the lower ramparts and Uther noticed that the main gate had already been closed and its locking beam set, leaving only the smaller gate for access. His men, under Sir Ector, would be ever vigilant upon this night, for no evil spirit nor indeed, could any Saxon be allowed to catch them unawares just because they were celebrating.

'It's beautiful, isn't it?'

The question crashed through his musings and Uther flinched in surprise and took a step away before stopping himself. The voice seemed to have come from nowhere, indeed, until that moment he had thought himself to be quite alone. Peering into the shadows, he saw that someone was standing closer to the wall, but it didn't look to be an evil spirit, although he couldn't be sure... no, it was a woman... he hadn't noticed her before. He felt his throat constrict as he realised that fate had brought him into the presence of Igraine, he swallowed.

'I always love the early part of the evening,' her voice was little more than a whisper, just another slight breeze upon the twilit air. 'When the stars begin to make themselves known with the first of their light. It's as if they have been waiting for the sun to hide beyond the hills and then, once they begin to feel safe, they peek out through the darkness and reveal themselves... it is quite magical, especially so tonight, on the Eve of Samhain.'

'My Lady, you took me quite by surprise, you are here alone? It is not seemly to be alone and unescorted. Do you not fear the spirits that will be walking amongst us this night?' He stepped closer to where she stood, a shadow amongst the shadows. 'Most people have a certain respect, if not a fear for the Eve of Samhain. They will cling to the firelight until the first glimpse of dawn has chased your stars away. Tonight, my Lady, it is dangerous to stay within the shadows.'

He heard her laugh and saw her hand move up to her mouth. 'Why King, Uther, do you really believe that tonight spirits, sprites and ghosts will pass through from beyond and walk beside us?' Her tone carried her smile and was slightly mocking. It was as if she were teasing a child and not talking to her King. 'I must confess that in all my years, I have yet to see any of these spirits, good... or bad.'

'Indeed, my Lady, yet I still think it best to hold with the Druid teachings this Eve. It is never wise to tempt the spirits and, truth be told, I have always enjoyed this celebration upon the first night of Samhain. It is the chance to commune with our dead and has always been a time of good memories for me. An opportunity to think that perhaps those I have loved and honoured have not been taken from us forever, so utterly and rudely removed from existence.' He stood beside her and looked back out across the celebrations below. 'As we always do, we have set places at the feast for many of our departed friends, those who have crossed into the Shadowland within this last year, Cunobelin of the Trinovantes, who lost his life upon our quest is amongst them. We shall honour them, welcome them to our table, boast of their deeds and seek their council. And I admit to you that since I was a small child, I have been among those who also believe that, on this one night of the year, there will be more evil spirits lurking in the shadows waiting to make their mischief and so I take care. Some will be spirits, but others will merely be men up to no good, waiting to blame the evil spirits for their wrongdoings.' Uther turned his gaze to the shadowy figure beside him and smiled. 'It is so hard to see you in this light. Perhaps, my Lady, I am speaking with an ugly, mischievous sprite and not with the most comely, Lady Igraine, should I be prepared to defend myself?' He heard the soft sound of her laughter once again and saw her glance back into the hall.

'Do not be distressed, King Uther, I am no sprite, yet I do fear that I have arrived at your celebrations a little less comely than when you saw me earlier today. With your permission, I shall keep to myself in the shadows. I have no wish to spoil the occasion. I shall not be taking part this year, but shall remain at a distance and then await your permission to leave with my people.' She turned as the sound of cheering erupted from below. Lit by the flickering light of the fires, dancers were leaping and turning to the sound of pipes while those watching laughed and clapped their hands in time to the deep rhythm of the drums and tabors. As Igraine leant out over the stockade wall, her face left the shadow and was momentarily revealed in the light. To Uther, she still appeared as beautiful as when he had first set his eyes upon her earlier that same day when she had moved through the crowd and he had felt his heart struck. But then she turned and he saw that the other side of her face wore a livid bruise and her left eye was swollen, almost closed.

'My Lady! What has happened? You have been injured, who would do this?' He felt a surge of anger flood through him, and he clenched his fists. 'If you were attacked, I shall make them pay, whoever it might be. You are my guest within this fortress and as such should enjoy your King's protection.' He reached out and took her by the shoulders, turning her towards him and bringing her face once more into the light, but she struggled and tried to back away.

'Please, King Uther, no.' She pulled further back to the safety of the shadows. 'It was a family disagreement, an accident, a misunderstanding for which my Lord has since offered his apologies. The fault for what befell me was mine and is mine alone to bear. Please... just leave me and rejoin the feast, you will soon be missed and...'

'You are wife to the Duc of Cornwall, to Gerlois?' Uther dropped his arms and stepped back. 'He beat you... I had heard that this happened, but had not realised that it was you of whom they spoke.'

'My husband is Duc Gerlois, and yes, he was most upset that I chose to leave his side and walk alone earlier today. I wanted to be amongst the people arriving and to see and enjoy the dancers, so after some time in his company, I slipped away without an escort. He was also angry that I allowed our children to leave his side, but since he departed on the quest the children have made friends here, as children will, and they wanted to join them in their games. Now that he has returned I sense he has changed for the worse.'

'This isn't the first time he has beaten you is it?'

'No, certainly not the first, he has struck me often, as any husband will to keep his wife to his order.'

'That is not an excuse to hit a lady of rank, not with such force. Nor to hit someone whom he loves.'

She laughed, the sound soft and musical. 'He does not love me, King Uther. I don't think Gerlois loves anyone or anything, certainly not me. Perhaps trade, he loves to trade. Anyway, now that he has returned from your quest he seems so agitated all the while. He would have his family standing beside him at all times. King Uther, I know something untoward took place upon the quest, something that has caused him to become angry and distressed and most eager to leave, but we have not had the opportunity to speak of whatever happened yet.' She sighed and looked down at the fires and the dancers. 'You must know that he is not such a bad person, King Uther, it is just that my husband can be a complicated man and has a terrible temper. He would prefer, and indeed deserves, a more dutiful and compliant wife than I am able to be. Our union was arranged by my father, who took much-needed coin for giving me over. I confess it has been a very suitable match for my family, and another trade deal for Gerlois, who also gained much land

and holdings from my father. Yet the arrangement has possibly been too restricting for me. I was spoiled. Once our match was made, I was allowed to occupy the fortress at Tintagel, the least favoured of Gerlois homes as there is so little trade to be done. Before this, I was living in my father's hall in the village of Tamara. My father was the chieftain of the Cornovii tribe and I am his only child, so I was an important girl,' - there was a smile in her voice and then she sighed - 'but he was old. He had debts to Gerlois and others and so he sold me along with his right to rule over the Cornovii. When I was young, I could go where I pleased, no escorts. I knew everyone and all knew me. Tamara is a beautiful village on the banks of a river. I remember riding on the raft that travellers would be taken across on, the ferryman was my friend. It was a nice place to be a child and when I grew a little older, I trained with the warriors.' She sighed and turned to face him. 'Let's just say I enjoyed a freedom in Tamara that is now more difficult to find,' - she leant a little closer and added in a near whisper - 'it is often a little difficult to live up to my husband's rules and standards.' She gazed at Uther silently for a moment, and he felt she was judging how much more she could confess. They were still in shadow, yet his eyes had adjusted, and he could now see some detail of her face as well as the darkness of her bruises. She came to her decision because she quietly confided: 'I am afraid after all these years he has little or no affection for me, I am an incumbent product from one of his trades. I often toy with the notion of disappearing into the crowd and never again fearing that he will beat me, or perhaps... no, I have said too much, none of this is your concern and I have overstepped my place, please accept my apologies.' Her hand brushed his arm as she withdrew, but he stepped forward and held her, feeling emboldened as she allowed him so close. He could smell her hair and feel her breathing, the warmth of her body against his.

'Perhaps our meeting was fated, Igraine.' He gazed down at her as she leant silently against him. 'I would take you from him, make you mine. I wish to protect you, to hold you always. I...'

'Igraine!' The shout came from just a short distance away, and the couple quickly stepped apart, with Uther turning to watch the dancers and Igraine withdrawing once more into the shadows. Uther glanced back and saw Duc Gerlois walking uncertainly towards him. The Duc was showing signs that he had been drinking heavily, he held a clay cup, carelessly spilling its contents as he walked, his head turning left and right, searching for his wife. Face flushed; he wore the familiar scowl set rigidly in place, but then his eyebrows rose as he recognised his King and he stopped short. The clay cup fell and broke as it hit the ground spilling a pool of the remaining liquid at the Duc's feet.

Uther began walking towards him, a smile set upon his face. 'Duc Gerlois, I was watching the people dance and taking a little air, but now I find there is a chill to the evening, and so I shall rejoin the celebration within the hall, please, join me.' Uther held out his arm to encourage the Duc to walk in his direction, and Gerlois did, but not before casting a frowning eye over the area where Uther had been standing.

'Have you seen my wife, King Uther? But then, how could you, you have not even been introduced to the bitch, so...' He shrugged.

'I am sure you will find that she is in the hall somewhere searching for you.' Uther took the Duc's arm and steered him back towards the sounds of feasting. 'I was told that you had some trouble, some differences with her earlier today?'

The Duc turned to Uther and studied him with red-rimmed eyes, the frown now back in place. 'She is wilful and needs to be disciplined. She can be like a child, wandering the paths upon Tintagel and even going down into the village without proper escort. It is not right, and if you had met her, you would understand.'

'I hope that when I do take a wife, then I will not have need to beat her.' Uther glared at the Duc, and Gerlois scowled back.

'I follow you as my King, and I followed you across the seas on the Druid's fool errand, King Uther, much to my regret, but I do not have to listen when you tell me how to treat my wife. The bitch is headstrong and deliberately irritating. I think I know best how to deal with her and do not need your advice.' He turned on his heels and walked back towards the hall.

Uther glanced back into the shadows where he knew Igraine had been watching and listening, and then made his own way to the hall, breathing deeply, his fists clenching and unclenching as he tried to release the surge of anger that had risen within him and attempted to think rationally. As he entered the hall, he was in time to see the Duc shouting at one of his men, then snatching a horn of ale. He watched as he swayed, drinking deeply, the ale dribbling down through his beard. When he had drained it, he threw it down and then turned to glare at Uther with a look of hatred and contempt that was barely contained.

Uther avoided him, choosing instead to join Sir Ector and Merlyn where they were already eating from a wooden platter heaped with a variety of different meats. Taking a large wooden pitcher of ale, Uther emptied its contents into first Sir Ector, then Merlyn's proffered horns and finally into a drinking horn of his own, and then banged the heavy pitcher down onto the table to draw the attention of those in the room. Cries of 'Silence for the King,' accompanied hushing sounds and expectant murmurs as all turned towards him.

'My friends, warriors of Britain. I welcome you all to the fortress of Pendragon and to this, our celebration of Samhain.' A cheer erupted, and Uther waited for it to calm. 'We accepted the challenge, we completed the Druid's quest, and we have come home to be amongst our own to celebrate our victory.' There was another cheer and loud drumming as feet stamped upon the floor and fists banged down upon the tables. Uther smiled around at his audience. 'We survived the seas and then we finally survived the Druids and their games...' He turned and raised his ale horn towards Merlyn, who smiled and raised a hand. 'We survived Uath the Stranger and his challenge... although a good man also died. Cunobelin, whom we honour at this table.' He raised his horn to the empty place set for the fallen hero, and a murmur filled the hall. Uther saw people turn in the direction of Duc Gerlois, who still stood glowering and flushed with a mixture of embarrassment and alcohol. Before the Duc could say anything or another in the hall should choose the moment to throw a challenge, Uther pushed on.

'We were once many tribes, scattered across this land of ours, kept apart by our Roman masters...' Angry calls and cries of defiance filled the hall, and Uther allowed the anger to build before going on. 'The Romans left, and then the Saxons came to call, seeking to become our new masters, but we rose and became one people, we united to become the Brittani of old, we became Britons.' Shouts and cheering filled the hall as Uther drank from his ale horn. After taking a long draught, he lowered the horn, wiped his mouth upon his sleeve and waited a few moments for the noise to subside.

'We must continue to be strong if we wish to banish these invaders from our lands. We must continue to be one people and show them that there is no future for them here.' Calls of agreement filled the air, echoing down from the rafters above them. 'Help the Saxons understand that this is our land, as decreed by the Gods of old.' He stopped talking and allowed the noise to lessen a little, waited, watching his closest men, the Lords, Chiefs and Elders of the tribes. 'This was no idle quest that sent us to Erin. When the Druids erect the stones at Stanenges, it will allow the spirits of those slain to seek rest, a chance to cross the great river of the dead and enter the Shadowland. It will also bring a new life to our warriors, new strength to their spear arms and a new future for our tribes.' A great roar arose within the hall as the warriors celebrated with their King.

'Before I allow you to return to your eating and to your drinking, let me ask you to take heart in the family of our union and to join with me again in the building of our future. Look to your brothers across these tables, look across the fields, rivers and streams of our land and seek your fellow Britons. Be clear in your friendship and in our alliance. Seek to gather those around you who would bring you strength, aid and friendship and offer them the same in return.' Uther stopped and gazed about the hall, allowing his eyes to come to rest upon the scowling Duc Gerlois. 'You have the birthright and are the strength, the law and the power to lead our people. Each of you within this hall hold positions of great responsibility. Treat your warriors, your villagers, your friends and especially your family well, do not bring them needless pain or suffering, for how you treat them reflects upon you. I salute you warriors of Britain.' Uther held up his ale horn and called, 'For Britain!'

As those within the hall returned the salute and then went back to the important task of eating and drinking, Uther glanced to Gerlois, who he saw was still standing, glowering drunkenly at him.

'I don't think you have made a friend with Duc Gerlois, Uther; he seems a little… upset.' Merlyn poured more ale into Uther's drinking horn and pulled the King around to look at him. 'You shouldn't antagonise him Uther; Duc Gerlois has been changed by our quest. He was not the most pleasant of people before we took to the boats, but now… he suffered much, and he will no doubt cause those under him to suffer in turn. Let him cool down and by the next meeting of the tribes, as we sit around your wonderful round table, much of what took place will have been forgotten.'

'He is not a good man, and he is weak.'

'That may well be, yet he leads one of our most wealthy and important tribes.' Merlyn's face creased into a frown when he saw how angry Uther was.

'He fled the challenge of the Stranger, killed Cunobelin…'

'There were witnesses, Uther… Gerlois cannot be blamed for the death of Cunobelin and as for the challenge he…'

'He beats his wife…'

'That is no crime, to beat a wife. A wife must know her place. You cannot…'

'She was the girl… earlier today. Her name is Igraine, I… I met her.'

'Oh, Uther, this is ill-advised, do not make an enemy of Gerlois of the Cornovii. You are the one who can, and is, uniting the tribes, something many thought could never happen. Please do not begin throwing all that away because a girl took a beating. Forget her, lead your people and you will soon find another girl, preferably unmarried and not yet a mother, to make your Queen… please.' Merlyn held his ale horn up, an invitation for Uther to agree with him, but Uther ignored the offer and glanced back in search of the Duc, but Gerlois was nowhere to be seen.

'My King, four warriors at the main gate, were overpowered, one of them was injured. The Duc and his party have fled, we think they left some time before first light.'

Uther sat up from where he had lain in a deep, yet troubled sleep only moments before and rubbed at his eyes; he felt groggy and thick headed from too much ale the night before. He glanced around, past the warrior standing beside him, and saw weak light seeping through the thatch above, indicating that it was indeed morning. The fire close by crackled and a flame rose into the new sticks the warrior must have placed upon it before waking him. He shivered and drew the sleeping fur higher and thought for a moment.

'Renew the guards at the gate and then send a party of riders after the Duc and his people with a request that they return. We shall ask Sir Ector to lead them. I gave orders that none were to leave until our celebrations here were complete.' He stood up on shaky legs, dragged the fur back around his shoulders, and crossed to the fire where he slumped down on a stool. 'That man is infuriating,' he muttered. He turned to the warrior. 'Please ask the Druid Merlyn and Sir Ector to join me, we need to deal with this properly.'

'Yes, King Uther.' The warrior trotted off, and Uther returned to the fire, poking at it with a stick before throwing on a few bigger pieces picked from a pile close by. 'It would seem that you are forcing my hand, Duc Gerlois, you should have stayed. We would have talked... Merlyn would have made sure that we parted as friends and that I leave any desires for your wife well alone, and perhaps I would have... perhaps, but now I am feeling less inclined to do so.'

Morgana shifted on her stool, unable to contain herself anymore. 'My father aided you; he sent ships on your ridiculous quest and, in an effort to gain your favour he even stood and took the challenge of Uath the Stranger. Just because you took a fancy to my mother, you turned his people against him and murdered him. Of course, he took his people and left. Was it not you who forced him to this point, King Uther? Did he have any other choice? He fled because he knew that you had deliberately brought him to this point, belittled and cowed him in front of his people and all the other tribal leaders… just so that you could satisfy your lust?'

Uther stared up into the shadowed face of Morgana as she sat beside his cot. The light had all but faded from the room and the chill of evening was invading. He heard another noise in the room and glanced across to see that Maude was trying to coax a flame amongst a bundle of twigs in the small hearth.

'No, Morgana, that is not how it was. I began that quest seeking only to bring my people closer together, and that included your father. He was a difficult man. You do not need to take my word for that, ask any who knew him. I thought at first that he was a good man, poorly judged by others, but I was wrong.' Uther tried to sit up and Morgana took his shoulders and lifted him forward roughly, put a bolster behind him, and he sank back gratefully, once more depleted of energy. After a few moments, he opened his eyes again and saw that she was staring at him silently, waiting for him to continue. He tried to find the right words so that she might understand.

'I am sorry, Morgana. I know you must hate me and for so many reasons, but also know that I wanted to help your mother, regardless of my feelings for her. He was beating her cruelly, and not just on that one occasion. Her life was endangered. She pleaded with me to help her, to aid her in getting away from a man who showed her no affection, no compassion. More often than not he just showed her the back of his hand.'

'And so you crushed him, stole my mother away, and I was sent to the nunnery at Laherne.

'I had no part in where you were sent, that pact was completed before I took Igraine to be my Queen. I have done many dreadful things in my role as High King of the tribes. Indeed, for my own reasons, I was also a terrible father to Arthur, my son. But believe me, when I tell you that I took no part in sending you away.'

'We shall see. Sleep, King Uther. Tomorrow you will tell me of the death of my father and the abduction of my mother, for now, you can try to find sleep.'

As Morgana rose and left the cell, the warrior Maude edged closer to her King's side. For a moment she said nothing, she simply gazed down at him and then reached out to brush a stray lock of hair from his brow, then leant down and whispered, her voice a soft breath against his ear.

'My King, I do not trust her. I fear for your safety here. You must try to gain a little strength for I think we must leave here soon. I will care for you properly.' She poured a cup of Morgana's brew into the clay cup, and held it close so that Uther could drink, and as the scent of it filled his senses his mind began to relax.

'Tell me something of you Maude? Where are you from? How is it that I am favoured with you as my guardian, my ever-present shadow?'

'There is little to tell, Sire; you should sleep.'

He stared up at her and smiled as she held the cup to his lips again.

'Very well. But I am just a simple person; there is little to tell. I am the daughter of a warrior, my father; he talked about you and the victories you shared at Mount Badon and Aegelsthorpe, he was a very proud man and very loyal to you. He told me of the early days when you were gathering the tribes. The difficulties that you had. My mother died birthing me, so I was brought up in a large communal roundhouse with many other children for company, so I had lots of opportunities to learn how to fight.' She smiled and raised the cup to his lips once again. 'When my father would return from his service with you, he would train us. It was all I ever wanted, to grow up and be like him, to fight near you... and now I am privileged to protect you while you heal. It is my honour to be here and look after you, my Lord, a very great honour indeed, my father smiles at me from the Shadowland, I shall not leave your side.'

Uther reached out and took her hand. 'Thank you, Maude, it is I who am honoured, to have you as my guardian in this, my time of need.'

Maude smiled and drew her hand away. 'Did Sir Ector bring back the Duc and the Lady Igraine? What happened?

'Let me sleep now. Tomorrow I will tell you of Igraine's experience, just as she retold it to me many years later. Morgana will be most unhappy if she doesn't hear of her mother's account. Poor Igraine was cold, confused and in a lot of pain.'

Chapter 17

Flight

There were six children and two women in the open cart, huddled together around the Duc's baggage and belongings, trying their best to keep warm in the late morning, which was cold and wet. The constantly rumbling, bucking cart was most uncomfortable, and so despite the softness of the bags around which they lay, the occupants were sullen and miserable. The party had moved at a rapid pace and this, coupled with the uneven, frost-hardened track, was making the boards beneath the occupants' buttocks bounce and jump alarmingly, leaving them bruised and hurting.

A man with little hair and fewer manners sat on the front bench. Igraine didn't know him and certainly had no wish to become acquainted. He was rude, stank of stale old sweat, oxen and horses, and it was obvious he thought nothing of his passengers' comfort. He was forever whipping the oxen that drew the cart, pushing them, again and again, to make them move faster, which made the cart bounce alarmingly. If that wasn't enough, he was being hurried further by the demands of the man who rode close to the cart astride a big white horse, Duc Gerlois. Igraine calculated that it must now be close to the middle of the day. They had been travelling like this for what seemed an age, and the pace of their flight had never ebbed, the poor animals must be exhausted.

It had been this hectic since they had first woken in the silent darkness of predawn. In the cold and dark they had been shaken awake and told abruptly, that they were leaving, no other explanation had been given. She had woken the children, who were naturally full of questions for which she had no answer, so they were left moving around in hushed whispers and confusion. All of it because her husband refused to explain, to stop, to rest, or even to slow down. It was obvious yet unthinkable that they were running away, fleeing from the fortress, from the King, without permission to leave.

Igraine ground her teeth, tried to endure, and wished she had found a chance to delay or refuse to leave her sleeping pallet altogether, but it had all been so fast and so early. They had been woken and sneaked away as if they were Samhain spirits returning through the veil between worlds, returning to the Shadowland. Except they weren't spirits, they were a frightened and confused group of people unsure of what was happening and why they were leaving.

Right now, in the back of the cart, Igraine felt numb as she peered out from beneath her course woollen cloak. It was wet and hung heavily over her, but at least it was still keeping most of the drizzling rain from drenching her further, but she would dearly love to stop and wring the water from it. Without any warning, one of the cart's wheels crashed into a pothole, delivering a jolting shock that made her flinch. Keeping her composure, she swallowed the pain, there was little else she could do, it wasn't the first time it had happened and no doubt it wouldn't be the last.

Gerlois was coming into view every time he came close to yell at the carter. She stared at him through her one good eye, the other still swollen shut from where he had hit her. What had happened? What had he done to make him like this? She hardly recognised him. He had never been the most pleasant of men, but a huge change had taken place while he had been away. He looked constantly worried and continually glanced back, obviously in fear that pursuers would catch up with them at any moment. She almost felt sorry for him, well almost. He kept yelling at the carter for not moving faster or the warriors on horses for not staying close; he appeared scared and that wasn't like him. She hugged Elaine, her second youngest daughter to her and smiled across to where Morgause her oldest, and Morgana her youngest, sat huddled close together. The other three children in the cart, two girls and a young boy with a wet, snotty nose who hadn't stopped crying since they departed, had parents within the circle of Gerlois' closest followers. She noted that Morgause still appeared tearful, yet Morgana was clearly untroubled by the rude awakening or the bumpy ride, in fact, she seemed quite happy.

The cart abruptly turned, bounced over some uneven ground and then rumbled through a grove of trees before slewing to a halt. Even though she couldn't see them properly over the sides of the cart, she was aware of the riders bunching up, clustering around. She could hear horses and men panting and horses' hooves stamping, muffled upon fallen leaves. Igraine and the children remained seated for a moment, expecting that the cart would start forward again as it had done on numerous other occasions this morning, but it didn't. They could hear more voices now, tired horses snorting and the jingle of harnesses as riders dismounted, and it became apparent that they had arrived at wherever they were heading. The warriors called and joked with one another, happy the ride was at an end, and she dared to believe that the ordeal might be over.

First one, and then a second loud bang made the cart jerk forward as both they and the oxen jumped, and then she watched as Morgana pulled herself up onto her knees and peered over the edge; that one was always first to jump up. Igraine waited for her daughter to report what was happening, but instead the child stood up and began cheerfully clambering over the side.

'Morgana, no… what are you doing?' Igraine pushed the sodden cloak to the side and tried to rise, but she was stiff and her body seemed to ache all over. She cursed and rubbed her lower back and then her legs, which were threatening to cramp. The needs of the children were suddenly being voiced, their calls of hunger and the wish to know, what was happening? Why had they stopped? Where were they?

'Shhh, my loves. Let us be quiet. We will find some bread and some cold meats for you soon, hush. Let us wait and see if we are to stay here or if we are moving on.' She glanced around to get her bearings and saw they had drawn up in a clearing amongst trees on the bank of a wide river. Three boats were moored close to where her husband was standing, two vessels tied hard against the bank and a third moored further upstream. Gerlois was paying the carter and they were haggling animatedly – he always haggled, the smelly carter didn't look best pleased. Most lords would leave this minor duty to one of their men, but Gerlois loved to argue about money with anyone.

Behind the cart, one of the warriors began gathering the horses, tying them to a long rope, probably so they could be taken back overland. The horses belonged to the Cornovii, but there was clearly not enough room to take them all on the boats, if that was indeed Gerlois plan, to sail – he had told her nothing of his plans.

It seemed they would be stopping here for a while at least, so she started to organise everyone out of the cart. A man called something as he ran down the heavy plank spanning the gap between boat and land; one of the loud bangs she had heard must have been as the crew had dropped the plank down. The boats were also Cornovii, she recognised several seamen and certainly the gnarled features of the boat master who was now helping several warriors persuade Gerlois' great, white horse to walk up the bouncing plank and onto the deck. The man must surely be close to fifty years. His skin was tanned dark, like old leather and crusted with the salt of all his years at sea. He was bent with age, had short grey hair cropped close to a mottled scalp, and piercing blue eyes the colour of a storm-whipped sea. Igraine was sure she wouldn't like him, which troubled her. She tried to like and get on with most people around her, be they from the higher groups of the tribal Council's warriors or one of the servants. She was even considerate to serfs and slaves. It was just some of the men Gerlois employed that she found so distasteful, she wasn't sure why.

She continued to rub at her back as she hoisted herself up on unsteady legs and watched as Gerlois' horse whinnied and stamped its hooves, its hot breath a pluming white cloud in the chill wet air. They had placed a cloth over its eyes, but its ears were twitching and it was snorting and prancing in alarm as it realised where they were trying to guide it.

'*Morgana, no!*' called Igraine, and then she sighed. The child was running over to help with the horse, but then it was highly likely the girl would be able to calm the beast better than the warriors, that one had a way with animals. Clambering down, she stretched her back which felt good, and glanced up through the cover of yellow and brown leaves at patches of grey cloud floating past high above. It was still cold, and the rain falling above the trees was dripping through the canopy; it was a truly awful day to be travelling far that was for sure. Gerlois must have his reasons, but she worried what those reasons might be and where he might be leading them.

'Keep away woman,' the carter growled irritably, as he strode past and pulled himself up to his seat. She drew the two girls back and cautioned the other children to stay clear as two warriors pushed past them to jump up while another held tight to the oxen's harnesses forcing the cart to stay where it was. The warriors quickly began unloading the bags and bundles, throwing them down onto the wet ground, even while the carter was cursing his low payment and lashing the oxen, trying to break them from the warrior's grasp. The bundles were picked up by others, quickly taken over to the boats and thrown up into waiting hands, all while the carter continued to grumble and complain.

'Get on board, Igraine, and hurry, we must be away,' called Gerlois as he walked towards her. He pushed her and the girls roughly towards the boat, causing Igraine to stumble. 'You try my patience, woman, hurry I said, we need to be as quick as possible. If you cause any delay then I will leave you all here, I mean it, so do not make to test me.'

Lifting her skirts so she would not trip again, Igraine did as she was bid and hurried the children over to the boat. Morgause was first to step onto the wooden plank and a warrior extended a hand to her before quickly pulling her up the three steps between bank and deck.

'Now you, Elaine, get on the boat so that your father and the men can finish the loading.'

'But I'm hungry mother. We still need to break our fast. It's been so long since we woke. Why are we...?' she stopped talking abruptly as the thumping sound of horses hooves echoed through the trees. Everyone in the clearing stopped what they were doing and turned towards the sound. After a brief moment's hesitation, the warriors quickly dropped whatever they were doing and gathered to form a wall, shield's held together, tightly overlapping with their spears pointing through towards the sounds of the approaching horses, a barrier of warriors ready to fight, a lesson in war learnt from the Romans.

'Quickly... up now.' Alarmed, she clapped her hands behind Elaine and cast about for her youngest daughter. 'Morgana, on the boat... please.' Thankfully, there were no protests and Morgana ran unaided up the wooden plank and onto the deck where she clambered up to find a better vantage point to hug the mast and peer over the warriors' heads as three rumbling chariots accompanied by a large band of horsemen entered the clearing. Igraine gingerly walked up the plank, arms stretched out to either side for balance, then glanced around to see that her youngest daughter was grinning, delighted by the distraction, seemingly oblivious to the danger or of the drama and heightened tension that was unfolding around them.

The horsemen had pulled up as soon as they realised that they had caught up with their quarry. The chariots that were following close behind drew back on their reins, and for a moment there was confusion as horses and chariots tried to hold without being pushed onto the Cornovii shield wall. Order was quickly restored and the horses stood panting great clouds of breath, harnesses rattling as they shook their heads, shivering their great muscles as adrenaline continued to course through their veins; they had clearly been ridden hard. The newcomers were showing a mixture of tribal colours and swirling blue tattoos, and as they quietened their mounts, they eyed the line of men, spears and shields that faced them.

Igraine could see that they were from several tribes, possibly it was so no reason of offence might be offered to the Cornovii from a single tribe. One of the mounted warriors of the tribe, Atribates, which was evident from his dark green cloak, and with his hair gathered back and heavily limed so that it appeared white and solid, rode a little forward and called over the heads of the waiting Cornovii.

'Greetings, Duc Gerlois, warriors of the Cornovii. We bring you greetings from King Uther Pendragon, High King of all the tribes. The King has sent us in search of you so that we can request your return to Pendragon fortress. The King is in need of your counsel, Duc Gerlois.'

Gerlois pushed through his men, stepped ahead of the shields, and gave one of his small bows and little more than a nod of his head. 'Please thank King Uther, but we have an urgent need to return to our own the lands. An… unexpected situation has arisen that requires that we make all haste. Please offer my apologies to King Uther and explain that it has become unavoidable that we should leave.' Gerlois spun on his heels and walked back towards the boats. Igraine heard him mutter to the boat master, 'Be ready to cast off at my command.' He glanced back at the riders and she did the same thing, seeing that a small group, the leaders of this combined force, were talking amongst themselves. In front of her, the Cornovii warriors remained in their shield wall; the spear ends waving to and fro through the shields as they waited to see if they would be attacked and be called upon to defend their Lord. At the front of the boat the last of the bundles were being thrown up into waiting hands and Igraine realised that Uther's men were too late, everything was aboard and they were ready to leave, there would be no return to Pendragon fortress today.

One of the chariots broke from the pack and rolled forward. 'King Uther has demanded that you return.' The man, standing tall upon the platform, wore Iceni blue, he was an older warrior, his exposed arms carrying many scars of battle. He pulled the helm from his head and Igraine saw that it was Sir Ector, the man Uther was known to trust above all others, save of course for the Druid, Merlyn. She felt a renewed flutter of hope rising within her chest; perhaps Gerlois could be persuaded to return. She realised that more than anything, she wanted to go back, to see Uther one more time.

'Nobody was given permission to leave while the Samhain celebrations were underway, this was understood by all. Your duty to your King is that you return, by not doing so you risk giving great offence, Duc Gerlois. We have been charged to escort you.' Sir Ector glanced to where Igraine and her daughters stood on the boat's deck and bowed his head in greeting before addressing her directly. 'My Lady Igraine. King Uther has reason to be concerned for your safety; we have been charged to escort you back to Pendragon fortress.'

Gerlois walked up onto the boat, the plank bouncing under his weighted steps, and glanced angrily towards her, then turned to speak to Sir Ector. Igraine could see that he was unhappy that Sir Ector had addressed her so openly, her husband's face wore an even deeper scowl than usual and his hand was gripping the pommel of his sword so tightly that she could see the whites of his knuckles.

'We wish no offence to King Uther, nor to you, Sir Ector of the Iceni, but we *are* leaving. My wife is in no danger, so neither you nor King Uther need fear for her. It is most unfortunate that we have had to leave, but we have a great need to return to our lands. Please offer my…'

'King Uther does not wish to have your apologies nor regrets, Duc Gerlois. *You will return to Pendragon fortress.*' This last was shouted by Sir Ector, which startled the chariot's horses making them step closer to the bristling wall of spears and shields, the warriors holding firm as the challenge hung heavily in the damp air. It began to rain harder, the sounds of raindrops bouncing from armour and shields mixing with the music of it pattering onto leaves and splashing into the river.

After a moment's brief hesitation, Gerlois voice rose above the sounds of the rain and announced decisively, '*No, we leave,*' then he called to his men, '*Board the boats.*' The wall began edging backwards to the river.

With an angry yell of, '*Damn you, Gerlois,*' Sir Ector whipped the reins down upon the back of his horses and the chariot leapt towards the wall. Behind him, the mounted warriors howled their war cries and kicked their horses into motion. Within moments, the clearing was reduced to confusion as the horses drawing the chariots hit the wall first in an attempt to break it or at least unsettle the spears, and then the mounted horses hit trying to force the wall apart. Unfortunately for Sir Ector, there hadn't been enough space to gain any speed, so the Cornovii wall was only made to step back whilst still remaining intact and stable. The wall began to push forward once more, the warriors grunting with effort, shouting and heaving and only slowing a little as one of the other chariots moved in, but it quickly became entangled with the first, making it difficult for Sir Ector to turn his chariot. Igraine could see the frustrated anger rise upon his face as he shouted at the other chariot to get clear, and then he whipped the reins down with a loud *'crack'* to drive on his own horses. Realising they weren't going anywhere with any speed, he turned and hacked down upon the upraised shields of the wall with his sword, trying to force them back while his warriors moved in to aid him.

The sounds of battle were deafening. Within the wall, warriors were shouting and cursing the horsemen and charioteers, stabbing out with their spears, aiming for the riders, but also seeking to strike the horses, trying to maim them so the mounted men and women attacking them could be dragged down. Pandemonium ensued as horses and men screamed and tribesmen from both sides cursed, spat and fought. Several fell from both sides, swallowed down amongst the madness of battle to die between a dark confusion of legs, hooves and chariot wheels. Gasping the last of their ragged breaths between gritted teeth and waves of agony as both friend and foe tripped and stamped upon them.

From the safety of the boat's deck, Duc Gerlois called out, his voice almost lost amongst the commotion. *'Please pass my regrets to King Uther. I am sure all will be well between us, but for now, we must sadly decline his request to return. Our stay at his court has been... most delightful.'* Gerlois nodded to the boat master, and orders were barked out, ropes untied, and using two of the long oars, the first of the boats was pushed towards midstream where it began to drift slowly out into the deeper, middle water. Sir Ector finally drew his chariot clear, and seeing that the Duc and his family had escaped, blew upon a horn. His men drew back from the Cornovii and the wall quickly broke apart, the warriors running to the remaining boats.

'*It didn't need to be like this, Gerlois,*' yelled Sir Ector. He drove his chariot close to the river bank. '*You are a senior member within the court of Uther Pendragon. Your quest went badly, but you would have survived, you could still survive this if you return. You do not have to set the Cornovii against the rest of the tribes; I beg of you to return.*'

Gerlois said nothing; he just stared, and so Sir Ector did the same. He and his men following along the bank keeping pace with the boats as they drifted with the current. From her vantage point upon the deck, Igraine watched them as the river widened, and the distance between the two groups became greater and greater. Sir Ector, she thought, seemed genuinely saddened that they were leaving. The river flowed, and the boats were carried faster by the swirling currents past reed beds and water birds. Silence filled the air save for the soft movement of water, the patter of raindrops, and a breeze that whispered through the reeds and the few leaves that remained upon the trees that overhung the flow close to the bank.

After some time, the horses reached a part of the riverbank where a small stream and marshy ground blocked their way. Unable to pass further, they halted and stood watching, horsemen and chariots gathered closely together until the river bent around and they were lost from sight.

Igraine drew her daughters to her, and they huddled together silently in what little shelter the vessel offered. They sat listening to the *chop, chop, chop* of the water slapping against the high prow as it began to meet small waves head-on. As the river widened before becoming open sea, oars were lowered, and the steady beat of a drum began to keep them in time. It echoed over the water, a sound as flat and featureless as the day. She realised it was going to be a long and uncomfortable trip back to the home settlement of Isca, at the heart of the Dumnonii lands where Gerlois ruled. Or perhaps, she reasoned, if the seas were fair, then they would sail past the Dumnonii moorings on the coast of Sumorsaete, and would instead travel further down the coast to beach at the small fortress and settlement upon the Isle of Tintagel in the lands of the Cornovii. Gerlois ruled over both tribes, but Igraine knew that Gerlois felt most safe and secure at the more easily defendable headland upon the coast, and with the current mood of her husband being so strange, it made more sense that Tintagel was their destination. For now, as the boat began to move with the rise and fall of bigger waves, and a stiffening breeze tugged at the big square sail that the crew had raised, she just wished she were back in the cart, or better still, at Pendragon fortress where for a short spell, life had finally seemed to be making a turn in her direction. Although, perhaps that had merely been her fancy, just an elusive part of a festival that everybody knew was filled with all manner of spirits and their trickeries.

The mood within Pendragon fortress had been sombre since Uther had risen early to hear that the Duc, his Cornovii, and of course Igraine had left. The Cornovii, allied strongly with their Dumnonii neighbours, were one of the larger, wealthier tribes and important to Uther's efforts to form one strong, unified nation that could hold back the forces of invaders like the Saxons and indeed the Romans, should they ever return however unlikely that may seem. It infuriated Uther that the Duc had left, and especially, he had to admit, that he had taken Igraine with him. There was clearly no affection between the Duc and his wife... but still. He knew he shouldn't dwell upon her but it was difficult, he had never felt like this before about anyone. He was consumed with an aching, angry desire to be with her, an emotion he reasoned, which could only be love, which in turn also made him angry that he should be struck so and at such a time. Added to his discomfort, was a chill draught that chased about his hall despite the numerous fires and hangings stretched across every opening. It was a day filled with frustration and reflection, and so his mood was as dark as the cloudy rain washed day.

When, late in the evening, Merlyn entered, followed by a wet and bedraggled group of Druids, the scowl dropped from Uther's face for the first time since waking that morning to be replaced by a smile. 'Why, Merlyn, you and your kin are most welcome, enter, enter. Does the presence of Druids in my hall once more tell me that you have already placed the stones?' Uther studied the small group. There were four newcomers, dripping wet, shivering, and each casting longing glances towards the various fires in the hall.

Uther waved the shivering group of Druids towards one of the fires. 'Please, warm and dry yourselves. I am sure we can find some dry robes from somewhere.' They turned to Merlyn seeking his approval, and he also muttered that they should warm themselves and pushed them forward before moving to Uther's side.

'No, Uther. The stones are not yet at Stanenges, even Druids cannot move that quickly, but they are being moved as we speak.

'Moved?' questioned Uther, 'How are they being moved this time, will they fly?'

Merlyn tapped the side of his nose and gave a twinkling grin. 'They will arrive in time and be placed correctly, ready for the sacred rites that will be concluded upon the festival of Alban Arthan, the shortest day and longest night of the year. The first of these rites will be performed as the golden sickle cuts the rope of mistletoe that binds the largest stone. Other rites will be performed by different Druids over the following days. However, I am afraid that you will not be permitted to bear witness to any of these events... but then, I do not think you would want to be there anyway,' he concluded in a lower tone.

'I have given up the thought of ever being made truly welcome by Druids, please do not fret.' Uther smiled at Merlyn, and the Druid frowned.

'You are, however, invited to attend the final rites of fire, which will be held four days after Alban Arthan.' Merlyn's face broke into a smile as he said this, his thick grey beard bunching up below the crinkling of his eyes. 'Very welcome you will be, and it's my favourite part… it gets a good deal warmer with all that fire.'

'Alban Arthan… I am sure we will be delighted to be there, Merlyn, but the longest night, the solstice, is well within the dark times of winter. The God, Cailleach, will be powerful in his rule by then. It will be cold, wet and inhospitable upon the grassland, and that will be if the snows have still held. Will you be making preparations to receive us, as well as do all that is necessary for your stones?'

'Two great halls are going to be constructed, King Uther,' called one of the visiting Druids. She rose from where she had been crouching by the fire. Uther noticed that her dark brown robes had begun to steam and that she had unbound her long hair to help it dry. The effect of the mist that shrouded her left her transformed, lit as it was by the flames of the fire from behind. She had taken on an ethereal quality. Whether she was aware of it or not, Uther didn't know, but it quite took his breath away and once again humbled him slightly to the mystery and sacredness of the Druids. She was probably no more than twenty summers and appeared to him like some goddess from the old times. Moments before, as the group had entered wet and cold, she had given the impression of being closer to fifty and almost crone-like.

Uther nodded his thanks and then leant forward to speak again to Merlyn. 'Is it necessary for you to be involved in these rituals personally? I have an undertaking that I believe might require your help.'

Merlyn's smile became a frown, and he moved closer to Uther, his voice dropping to match Uther's lower tone. 'What do you mean, an undertaking, what sort of undertaking? What are you planning, Uther?'

'Earlier today, I sent Sir Ector after Duc Gerlois and his party; they departed without permission, and against my orders, before dawn. Sir Ector is to request that the Duc returns at once. I have taken about all I am prepared to take from the Duc. I have found his surreptitious departing to be most offensive, especially in light of recent events upon the quest. I am sure you will agree that it would be far better that we reconcile our differences here, rather than allowing this latest act of disrespect for his King to cause us to clash.'

'Clash? You seriously intend to allow your infatuation with the Duc's wife to bring us to a point of war within the tribes?' Merlyn stared at him. 'Do you not think we have enough of a problem with the Saxons? I had thought you a far bigger man than that, Uther. You are the unifier of the tribes. The leader that has done away with the centuries of squabbling and differences, but now you will have us throw all of that away because of a woman... a woman... because we both know that it is her that this is all about, have you been taken by madness? Perchance, did you drink too much seawater while we floated amongst the stones, has it scrambled your brains?'

'Careful old man.' Uther scowled. 'You forget that I am your King, and you overstep yourself. I would not throw our alliances to the side, but neither am I able to allow this man to lead one of our largest tribes without bringing him to account. He has shown himself to be untrustworthy, cowardly, and also it now seems, a man unwilling to remain with us at his King's request. Don't think I haven't forgotten that he cut the rope back on the boat and nearly killed both of us. He is the runt within our litter, and that is regardless of my personal feelings for him, or for his wife. If the Cornovii do not return with Sir Ector, then we shall visit the Duc to hear his excuses and then decide if a new ruler of the Cornovii and Dumnonii is required.'

'And the woman has no part in your decision to make this war upon the Duc's tribes?'

'Care for your fellow Druids, Merlyn. They are tired, wet, and in need of our hospitality, something we offer in abundance to those who are part of our Kingdom.' Uther rose and walked from the hall while Merlyn shook his head, a sad frown upon his face.

'King Uther... the Abbess has gone... she left a short time ago. Please, stop now. You keep on speaking. You talk and talk, but you need to rest.'

Uther focused his eyes upon the face of Maude and ran his tongue across dry lips. The present world swimming slowly into focus. He looked up into the face of the warrior maiden as she seemed so concerned, so worried, were those fears for him? He smiled and reached a hand out to her. 'I am well. The Abbess was right; it feels good to tell of those days. I feel myself lighter, unburdened as the words come from deep down inside me. It is as if I am watching the story of my life unfold before me while I listen to a distant voice that isn't really mine. I had not realised how heavily those events have weighed upon me all these years.'

'King Uther, please, drink water.' She helped him rise, lifting him from the bed, and then held the bowl to his lips. He sipped, the cold water felt good, then licked his lips again feeling them dry and cracked. She was watching him closely, smiling, obviously pleased he was back in the present and that she was able to care for him herself now that Morgana was away.

'I fetched it from the well, myself. I do not trust this herbal infusion that the Abbess brews for you. She is always so anxious for you to drink it, yet when she caught me smelling it, she became most incensed and warned me never to touch it. King Uther... she was furious, which I think is strange. I think it would be best if you do not drink her potion; in truth, I fear for you.' She bent down and whispered in his ear, 'I do not trust her, but worry not, for I am here to watch over you.' She sat back up and smiled once more. 'I shall fetch food... some broth. You will get stronger and then soon we shall leave this place, you and I.'

He drank more from the offered bowl and watched her as she fussed over him. He couldn't really comprehend what she was saying; the infusion was good, sweet with honey and he felt that it was giving him strength. Morgana could be no threat, surely. But Maude was right when she said he needed to regain some small part of his former health because he still felt terribly weak. When he was stronger, he could decide what was to be done. For now, he felt exhausted and drained of energy. His life was weighing so heavily upon him, as if it was pulling him down, down into the depths of a darkness where he knew his dreams were waiting to torment and confuse him, but he was unable to avoid it any longer, Uther slipped down into the blackness within his mind and slept.

Chapter 18

The Lament of a Wife

Uther waited, roaming his hall and corridors, churlish and irritable, snapping and bad-tempered with any of the servants and slaves he happened to meet, which was not normally his way. He knew what he was doing, hated himself for it, but his mind was spinning, and he couldn't help it. Consequently, people avoided him and those needing his approval or consent for anything, quickly decided to leave the King to his moods and await the return of his more personable disposition. Therefore, he was left alone in his hall with none but the dogs for company.

The shadows of night were closing in when his waiting finally came to an end with the return of Sir Ector and his warriors. The clatter of the horses' hooves and rumbling chariot wheels echoing loud from down in the lower yard. The sound rising above the dripping of rain and the clamour of fortress life, jerking Uther from his sullen mood. A surge of anticipation flowed through him, and he stood up and paced the floor, the rushes rustling and whispering beneath his feet, waiting expectantly for news of Duc Gerlois and far more importantly, of Igraine. Moments past, and stretched into even greater spans as Sir Ector did not show. Uther returned to the fire and stabbed angrily at it with a stick. It spat back and sent up a plume of crackling red embers. After what to him seemed half the night, a weary Sir Ector finally walked into the hall.

Uther glanced up and frowned. 'Why do I not see Duc Gerlois on his knees begging me for an apology? What happened, Ector? Did they outpace you? Or were they joined by an even larger Cornovii force, which even now are beating at the gates threatening to take possession of my fortress?' He threw the stick onto the fire and rose to face Sir Ector. The older man was tired, he could see that, but impatience and disappointment had caused his anger to rise again. Biting back another barbed comment, because he knew he was being ridiculous, Uther drew in a breath, waved Sir Ector towards a seat across the fire, and waited for an explanation.

'They took to their boats. We caught up with them just as they were finishing the loading and were about to depart. Words were exchanged. The Duc was firstly invited and then instructed more firmly to return. However, he refused, and we felt compelled to use force, a fight of sorts ensued, but it was too late. We lost a horse, and two of our warriors were injured in the skirmish. He was not going to return, Uther. There was no persuading him, and they were already beyond our reach when we arrived.'

'Did you see the Lady Igraine? Was she...?' For a moment, Uther didn't know what to say. He was probably unaware of his hand held out as if waiting to be given something, some token of knowledge that Igraine had been seen and was well. He stared at Sir Ector and could see that he was uncomfortable. He sighed and dropped his hand, aware of how foolish all of this must seem.

'The Lady Igraine... the Duc's wife was on the boat with her daughters. I did as you instructed and explained that we had reason to fear for her safety, but we were too late. All the vessels were away and midstream very quickly. I couldn't get to her, and she remained silent throughout. I could not tell if she wanted to return with us or remain with her husband, I am sorry, King Uther, I have failed you.'

'No, Sir Ector, the Duc has failed us all. No fault lays at your feet. We will deal with our errant Duc, now, during this winter before the Saxons stir from their cold sleep and bring their troubles upon us once more. I shall call a special meeting of the lords and chiefs tomorrow morning before they depart for their halls and tribal lands. By Beltane, we shall have a greater understanding between us, or a new ruler shall hold court in the lands of the Cornovii and Dumnonii.

The blow took Igraine quite by surprise. She had been sitting beside Morgause, holding her daughter close for comfort and warmth, staring out across the featureless horizon as cold wind tousled the shawls that they clutched over their heads as the boat rose and fell beneath them. Her attention had been far away, dreaming and wishing she were anywhere but on this boat. The very next moment she found herself sprawled across the deck, her head ringing and the side of her face screaming in pain. She heard a wailing cry and realised it was coming from her and that Morgause was trying to roll her over.

'Mother... Mother!'

Igraine cut her cry short and tried to gather herself. She drew in two, deep, ragged breaths and then glanced up past her daughter into the angry face of Gerlois as he towered over them both, his feet set wide apart to brace against the roll of the waves. Just past him, at the far end of the boat perched upon the prow, she could see Morgana; thankfully oblivious to anything but the joy of being at sea and the spray of the waves. She was glad her youngest had been spared seeing her mother struck, but the other children, Elaine amongst them, were staring at her with different mixtures of fear and horror written upon their young faces. One of the other women was trying to hush the little boy who was sobbing again.

Gently pushing Morgause to the side, Igraine heaved herself into a sitting position. 'I will be all right, child. Go, join your sisters. Your father wishes to speak with me, he...'

Gerlois stepped closer and bent down beside them. 'Her father wishes to know why Uther Pendragon takes such an interest in you, bitch? Did you lay with him? Is this why he spurns and dishonours me so? Why he sends his dog, Ector, in search of us? They came after all of us, yet it was you he sought out... don't think I didn't notice that. The Lady Igraine is in danger, he said... but danger from whom, from Saxon raiders? Samhain spirits? Me?' He stared down at her, his face angry and flushed red, the cold wind tugging at his hair. 'So help me, woman, I will kill you rather than lose you to that whelp of a King, and I will take out your eyes if I find you have been unfaithful to me. Do you hear me, bitch? I own you, don't you ever forget that.' Spittle sprayed as he spoke, she felt some alight upon her face, and she stifled the impulse to wipe it away.

His face loomed so close to hers that she could smell onions upon his breath, and part of her mind asked when he had found time to eat them. 'Do you understand what I am saying, Igraine? You will abide close by me from this day forth and not stray. I will have you faithful, like the bitch you are, or there will be an end to our union, and you would not like the way that I would end it. Now get back to the children and shut those snivelling brats up or I will feed them to the fish.' He stood and glared at Morgause, who remained defiantly close to her mother, trembling, and then he stamped his foot close to the small weeping boy who shrieked and hid his face, which only made Gerlois growl at him and then laugh.

As he rejoined the warriors at the steering oar, Gerlois snatched the small brown goat being held out to him by one of his men and crossed to the side. Drawing breath he bellowed out across the waves.

'Hear me, Lyr, great God of the sea. I ask that you aid us by soothing the waters and allow our passage to pass without hindrance.' He held the goat up by the skin of its neck in one hand, high above his head while in the other hand, he held his knife. The goat gave a weak kick and then stopped moving and hung still as if resigned to its fate. 'Bring us fair weather and allow us to pass across your Kingdom in peace. I offer you this life in payment for our intrusion.'

With one swift movement, he brought knife and goat together and slit the goat's scrawny neck. Blood splattered down upon him and across the boat's side, and then out over the sea as he held the little carcass above the waves, it twitched feebly as its spirit was released. After a moment, Gerlois turned his blood splattered face towards Igraine, who still lay upon the deck, half raised upon one elbow. The goat was hanging in his hand, still now, a trail of bright red blood dripping to the boards. He stared at her for a moment, then he tossed the frail body over the side and returned to his men.

Igraine crawled back to her daughters and held them, as the boat rolled and the cold, salty spray mixed with a drizzling rain continued to soak them. She could hear Gerlois' horse whinnying in alarm and the stamp of its hooves. A soft voice tried to calm it and after a short while, it did indeed quieten down. Drawing her daughters closer still, she stifled a sob and wondered at the madness of her husband and what the spirits truly had in store for her.

Night was always the worse time to be travelling by sea and was more often an experience to be avoided. As the light bled from the sky in a weak mockery of a sunset, Igraine waited in vain for the boat to change course towards the coast. After a while, she felt her spirits fade, and a shiver of fear and resignation run through her as she accepted they would be spending the hours of darkness at sea. It left her feeling numb, unsure how she was going to be able to cope. There would be no rest from the discomfort, the constant movement or the gusting wind that howled through the ropes and across the deck, driving the wet, stinging salt of the sea, robbing them of all warmth. On almost every other voyage that she had been forced to endure, when the day had been done they had headed into the coast and beached the craft or found some river inlet to drop an anchor stone. They had found a place to rest, to change into dry clothes, find comfort and seek the warmth of a fire, but it obviously wasn't to be on this night. Gerlois was indeed a driven man, possessed with the need to be back within his own lands and so they sailed on.

Darkness gradually consumed them. It robbed them of any sight of the coast and the familiar landmarks she knew the boat's master would normally need sight of so he might know where they were or how close they may be straying towards any treacherous stretch of coastline. She watched as shadowy figures crossed towards them and tugged the small, whimpering boy from the clutches of his mother. The child's voice rose in a wailing protest as the men dragged him away, the mother screaming, hands held out trying to get a grip upon her son.

'Nooooo… no, no no…'

Igraine couldn't quite believe what she was seeing, even as it happened before her very eyes. It took her a moment to react from the listless apathy that had been holding her. The boy was handed across to Gerlois; the mother shrieking hysterically was pushed down to the deck as Gerlois produced his knife and held the child by one foot to dangle headfirst above the dark, inky waves, just as he had done with the goat earlier.

'*Gerlois, no!*' Igraine found her voice and tried to rise to her feet but she was stiff and slow. 'Gerlois. Have you lost your senses…? He is a child; this is no goat. What possesses you? Let him go, please… please.'

Gerlois turned and looked back at Igraine, he was just a shadow against the darkening sky, but she knew the look of loathing that was directed at her and she shrank back, hating her inability to do something…. anything to turn him from the abhorrent act he was about to commit.

'His father died back there on the riverbank,' called Gerlois, 'and now this child is nothing but a worthless wretch that will die of hunger, or the sickness before the winter is done.' The child wailed again, and Gerlois shook him. 'Silence you little shit.' He slapped the child to stop him moving, but the boy screamed even more and kicked, showing more fight than anyone might have given him credit for, squealing like a speared pig before subsiding to plaintive sobs, calling for his mother, strings of snot trailing in the wind.

'Now he, at least, has a purpose. Go talk to Lyr, and now also to Dylan, who is God of these seas hereabouts, and ask him to grant us safe passage.' The shadow of Gerlois' arm raised, there was a quick motion towards the boy followed by a gurgling scream, and then Gerlois let go of his charge and leant over the side of the boat as the water claimed the body.

'I give this offering to you, oh great God Lyr, and to you, Dylan. May this, oh so precious life, be payment for your good favours and protection of this vessel and all who journey within it.'

Gerlois turned, his task completed, wiped his hand on his cloak and then crossed to stand before Igraine.

'We do what we need to do to complete our journey. Now shut your hole and stop that stupid bitch from screaming too, or I will have my men plow her and give her another son to make up for that worthless little shit.' He laughed as he walked away and Igraine felt a burning hatred, the like of which she had never experienced before. She did not know this man, this man whom she had called husband. She crawled across to the boy's mother to try and give some small comfort, although she knew not what she could say or do. To take the life of a child to placate a God, or Gods, yet surely these Gods must now look upon them with less respect, not with more.

'Shhh, hush now.' She held the woman against her chest feeling the sobs and grief shake her.

'Your boy has gone to play with Dylan, I know of this God, do you?' There was no answer, but she decided all she could do was speak and hope the sound of her voice brought comfort.

'The God Lyr is well known to all of us who sail upon the God's waters, but Dylan, he is less known. He was born a mortal child, to mortal parents and loved the sea. He grew up to love it so much that stories tell that he swum with the fish before he could walk and then one day, so the tales go, he escaped his parent's arms to remain deep in the depths where he joined the ranks of the Gods.' The woman's sobs continued as Igraine rocked her, but the trembling had calmed a little as she listened.

'Dylan is known to call these waters where we now sail, off the coast of Cymru, his home. He plays with ships the way small boys are often playful with bugs as they pull off their legs, your boy will swim alongside Dylan and they can play together now.' She knew it was important that they request both Lyr and Dylan to allow them to pass and that Dylan play fair, but to call upon the God's favour with the life of a child? Gerlois had not only changed; he had now become a monster in her eyes.

She rocked the weeping woman and patted her back wishing there was more she could do. A surge of resentment swept through her as the darkness became almost complete, robbing her of sight. It was an anger toward her murdering husband and his stubborn foolhardiness, forcing them to remain at sea and bear this ordeal when she could see no necessity to inflict any of this upon them. There were women and children on board, not just some party of raiding warriors. Why could he not understand that and show some shred of compassion? The cold wind tugged at her wet hair drawing it from under her headdress and making it dance about her exposed face, but she felt too tired to try and cover it again. She hugged the boy's mother to her and welcomed her daughters with her other arm as cold tears slid down her face unseen, but then after a short while, she sniffed them back. Staring up into the gloom, she softly implored Lyr to clear away the clouds and take the drizzling rain away. If the clouds departed, then the stars might be revealed to guide them or, best of all, the moon might light their passing

Despite her discomfort, at some point, she must have dozed because she woke with a start and for one blessed moment didn't know where she was. She had been dreaming of Pendragon fortress, of the music and dancing at the Samhain festival and of course of the moments when she had shared such an intimate conversation in the shadows with King Uther. In the dream, they had laughed, and he had taken her hand and implored her to dance with him, drawing her from the darkness out into the light. She had felt happiness surge through her body, but then she had awoken and realisation struck as her body quickly reminded her that she was wet and sitting upon a hard wooden deck. Then before that, for most of the day, she had sat in the back of an uncomfortable cart, so her buttocks were both numb and bruised and would be aching for days. She sighed, much longer like this and the bruises would be turning to sores, which renewed her worries for the children and invoked another softly muttered curse upon Gerlois.

Then the pains in her back made themselves known, and she tried to move a little, this drew a weak moan from Morgana. Oh, this was just intolerable, sitting for so long without the chance to stand and stretch. She shivered, squeezed water from her shawl before wrapping it back around her and Morgana, and wished she had stayed asleep.

She could hear the horse moving, feel through the boards beneath her when its hooves stomped upon the deck. Poor creature, she had forgotten that it was suffering too. Drawing a deeper breath, she tried to shake the feeling of despair. Tried to believe that it really would all be over soon. Grimacing, she turned her neck, rocking it slowly from side to side to work out the stiffness and ease the discomfort. About her, just visible in what little ambient light there was, were the shapes of the women and the children in her little group, bunched closely together. The whimpering of one or more of the children could be heard as they slept, mixing amongst the other sounds of the boat as it creaked and splashed, rose and fell, meeting the waves, with the wind and water hissing about them.

Oh, by the spirits, but this was a wretched experience for all of them, and she knew it. There would be at least two more nights at sea if Gerlois didn't have a change of heart and head for the coast, who else might he sacrifice in his demented need to sail on? Were her girls safe from their own father? Was she? She fretted and fussed, and then her eyes were drawn upwards as without any warning, the night sky seemed to awaken, the clouds slowly drawing apart, allowing the first moonlight to break through and reveal the churning sea, painting the waves and the boat in its cold, silvery light.

Looking out across the now visible seascape of rolling white-capped waves, she wondered at the beauty of it all, and then glanced up and felt her feelings of despair slip further away to be replaced by awe as the full majesty of the stars was fully revealed. A vast scattering of constellations, their light painting the edges of the retreating clouds. It lightened her heart, and she drew in a breath of cold salty air, her eyes flittering from one group of stars to the next. At the highest point overhead, the stars seemed to be grouped much closer together, appearing as a river flowing wide across the dark sky. The Druids, she knew, called it the white river and told that it was governed over by the Goddess Arianrhod, who they said was the true mother of the sea God Dylan. It was along this silvery pathway that they said the spirits of the dead must be carried on their way to the Shadowland.

Feeling better than she had in days, she realised how small her problems were in the eyes of the Gods and that anything and all was allowed to be possible in this life. She had been born in a village to the chieftain of the Cornovii, been married to a Duc, born beautiful daughters and travelled to the ends of the land. And now she had a King casting his eye towards her. She may be cold and wet, and in the middle of the sea, but what future might possibly lay before her, she could not even begin to imagine, but for now, at least, she could dream...

They saw the stones being transported to Stanenges by the Druids or at least some thought they saw them. It was late on the fourth day after leaving Pendragon fortress, the long line of men and women, chariots, and carts trudging one after another beneath a featureless white sky. Uther was tired, riding slumped in his saddle and having ridden since daybreak, he had been dreaming and thinking, anticipating their arrival at the camp that his men would have prepared to await his arrival.

A whisper of excitement seemed to travel down the column as word was passed from warrior to warrior. Apparently some of the slingers, a group of warriors who were marching on foot at the rear of the long column, had seen the huge stones on the horizon, passing over the distant hills. The buzz of speculation and interest ran up and down the line with calls of confirmation and disbelief sounding in equal measures, it was the most interesting thing to have happened all day. Uther, sitting high upon his horse, gazed out at the hills, scanning along them for any sign of movement, but nothing caught his eye other than wet trees. He continued to watch for a few moments, eager for some glimpse of huge stones floating one after another, or more than likely pulled upon horse and cart he reasoned, because he knew Druids to be tricksters. As eager to pull the wool down over your eyes and confuse you whilst calling it magic, than show themselves to be doing things as any normal person might do. But then, he reasoned, whatever Merlyn had done to those stones to make them float was still rather magical, not to say getting them down from up on the mountain all by himself, so maybe they were flying, who was he to say that Druids couldn't make huge stones fly...

He returned his scrutiny to the horizon, but still couldn't see any sign of them. After a while, as the chatter about stones and Druids lessened around him, he returned to pondering the muddy path, the possibility of a dry pavilion for the night, and thoughts of Igraine. The worst thing about travelling at any time was the mind-numbing monotony of being on horseback for day after day. This close to the winter solstice, the boredom was made worse by the cold and rain. At least, thought Uther, I am not walking and have a comfortable living space being prepared for my arrival. He looked about at the chiefs and warriors riding around him who would also be closely cared for as soon as they arrived at camp, and then he glanced back to the tide of men and women who were walking to the rear of the column with the carts. He knew their number would be close to five thousand and provisioning for the march was a taxing task, one that he was glad could be passed to more competent men than himself. The warriors marching on foot would be setting their own camps when they arrived, finding their own areas to light fires and would erect shelters from materials carried on the carts and from what they could cut from the trees. He also knew that a large number of them would simply enter the forest to seek shelter. It made him reflect on the time when Cal, Nineve, Merlyn and he had travelled through the forest of the Wield, sleeping out amongst the trees with no cover from the rain and cold other than their cloaks and a bed of gathered moss and bracken.

It wasn't a bad memory, not when compared with other events that had assaulted him from before, during and after his rise to be King. Sleeping out in the rain had been cold, and of course wet, but it was a pretty good memory of simpler times. He looked up, startled from his reverie by a rider forcing his way towards him through the flow of carts, warriors and horses. It was one of his scouts, a man of the Iceni; Uther could tell from the blue cloak and swirl of wet blue woad upon his bare chest, he held up his hand in greeting as the warrior approached. The man jumped to the ground to kneel, but Uther quickly called for him to stand.

'There is no need to lay in the mud, my friend. You have ridden hard to find me, what news do you bring of what lies ahead of us?'

The warrior rose and swung himself back up onto his horse's back before answering.

'A temporary fort has been built awaiting your arrival some short way ahead, Sire; all shall be ready for your arrival. But we also have word on both the Cornovii and the Dumnonii as you requested. Word has been sent to all their villages to gather their spears and amass both at Isca and also Dimilioc. None have been told why, save that they gather in defence of their Lord. We were told that thousands are gathering at the two fortresses, it seems that they received their calling almost half a moon ago.'

Uther nodded. Gerlois hadn't wasted any time. He must have sent his orders almost as soon as the boats had beached after their quest. He had known they would flee but delayed their departure until he was sure his warriors would all be gathered together upon his return. Uther ground his teeth and tried not to show his frustration to the warriors that were marching past them, all staring openly at their King, as he discussed matters far beyond their ken. It would seem that the Duc was more prepared than he had given him credit for, but why call his warriors to two different fortresses more than a day's march apart, was this just to cause confusion to those he knew would be pursuing him? The planning was something Uther reluctantly admired, but it also left him with a feeling of irritation, Gerlois should not be the enemy, but he was clearly preparing to confront the combined might of the British tribes. He tried to shake off the feeling and thanked the man, then he rejoined the movement of the warriors and pondered deeply. There was much to be settled, firstly at Isca, it would seem, and then possibly on to Dimilioc.

The raven flew across frost covered fields, above woodland already sleeping its winter sleep, and hovels with smoking fires, housing peasants trying to survive winter's harsh grasp. It knew where it was going; there was a path but a short distance to the side, making it easy to find its way, with a few peasants making their way between villages in the early morning light. It meandered across the countryside enjoying the freedom and sensation of flight, the wind making a soft, pleasing hush across its glistening black wings as its head turned from side to side taking in every detail of the land, all its features and especially the people it passed.

As it came to hamlets and villages both large and small it flapped its great wings to gain height, before gliding down to flit softly once more over fields and rivers, until finally, it crossed the unmarked border into Saxon lands that, to the eyes of the bird, were little different to the lands claimed by the Britons, yet it knew this to be the current boundary between the two. Then a burnt out hall confirmed it; it flew on.

Recognising the settlement that it sought, the raven alighted high in an old elm tree, its branches bare of leaves this late in the year. It gripped the branch with its claws and turned its head to peer down at the warriors gathered below standing around their small mean fire; the village guards such as they were. They were stamping their feet for warmth and blowing steam from their mouths over cold hands as they joked and chatted and bemoaned the chill in their harsh, abrupt speech. Swords, spears and axes were left piled to the side of the fire along with their shields, ready for an attack that clearly none of them expected to happen.

With a loud *'cawww'* the bird swooped over their heads, barely noticed, and then down between huts towards the largest of the grouped dwellings. As the raven approached the ground it shimmered and grew, and moments later, Morgana le Fey was stooping to push past the low doorway.

She rose and drew down the cowled hood of her cloak. The occupants glanced up as the door banged shut behind her, the only announcement of her presence. They were the same group as had previously occupied the roundhouse; the two women, a small group of children and the man by the fire, the dog even now shrinking back with a soft growl. They all stared at her as she pointedly ignored them all and stepped towards the fire, to warm her hands.

'You bring news?' Octa glanced at the door, a frown set upon his face, and then stood up from where he had been crouched, sharpening a seax. He quickly sheathed it, then slipped the stone into a pouch tied at his waist. 'We had not expected you... not so soon.' She could tell he was unsettled; perhaps he had expected his men to announce her, the thought made her smile. It was good that she could ruffle the man just by appearing when he least expected it.

'The King still dies, I become weary of tending him and listening to his lies. He is fevered, delusional, and has no recollection of truth as it indeed was, regardless of the strength of the potion that I give him, his mind has broken. I have come to summon your warriors to take him away.' She looked up and smoothed the front of her black robes before fixing him with a frowning stare that she knew would continue to unsettle him. After a moment, she said, 'You promise to make him suffer? You said that if and when I delivered him to you, that you would take him away from his people and draw out the moments of his death until it became a long, unending scream... can I hold you to your promise, Octa Hengistson? Can I pass this burden to you so that the spirit of my father can finally lay in peace?'

Octa gestured for her to take the seat by the fire, and then resumed his own, letting out a sigh as he sat down. 'We will take the King from you, of course, but you promised to deliver the son as well. We need

Arthur so that the Britons have no leader. The King is the King, yes, but with the Druids help, the boy is already ruling. Some might ask what use a dying man could be to me when the whelp is already leading the pack, don't you think?'

'The dying man is still the King, and he can be taken easily, taking the son will need a little more finesse, he is forever within sight of the Druid, Merlyn; he never allows the boy to be alone.' Morgana accepted a clay bowl of steaming liquid from one of the women and smiled her thanks. The rich earthy smell of chamomile greeted her as she inhaled. Sipping it tentatively, she found it had been sweetened with honey and was delicious, but a little too hot. She lay the bowl beside her to cool and turned her attention back to Octa as he began to speak.

'We know well of Merlyn; we are told that the Druid wields the most powerful of magic, and he has a deep hatred of my people for some strange reason.' He smiled, and then his face became serious once more. 'We will come for the King, but it is for you to deliver the boy. Then both of them shall disappear. They shall never return to trouble either of us. Without them, the land will quickly fall to Saxon rule, which I assure you will benefit both of us. Bring us the boy who would be King.'

Morgana spoke calmly as if she were talking to a child. 'You must have patience. All will be done, everything completed. Firstly, you shall rid us both of the father, the pup I shall bring you when the time is right; I will not rush this unnecessarily. Your men will come to the Abbey upon the next full moon; this is in six days. I shall allow a small group to enter the Abbey and take the King. Only one guard watches over him, a woman, a tiresome creature whom I shall deal with in my own way.' She picked the bowl up and sipped her infusion, feeling the warmth of it fill her, before continuing. 'This is the way of things and how it shall be done, are we in agreement?' She waited for Octa to nod, and then glanced up towards the hole in the centre of the roof where the smoke from the fire lapped lazily around the thatched edges before being drawn out by the soft morning breeze. She placed her bowl on the floor and returned her gaze to Octa. 'Do I have your word, your blood bond, that you will come... do we need to cut thumbs to seal the oath?' Her head tilted to the side, much as the raven's had, as she waited for him to answer.

He shook his head and sat back before clearing his throat. 'There is no need for blood or oaths; we will come. For what greater prize can I ask, but the living body of the King of the Britons?'

She nodded, raised her hands, and with a crackle of energy and a flutter of robes, the raven was flapping up towards the smoke hole, the dog having found its courage at last, barking furiously below. She flitted through and then sat on the edge, her head once again turning to the side, beady black eye staring down into the shocked, upturned faces of the Saxons, and with one last *'cawww,'* she was gone.

Chapter 19

A Conflict of Interest

The hills and woodland, the paths and lanes, every animal, man, woman, and child steamed and gave forth a rich aroma of unwashed and foul odours in the early morning light of dawn on this, a new winter's day. As it frequently had over the past ten days of their march, it had rained for much of the night making rest and sleep almost impossible. Thankfully, the clouds had finally fled before the appearance of a brilliant sunrise that lit the misty world about them with soft orange rays. The weak but welcome warmth now bathed the steaming, bedraggled column.

Uther was riding close to the front, exhausted by the journey, the rain and even more by the constant sticky mud that caked the feet of those marching, it bogged down chariots and carts, and it even made progress difficult for the horses.

The seemingly endless procession of warriors had spent the best part of each day slowly moving forward in numb resignation as they travelled towards their goal, which for most was simply the hope of a hot meal and dry place to sleep. With such a large force it was often difficult just to follow on, as those in front were in turn slowed by impassable puddles big enough to be called ponds and paths filled with mud. They tried to ignore the rain as it lashed down upon them in the open or dripped upon them from the trees, below which they sought shelter, as water found its way into every item of armour and clothing that they wore or carried.

The previous night they'd sought rest after darkness had already fallen and it was finally decided that they were not going to reach the next camp. Once again between planned resting places, they had been forced to make do with very little shelter and no chance of lighting fires. As the light had faded to darkness and the cold had crept in to wrap chill fingers about each and every one of them, regardless if they were warrior, Lord, or King, they had huddled beneath trees and bushes in sad little groups. Uther had spoken with Sir Ector and Merlyn, but it had been hard to find the energy to converse.

Sometime in the early light of dawn, knowing that no one had found sleep or any real rest, Uther gave the order that they would soon be leaving. Since then, they had been forcing one foot after the other in the misty gloom in the hope of reaching Gloucester some time later in the morning. It was in the settlement of Gloucester that Uther knew they could finally find rest for a few days in the well-established settlement and hill fort.

'Do you know much about where we are going, Gloucester?' Asked Uther with little enthusiasm for the answer. 'It sounds like a Roman name, what did we call it before the Romans, do you know?'

Merlyn looked up from his reverie and smiled, happy at the opportunity to converse.

'Yes, Uther. I know it well. I knew it before the Romans were here… but that is another story. Before the Romans there was a settlement and an ancient fortress, even older than me, called Kingsholm; had a good sized settlement around it. When the Romans arrived, they subjugated the local tribes and renamed it Gloucester. Ignored the hill fort and built their own strange villas and buildings on the lower slopes as the fortress on the higher ground fell into decay. Once the Romans left, the fortress was reclaimed by the local tribesmen again and today it endures once more.'

'So a King once lived here?'

'Most probably, sometime in the mists of the past, but the Roman name Gloucester seems to have taken a good hold, so unless you want to live here let's just keep calling it Gloucester. I doubt the locals would wish to have their town's name revert to Kingsholm anyway.'

'That's fine by me, I just hope it is close and ready to receive us,' said Uther as he pulled the hood of his cloak, lower.

'I know that Sir Ector sent riders ahead to warn of our approach several days ago. I am sure so that all necessary preparations have been made to house and feed our warriors, even if the weather has not been our friend and delayed us.'

'It is difficult, but we will endure and become the greater for it,' said Uther. 'There are many sound reasons that war is fought in every season other than in winter. We should all be sitting out the winter, warm and dry.' He dammed Gerlois for the tenth time that morning as he realised that the sun was barely over the treeline. Lately, he had spent far too much time damning the man he sighed; oh, but damn the man indeed, for at least one final time this morning. He really should be back enjoying the comforts of Pendragon fortress, warming his feet by the fire, thinking of a boar hunt or planning what actions to take against the Saxons come the Spring thaw, not splashing about in mud, wet through to the skin in anticipation of bringing the tribes together for war.

Thankfully, for the remainder of the day, the weather remained fair and the warrior's spirits seemed to lift as they warmed from marching and their clothing and leather armour dried.

By midday, the path they were travelling merged with a Roman road. Uther's horse clattered up onto the well-packed gravel surface and he noticed that while some of the warriors walked on the mud-free stone surface, others still chose to struggle along the muddy path at its side. 'Lest they lose contact with the spirits of the earth,' he knew. He remembered his own misgivings when he had first encountered the strange flat surface of stones many, many years ago and his own belief that if he trod upon its surface for too long, he would lose contact with the spirits of the land and his ancestors that watched over him... but it did make for faster easier going.

They passed a milestone with carved lettering indicating that the fortified settlement of Gloucester was just five Roman miles distant. Uther looked at the marching men in front of him and tried to picture the distance and how long they still needed to travel before he might change his clothing, eat a meal, and perhaps sleep before dealing with the boundless questions and requests that would be waiting for him. One Roman mile was a thousand paces, with two steps making a measured pace… he watched the closest marching warrior and counted the steps as he walked… after a few moments, he concluded that it would be a short day of travel before they arrived, which cheered him greatly.

'You appear pleased, King Uther,' said Sir Ector after noticing Uther smiling. 'There are few things to smile about on a march such as this, would you care to share what amuses you?'

'Little amuses me, Sir Ector. I was merely noticing that while they have long left our shores, the Romans' legacy still lives on in our Britain, even though it has been years since their legions marched here.' He pointed back at the milestone. 'To know where you are upon the road is valuable information, we must be sure these markers do not fade into insignificance. We would do well to continue the job that our old Roman masters started and keep the stones clear of weeds. The stone tells me that we are but a short stroll to the camp at Gloucester, and I think we shall be breaking our night fast upon meat and eggs.' The two men smiled at the thought then nudged their mounts into a trot, to pass the warriors in front of them.

Some time later, the sprawling camp covering the hills and fields about the fortress came into view. The smoke of hundreds of cooking fires drifted languidly up towards the clouds, filling the air with the smell of food being prepared. Uther looked out from the hill fort across the warrior's camp towards the southern forested hills. He could see the thin line of the road crossing the fields and disappearing into the dark treeline. He knew that beyond the forest, where it emerged and within just a few days march, lay the lands of the Dumnonii and Cornovii tribes.

As the boat left the more turbulent open sea behind and slipped into the calmer waters of the river, Igraine felt an impatient need to feel solid earth beneath her feet.

She had feared they would spend a third night at sea, something she felt would test the boundaries of her sanity beyond the point of breaking, but just as the light was beginning to fade from the sky the little boat had turned towards the coast and she had felt her spirits lift.

Everyone sprawled around her had sat up, several children jumping to their feet and all had begun to chatter excitedly as the abrupt course change had been made, and it became apparent their journey would soon be at an end. They had only resumed their places and quietened down when Gerlois had growled at them to stop clucking like excited chickens and keep out of the crew's way.

And now trees, drab looking water reeds and the deadheads of last summer's bulrushes were slipping past closer and closer to the side of the boat. It was steady for the first time in days. They were no longer rising and falling as they had when on the open sea. Now as they were passing achingly close to firm land, they could smell the earth and slightly pungent aromas of rotting reeds. Sliding cleanly through the river water with a hiss, thanks to the heaving efforts of the oarsmen, they drew closer to the distant mooring posts, the oars rattling against the side of the boat after every measured stroke.

Raising her head a little, Igraine tried hard to curb the excitement she felt, but still had to exchange furtive grins with others in her group as they whispered their questions and exclamations. They were all craning their heads to see better, like so many chicks in a nesting box she thought, but she was doing it too. Horsemen were waiting for them, a small band, their leader standing alone on the bank while the others remained mounted some way behind him. She hoped that they would be welcomed into an established encampment with food cooking and comfortable sleeping arrangements already waiting. She was as exhausted as she could ever remember being and felt she could sleep for days. She smiled down at her daughters and hugged them close.

'Oh, girls, soon this will be over, and we will get off this boat. We will be able to look after each other, comb our hair out and clean ourselves, and surely eat a proper hot meal.'

'I want hot pottage, oatcakes and roasted meat,' said Elaine, her eyes wide at the thought. She held a hand to her belly then grinned.

'I want to ride the horses,' said Morgana excitedly. She pointed to the waiting horsemen. 'Do you think they brought us all horses to ride? Do you think they brought Blackberry for me?'

'Don't be silly, Morgana,' chided Morgause, 'why would they bring your pony with them? We shall travel by cart...'

'Or chariot! I wouldn't mind driving a chariot.'

'Hush, both of you.' Igraine pulled Morgana down and hugged the girls to her again. She glanced across to Gerlois, but he hadn't heard Morgana, he was talking to the boat master, helping guide them through the narrowing river.

'Raise oars,' called the boat master, and eight dripping oars were raised overhead and then brought into the boat and stored. As the vessel came close to the bank, one of the crew jumped ashore and heaved back on a rope slowing the craft as it neared the bank where the mounted warriors waited. Another line was thrown, and the boat drawn to a final rest bumping close to where one of the other two boats that they had departed with was already moored. Igraine looked to Gerlois, waiting anxiously for permission to leave the boat, but he ignored her and instead jumped down himself. He walked to the front of the vessel and held his arms out; Morgana jumped down happily, and they walked together to the waiting warrior. As the white horse was led ashore, Igraine glanced around. There were no slaves or servants waiting. She could see no pavilions erected with dry cots, nor smoke from fires cooking, preparing hot meals. She stood, confused, there seemed to be no preparation for them at all.

'Gerlois?' she hadn't meant to call him by name, he would be angry, but she didn't understand. He glanced back at them on the boat as several other warriors joined him on the bank, and then as she saw horses brought for them she noticed the boat was drifting back out into the river.

'Gerlois... please... what is happening? Morgana... why are you taking Morgana? Gerlois, can we not come ashore and make camp? Can we not rest and cook a meal... for the children?'

Gerlois swung up onto the back of his horse, pulled Morgana up to sit behind him and called, 'You are being taken to Tintagel, Igraine. You and the girls will be safe there while I go to meet the King at Isca, we have some business to discuss that I think will be better done without you there. Morgana will accompany me.' The boat was moving quickly now, caught on a current being drawn back out to sea.

'No... Gerlois, please. Why keep Morgana with you? Let us rest here for the night, I beg of you, Gerlois... *Gerlois?*' She shouted this last as he wheeled his horse and the group of mounted warriors disappeared from sight amid a chorus of yells and shouts. Igraine watched as Morgana turned in the saddle, to look at her while clinging onto her father as they rode away. Then Igraine collapsed back down into the arms of her remaining two daughters and they sobbed together, the whole group of women and children crying as they slipped back out towards the sea.

'Why did he take Morgana, Mother?' asked Elaine. 'Why does she get to go with Father?'

'Hush Elaine, I'm sure your father has good reason to take Morgana with him.' She said this but knew that Gerlois had taken her daughter as another way of keeping her, his wife, docile and obedient. It was a harsh lesson, but surely he would care well for his own daughter... wouldn't he? 'Please,' Igraine found her voice as she noticed pity on the face of the boat master. 'Please allow us to put ashore and rest for the night. We can sail again at first light; we would not lose much time... we need to rest, can we?'

The old man shook his head sadly. 'Duc's orders, Lady. We are to take you to Tintagel making all haste and see you enter the fortress before dusk tomorrow. To do that we must sail through the night.' He glanced up at the cloudy sky and shook his head. 'It may rain, but there will be no storm. I have no reason to cross the Duc; I'm sorry to say. I see you have a powerful need to rest, but for now, this is the way of it, we sail.'

And so once more they put to sea. The women and children on board, gathering together to endure another winter's night, exposed and wet on an open deck, it would mark their fourth night at sea.

It did rain, soaking them all, chilling them even further if that was at all possible, as they clung to each other in a tight little group so that Igraine felt they might all die of exposure, but it didn't storm and by dawn the next day the rain had ceased.

'While you lot were still sleeping, at first light, we passed the Dumnonii trading settlement of Appledore, a pleasant place with a pleasant name, passing it already means that we're being carried by good winds and is proof that the Gods smile upon us.' The boat master appeared pleased as he said this, he passed around dry oatcakes taken from a greasy looking sack.

'If yer have a mind to, keep an eye down the coast and yer may shortly see the fortress of Tintagel coming into view.' Everyone turned to look, but there was little to see but grey water, a grey coast and an even greyer sky.

'For those of you who haven't seen Tintagel from this vantage, tis set upon an islet that juts out from the coast. Up upon its own little headland, so it is. The watchtowers are what you'll see first.' He turned away and went back to his business, minding the steering oar, gazing up at the big sail as he teased as much speed out of his vessel as he could. Without Gerlois on board, he was more relaxed with his charges, and the little group of women and children were able to stretch their legs and stand at the windward side of the boat to watch the coastline slip past, each eager to catch the first glimpse of the fortress.

'I'll be the one to see it first,' called Morgause running to the side of the boat. She crammed oatcakes into her mouth and pushed past her sister.

Igraine allowed herself to be drawn to the side of the boat by Elaine to see a distant sail. It was probably one of the vessels carrying tin for trade goods, its sail a dull brown smudge in an otherwise grey day. Igraine shivered and cast her eyes down the coast, but Tintagel was still nowhere to be seen.

It was past midday when Morgause gave a shout, saying she could see the towers of Tintagel in the misty distance. Everybody strained to see, but none save Morgause could make out anything, all but Igraine voiced their doubts. If Morgause had said she saw the towers, then Igraine knew she had seen them. The voyage would soon be over and rest not far away. She gripped the side of the boat, her nails digging into the wood, and stared along the coast until finally, she too saw the protruding headland, waves foaming white upon the rocks at the base of the cliffs, and knew they were almost there. Her thoughts turned for a moment to Morgana and hoped she wouldn't irritate her father too much. It scared her more than she cared to admit that her daughter was out of her sight and in the company of such a man as Gerlois, even if he was her father.

Maude crept silently along the reed-strewn passageway, moving from memory through the darker parts, ignoring the rustling and squeaking of the rats that she couldn't see, but was all too aware of their presence. She refrained from taking a candle of her own; wanting to be as silent and unseen as possible and moving about with her own light would have announced her presence to any of the nuns who might be up and moving about on their own nocturnal business. They kept strange times these nuns, even now in the darkest hours of the night they would all wake to attend prayers.

Reaching the part of the Abbey where she had hidden the growing pile of provisions, she pulled the bench carefully to the side to reveal the hidden stash and added a leather satchel. She scanned the darkness about her, listening intently until certain she was alone. The satchel contained a few coins from the bags the King had arrived with, his rings that she had managed to hide, and some documents she had found beside the cot. She hadn't quite known what to take, or what the King would need, but she was intent upon taking him away and knew she had little time to prepare. Warm clothes, some blankets... what else, where would she go?

Maude retraced her steps until she was close to the room where the nuns prepared their food and decided to see what she could find to bring the King. A low fire was burning in the hearth, the glow of a few bright embers enough to allow her to search the tables and boxes that she could see. There were plenty of vegetables and herbs hanging in bunches. She found a hunk of hard bread wrapped in a cloth and then when she took the lid from a pot she smiled as the aroma of barley pottage filled the air. She scooped some up with her fingers; it was still warm. Taking another mouthful, she replaced the lid and began to search for a bowl; tonight, the King would eat, and soon he would become strong again, and they would be leaving.

Chapter 20

Dead Echoes of Winter

It was as Duc Gerlois and his party were approaching the main gates that the first snowflakes of winter began to fall upon the Dumnonii settlement of Isca. Above the high walls of the fortress, constructed from huge tree trunks fitted tightly together with their bases buried deep in the earth, the dense grey clouds began to let go their burden as if they had swollen and held their load for as long as they possibly could, but the time had come when they must softly, and silently burst, to slowly release their burden.

Isca was one of the largest trading settlements within Britain. Within the walls were hundreds of roundhouses, huts and halls of many sizes and it teemed with merchant representatives from the many tribes of Britain and also from tribes across the sea who wished to trade with both Britons and their Saxon invaders. The main strength of Dumnonii and Cornovii warriors were camped here to offer protection for the trading settlement, its inhabitants and also for the travellers and merchants who journeyed upon the surrounding paths and roads. At its centre, a large market square dominated the settlement, as a place where goods and livestock that were brought from all over the Kingdom and from across the seas could be traded and sold to its multitude of visitors.

As the small band of horsemen clattered up the hill, a few solitary flakes floated down from the oppressive grey sky. Out of the corner of his eye, Gerlois noticed Morgana's little hand reaching out to catch them.

'Hold still girl, or you will fall just before we reach the town and embarrass me.' The hand was snatched back and he felt Morgana hold him tighter.

Other flakes were following the first few, the snow was increasing quickly, holding a promise that winter had arrived and that it would worsen severely before it was over and done.

During the night the temperature had dropped quickly. When just after first light the Duc and his men had awoken, they had emerged into a world without a breath of wind. It was deathly cold, painted white with frost, puddles covered in crackling ice, bare trees hard and still as if frozen in place. Gerlois had smiled, his breath misting in the chill air. Winter was finally making itself known and this would only hamper the efforts of Uther, if and when he arrived with his mighty force of warriors. Gerlois knew that if the King could be held at arm's length between Isca and the fortress at Dimilioc until Beltane, then the Saxons would begin their raiding once more and his Dumnonii and Cornovii would be left in peace to fortify their borders and continue their trading while Uther returned to the conflict with the Saxons, if that is, he and his army hadn't starved or frozen to death in the meantime. Either a new peace with Uther Pendragon would be made this winter season, or the King would be forced to recognise these lands as a separate Kingdom.

Now at Isca, the snows of winter had begun and those first few snowflakes were quickly and silently filling the sky, settling in his horse's mane and on his beard so that it tickled his chin as it melted. It was already dusting the open, levelled land all around the settlement, turning pig runs and turnip fields into a soft white, bringing beauty to what had been a stark muddy world brief moments before. This was no weather to make war, he kicked his horse into a trot and grinned at the thought of Uther Pendragon shivering, camped beneath a tree while he was warming himself by his fires eating goose, yes... that was it... he had an appetite for goose this cold winter's day.

'Make way for the Duc,' called his man, Peder, as they approached. Peder, an older man past his fortieth year, was in charge of fortifications and defences of all of the Duc's fortresses including the largest of Isca, Dimilioc, and of course Tintagel, he had been a faithful servant of the Duc for many years. With his hair and beard showing more grey than the glossy black he had been so proud of for years, he was fastidious in his dress sense seeking out the finest furs and fabrics that the traders brought from Gaul. It was often a point that his men found amusing but never mentioned within his hearing. He was a big man who carried his years well and was feared amongst his warriors as having a quick temper and excellent fighting skills. He had also been the warrior who had travelled to meet the Duc as his boat docked.

'I see the land has been cleared, prepared in case we are attacked,' called Gerlois to Peder. 'Did you have to remove many of the surrounding halls and dwellings?'

'A few, in fact, several, but now all the land around the settlement has been emptied for two hundred paces, my Lord Duc,' replied Peder. 'The area directly around the main gate was already clear of course, except for a few bushes and small trees between the fields that have now been removed, however, we were forced to do away with a number of huts and roundhouses close to the southern gate. Because of this, there were a number of unhappy merchants who lost property there, but they were assigned land within the walls and therefore gained by the action, so all ends well.'

As the two massive fortress gates swung inwards, twenty warriors ran out to line the road in honour of their returning Duc. Gerlois and his retinue rode past, he raised a hand in salute, and then they were entering the settlement, the clattering of the horse's hooves echoing in the still air. Warriors came forward and held the horse's reins, as first Morgana dropped down, and then the Duc and his men dismounted. The horses were led away to be tied up, watered and fed, and as the gates were closed behind them, Gerlois smiled in satisfaction and sighed, finally feeling that the need to run had left him, he was safe... or at least safe enough until he decided to make his final move to Dimilioc and by then, time would have run out for Uther Pendragon. He turned to Peder.

'See to it that the sentries keep a good watch. There will be scouts coming soon, sent forward from Pendragon's warriors. I want to know when they are seen… and send out our own riders to get information on just where our King and his men have already reached on their march. They will be tired and cold and should have very little appetite for war.

'Yes, my Lord,' muttered Peder, 'we will soon know.'

'It appears that the weather is on our side, at least,' said Gerlois, holding out his hand to catch a snowflake. 'With the grace of the spirits, we shall either have Uther Pendragon as our guest in a few days, having apologised for his treatment of me, or they will have retreated, back north, and will be more concerned with provisioning their people through the winter months and preparing for Saxon raids after the thaw.' Gerlois turned and began to walk towards his halls with Morgana skipping along at his side. There were two halls, built side by side, set in the main part of the fortress, close to the market square; he liked to be close to where the gold and silver changed hands and where he could entertain visiting merchants.

'My Lord,' called Peder, 'there is an envoy from the Veneti awaiting you. He arrived by boat from across the water several days ago and asks to be brought to you as soon as you arrive.'

'An opportune arrival,' Gerlois smiled and rubbed his hands together in anticipation of a good trade deal. 'Send him to my hall; I shall await him there. Have a goose prepared and bring pots of their good Veneti wine and of course, Saxon ale. Uther Pendragon can wait, we have trade to discuss.'

They had thought they were already in the depths of winter, until the night when it really arrived. Only one day out from the relative comfort of their encampment at Gloucester, dark, ominous clouds began to gather overhead, and the temperature dropped along with the fading light.

'I don't much like the look of this, but 'tis too cold to snow, surely.' Sir Ector pulled his furs around him and scowled up at the clouds.

'I wouldn't be too certain of that,' said Merlyn as he held out a hand to catch the solitary snowflake drifting down towards him. Other flakes were already appearing around them, and a disgruntled murmuring was moving up and down the line of marching warriors.

'We shall build our shelters this night within the forest,' said Uther. 'Like as not, it will be done by morning and we shall be able to move on. For now, let us prepare for the worst, make our shelters and put some hot food into our bellies.'

'To the trees and make camp,' called Sir Ector, and the word was repeated up and down the line. Chariots, carts, and horsemen began heading towards the trees with all the warriors on foot following behind. Sir Ector sent several warriors to set up guard points on a perimeter and others to scout the forest in the direction of Isca.

'Our scouts report that we are approximately two days march from the fortress of Isca.' Uther walked his horse closer to where Sir Ector and Merlyn rode. 'As they have already met with several of Gerlois warriors, we can assume that he is well warned of our approach. The gates will be closed to us. I would have your counsel as how best we can proceed.'

Merlyn turned in his saddle, to look at Uther, a bemused look upon his face. 'Now you wish our guidance, King Uther? Possibly it is a little late for us to add our counsel. What exactly is it that you wish to accomplish by bringing so many warriors half way across the Kingdom, in the dead of winter?' He took a look up towards the clouds, snowflakes catching in his beard. 'The Gods conspire against us for they are now sending us a full winter it seems.' The three riders reached the edge of the treeline and warriors took their horses as they dismounted. Fires were already being lit, the smell of smoke drifting around them promising an escape from the cold. Shelters were also being constructed, hurriedly, the sound of branches being cut echoing through the forest.

'I know that both of you, as well as many others, believe that this is a mistake born out of your King's infatuation with the Duc's wife, which is something that grieves me to be so misunderstood.' Uther ignored the raised eyebrow and amused smile upon Merlyn's face. 'There are two things that need to be accomplished by our intervention in the affairs of Duc Gerlois. Both the Cornovii and Dumnonii tribes are ruled over by the Duc. Combined, they are one of the richest tribes within our alliance. We cannot have them led by a man who is not a true member of our union, an honourable member of the round table. A man that at the moment, we cannot trust. Duc Gerlois must go down upon his knees to me, his King, pledge himself to our cause and take up the responsibility that his position dictates, or he must be replaced. If he is to be replaced, then it must be now, not later when all his misdeeds have become nothing more than old memory.' Uther looked into the eyes of his two friends, one after the other, seeking some understanding.

'I agree, King Uther,' said Sir Ector. 'The Duc is both infuriating and also untrustworthy, his conduct upon our quest was embarrassing, and he then offered great insult by not returning when you commanded; he must be brought to heel.' Uther smiled placing a hand upon his friend's shoulder, silently thanking him for his understanding.

'Pah!' Merlyn grinned and slapped his knees while Uther scowled across at him. 'We could have waited until spring, to march down here for that. The Duc will do little between now and then, a little trade maybe, that's what his greedy heart desires, but even trade is hard to accomplish in winter.' He waved his arm around at the cold, bleak woodland. 'The only reason that we have marched down here, and will spend most of the winter freezing our bottoms off in this forest, is that you have desires upon that girl.'

'Keep your voice down and control yourself.' Uther drew Merlyn over to a fire that had been lit for them and they sat together on a fallen log, holding their hands out to the flames while Sir Ector sat opposite them and frowned at Merlyn.

'It is fine, Uther. You are a King, and a King gets what a King wants, that is the way it should be. I am not going to argue the pointlessness of marching such a mighty host of warriors half the way around the world, in the middle of winter, to win your girl. It is a little late for that and, quite frankly, not my place to do so.'

'You have never been shy before about telling me what you think, certainly you have called me a fool many times. I'm sure you have your reasons why you are not berating me right now, but I don't care, because after the quest to Erin, which was also pointless and an incredible waste of time,' Uther held a hand up to Merlyn, as the Druid made to argue. 'After that, oh so noble, quest, we agreed that you were very much in my debt. You will soon be repaying that debt by helping me to bring the Duc to heel or Igraine back to Pendragon fortress.'

'And how am I, a mere Druid, supposed to accomplish that for you, Uther?'

'You are not a 'mere' anything, old man. I do not know how you will aid me just yet, but I will surely think of a way. Firstly, we have the Duc and his walls to deal with, which is why I need both you and Sir Ector.' He looked across the fire to Sir Ector. 'We will need to get into the walls of Isca, or we will need to bring our Duc out... any suggestions?'

The warriors of the tribes dug in, huddling close around their fires for three days while the winter threw its cruellest, coldest weather at them. The shelters they had constructed, for the most part, were made from a large number of supple saplings that had been carried upon the carts. They were placed in a circle, bent and fashioned into the shape of a hut, covered with animal hides and then thatched with gathered branches. They were warm, dry and with a fire at the centre of each, the warriors were able to cook their staple of barley pottage. The ingredients of the pottage in each hut differed slightly, but as very few were able to add any meat, most of the differences came from the variety of seeds and vegetables being carried by the warriors in each hut.

They told stories, sang songs, and joked with each other to relieve the boredom and keep chills at bay, whilst the pottage continually cooked.

Merlyn and his Druids did their best to try and appease the blue faced hag, Cailleach, Goddess of winter, by making offerings of hastily gathered roots, dried flowers, and of course, blood, the meat from each sacrificed lamb, goat or chicken being offered for the pottage in different huts. Uther regarded their ceremonies with interest and hope, but a look to the cloudy sky showed that the Goddess still had a mind to torment them and that the Druids were being ignored. Snow continued to fall without let, covering the forest and all its surroundings in a thick, if not beautiful, blanket of deadly cold. Thin trails of smoke rose from white mounds beneath which the warriors huddled in their huts, praying to their Gods, and waiting for the hag to lose interest in her game so that the cold might end.

At dawn, on the fourth day of their forced confinement, the warriors emerged to find that the snow had finally stopped falling. A cold, crisp morning lay under a deep blue sky suggesting that the hag had finally turned her attention elsewhere and that a change had occurred in the weather, hopefully, she had found some Saxons to chill.

Merlyn, of course, claimed the change was because of his devotions. At his request the spirits of the ancestors had intervened on their behalf, Cailleach had been persuaded to leave, and the Gods were once more smiling upon them.

As Merlyn and Uther mounted their horses and moved off to be at the head of the column, they passed carts and chariots being dug from the snow and being piled high with the hut building materials and all the many other entrapments that the mass of warriors needed on the move. While huts were being dismantled, many of the tribesmen travelling on foot were already being led onto the path between the trees. Horsemen and chariots would follow and soon pass them with Sir Ector at their head, having sent out bands of scouts at first light to clear the way and send word back should they encounter the Cornovii. All knew that this was to be the final part of their journey to Isca, this was the day they would encounter the combined might of the Cornovii and Dumnonii, and their King would face the Duc.

Tintagel was an important part of the Cornovii, Dumnonii trading empire. Many boats anchored in the bay below the fortress to bring goods ashore, boats that had journeyed from all over the known world. It was a second home to Igraine and without Gerlois there she finally had time to heal, to be with her remaining daughters and to walk wherever she wished without the restriction of the Duc's rules and his demands that she stay constantly by his side. Although her father's village of Tamara was less than a day's walk inland, she had not seen him in many months because of Gerlois' rules, in the spring thaw, she would visit. She felt more content at Tintagel than in the larger settlements of Isca or Dimilioc; it was home. Isca was two days travel east by cart, where her thoughts persistently were as she thought of Morgana and worried for her safety while Dimilioc was just half a day's ride.

The Isle of Tintagel was home to the small wooden fortress, which comprised of a stone and wood palisade that surrounded four small halls and her own larger hall. There was also a small community of traders, shepherds, and fishermen who lived in the huts and shelters that dotted the isle. She was well liked by all who lived there, both amongst the people upon the isle and also in the village of Tintagel itself, which was over on the mainland. Whenever she was there, Igraine would spend time roaming the windy isle, either alone or accompanied by one or more of her daughters. On fine days she would cross the bridge that spanned the defensive ditch, either to stroll along the cliff path or to walk on into the village, to meet and talk with the villagers, many of whom she called friends.

Now, however, the weather confined her to the fortress, the wind howling as it drove sleet and snow against the shuttered window openings and rustled through the thick thatch above their heads. They gathered around the central fire and sang songs, roasted nuts, told stories and thanked the spirits that they had survived their sea voyage.

'When the snow stops then the sun will come to warm us,' Igraine smiled around at Morgause and Elaine. 'Shall we climb down to the caves? Would you like that?'

'It smells down there, and it will be slippery on the rocks,' said Morgause in a sulky voice.

'I think I will stay here, by this fire until Beltane, and it is time to come out and dance,' said Elaine with a giggle. 'I hate the cold.'

'You know that Morgana would call you both babies,' said Igraine, smiling at the thought of her missing daughter. She would want to climb down the path and take a boat, even if it was still snowing.

'The big cave is magnificent,' conceded Elaine. 'So much bigger inside. Morgana always says that a great sea serpent calls it home. You don't think that do you, Mother?' Morgause looked to Igraine for reassurance.

'Morgana only says that because she enjoys scaring you,' said Igraine with a smile. 'There are no monsters in any of the caves, so nobody needs to worry or even think about it.' Both Morgause and Elaine looked relieved. 'Anyway, today is not a day to go down to the caves. It will be some time before we can comfortably leave here. Now, I know that we have some honey, would either of you like to bake hearth cakes?' The girls squealed in delight and preparations were made to bake the cakes. It was always difficult filling the time when the weather held them captive, but Igraine could only thank the spirits that the cold weather had waited until their sea voyage was over. One of the Gods or some great spirit was watching over them she felt, that was for sure. She hoped Morgana was faring well and was warm, dry and happy with her father.

The first stones of the conflict were slung just as light was fading and the Duc of the Cornovii had thrown his final insult of the day.

They clattered against the solid trunks of the palisade and didn't strike anyone.

'No more stones,' called Uther as he walked back towards his men shaking his head, 'he is not worth it. The man is pathetic; he knows we're here and that we will have to reach an agreement. He is being obstinate, trying to be something he clearly isn't in front of his men, that is all.' He walked back through his ranks with Merlyn and Sir Ector quickly falling in behind him.

'Sir Ector, I tire of playing games with the Duc. You will not like what I propose, but I have a way of getting information. I will need two of your men to accompany me while you create a distraction here at the gate. We shall end this matter quickly I think.'

'Uther...' Merlyn took hold of the King's sleeve and forced him to turn around. 'Uther what are you planning and why won't we like it?'

'Fear not,' replied Uther. 'All will be well, and we won't be too cold while we wait on the Duc's pleasure. We're going to burn his gate. It will keep us warm, upset him, and make a nice distraction.'

Upon arriving at the fortified town of Isca, for that was what it was, a fortified town rather than just a fortress. Sir Ector had approached the gate and called for Duc Gerlois to show himself so that King Uther Pendragon might speak with him. Behind Uther and his small group, the warriors of the tribes were making their camp in the forest, some five hundred paces from the wooden palisade of the town. Standing over the gate, Cornovii warriors stared down at Uther and his party saying nothing, Uther only had to assume that the request for Gerlois to show himself would, in fact, reach the Duc. After quite a significant period of time, they were beginning to wonder if word had actually been sent or they were in fact being ignored when the Duc finally showed himself, standing beside his men, one hand resting casually upon the shoulder of a young girl whom Uther recognised as one of his daughters. The Duc held a haunch of meat that he waved around between bites to emphasise that he was about to start speaking just as soon as he had finished chewing.

'King Uther, I am heartened to see you. I did explain to Sir Ector there,' he waved the meat towards Sir Ector, 'that I was bitterly disappointed at having been called away from the celebrations at your fortress. I was told of events here that demanded my immediate return... I did try to explain.'

'Duc Gerlois, please open your gates so that I might enter with my retinue. I think it best that we discuss the problems between us in a little more comfort than this. You have caused me to march many days through the foulest of weather, will you not bid me enter and offer me hospitality?' Uther's horse had edged forward, it stamped at the ground and shook its head, clearly aware of the anger that Uther was barely keeping in check as he looked up at the Duc and his daughter.

'King Uther, the town is full, I shudder to think of what paltry accommodation I might be able to offer you should I bid you enter now, we are so unprepared, and you sent no word of your coming.' Duc Gerlois peered down at Uther and offered a sickly smile. 'If you could come back in a few days I am sure we would have something more suitable prepared for you. For now, I think you would be much more comfortable in your pavilion.' He dropped the bone he had been gnawing over the side and sucked on his fingers, one after another, still looking at Uther.

'How dare you speak to your King in this...'

'Do not banter with him,' Uther, cut Sir Ector off, 'he understands only too well how he insults me while he hides behind his daughter.' Around Uther, the warriors with him began to spin their slings, the sound a whirr in the air like a hive of angry bees, the war hounds at their sides growling, hackles raised in anticipation of being set loose. Uther raised his voice to be heard above the sound. 'Perhaps, Gerlois, I may indeed be more comfortable amongst my own after all, but I am very sure that I shall be sitting at your table presently. Just as soon as the Dumnonii and Cornovii are once again counted amongst the allied tribes. I wonder if it will be you sitting at that table beside me; you play a dangerous game.' He turned his horse without waiting for a reply and heard the slingers stones clatter against the palisade.

'No more stones,' called back Uther angrily. 'Did you not see the girl? That man is pathetic.'

Chapter 21

Isca

Dawn brought another crisp, cold and beautiful morning, beautiful at least to any who could appreciate it after such a frigidly cold night. As the last of the darkness retreated, the stars were replaced with a sky, the rich blue of tribal woad paint. Snow still lay thickly and showed no signs of melting, but even the winter chill could not dispel how perfect the morning was as Uther walked from his pavilion in search of food to break his fast. He pulled the woollen shawl more tightly about his neck as a chill wind danced about him, sending small puffs of snow falling from the branches above.

'Greetings, King Uther,' - Sir Ector rose from where he had been crouching feeding wood to a crackling fire - 'a fine day for a battle.' He turned and pointed out towards the palisade walls of Isca. 'We've watched several deserters drop from the walls, quite amusing as they scuttle off into the forest. There must surely have been more of them during the night. I've sent some warriors in search of a couple so we can ask a few questions. I can only imagine that Duc Gerlois is also feeling the strain of us being here, he may be a little more open to speaking this morning when we approach.'

Uther smiled and sat down beside Sir Ector. 'Let us hope he has spent a night worrying and lying in remorse at his actions, I doubt it, but we shall surely see. It is my fervent wish that he throws open those gates, and we are welcomed so that we can discuss cooperation and the solidarity of our tribes, but firstly I wish to eat, so let him keep his gates closed a little longer.'

As they rode towards the gate, a warrior leaned over between the spiked palisade tops and called down to them. 'The Duc is indisposed, King Uther. I am to ask you to await him while he attends to business within the town.' The speaker gazed down and appeared genuinely sorry that he could not bring Duc Gerlois to speak to Uther. 'He said that you would come and that he would join with you as soon as he was able.' The man shrugged as if saying 'what can I do about it?' There were several warriors of the Dumnonii and Cornovii grouped there; Uther couldn't easily tell them apart, their tribal colours and armour very similar and their speech carrying the same heavy burble no matter who spoke, male or female.

Uther and Sir Ector had ridden to the gates of Isca after breaking their fasts and were accompanied by just a small group of mounted warriors. 'I have no arguments with the warriors of the Cornovii and Dumnonii tribes. We are all one, united under the name of Britons. Yet you know your chief and leader Gerlois is hiding from me, disrespecting me, his King. He cowers behind you as he throws his insults at me and leads you all to shame.' Uther's horse shook its head and danced to the side, its hot breath steaming in the cold morning air. He took a moment to pat its neck and whisper softly to calm it before continuing.

'The Dumnonii and Cornovii are valued members of the united tribes. We have fought the Saxons together and together we will fight them again. I am asking you to open the gates and let me ride into your fortress. The Duc does not deserve your loyalty; you may aid me in choosing a new leader for your tribes and together we will...'

'Together we will what, King Uther?' Duc Gerlois appeared next to his men and sneered down at Uther and Sir Ector. 'Allow us to bow and scrape to you while you lead us on more ridiculous quests, then turn tribe against tribe with the Druids' games and attempt to make off with our women. In Dumnonia, we are free men, as we were before the Romans, as we were under the Romans and as we will continue to be without your interference. Leave us and perhaps we will speak again once the winter thaws.'

'You condemn your men and women with your words and with your actions, Gerlois.' Uther sat straighter in his saddle and raised his voice so as many within earshot could hear his words. 'Hear me warriors and people of the Dumnonii and Cornovii. You are hereby instructed to hand over Gerlois, former Duc of those tribes to face judgement before me, his King. If you do not surrender the coward Gerlois, then we shall have no regress but to bring war to your fortress and take him. You have until midday to hand him over.' Without waiting for any reply, Uther wheeled his horse and rode back to his camp trailed by Sir Ector and his men.

Moments after Uther entered his own camp his drums began to beat the call for war, and the horns rose to send their long melancholy wail across the snow filled expanse between the two groups. It seemed to all the world as if blood was soon going to be shed.

The walls of Isca were not the mightiest of barriers, but the trouble that Uther had, he soon realised, was his lack of any war machine capable of bringing them down. They had all heard tales of the Roman siege machines, onagers – large travelling platforms with slingers capable of sending a number of rocks, each bigger than a man's head, into wooden gates and breaking them asunder. He knew that in the days before the Romans had occupied Britain then his ancestors had their own siege machines, but times and the art of war had changed, and now he had none. Uther's troops were quick, mobile groups that could raid, fight from horseback or from chariots, could stand side by side in a shield wall and scream into the face of their enemy while exchanging blows, which was a fine tactic against the Saxons who fought in much the same manner, but the gates and walls of Isca were a problem. Uther knew it and obviously, Gerlois knew it too.

'They give us the answer within the problem they present us.' Merlyn smiled as he gazed about the fire at the gathered Council of War, and then frowned as he was met with blank questioning looks. 'We are held back by the walls of Isca, and so, in turn, we should build our own wall around the town and close the fortress off from the world.'

'A worthy plan, Merlyn, yet I hadn't planned on this taking years,' broke in Uther. 'We need to humble the Duc and have his people deliver him to us as quickly as possible; there must be a quicker way.'

'We need to scale the wall, this is all,' muttered Sir Ector. 'Once we have men inside, then they will give us the Duc. I have fought with these warriors many times and each time it was under the banner of Pendragon; they have been loyal to you, Uther. These men and women have stood shoulder to shoulder in the shield wall facing the Saxons with us. We have laughed together, spilt blood together, cared for each other, these are good warriors. They must surely be feeling some confusion between their loyalty to you, and their loyalty to the Duc. They know by now of what transpired upon the quest to Erin. The Duc's hold over them must surely be weak. I feel that once we have men the other side of those walls, then they will begin to break and more and more will come across to join our ranks.' Sir Ector pointed to the walls behind them. 'I suggest we cut trees and branches and construct a hill against their wall, something our tribesmen can scale. Or ladders, big enough for many of our men and women to climb. We will set our archers to protect those climbing; we don't want them speared from the wall.'

'Another good plan,' said Uther. 'What I am hearing is that we need to give them time to turn from Gerlois and join us, and I agree. I don't want to kill our brothers and sisters. It's not their fault that the man who leads them is a self-obsessed fool. We require a plan to break the Duc, but not the Dumnonii or Cornovii; we will kill as few of their warriors as possible.'

'If the Duc were a warrior,' said Sir Ector, 'then it would be a simple task to call him out and challenge him to single combat.' He shook his head and spat into the fire, it hissed angrily, 'but our Duc's warrior days are past him, we have recently seen more than enough evidence of that, he will not be lured onto the battlefield.'

Uther stood and looked from Sir Ector to Merlyn as he tightened the belt holding Excalibur. 'Cut the wood, lots of it. We will provide the Duc with a little entertainment and warm his feet at the same time. I want wood piled by the gate, make it as high as possible, and Merlyn...'

'Yes, Uther?' asked Merlyn warily. He looked up at Uther, his bushy white eyebrows raising in question.

'I will want a little of your Druid mystery sometime later. We will upset our Duc and perhaps provide the distraction that I need. I have always found that you're the master of upsetting and distracting people, Merlyn, so let us use that talent of yours to our advantage.'

The lone Briganti warrior dragged his spear against the snowy ground. He rode a dappled mount that flicked its head in annoyance at how slowly it was being forced to walk. They were keeping just outside the range of any arrows, along the line of the palisade. The warrior's head was turned to the side and wore an evil grin under his blue woad paint as he watched the Cornovii and Dumnonii warriors lining the wall, pushing past each other in their haste to match his progress. He was bare legged below leather riding shorts and a cloak and tunic decorated in the blue-green plaid of his Northern tribe. He hadn't been the first warrior to seek single combat that morning, two men had died, one from each side and a Dumnonii woman had been taken back within the fortress after her fight with a female warrior of the Trinovantes had not gone so well for her.

The Briganti stopped and turned towards the wall. 'Come, I tire of waiting. Who will face me? Who will join with me in the warrior's dance?' He raised a skin of ale and tipped it, so the liquid fell into his open mouth. Unfortunately, as he lifted the skin the horse danced beneath him, and he coughed, dropping the skin to the floor where it landed with a loud splat to spill the remains of its contents in the snow. Laughter and jeering rang out from the palisade as the Briganti tried to regain control of his horse, which he did remarkably quickly and then snatched up his spear and yelled even louder.

'*Cowards...* will nobody answer my challenge or will you keep cowering behind each other whispering and crying? Send me a challenger or surrender your fortress to me... I would like that.' The horse turned beneath him again, almost spilling him to the ground, but he held on, controlling it once more. He was clearly intoxicated, but then most of the warriors on both sides had been drinking some form of alcohol since the moment they had awoken to lend them strength and fire as tensions were raised.

The sound of wood grating against wood rumbled as the gateway to the fortress was unbarred and then heaved slowly open, creaking in protest as it moved. A lone horseman emerged riding at a canter and the gates dragged closed behind him. His colours of deepest red and the dull yellow of a late summer flower reflected the Dumnonii tribe. Leather greaves were strapped to his legs and forearms, a plain conical helm with nose guard and cheek flaps protected his head, and at his left side, he clutched an oval shield. He rode well and with confidence, a roar of approval coming from those spectating from the palisade as their champion hefted his own spear in mocking salute of his Briganti opponent.

'I, Withel, of the Dumnonii answer your challenge. Prepare to enter the Shadowland.' He kicked his mount into action, and it jumped forward as he let out a cry, '*Hahhh!*'

Some fifty paces away the Briganti did the same, '*Yahh, yahhh,*' lowering his spear as his horse powered forward, seemingly as eager as he to attack the foe, clouds of snow kicked up by its hooves. The watchers on the palisade screamed and cheered, driving their champion on while warriors emerged from Uther's camp to add their own encouragement, calling their support whilst jeering and taunting those within the security of the fortress.

The riders clashed amid an explosive confusion of snow and loosened bits of armour. Horses clamouring for footing, warriors swaying trying to keep their seats, a mental reckoning of damage as the shock of the moment seeped past, and the horses walked on. The Dumnonii had lost his shield and swayed upon his horse having almost fallen, whilst the Briganti was shrieking and cursing, trying to pull his pony round to face his opponent once more. Blood was streaming from a wound to his side, but he seemed not to have noticed as he raised his spear once more.

'Again you stupid goat, find your spear and face me again.'

'The Dumnonii rode back to retrieve his spear, leant down and scooped it up without dismounting or slowing, then held it above his head as more enthusiastic cheers echoed from the crowd on both sides. The riders wheeled their horses and rode at each other again.

'Keep the challenges going and take the fortress if the opportunity presents itself.' Uther mounted his horse and cast an eye to the two warriors who had just clashed for the second time. The Briganti was down, rolling in the snow, his horse which had cantered a little further had stopped running and was now looking back at its fallen rider. The Dumnonii, although still mounted, was slumped in his saddle and looked to be wounded.

Uther shook his head and mumbled, 'At least while the single combat continues there are not hundreds being injured or slain. I wonder if the Duc would deign to match swords with me?'

'I doubt it very much, but perhaps we have someone here who may be able to answer that question,' said Merlyn as he rose from his seat on the log. Uther and the gathered Council all looked on as two warriors pushed a female Dumnonii forward. She was a warrior, as could be seen from the oddments of armour she wore, yet she carried no weapon.

'I was leaving, returning to my village when I was captured by your men, I decided that I have no appetite for this conflict.' The Dumnonii slumped on the log and tried not to be distracted by the fire. She was obviously cold and the flames of the fire danced amongst glowing embers that gave off a comforting heat, but she was being questioned by her King and knew she must give him her full attention, even so, she edged a little closer.

Uther leant forward and smiled, trying to put her at ease. 'You have not been captured; we are not at war with your tribes. I asked my men to bring me some of the warriors that we saw leaving the fortress so that I could ask a few questions, most we are allowing just to leave unmolested. I apologise for delaying you, but you can depart for your village just as soon as you have warmed a little and we have had a chance to talk. I am Uther, what is your name?'

The warrior glanced about at the few people gathered around her, Sir Ector, Merlyn, and a few others, before looking back to Uther.

'My name is Rozen, Sire, and I know who you are. I fought close to you when we met with the Saxons last Samhradh. It was a hot, still day and there was a strong Saxon force, but we had little fear because it was you who led us that day. I was not one hundred paces from where you sat your horse.' She smiled as she remembered. 'I can recall seeing you riding a white horse and us listening to your fine words before the battle, telling us they were no match for the warriors of the tribes. We stole a victory from the Saxons that day, but I also lost a good friend.' Her smile dropped and she drew in a breath, to stare at her feet for a moment before looking back up to Uther. 'I don't understand what's happening here, why we are being asked to oppose you?' She sniffed and shook her head. 'I have a sister with child and my little brother talks of taking up a spear alongside me, but he is only ten summers, he needs me, my family needs me and I don't want to be here.'

'I'm sure you are not alone thinking like this. We have seen quite a few warriors leaving Isca during the night. The Duc's hold upon his warriors must be slipping, do you think many would follow him into battle against us?'

The girl glanced up at Uther and then back down to her feet. 'Many don't comprehend why they might be told to fight you, but Duc Gerlois is our Lord. He has been a good Chief and brought us prosperity; many will still follow him... but not all of us.'

'I do appreciate your situation,' said Uther, 'I understand the confusion and I don't blame any of you. This whole conflict is beyond the understanding of the best of us. Duc Gerlois has much to answer for.

Is he with his family in Isca? We have seen one of his daughters upon the wall with him, but no others.'

'The Duc keeps to himself in his hall doing his trading, and yes I think I have seen his daughter, but they do not come out much, it is too cold... too cold for them, they are not warriors.' She smiled.

'Will you tell me where in Isca their hall is?'

'It is close to the trading square in the centre of the settlement; that's no secret. It's the largest hall; there are two side by side. Can I go now? I just want to return to my village.'

'Yes of course, and thank you, Rozen.' Uther glanced around and beckoned to a waiting warrior. 'Please guide our friend here through our ranks and onto the path to her village.'

The girl smiled her thanks and headed off with the warrior.

'So what did we learn there, Uther?' Merlyn watched the girl departing and took her place on the log.

'We know that they are not happy with their situation, but we also know that we will have to fight. I want you to create one of your potions.' Merlyn raised an eyebrow in question, but Uther continued. 'I remember some years ago, during the winter solstice celebration, that you produced some magical branches that burnt long and fiercely for our entertainment. They spluttered and smoked and almost set the hall on fire, rather impressive.'

Merlyn nodded his head and then smiled, stroking his long beard as he remembered. 'That was several years ago, yes, and I recall that they were quite hard to put out once the flames had got good and started. It is still something I would like to work on a little more, but I imagine we are talking about this because you want me to cover the Duc's gate with a solstice flame, not for me to entertain your warriors. I might be able to come up with something, but I cannot guarantee that we will not burn the whole of Isca to the ground, if we do, I don't think it will make us very popular.' Merlyn frowned and thought for a moment before continuing. 'It is a good idea. Let me see what I can come up with; I have most of the necessary ingredients to make a small amount. It might be rather fun... what colour would you like it to be?' He raised a bushy eyebrow in question and then shook his head as Uther frowned at him. 'I shall set to it immediately, Uther.' He stood up and headed towards the small hut he had constructed with the other Druids, mumbling to himself as he walked away.

Morgana skipped along the walkway gazing out at the vast encampment of warriors surrounding the settlement. She wasn't sure what was happening, but it was all very exciting, much better than being stuck with her mother and sisters in boring old Tintagel. She knew it was best to keep away from her father. He was busy talking of trade with the man with the strange accent and instructing his warriors about protecting the walls and gateway. She had heard him talking with Peder, the man who organised things for father, saying that the King would leave shortly, and trade would continue presently. She hoped they wouldn't leave too soon; it was exciting seeing them out there and she hadn't minded in the least when the slingers had shot stones at them after her father had been talking with the King. She stepped to the side as a group of warriors pushed past, there leader growling at her to get off the wall, but one of the women in the group flashed her a smile which she returned. The warriors were heading towards the gate where much of the activity was taking place, as it was where her father shouted down to the King when he came out to speak, maybe it was going to happen again?

'Get out of the way, girl.' She stood aside as three more warriors pushed past. 'You shouldn't be here, get down somewhere safe before you catch a stone.'

That was silly, the King's men weren't slinging stones at anyone right now. She looked over the edge again to see; there was an awful lot of noise coming from the trees. It sounded like they were chopping them all down... she couldn't see anything unusual happening over there, just the sounds. She reached out and took hold of the palisade wall as a gust of cold wind rocked her. It was getting darker, clouds coming in again, maybe more snow was coming. She decided to go down into the settlement and see what else might be happening; it was boring just staring out at the visiting camp, but it was still more interesting than being at dull and dreary old Tintagel where nothing exciting happened. She climbed down one of the ladders and went off to explore. It might be days before any fighting took place, but she hoped it wouldn't be too long. The smell of cooking drew her through the small passages between the huts and into the trading square where she joined a group waiting for cuts of meat to be distributed by her father. He was smiling and laughing with everyone, making jokes about the King and his warriors encamped around them. She watched him; he had never handed out meat before and she wondered why he was doing it now?

Three men broke from the cover of the treeline and silently loped through the darkness towards the palisade of Isca, their footsteps crunching softly in the snow covered ground. Between them, they carried the burden of a small tree, most of its branches stripped from it with smaller branches lashed to the trunk in the fashion of a simple ladder. As the three reached midway, four others broke from the trees and followed.

Above the town, an orange light was beginning to grow, slowly at first. It began to reflect from the low clouds hanging overhead giving the runners greater reason to cover the exposed open ground more quickly. Shouts of alarm could be heard now, and a bell was ringing frantically, meaning Merlyn and Sir Ector must have done a good job.

Ahead of Uther the warriors reached the wall and heaved the ladder up against it, it bumped softly, which in the silent night air sounded disturbingly loud to Uther who was still thirty paces away. He flinched, and with his steaming breath heavy in his ears from the short run, he glanced upwards to see if Cornovii warriors were guarding this remote part of the palisade. The night sky was bright now, the spiked edge of the wall a black silhouette against it showing no warriors standing, but it was hard to see if there were any hiding, crouched down, watching and waiting to heft spears and bring pain and death in the shadows. They just had to climb the ladder and hope the spirits were looking over them.

The first warrior reached the base of the tree, his spear slung over his shoulder tied with his sling, it swung from side to side as he scampered quickly to the top, the tree flexing and bouncing under his weight. Uther saw him hesitate, peak carefully over the edge, and then raise and dip his head quickly in case it should meet a sweeping blade, but then he was up and over and the other two in front of Uther were on the tree and climbing too.

With Excalibur slung across his shoulder, Uther ran up the bouncing tree, falling forward half way up to use his hands to hold on and help him balance as he continued to climb, moving from one handhold to the next. Within moments, he was clambering between the sharpened tops of the stockade and crouching with his men on the walkway, his breathing loud in his ears and his heart thumping in his chest, hands freezing cold, but they were inside.

Morgana stood up abruptly and left the cell. She could still hear the half-dead King talking on and on in that dreary, feeble way that was close to sending her mad; she just wished he would hurry up and die. He had as good as admitted that he had marched his warriors after her father, for no other reason than he was in pursuit of her mother like a slavering dog chasing a bitch in season, fighting off all and any other drooling dogs to slake his lust. He was calmly describing how they had attacked her father in Isca, laying his crimes bare. Well, now it was enough, she had heard everything she had needed.

Moving through the dim corridor, she made her way to her chamber and began to prepare a final broth. Her brow creased as she gathered the ingredients. It was somewhat vexing that the King had eaten very little the last two times she had prepared it. It was possible that he was losing his appetite as his time to die came closer, and yet he didn't appear any closer to death, in fact, he seemed to have gained colour. She stopped chopping as her thoughts gathered. She must make the potion stronger and insist that he eat, hold his nose and choke it down him if necessary. The Saxons would arrive on the morrow when the moon was at its fullest. She would be rid of him then and also that bitch warrior who sat swooning by his side watching her every move, the Saxons would kill her before taking the King. Morgana smiled at the thought of the warrior, Maude, jumping up as the Saxons entered, the sad cow would be unarmed, she would see to that. As she tried to stop them, she would be stabbed and lay dying on the floor, her blood soaking into the rushes as Uther was dragged out, never to be seen again. Morgana spat into the infusion as it steamed upon the fire and smiled. One more day and vengeance would be hers; they would be gone.

Chapter 22

Avoiding the Path of a Mad Dog

Uther glanced along the walkway in either direction and then down into the dark shadows within the settlement below. Nothing was moving, no guards patrolling the wall or anyone in sight amongst the huts, as far as he could see the spirits were watching over them and they had been unobserved. Plenty was happening on the far side of the settlement, around by the gate, which was what must have drawn any guards away. Flames were fluttering, already licking the pointed tops of the palisade, it looked like the whole wall and the gatehouse itself was ablaze. He could hear cries of alarm, calls for water and the first buckets were being filled from the horse troughs, ready to be passed up to warriors calling for them from atop the wall. A crowd of onlookers was also gathering to watch the spectacle unfold.

'Come on, let's go.' Uther ran towards the closest ladder and climbed down, waiting at the bottom for his two companions to join him. Pulling Excalibur from his back, he tied it to his side and then blew warm breath into his hands before rubbing them together to warm them; it was cold, especially this far from the fire. Uther smiled imagining the fury and distress that Duc Gerlois must be going through at the moment. The wood of the palisade was made up of thick, heavy logs, and they were wet from all the rain and snow of late. The Duc must have thought them very tough to burn, unaware of quite what

255

Merlyn could concoct from his potions. The two warriors joined him and they set off through the huts with Uther leading.

There were several hundred huts and halls within the walls of Isca, but as the populace slept it was mostly deserted. Twice they came across groups of warriors, but on both occasions they weren't challenged, the warriors being too intent upon reaching the flaming gateway. Moving between the huts, they kept to the shadows as much as they could and it didn't take long to find their way to the central trading square where Gerlois allowed merchants and traders to set up and meet. Three women, cloaks wrapped tightly about them to guard against the night chill were the only people there. They were talking in hushed, excited voices, staring at the flames rising above the distant gateway. Uther signalled his men to stand back and they melted into the shadows as he approached the women.

'I beg your pardon. I am newly arrived in Isca and not too familiar with where I should be going. I have messages for the family of Duc Gerlois, will you please direct me to his hall?' Uther gave a bow and the three women did the same in return. He knew they would be able to see, even in the flickering light cast by the distant flames, that he was no mere warrior, but of a higher caste blood. Yet he was also confident that they wouldn't recognise him as their King.

'I think you'll find that Duc Gerlois is at the gate, Lord. You need merely follow the light of the flames to find him.' The three women giggled and the one who had spoken, tilted her head as if waiting for his reply.

'I'm not actually looking for the Duc,' replied Uther. 'I understand that his family is here, I seek the Lady Igraine. I have word from her father and was told to deliver it to her in person. Surely she will not be fighting the flames at the gate as well?' It was his turn to make the women laugh.

'No My Lord, the Lady Igraine is surely not passing buckets of water, but I fear your journey has been in vain, for the Duc's wife is not here at Isca.'

'Not here?' Uther felt anger and confusion grow within him. 'What do you mean not here? I saw her daughter here earlier today; she is surely not far from her daughter?' He was becoming louder but didn't care. 'Did she not arrive with the Duc?' The woman he had been speaking to, gave a little squeal and Uther looked down to see that he had grabbed her by the wrist without realising; he let go. 'My apologies, your news caught me unawares. Where can she be, if not at her husband's side and close to her daughter?'

'Who are you that wants to know?' The women all began to step back from Uther, one of the others looking around as if seeking someone to call, becoming alarmed by this stranger's gruffness with them. Uther cursed his lack of control and took a deep breath to calm himself.

'I apologise once again. The Lady Igraine's father sent me, what I thought would be a simple task of confiding with her and her alone. I confess I had thought my quest an easy one, yet now you are telling me that this is not to be the case. Please, do you have any knowledge of where the Lady Igraine might be? I just wish to complete this quest and pass her father's words on to her.'

'That's the Duc's hall over there,' said the girl indicating with a nod of her head towards a large wooden structure the other side of the open market area,' but she's in Tintagel.' She rubbed at her wrist.

'Kerra!' exclaimed one of the others. 'You shouldn't tell him anything; we don't know who he is.'

'Please,' said Uther hurriedly. 'I only intend to bring the Lady Igraine word from her father. I have no wish to cause distress and will not trouble you again.' Uther backed away into the shadows, and the women scuttled off chattering excitedly.

'We can leave.' Uther rejoined his men at the far end of the hut and waved them on towards the wall. 'I've learned what I needed to know; we have to get out of here.' They tried to retrace their steps, jogging through the huts, but as they splashed through several larger puddles, the thinnest surface of ice breaking under their feet, they realised they had made a wrong turn.

'It must be this way, Sire,' whispered one of the men, and they set off again through a number of twisting turns before entering yet another narrow passage between halls, huts, and roundhouses, this one with the dim outline of the palisade looming up at the end. Unfortunately, before they had passed more than three strides, a low growl came from the shadows and a huge war hound moved slowly to the centre of the track. In the dim flickering light that lit the passage they could see that its hackles were raised, its ears flattened against its head, and its mouth was dripping foaming saliva. This hound was sick, sick in a very dangerous way, with weeping evil eyes that showed pain and anger. It shook its head sending white spray high into the air and then took two more steps towards them before the chain holding it clinked and became taut.

'Go back, this animal is cursed,' hissed one of the warriors.

Uther made to turn around, but heard something, he quickly drew close to the side of the closest hut, pulling the sleeve of one of the others to do the same, then held a finger up to his lips signalling silence. They stayed motionless, straining their hearing for a few seconds as the hound growled softly behind them. Sure enough, a few moments later, three Cornovii warriors appeared, each holding short stabbing spears.

'Something spooked the dog,' hissed one in a whisper, 'they may be down here.'

'Anything will spook that hound, Sithny, and if they were down here, they would be screaming for their lives, that animal is as mad as a full moon. You should have killed it days ago and had done. Tis filled with evil spirits and no good to anyone, nor itself neither for that matter.'

'He was a good fighter and loyal to me that hound, for many seasons we fought side by side, it saved my life more than once. The spirits may leave it and... hey, who's that there? Hey, you...'

'We have no wish to fight you, let us pass, and we will vanish into the night.' Uther stepped out of the shadows, and the three Cornovii warriors took a step back, their spears coming around to point at him. His two companions came alongside, and the three Cornovii tensed.

'How did you get past the wall? You're burning the palisade, and now you think we will just let you walk away? How stupid do you think we are?'

'I am Uther Pendragon, your King. Let us pass, do not make me kill you.'

'We are the Duc's men; we don't answer to you and you can't just…'

The warrior didn't get a chance to finish his sentence as Excalibur snaked out in one fluid movement and stabbed the lead warrior in the throat. The man went down uttering a gurgle through spouts of blood as Uther's companions leapt past him to take on the other two warriors. It was regrettable to kill any warrior here, but they had known they may have to before getting away with their lives, and Uther had been forced to make his decision quickly. Behind them the dog began barking savagely, just as Uther attacked and killed a second, his sword slicing down through the man's guard to cut deeply through his neck and into his chest.

'Alarm, alarm!' screamed the last Cornovii as he backed out of the passage.

Uther and his men rushed him; Uther kicked out as one of the others matched him with his spear and the Cornovii fell. Without waiting they dashed past, but then two more appeared, one with a spear the other with a huge war axe that he swung in a huge arc around his head. With a glance to their fallen comrades, both began yelling loudly to draw others to them. Then a spear throw took the axeman in the chest, and the other began fighting for his life with Uther. The spearman continued to shout out for help, his eyes darting around seeking others, but he was holding them at bay on his own within the narrow passage. Uther was unable to retreat because of the war hound and unable to go forward because of this one man.

'Kill the hound,' said Uther as he advanced on the spearman. Behind him, he heard a scuffle and curse.

'It has my spear, it's bitten it… get off yer damn dog.'

This was taking too long; they had to get out. The noise from the front gate was getting louder, roaring and crackling as the fire took greater hold while masking most of the calls from the warrior, but others were sure to come soon. Uther dropped his stance and stabbed out, his thrust coming under his adversaries spear, and he felt Excalibur crack through the man's ribs and enter his chest. The man's shrill scream rose above the noise from the fire and the barking dog, which had dropped the spear and was now frantic with blood lust, straining against its bonds in its effort to break free, desperate to follow its basest instincts and attack, bite and tear flesh.

'Move… to the palisade,' hissed Uther. 'Find another way.' He heaved Excalibur from the dying man's chest and led them on past huts and halls in what he thought was the right direction. Hearing shouts and the sound of running feet, they turned into another passage that he hoped desperately would lead them to the wall. The three men ran through a small open area and jumped the smoking remains of a small cooking fire, landing hard they startled several chickens into a squawking, flapping cloud and then past a goat, which bleated plaintively, as they knocked into it in their haste to get past. They seemed to be enveloped in a growing cacophony of noise until with a howl of glee, easily perceived above the din, they heard the dog break loose, the sound of the chain breaking quite audible above everything. It was soon followed by people shrieking and the terrible growling as the hound of war found its first victim to savage.

'That's a war hound,' said Uther, 'it will kill and move on quickly. We have to get out of here now… there… down here…' He pushed the men on, and they ran to the end of yet another narrow passage and were rewarded with sight of the palisade wall. Unfortunately, there was now a warrior upon it, drawn by the noise and confusion erupting between the huts. He stared down as Uther, and his men ran towards them, uncertain of what was taking place.

'There is a war hound loose, its attacking people,' called Uther. 'It's sick, gone crazy, help us get up, it's coming, quickly…' Unable to see exactly who they were in the low light, the warrior leant down from the parapet. Uther hurriedly put Excalibur into its scabbard and reached up towards the hands, he jumped and felt a strong hand close around his wrist. As the Cornovii pulled him up, he swung his legs onto the platform then quickly turned to help the others. One of his men jumped up, and he managed to catch his arm and pulled. The sounds of the huge hound were getting closer, its barking now at the passage by the closest building, and then it emerged at a full run, less than twenty paces away. As it closed on them, Uther could see the madness in its eyes, the foaming mouth and blood dripping from the huge maw of white teeth.

'Swing your legs, do it,' shouted Uther. Below him, the warrior dropped his spear, clamped his hand around Uther's wrist and swung his legs up onto the platform. Just in time, as his arrival was preceded by a huge crash which rocked the walkway as the hound leapt, just missing his legs and hit the wall. All went silent for a moment, or it seemed to, they all leant over to see the hound getting groggily to its feet. It shook its head, then spun around growling then launched itself at the last warrior, still hanging from the Cornovii warrior's grasp, unable to get up. Its massive weight slammed into him as he struggled, its teeth clamping upon his thigh. He screamed as he fell and then was dragging down into the shadows, screeching shrilly as the hound took out all its pain and frustration by tearing into him; his screams only ending when his throat was ripped out.

Uther pulled himself away and exchanged looks with his surviving accomplice. 'We have stared death in the face together this night, my friend. What is your name?'

'Halwyn, Sire.' They grasped forearms and smiled grimly at each other, united in a common grisly bond, and then turned to the warrior that had pulled them up as two others arrived. Three of them, who were now looking questioningly at Uther and Halwyn, waiting for some sign of an explanation.

'You have to be careful with that hound, it's likely to hurt someone else,' said Uther.

'Who are you?' The warriors could see that neither of the men pulled to safety were Cornovii or Dumnonii as neither wore tribal colours.

'You saved our lives,' said Uther. 'We thank you and would prefer to leave you alive and unharmed. I am Uther Pendragon, High King of the British tribes; I am your King. I am going to pass back over this wall, and you are going to let me and my friend, Halwyn here do so without trying to stop us.' He glanced back down into the eyes of the snarling dog. It had finished with the fallen warrior and was now circling below them. It jumped and snapped at him as it saw he was watching. 'Neither you nor I wish to be food for the hound, so let us pass.'

'But the Duc has ordered that you and your men are to be stopped. I cannot let you leave, King Uther, I am sorry.' The warrior took hold of Uther's arms, but in the same moment that he was held, Uther sidestepped, lowered his left arm, caught the man's elbow with his right hand and turned so that the warrior tripped and fell over the side, scrabbling to hold onto Uther as he dropped away. The warrior landed heavily, close to the hound which spun quickly and took a step towards him, snapping its jaws as it barked furiously. The warrior got shakily to his feet, and Uther called out, 'Hey, your spear, catch it.' He scooped up the man's fallen spear and dropped it down to him.

'And you can go help him,' said Halwyn, pushing the other two over the edge as they peered down. They didn't expect it and fell, spinning their arms, yelling in fright and anger at the action, but they landed well and turned with impressive speed to face the war hound along with their friend. Uther and Halwyn watched for a moment as the hound leapt and the three warriors did battle. They spread out around the hound so that it growled, turned and spun around from one warrior to the other, confused as each stabbed out when its side was presented. As a spear glanced off its ribcage, it howled and turned snapping at the warrior, but he stepped back allowing one of the others to enter and stab. It would be a short-lived fight as the animal was outnumbered and unable to effectively attack one on one.

Uther turned his back on them, glanced over the side of the palisade into the night and whistled. A few moments later a tree ladder bumped up close to them, and they readied to climb over. From below came a high pitched whine and they looked back to see that the hound had finally been dealt a mortal blow. It lay, chest still heaving, a spear protruding from its chest, twitching its life blood away as all three Cornovii ran towards the closest ladder some thirty paces away.

'Go, Halwyn, you first,' said Uther and then readied to climb over.

'Wait…' Uther turned at the sound to see a young girl running towards them along the palisade walkway. Surprised, Uther saw that it was the Duc's daughter, and she was apparently alone. She walked quickly, gazing down wide-eyed at the dying war hound and the running warriors, arms held out for balance on the narrow boardwalk.

'I saw you,' she said, her words breathless from her run. 'They made me stay away from the fire by the gate, said I would get in the way, so I was crouching down over there,' - she pointed someway back down the palisade - 'when I saw you climb up away from the dog. You almost didn't make it.' She stared at Uther then back towards the warriors who were now on the ladder, climbing up towards them. 'Now they are after you and they're cross, but you did push them off, so I suppose it's to be expected.'

'Your name is Morgana, isn't it?' Uther smiled and went on as she nodded. 'I'm afraid we have outstayed our welcome here, Morgana; we have to leave. You keep out of trouble and stay away from any fighting; it will all be over soon. Oh, here…' He reached into his jerkin and pulled out the pebble she had given him on the beach just before they had boarded the boats for their quest across the sea to the Isle of Erin. 'You gave me this token to keep me safe on our quest, do you remember?' She nodded and took the proffered stone. There was little light and what there was came from the burning gate and palisade behind her, but as she looked down at the stone, he could see her smile. 'I think it is you who needs our talisman now, Morgana, to keep you safe through the coming days. It worked well for me, and now it will work well for you.' He turned and hauled himself up, over the palisade and onto the ladder. 'Stay safe, Morgana, this will all be over soon, do not fear.' He began to climb down, and she looked over the side to watch him go.

'I will keep it for protection, King Uther, but we are leaving soon, so I am not scared. I'll return the talisman to you when you have need, have no fear.' She was shoved rudely to the side as one of the warriors arrived and angrily stared down into Uther's eyes. Uther felt a momentary tremor of fear at being so close, so vulnerable and balanced as he was so high above the ground. He tried to calm his fears and continued to descend carefully, hand over hand, step by step. He watched the man smile, raised his spear and prepare to throw, but then just as he brought his arm down; Morgana came flying back into view and pushed into him, then she ran off as he cried out angrily, his spear dropping harmlessly to the side.

Uther smiled and descended the last few spans, before retreating back into the darkness of the night. Only the niggling echo of Morgana's words, *we're leaving soon*, causing him concern.

'She saved my life that night. If Morgana hadn't pushed that Cornovii warrior, he would have...'

'Please... King Uther, you must hush now. We have to leave... quietly. Put this on; we need to keep you warm.'

He knew his eyes were open, but it was difficult to see in the light cast from the small guttering candle. He felt woozy and tired, completely exhausted. Maude steadied him as he felt himself sway. She had pulled him up into a sitting position on the bed, he could see his knees and knew his feet were on the floor; it all felt odd. She was pulling something over his head, it felt like an under-tunic, but wool, not linen. It was stiff and scratchy against his skin.

'It will keep you warm my Lord, pull your arms through.' She was whispering, why was she whispering?

'If Morgana hadn't pushed that warrior out of the way, I would have been a dead man that night at Isca. Nothing else would have happened. No Igraine, no Arthur… it would have been…'

'Please, King Uther, you must be quiet. We have to leave, and we don't wish to attract the attention of the nuns. You have to stand for a moment. I'll help you up, and then you must hold against the wall while I get you into these.'

He felt her pulling him up and placing his golden torque around his neck; it felt cold and heavy. He tried to help, tried to stand, but he was so weak, and when he did make it to his feet, he swayed and his guts felt as if they might decide to empty in some spectacular fashion, and then his head began to pound. A rush of heat flushed through him and a sheen of sweat made itself known upon his brow. Steadying himself against the wall, he looked down at the top of Maude's head. She was pulling on leggings, lifting his foot trying to pull the unyielding material up his skinny leg. He giggled, and she looked up at him, a frown upon her face. The leggings were past his feet, and she pulled them up his legs and tied them off, tucking in his tunic. He dropped carefully back down onto the bed feeling a wave of relief, and she pulled his legs out, lifting them to wind linen strips about his calves.

'Why are we doing this? Where are we going?'

'Away from here. It is not safe. I shall take you somewhere safe and then fetch the Druid, Merlyn, but we have to get away from the Abbey tonight.'

Pulling a heavy wool cloak about him, she tied it at the neck then drew the cowl over his head before heaving him back up into a standing position where he swayed once more.

'Let's go. Lean on me and please keep as quiet as you can.'

He allowed her to guide him out of the cell. Her arm was around him, lending him support as he concentrated on placing one foot in front of the other, it was exhausting, but he persevered, knowing it was important to Maude and he was inclined to trust her even if he didn't truly understand why any of this was necessary. He couldn't help making noise. His breathing was laboured, and his feet were shuffling in the reeds that covered the passage floor. It sounded loud in his ears and he knew he must present a pathetic and ridiculous sight. He surely was the half-dead King. He heard himself giggle again and then managed to stifle it quickly as she cast him a frown in the low candlelight. A wave of nausea ran through him, but he kept going.

They had managed to pass down several passages when the sound of muttering voices reached them; distant at first but getting closer. There was a moment of uncertainty, and then he was being hurried off in a different direction, stumbling in the darkness until, moments later, he found himself crouching against a wall in a small room with his head pounding and Maude's hand clamped across his mouth. He felt the urge to giggle again at the ridiculousness of the whole situation; he was still a King after all, and here he was hiding in the dark with a female warrior he hardly knew. Her breath was hot against his ear; it tickled as she breathed. The voices were getting closer until they finally passed close by, not two or three steps away, accompanying the heavy tread of four or five people... the voices were just harsh whispers, but within them he recognised the Saxon tongue.

Uther suddenly realised the seriousness of the situation; Saxon warriors were in the Abbey.

Chapter 23

The Druid's Well

'What do you mean, gone?' Uther gazed down into the face of the Dumnonii warrior. He was an older man with grey in his beard and a squint that probably told that his eyes were failing him. He was bleeding from a wound to his head, the blood matting his hair and soaking the wool of his cloak and tunic. He was also cradling his left arm, although Uther could not see any blood, it was probably broken. Three Dumnonii had been captured in the early morning light by one of his patrols to the south, and the news they brought was not welcome.

'The Duc has departed Isca with the main force of warriors that were encamped here.' The man sounded tired and resigned to whatever fate might befall him. 'They travel to the fortress at Dimilioc where they will join with the main Dumnonii and Cornovii forces. They left us here. I have told you all that I know, King Uther. I am a loyal warrior of the Britons and have fought against Saxons, Jutes and Angles under your banners for many seasons, but I am also Dumnonii and must follow my Duc, do what he tells me, but I can inform you that he journeys to Dimilioc, it is the stronghold of the Dumnonii lands.'

Uther nodded and indicated that the warrior should rise, but the man stayed upon his knees, the two warriors that had been caught with him dropping down alongside him.

'We have been captured and fairly treated by you. Allow us to live, to leave and return to our villages. We are no threat to you and will come fight alongside you against the Saxons when you call; when you have defeated the Duc, as you surely will.'

'Releasing you will depend on how you are willing to help with a few questions,' said Uther with a frown. 'Firstly, tell me how many warriors remain within Isca?'

'There are just a few, perhaps thirty, to maintain the pretence of the fortress being occupied, they have stayed to buy time so that the Duc could make his way to Dimilioc freely.'

'But how did he escape the fortress with so many warriors? I do not understand how we did not see such a large force leaving.' Uther turned away and paced a few steps, his fists clenching and unclenching as he pictured the Duc's smiling face knowing that he was slipping away, evading conflict or capture, forcing Uther and his warriors to endure further hardships if they chose to follow him.

'The settlement here is large and not so easy to defend as you have already seen. The palisade conceals several gates that are all but hidden from your patrols. Your forces were at the gates of Isca, but the Duc could have chosen to withdraw any time he liked. And so soon after the fire was put under control at the main gate last night, the Duc became worried and gave the order to leave.'

Uther sighed and shook his head in resignation. 'Thank you for your information. Your King appreciates your situation and that you have chosen to say what you have.' He signalled for the warrior to rise and began to turn away.

'King Uther.' The warrior stood and looked back at his two companions before continuing. 'Most of the Dumnonii and Cornovii that were questioning the Duc's decisions have now deserted him; they have been leaving over the last few days since your arrival, unwilling to cross swords with you. But the warriors that now travel on with the Duc, and also those that await him in the fortress of Dimilioc, are the most loyal to him. Those warriors within the fortress will here will resist, and they will fight you, and that is what the Duc is now preparing to do at Dimilioc. However, while the settlement of Isca is merely a trading settlement, you have to know that the fortress at Dimilioc isn't for trading, it is a stronghold of war.

'Go, child, I will come for you when all this nonsense is over and the King has stopped his persecution of us.' Gerlois pulled Morgana's face close to his and wiped the tears that flowed down either side of her dirty cheeks with his thumbs; he was trying to be tender, but was scowling as always she noted. What had she done wrong?

'I am sorry, Morgana, I know you understand little of what is happening, but all that you need to know is that we have been maltreated by the King. There is no reason to weep. Find courage in your heart and know that we shall prevail in this disagreement. We shall defeat Uther Pendragon at Dimilioc and force a peace between us. He will know that our family cannot be torn apart, that he cannot hope to humiliate me as he did and expect me to smile and nod my thanks. It is fast coming to the time when we must fight, and so you must be away from this trouble. Hold strong, child, go.'

Morgana sniffed and broke away from her father's hold to drag the coarse wool of her sleeve across her nose; she sniffed again then drew in a breath and steadied herself.

'I will be strong, Father, but I can still come with you, you do not need to send me away... please?' Morgana took hold of her father's arms again and stared up into his face, willing him to keep her close.

Gerlois scowl deepened and he pushed her arms away in irritation. 'No child. Your mother and sisters are already away from all of this, safe at Tintagel, and I have made arrangements for you to stay with the holy sisters at Laherne. The King's men will not find you there. You will be safe and when this is over, I shall come for you, it will be a matter of only a few days.'

'No, Father, I will not go, I want to be with you... please let me come, Father?' Behind Gerlois hundreds of mounted Dumnonii fidgeted silently, watching and waiting for the exchange to finish, silent in the early dawn light save the snuffling of horses and the occasional jingle of a harness.

Aware of the spectacle they were creating, Gerlois shook his daughter, only stopping when she cried out in alarm. 'Do not defy me, girl, be strong. This is no debate; I don't have the time for this. Go to Laherne and learn some obedience.' He pushed her roughly away, and she tripped backwards almost falling but was caught by the arms of a waiting warrior who lifted her up upon a horse. She didn't resist. Taking up the reins with reluctance her tears returned to fall glistening upon her cloak while she trembled and stared at her father. As the two warriors accompanying her rode away, she kicked her heels into her mount and followed, staring back, unable to stop the feelings of loss and grief at being taken from him from overwhelming her. She watched as he led his warriors along the misty road to Dimilioc and the certainty of war without sparing her a further glance.

The three Druids slipped quietly through the wet undergrowth and the yellowed, dead remains of summer bracken. They followed a trail that only they could see having left the paths of man and beast some time before; they were guided now by something far more ancient. As they walked, they chanted softly, the sound falling flat in the dead air of the forest, it surrounded and protected them as it mingled with the ground mist that wafted from their path by robes that had become wet and heavy.

They walked unerringly through the trees for some time until they came across the grove. The entrance was marked by a large upright stone, its surface mottled with moss and lichen, the runes cut into the surface in a bygone age almost invisible beneath. As the three stepped past, each placed a hand upon it and then touched heart and head, muttering a blessing and a request for the living spirit that dwelt there to welcome them, to aid their searching and bless their visit.

Past the stone, the path dipped down around a stunted, gnarled elm. Tied into its branches was an assortment of rags, tokens torn from the clothing of those who travelled to worship the spirits here. The tree appeared to be rising from the forest floor in tortured agony as if desperately trying to tear its roots free from the clinging dirt with its movement frozen in an ancient time. The Druids stepped carefully past, bending low to avoid breaking the delicate thread of a spider's web that glistened with droplets of water. Dipping into the darkness of overhanging vegetation their feet found four stone steps, that once descended, finally brought them out into the sacred grove itself.

The air was still and thick as if it never felt the release of a breeze. It was fetid, ripe and pungent with the damp smells of struggling life and rotting decay. A ring of oak, elm, and holly trees marked the boundary of the grove, the dark, gloomy depths of the forest drawing outward and away as if the trees were trying to drag their roots from the soil and flee. Within the grove was a simple earthen clearing, its surface dusted with snow, at its centre was a small, almost perfectly spherical, pool, its depths as black and still as the darkest dreams of night.

Crossing to the pool, the Druids chanting became louder before stopping abruptly; they dropped to their knees at the pond's edge, and the surface rippled, droplets of water rose and danced and within moments it was as if a silent storm was lashing the pool with driving rain, yet neither wind nor rain fell.

Merlyn clapped his hands, the sound cutting through the air, all noise and movement ceased and the surface of the pool at once returned to a mirror calm. Now in silence, the three Druids raised their hands, pulled back their hoods and bent slowly forward, their faces looming up to be reflected perfectly in front of them as they closed the distance, appearing as if entering within themselves... and then the illusion was broken as noses and lips touched the surface, and they sucked noisily at the water, drawing it into their mouths then swallowing it down deep into their bodies. After a few moments, each sat back and remained motionless, kneeling, eyes closed, hands resting in their laps as the water of the grove invaded their beings.

Uther idly touched the heavy golden torc at his neck, something he would invariably do while his mind contemplated and weighed a problem. His fingers traced the smooth flow of the spiralling metal, each of the many fine twisted strands coming together to forge a whole that was far stronger and more valuable than any of its individual pieces, much like the tribes of Britain as they had been brought together to unite against their common enemies, he had often mused, but his thoughts were not upon the torc nor the united tribes this day. As his fingers came to the twin dragon heads that were formed at either end, he drew in a deep breath and sighed, dragging his eyes away from his first sight of Dimilioc. Its defences were certainly far more intimidating than the wooden stockade of Isca; there was no doubting that. He had known of the fortresses construction, but Gerlois had obviously been keeping any magnitude of the details to himself, he had spoken of Isca and Tintagel, but rarely mentioned Dimilioc.

It had taken three precious days to move his warriors and their encampment here, and now they were arriving to find this. Standing proudly upon a coastal hill with the deep grey of the ocean behind it, Dimilioc fortress comprised of five separate earthwork rings that circled a white central fortress, the stockade walls daubed with mud till hardened and then painted with a mixture of lime and water so that it shone in the pale winter sunlight. To reach and attack the fortress, his warriors would need to break through these five separate levels. They would first have to enter the low ditches and then clamber up the steep, slippery earthen banks opposite while the Dumnonii warriors who would be defending the higher ground with rocks, spears and abuse hurled down at them. Fighting their way to the crest of each earthwork they would reach the Dumnonii shield wall and the defending warriors would begin stabbing down with their long, leaf-shaped spears through the seemingly impenetrable wall of shields that defended them against any slinger stones and spears that Uther's warriors might use to try to break them. If his warriors did finally reach the summit of the first ring and it was successfully taken, leaving behind the dead and the cries of the dying behind them, it would only be to see that the defenders had withdrawn to the next defensive mound. Once again they would be taunting the attackers to come and die, welcoming them to enter the Shadowland upon the end of their spears as they defended the higher ground once again. And all of this would have to be accomplished five times if the attackers wished to reach the gleaming white plastered palisade of the fortress itself. It was an all but impossible task that called for the death of thousands if the fortress was ever to be taken.

Uther glanced about at his forces as they assembled around him. Warriors were emerging from the trees, gathering to gain their first glimpse of the challenge ahead. He saw their looks of wonder and resignation. Watching them, he thought of the number of warriors he would need to sacrifice if he were ever to take this monstrosity of a fortress and then saw his frustration and concerns mirrored in the face of Sir Ector.

'I do not relish the task of assaulting those banks,' muttered Sir Ector as he removed his helm and scanned the earthworks of Dimilioc. 'I have faced many a shield wall and stared into the face of countless warriors as they tried to kill me, but this… many will die here if our actions are not calculated correctly. This is an impressive defence our friend Gerlois has created. Anyone would think him a little paranoid.'

Lines of Dumnonii warriors began to form upon the first earthen bank. Each was wearing some mixture of yellow and red, the tribal colours of the Dumnonii. As their shields began to come together to make the first stage of their shield wall, he saw the shields were painted with the same bright colours. They began to bang spears, axes and swords against their shields calling their taunts and challenges to the attackers as they arrived and formed around Uther.

'We cannot attack them unless they force us to do so,' muttered Uther. 'It would be a foolhardy act to spend so many lives here, warriors that need to face the Saxons in just a few turns of the moon if we are to regain our land. We will not lose the struggle for our Kingdom here. Where is Merlyn?' Uther glanced around looking for the familiar figure, but could not see him.

'The Druid sent word that he will be delayed, he said he would join us in two days,' said Sir Ector avoiding Uther's gaze.

Uther shook his head in frustration at the Druid's absence and gave orders to make shelters and to set guards. 'We do not allow any of them to leave, that much we can accomplish. They have the sea at their backs and few routes to escape by; we won't be letting the Duc slip past us again. I want chariots patrolling the battle line night and day.'

The first challenges began a short while later with another Briganti warrior striding out from Uther's lines to shriek a challenge up to the Dumnonii as they strutted upon their earthen wall. For a while, the roar of insults flew from both sides until a female warrior from the Dumnonii ran down the embankment and declared that she accepted the Briganti's challenge. She carried a small, rounded shield and a short spear that she spun in a dancing blur with expert ease while she grinned at her opponent. The watchers from both sides roared their approval as the two warriors circled, the female quickly showing she was the faster of the two. She skipped around her foe, easily avoiding his spear thrusts, deflecting them with her shield for a while without making any effort to strike him with her own weapon.

'Take his manhood, Liset. Geld him and make him squeal like the Highland pig that he is!'

'Send this woman back to make babies. Teach her some respect, Aris.'

The two fighters continued circling, stabbing and thrusting as their comrades' screamed support and derision in equal amounts until the woman was nearly toppled as the Briganti rushed in on her and stabbed. She staggered back turning his spear with her shield just in time, but then he dropped, turned a full circle and swept his spear around in a swishing arc that took the female warrior's feet from under her. She saw it and almost timed her jump in time, but the spear just caught the heel of her left foot making her cry out in pain. The Briganti sprang up, a grin of triumph on his face, and stabbed, but she hopped to the side and brought her shield down upon his head with a crack that could be heard above all the noise and sent him stumbling away, she limped backwards wincing in pain. He rolled, regained his feet and when he saw that she was not rushing in to finish him, he reached up to feel the blood streaming down the side of his face. He nodded his appreciation of her fighting skill; she nodded in return and they separated, returning to their own lines amid a chorus of calls both of support and condemnation for ending the fight so soon. Others took their place and there were soon three separate trials of combat taking place between the two opposing forces.

Uther knew this posturing and testing of each other's strengths would continue for some time until the two sides either calmed and separated to their two positions or enough adrenaline was built so that shield walls were formed and the battle was fought by all.

'Bring me a guide, someone who knows the area. I am going see where Tintagel is upon this coastline, and also, try and find Merlyn. If he returns, send him after me.' Sir Ector nodded and Uther walked back into the trees leaving the warriors to their trials.

'This way, Sire,' Maude's whisper tickled Uther's ear. She pulled at his shoulder, trying to get him to rise, but it wasn't easy. They had been squatting down listening to the fading Saxon voices for only a few moments, but it had been long enough for his joints to stiffen and his consciousness to retreat into a softer warmer part of his mind, and he was having a little trouble.

'Stand, Lord.... please... we must flee this place or we will both surely die here tonight.' She tugged at him and he managed to push himself up, forcing his legs to respond. His head swam, the world swirled around him and he leant against the wall for support, but she quickly gathered him to her and he felt himself being hurried along the passage once more. At one point she left him and he stood swaying against a pillar wondering what he was doing out of bed, and then he remembered the Saxons and his mind sharpened. Wiping a hand across his brow, he tried to peer through the darkness, to see where Maude had gone. He could hear movement, but then there was movement, rustling and squeaking coming from all around, in the rushes underfoot, and also above him, either, in rooms or possibly the roof thatch, he had no idea. And then she loomed in front of him, and supporting him with a strong arm, swept him along through the Abbey once more.

At an outside door, they rested, while she left him to see if anyone was watching for them. The cold night air teased as he looked out, sending a chill through him as he gazed out and up into a star-filled night sky. A white full moon floated just above the roofline opposite. He drew in a deep breath, smelling wet earth and the musky aroma of horses. Beginning to feel a little more alive, he dared take a step forward to see a little more of where they had emerged. It was indeed in the Abbey's courtyard; several puddles shone silver in the moonlight and water was dripping from the thatch in several places adding music to Uther's waking experience. He took another step, releasing his hold upon the doorframe and gazed up at the stars once more, and then Maude was with him again, moving him across into the shadows.

'There are Saxons in front of the Abbey, Lord, a small band of them... we must hurry.'

They entered a covered area for horses and Uther was left while Maude unlatched a doorway set in the opposite wall, two horses stared at them as they passed and snorted softly. He saw her silhouette as she peeked outside, and then she was pulling him out and pushing the door closed behind them. A dog barked, far off in the distance, and then he heard a cockerel cry a little closer, a little premature in its greeting of the dawn.

'To the forest, we have to make it unseen to the trees, Sire, can you do it? Please, lean on me, it will soon be over and you can rest, but we must make it to the forest before we stop.'

They strode through grass that was thick and wet but lying low, mostly dead and beaten down by the rain. It still soaked his leggings, the wetness making its way to the skin of his feet and ankles, chilling them quickly. Maude was pulling him along, glancing back from time to time at the Abbey, he could feel her doing it. He half expected a cry to come or the galloping of hooves to fill the night, but none did. After some effort and a little time, they were entering the forest and Maude allowed him firstly to slow and then to drop down beside a heavy tree trunk to gather his strength.

'Here...' He felt a flask offered to his lips and then the sweet fire of mead was washing into his mouth. He coughed, spilling some, but then drank again feeling the spirit fill him, giving him more clarity and the energy to look up at Maude; she was just a shadow in the darkness.

'Thank you, Maude. I think that tonight, you have saved the life of your King, I hope that soon I can reward you properly, but for now, you have my utmost thanks and gratitude.'

Chapter 24

The Druid's Pact

Merlyn pushed his fingers through the slick, wet entrails of the young goat that, until recently, had been suckling at its mother's teat. The Druids had disturbed the sleep of its peasant owner by banging noisily upon his hut and paid for the animal with a small sack of grain and a blessing upon his family. These were received as if they were gifts of gold and silver; he had also been told that they would return the body of the goat to feed his family when they had finished, altogether not a bad reason to be dragged from your dreams in the middle of the night.

They walked some distance from the peasant's hut, placed the struggling animal upon a rock and the three Druids had gathered around to see what knowledge its death might bring. Merlyn had slit the goat's throat with a swift practised movement using a small curved blade, and they watched with interest as the struggling carcase had twitched the final shreds of its brief life away. Merlyn's blade had then cut the soft skin of its belly and allowed the contents to ooze out, glistening and grey in the cold moonlight. The steaming organs were separated and examined, tubes and veins prodded, the heart, liver, and kidneys studied before they, in turn, were cut and dissected. Unaffected by the smell or the cold within which they worked, the Druids chanted and called upon the spirits to guide them and show them the different paths that may lie ahead. However, it was only when the last of the entrails were scooped from the belly of the beast, that they finally found what they had been searching for. The chanting ceased abruptly, and the

Druids pointed, exclaiming excitedly about something within the little body now stiffening in the cold grip of death. The spirits had spoken, a sign given, a path laid bare to be followed, the King must now be found.

Uther felt a surge of exultation as he released the strain on his horse's reins and gave them their head. The chariot leapt, the hazel and yew construction creaked and groaned as they splashed through ice-encrusted puddles and thundered down the narrow path, forcing both his companion and himself to duck beneath overhanging branches and burst through clouds of dislodged snow. Ahead of him, the horses' tails were up, their heads rising and falling, the muscles along their huge bodies writhing as they were allowed their freedom, hooves drumming hollowly on the frozen earth.

He was aware that behind him, the two chariots that followed would be having difficulty keeping their King in sight and it would be troubling them greatly. In fact, he could hear concerned shouting as they called for him to slow, but Uther was feeling as free and as released as the horses after so many days of marching and the confinement of the camp. His worries and frustrations were falling behind along with the mad rush of the chariot; it was good to be away, and he wasn't about to stop.

They burst from the trees into an open, rolling, snow-covered hilltop, the fall of the cliffs a safe fifty paces or so to their left side with the white-capped waves of the sea visible beyond beneath a cloudy, grey sky. To their right, the forest continued, dark, dense and endless. Pulling back on the reins, Uther managed to slow the horses to a canter and looked back in time to see the first of the chasing chariots emerge from the trees, its occupants waving to him; he slowed further.

'That was a good run.' He grinned round at his companion, an Iceni, who would have been the regular charioteer before Uther had usurped his place. The man was holding on to the sides, his face as white as the snow around them.

'Yes, Lord. You set a brisk pace to be sure.' He stood, pried his grip from the side rail, and tried to relax and then returned Uther's grin. 'You are a fine charioteer, Sire.'

'I learned from one of the best a long time ago. Here come the others.' Uther waved to the other chariots as they approached and then flicked the reins and the horses picked up their pace again to canter along the clifftop path. There was a chill wind blowing in from the sea, and below them, as the path neared the ragged cliffs' edges, they could hear the booming crash of the waves. It was cold, but it just made Uther feel so alive and at one with the world around him. He laughed out loud and cracked the reins down onto the horses once more to bring them back up into a run.

It was past midday when they sighted the three Druids. They were standing some way from the path, on the very edge of the cliff facing the gusting wind, gazing out past the turbulent waters that crashed far below them. They didn't move when the chariots came to a halt some twenty paces behind them. Uther jumped down and walked over.

'Merlyn… is that you? I sent out riders to find you but…' Uther stopped as, without turning around, one of the Druids held up a hand and then beckoned Uther forward with a gesture of his fingers. Uther ambled over feeling somewhat like a naughty boy about to be chastised. He stood to their side and tried to look into the Druid's hoods to confirm that it was indeed Merlyn, it was. He could see the Druid's nose, and the familiar grey whiskers were being blown all about his face while the hood held gamely on. Merlyn's eyes were closed. Uther got closer and raised his voice over the sound of the wind.

'Where have you been? I was waiting for you, and they told me you had…' He stopped speaking as Merlyn raised his hand again. As he slowly lowered it, the gusting wind dropped to a soft breeze, and the three Druids opened their eyes. Merlyn turned to Uther and smiled.

'Uther, there is no need to shout. You're late; we have been waiting here since just after daybreak. Did you get lost?'

'Lock shields.' The cry carried over the screaming and chanting of warriors awaiting their release and on both sides of the lines, the call was repeated. The front rank of warriors crouched and locked their shields so they overlapped, low to the ground, to protect the legs of those within the front line of the wall while the men and women behind, brought their shields forward, over the top of the first to form a high, strong and very solid wall. The third row of warriors leant forward to add their shields to the upper part of the wall which would protect from arrows and stones. An almost identical wall was being formed amongst the Cornovii ranks, they moved forward to the beat of drums, and the two bristling walls came slowly, almost hesitantly together.

Shouts and demands of help and encouragement rang along the lines of each to '*Keep the line!*' and '*Hold strong! Be ready for the bastards!*' Spears, swords, and axes were banged against shields, horns moaned and the whirring sounds of hundreds of slings being twirled filled the air like swarms of angry bees until the walls moved quickly over the final two paces to meet with an explosive boom that sent a shock through the frigid winter air.

Thousands of voices screamed in anger and determination as the two sides heaved and pushed against each other, cursing and insulting those just a short distance away behind the layers of shields. Time passed as the walls matched each other in strength, straining and shoving. Cries rang out from both sides as a crack was detected in the other's wall and a spear or sword was forced through to wound or kill. In a few places, the contest of strength was outmatched and, with little warning, the wall broke, and a flurry of fierce fighting would erupt. It was quick and bloody but was soon over as the wall on either side became whole once again. Amongst the shouting, screaming and roaring, a sharp horn blast sounded to those who were waiting to hear it. It sent a new order down the line of the King's warriors to, 'ease... ease.' As one, the heaving, sweating warriors within the wall took a single step backwards, which to the individual pockets of Cornovii warriors gave the appearance that they were beginning to push the invaders back into the forest and their voices raised even higher 'Kill them all. Push, push! *Kill, Kill, Kill!!*' Another and then another step was won, and the excitement of the Cornovii became ecstatic. Wiser, older voices with their ranks called for caution, to *'Hold the wall,'* and *'Stand fast.'* But the Cornovii warriors, less accustomed to the ways of battle, their tribal lands being so far from the Saxon borders, already felt they were winning, and so their wall of shields began to dismantle so that the warriors could hack and pull at the enemy shields across from them. As this happened, the lower half of the invaders wall slipped open to allow spears and swords to flash out, cutting and wounding the now exposed legs of the Cornovii until it was their lines that were faltering and the order being bellowed along the invaders line was to advance, all the while keeping their wall solid and impenetrable, practised and perfected so many times against the Saxons, taught to them so long ago by Ambrosius and his Roman trained warriors.

The Cornovii were in disarray. Their leaders ran along the line, calling for the shield wall to reform, but there was little chance or respite from the steady advance of the better-seasoned warriors within the attacker's ranks. The Cornovii turned and retreated up the first of their mud banks, quickly followed by Sir Ector as he led his men up the earthen embankment and then managed to continue on, chasing the fleeing Cornovii. They pushed them on, and then from the second earth bank as well before they were able to reform until the third bank, where the invaders were met by a solid wall of defence once more.

'*Shield wall, shield wall.*' The two groups gazed at each other across the short divide while stones, spears and arrows rained down upon both.

Sir Ector stood panting, his chest heaving at the effort of the battle and laughed. 'We have done well. We have won two of their lines of defence with few losses to our side. He looked across at the Cornovii wall that had formed up on the opposite bank just some thirty paces away, then raised his shield, deflecting a slinger's stone that hit with a solid '*thwack!*'

'We have taught them a lesson in battle and we will not gain the third embankment so easily, but nor will we lose this, our new line.' He turned to the warrior next to him. 'Keep the line, rest any that need it in the front ranks and move the wounded back, we move forward and will attack again shortly. If Uther were here he would be satisfied, for now, we have given Gerlois and his Cornovii much to contemplate.'

You say things like that just to annoy me, don't you, old man? I can't be late for something that was never planned; we were looking for you and now we have found you.' Uther grinned at Merlyn and saw that the old Druid, staring back out from the folds of his hood, was attempting to keep his own smile from showing.

'Well, I knew you would be here, and you are late,' said Merlyn, banging his staff on the ground making the assortment of bones and shells rattle. 'I have been on your errand, calling upon the spirits to aid me in the demand that I know you are about to place upon me. You wish to enter Tintagel, and you wish to do so swiftly and without shedding blood.'

'Yes,' Uther frowned. 'I'm calling upon the debt you owe me to be paid. You know Tintagel; you must know a way that I might enter, a path that is little known or a tunnel beneath the rocks. You are familiar with the island, aren't you?'

'I am, Uther. I have passed time there, and I shall help you enter, but I will do so based upon one condition.'

'No conditions, Merlyn. We completed your quest; I fought your monster and we brought back your stones. It is not I that owes a debt, but you.'

'I understand this, Uther, but come... walk with me. It is not so much a debt to be paid as an understanding that I wish us to agree upon.' Merlyn started to walk along the narrow path close to the cliff and Uther followed. The Druid began to chatter firstly about the beauty of the day and the wonder of the elements that were so exposed around them. The energy within the waves and the breath of the spirits within the wind. Once they were a good distance from the chariots, he beckoned Uther to sit beside him upon a rock. Together they stared out to sea and watched as the clouds slowly parted and a brilliant ray of sunlight firstly lit the clouds' edges and then struck the water below in a patch of dazzling glory.

'I ask very little for the gift I shall bestow upon you, Uther. I shall help you to walk freely amongst your enemies, find your Queen and make your match; for the spirits have shown me that this is the way that things should be and how it may be accomplished. You ask of me to repay a debt, but I will aid you freely, with joy and happiness in my heart. I only require that should this union be blessed with a male child, that you allow me to be his tutor for the first twelve years of his life.'

Uther turned to Merlyn and looked into his brilliant blue eyes, trying to understand what he wanted, to see where the Druid was leading him. Any child he might bring into this world would need tutors, and Merlyn would, of course, be a natural and undeniably valuable tutor to his son, or indeed a daughter if he were blessed with one, as indeed he had been to him for many years.

'I would surely wish you to be a tutor to my son, Merlyn, if I were ever to have one. I would always have expected this to be the case, you do not have to make me promise anything, you know that well... and so I do not understand.'

'I shall help you enter Tintagel and gain your Queen... but your first son will be given over to my keeping from the moment of his birth... you would, however, be allowed to visit.'

'To visit!' Uther stood up. 'You want me to give you my son?'

'Uther, I want you to allow me to look after your son, to guide him as he grows so that he might become the King that can lead our people after you... you know, after you...' Merlyn waved his hands in the air as if wafting away a bad smell.

'Oh, wonderful... I think sometimes you forget that I am King.' Uther shook his head in disgust as Merlyn smiled up at him, then sat down.

'Am I truly going to have a son?'

'I didn't say that. I only said if... it may never happen... perhaps she won't even like you... or you may be unable to have children or...'

'Oh, leave me with some dignity, old man. I suppose that if you are able to get me in and Igraine is there... and yes, if she agrees to become my queen... then I suppose you being my son's tutor...' Uther smiled at the thought of having a son. It all seemed so impossibly far away if it were indeed ever to happen. 'Why not tutor him in Pendragon fortress, so that we can all be together, would that not...?'

'No, Uther.' Merlyn interrupted. 'If I am to aid you in entering Tintagel, then you must give over your first born son to my care from the moment of his birth. I will bring him to you several times each year so that you may come to know him, but he must be cared for by the Druids, it is most important if he is to become the King of all Kings. This is how the spirits will it.'

'Several times a year, that's good of you,' muttered Uther. 'You would have me give up a son that I have never seen, to hand over my newborn son.... this is madness, and I will not do it.'

'You will not be able to enter Tintagel without my help, and you will never take Igraine to be your Queen, this much I do know. This is the moment in time where the spirits have brought together all that is necessary to make this future happen. If you do not agree, then another future will take its place. I will not pretend to you that I know what this future will be or what it holds, but I do know that it is a future where you and Igraine are not together. There will be no son, and there will be no King of Kings. Choose Uther and choose wisely.'

'You do not give me much room to argue. Nothing is ever simple with you, with Druids. You have manipulated me my whole life, and already you set out to manipulate my son who is not even born, not even conceived!' Uther stood and pushed his hair out of his face. He shook his head and then turned back to Merlyn. 'You owe me a debt, yet you repay me with this... this shallow choice, which is no choice at all.'

'It is true you have little decision in the matter, the spirits guide both of us in this, Uther. It is not me. I am just their hand. The choice is best for you, for your son, and for your Kingdom. Do I have your word and promise, Uther?'

Uther stared at him for a few moments, hating him more right then than he ever had before, or so it seemed. 'Very well, get me in and yes, you have my word.'

They stood and began to walk back to the chariots. Merlyn patted his hand on Uther's back. 'All is as it is meant to be, do not fret. I shall get you into Tintagel and you will find Igraine, all will be well.

'I don't know how you are going to get me past the Cornovii warriors that will be guarding it, Merlyn. I've been told that there is a very narrow pass, Tintagel will be very difficult to enter uninvited. Am I going to get wet?'

Merlyn smiled and skipped a few steps then peered over the edge of the cliff at the grey, pounding waters below. 'Wet... yes, possibly very wet indeed. That water does look cold down there, and rough too... could be quite dangerous, are you sure she's worth it?' He turned and walked back towards the chariots without waiting for Uther's answer, his shoulders moving as he laughed. Uther could hear him muttering, '...possibly very wet indeed.'

The forest was crisply cold. Uther looked up at Maude as she scanned back through the trees, her breath catching in the moonlight filtered through the leafless canopy above becoming a soft white cloud, ghostly in the near darkness.

'I do not hear pursuit,' he whispered, 'and I have been pursued through a few forests in my time. Did I ever tell you about...?'

'Shhhh...Sire, please.' Maude crouched beside him. 'We have not come far enough and will have left a trail across that field for someone to follow. They will come soon; we must keep moving.' She pulled him up onto his feet, and they set off again down the forest path that they could clearly see shining in the light of the moon, a silver trail passing through the black skeletal shapes of the trees. As they walked, Maude unwrapped a fold of cloth and gave Uther a cold hearth cake and then some nuts and dried fruits. Despite the cold he was ravenous. As he ate, he began to feel a renewed energy he hadn't felt in many months. He was by no means strong; he repeatedly leant upon Maude for support, but his mind was finding a clarity he hadn't felt in some time, and he realised he felt... better.

It was after they had walked for some time that they heard the beat of horse's hooves. Maude quickly pulled Uther from the path and they stumbled about thirty paces into the forest before slumping with their backs to a huge tree. It was ancient, its roots rising from the earth around them as if one of the ancient gods had thrust his arm down from the sky to grip the earth, gnarled fingers and knuckles bones caught frozen in time, rising from the forest floor. As they gathered their breath from the exertion between two huge fingers, Uther gazed up into the branches and felt the knobbly bark beneath his hand thinking that Merlyn would probably know the tree's name and want to tie a scrap of his cloak in its branches. He closed his eyes and made his own request upon the spirit of the tree for its protection.

He was glad for the rest. The air was rich with the smells of the forest, rotting leaves, and wet earth, he breathed it in greedily, his senses continuing to awaken as if he had been asleep for a very long time. After the confinement of the Abbey, it was refreshing and welcome.

Two horses came at a steady trot. They passed without stopping, and Maude made to rise, but Uther reached out a hand and stopped her. He couldn't see her in the darkness, but he could imagine the look of question she was giving him.

'Wait,' he whispered, 'there might be...' but he didn't get a chance to finish before the sound of more horses, harnesses jingling, could be heard through the trees. These riders were moving slower, the sounds of voices speaking, drifting through the trees. Uther wondered what clues they might have left, in their haste to get away from the path, but all they could do now was wait and see. Thankfully, the searchers moved on, but again, Uther placed a hand on Maude's shoulder. He peered around the tree, rising up onto his knees, the sound of cloth rasping against the tree bark, loud in his ears, the riders had gone. Looking back further down the pathway, he couldn't see any others coming, but then, he reasoned, it was very dark. Probably best to keep still and wait a little longer. A sharp sound made him turn back to where the trail came closest. He felt Maude rise next to him. It was a bird. In the middle of the path was a large black bird, its head turning from one side to the other, its beady, black eye studying the undergrowth through which they had pushed. It hopped up onto a low branch, stared in their direction and gave a loud *'caaawww!'*

Chapter 25

Tintagel

'They are priests, followers of the nailed God. They are likely to spit upon me, a Druid, and force you to sit with them while they chatter about miracles, fish and how they want to take you to the river, to get wet.' Merlyn frowned at the roughly constructed hut; a crude cross erected before it proclaiming that it was a Christian church, although it looked as if it would be hard pressed to hold the priest and ten worshipers. It had been constructed directly upon the well-trodden road and would be difficult to pass without making the Christians aware of their presence. There was no clear way to Tintagel without riding directly around it. In the distance, just a little down the coast, they could see the rocky Isle of Tintagel, the white foam of waves crashing upon its rocks, its slopes upon the top, green and dotted with sheep. Huts also covered the grassland and Uther was sure he could make out the highest part of the fortress, built upon the furthest side from them. More importantly, he could just see the wooden bridge that connected the isle to the mainland. It spanned the short distance allowing an easy passage over a difficult drop. It would only be a walk of thirty paces, but if the defenders decided to protect it, or even destroy the bridge, which they could surely do quickly and efficiently, then the fortress was as good as unassailable however large the invading force. He sighed and drew his attention back to Merlyn.

'The priests won't spit on you. You have been in the company of priests many times, Merlyn, they are harmless.' Uther climbed back up into his chariot and held out his hand to pull the old Druid up beside him. 'The only risk we run is dying of boredom if we stay and listen to their stories, come on, up...'

'They are a disease upon this land, Uther. They invade and usurp our groves, our sacred places, they build their churches upon ground sacred to the Druids and claim it as their own. You should banish them all. One God...pah! I ask you, you who knows the truth of the spirits and the Gods, the many, many Gods who live amongst us and also in the Shadowland; how can you tolerate them? It may have been the Romans that killed most of the Druids; surely few remain upon Ynys Mon to pass on our ways, but these vile creatures are the spawn of Rome, and they have come to finish the task.'

'They mean us no harm. I choose to allow them here because I be-lieve that every man has a right to follow his own heart. They will not destroy the Druids if you do not let them, be calm old man, it is surely beneath you to feel this way.' Uther flicked the reins and the chariot moved forward, bumping over the frozen rutted mud of the road.

'I have seen the future, Uther, this is what saddens me, and I do not like what I see.'

The three chariots rumbled past the small church and contrary to Merlyn's fears; no priest ran out to assail them, either with his teach-ings or with one or other of his bodily fluids.

'Uther will not be pleased.' Sir Ector looked up and down the shield wall and saw the line his warriors held was secure. 'He did not mean for us to attack.' The warriors, tired and bloodied, had now reached the fourth defensive mound, but it had cost them dearly. He looked back into the ditch behind and saw the dead lying in mud churned by hundreds of feet, coloured a rich red by the blood spilt from so many. He saw that the injured were helping each other back up and over the previous mounds, but it was not an easy journey. The frozen ground had been churned into a thick ooze, thawed by warm blood and the men and women of the tribes making battle. Many of those attempting to return to the forest camp were slipping and falling; others cried out in pain and despair at their injuries. He glanced back to the Dumnonii and Cornovii on the opposite bank. They were equally tired and their ranks fewer, but those remaining were still several thousand and were standing ready for the next wave of attack. Three lines of shields raised against the constant rain of slingers' stones that his warriors were hurling at them, the sharp sounds of contact loud in the air.

'Damn you, Gerlois, you stupid bastard,' he muttered. One more bank to go and then they would be at the fortress. Gathering his resolve, Sir Ector stared up at it, huge this close, the fortress of Dimilioc must surely be as big as the ancient fortress of Maiden. Warriors already lined the walkways at the top ready to sling their stones and throw spears and rocks as his warriors came within range, and they would be in range should they manage to take the final defensive bank. They were going to kill themselves winning these muddy hills only to destroy those who remained against the white walls. Uther was right, attacking had been madness, but they had been forced into the conflict after the challenges had escalated and groups of warriors had formed to fight. Shield walls had quickly followed, and before he knew it, they were assaulting the first mound. At the time, he had thought they had been winning, snatching a quick and easy victory, but now looking around at what the costs had been and what was still to be done…

'*Your Duc is a coward!*' Sir Ector pushed to the front of his ranks and raised his voice, bellowing over the incredible roar of battle. As his warriors saw he was standing alone and was trying to speak, the noise lessened enough for his voice to travel some small distance. 'Your Duc is a coward… he is responsible for all of this madness. Gerlois, you scum, you coward. You are killing our people. All of their deaths will weigh upon your spirit as you enter the Shadowland. The Gods and your ancestors will hold you accountable.' The noise lessened as more warriors on both sides stopped their fighting, yelling and screaming as they became aware that something new was taking place. In the distance from the outer edges of the battle the noise went on, but this close to the centre, it was becoming eerily quiet. Around him, the men and women of the tribes made space as Sir Ector continued his angry calls, driven to this point by senseless death and suffering to call the Duc forth.

'Deliver the Duc, bring him forward. Do not let him shelter behind your friends, your brothers, and sisters; they are all dying for his wrongs. Where are you hiding, Gerlois? Fight with your warriors... come and fight me. If you are no coward as you say, fight me and let the good men and women of our tribes live.'

A murmuring filled the air as all within earshot of Sir Ector lowered their shields and spears. The stones stopped falling and on the opposite bank the Dumnonii and Cornovii warriors parted and Gerlois pushed through the ranks, to stand, hands on his hips, scowling across the narrow divide at Sir Ector.

'So now the old dog chooses to bark. Where is your master, old dog? Why does not Uther Pendragon come forward to challenge me, why does he send his cur? You will not take this fortress, Ector. You may reach the walls, but you will go no further and just reaching them you will incur a terrible cost. You know we will make you pay for every step.'

'And whether we reach the walls or remain here, you will never be allowed to leave your precious fortress,' screamed Sir Ector. 'We go no further, this battle is done; we are staying. We will wait for you to either starve, surrender or die of old age... or you and I can fight, here and now, so that others may live, no one starves and none of our warriors become food for crows.'

Duc Gerlois stared at Sir Ector, weighing up the possible outcomes and choices left to him and then with a shrug of resignation, he took a shield from a warrior close to him, drew his sword, and stepped forward to slide his way down into the ditch towards the waiting Sir Ector.

The wind snatched Igraine's headdress and she watched as it fluttered away, out across the rocks towards the sea. She tried to gather her hair; it was blowing about her head in the strong, icy wind making it impossible to see properly. Once gathered, she was able to look out from the tower and observe the land and surrounding sea for some considerable distance; it was a magnificent view and she never tired of it. On the seaward side, dark, turbulent waters around the little isle spoke of violent storms taking place out at sea amongst far distant lands. She was not surprised there were no boats to be seen amidst the whitecaps that danced amongst the waves like white horses, rising and falling as they galloped, only a fool would take to sea in the winter season. Her gaze turned back towards the rugged coastland in its winter colours of grey and brown and just the barest shreds of green. There were a few patches of white on the cliff, lodged amongst the rocks where the snow had not been blown away. This was a cold and desolate place to be sure, but it felt good to be out in the open like this, even if it was so bitingly cold. She wrapped her thick woollen shawl more tightly about her and drew in a deep breath; she would bear it and stay a little longer.

Upon the isle below her, a few people from the fortress were set upon their errands, hurrying between huts, and further down towards the narrow bridge she could just see a group of warriors, they were huddled around a fire set against a large rock to protect its flames from the wind. Upon the mainland cliffs opposite, near the village, she could see two villagers. It looked like they were collecting firewood from a large stack, yes... they were gathering the branches into bundles. She kept watching as they heaved the bundles onto their backs and made their plodding way slowly back up the slope, bent under the weight of their burdens.

A strong gust rocked her forward and the whole wooden tower beneath her creaked and groaned as it moved in protest against the strain of the wind. Gripping the edge for support, she glanced back for reassurance from the two warriors stationed as lookouts. They were watching her, smiling.

'This is a well-built tower, Lady, it will not fall… just moves a bit in the wind is all.' She smiled and nodded her thanks and returned her gaze to the coastline, still unwilling to go back to the warmer confines below lest they think her scared. It was a silly reason to stay, she mused, she'd remain just a little longer. Movement further along the clifftop caught her attention and she tried to make out some detail in what appeared to be a small group of riders…. no, chariots, upon the coastal path. She studied them for a few moments, but then they disappeared back inland and were lost from sight. Visitors perhaps? A little distraction from the games and arguments of her daughters would be most welcome unless it was Gerlois. The thought sent a cold shudder through her that was nothing to do with the chill wind. She crossed to the stairway, the warriors lifted the heavy trapdoor for her and she descended into the fortress silently dreading the possibility that her husband may be about to visit.

'I have agreed, will you please stop asking me. I, your King, request most respectfully that you cease your demands and just get on with whatever it is you are going to do.' Uther glanced down the path towards the village of Tintagel and wondered at the madness of trying to enter the fortress. These people would be loyal supporters of Duc Gerlois and they would no doubt be very aware of the current conflict. Gerlois seemed to have been a step ahead of him since before the quest. So to believe these warriors would be unaware of who to allow onto the Isle of Tintagel and who not to, well…

'Not another word on the subject shall I say, Uther. You have my word on this. Just know that when you place the babe into my care, it shall be an act of kindness on your part, you entrust his care not only to me, but to all of the Druids, both here and…'

'Yes, yes, but you're talking about it again, Merlyn. I still think the probability of my entering the fortress is very slim, to say the least. There is a veritable gale blowing, snow will no doubt begin to fall again before darkness, and any path you may know onto the Isle is going to be either closely guarded or far beyond extremely treacherous. The chances of my fathering a child anytime soon seem extremely remote. Perhaps we should rethink this whole thing and... what are you doing?' Uther eyed the dirty thumb that was being pushed towards his forehead.

'Oh, stand still boy, I won't hurt you.'

'You called me boy again, old man. I thought I had broken you of that habit.'

'Behave like a little boy,' - Merlyn smudged his thumb a few times on Uther's forehead, it felt cold and wet and then hot - 'and you shall be treated like a little boy, whether you be the King or not.' Merlyn studied his handiwork, reached out to make a small change and then rubbed his hands on his robe to clean them. 'There, perfect. Don't touch it, let it dry, and then walk through the village as if you owned the place and then cross over the bridge to the fortress. You are alone from here.'

'Walk right in there?' Uther made to rub at the wet burning mud on his forehead and Merlyn slapped his hands down.

'I said don't touch it. If you rub it off, then it won't work.'

'What won't work, explain yourself Druid?'

Merlyn reached into his robe and pulled out a flat shining plate; Uther recognised the decorated edges as Roman. As Merlyn tilted it towards him, he looked at it and then jumped back in surprise when he saw a face looking back, it was Gerlois.'

'Be careful, don't make me drop it!' Merlyn snatched it back but then proffered it once again. 'One of these plates is very hard to come by and even harder to make, they break easily.' Uther glanced around, but the Duc wasn't to be seen, however, when he stared back into the glass, the Duc stared back.

'It is you, Uther.' Merlyn was grinning and Uther could tell he was about to hop from one foot to the other as he did whenever he was especially excited by one of his own tricks.

'You've made me look like Gerlois... I hope it isn't permanent.' Uther turned his face from one side to the other and reached up to touch a fat bearded cheek.'

'Be careful not to damage the rune upon your head. If you disturb it, the magic will end and then you will be plain old Uther, King of all the Britons once again.' Merlyn grinned happily then took back the glass depositing back it into the folds of his robe. 'Go on. This is what you wanted, now go see your girl.' Merlyn thought for a moment and then held Uther back by his sleeve. 'Do you need any...' - he waved his hands about and puffed out his cheeks, which he did whenever he was uncomfortable about something, and which to Uther's mind was a rarity - '...do you need any other advice....about what to do when you meet the lady, I mean as a Druid I can explain a thing or two... possibly give you a potion to... you know... give you a little...?' he patted his robe searching for a potion.

'No, Merlyn, I'm all good now. Do I still look like Gerlois?'

'You still look like a fat, bloated toad to me, maybe frown a bit more and get cross with a few people, go!'

'Uther walked off down the lane into the village of Tintagel thinking about how Gerlois used to walk. There was a definite swing of the hips and his stomach was always thrust forward. Uther glanced down at where a huge stomach should be if he truly were Gerlois, but saw only his normal, solid and immensely thinner frame. 'Oh, Merlyn, what faith I put in you!'

Sir Ector sidestepped the flashing blade only to be knocked backwards by the heavy shield, he stumbled but kept his footing. The blade was coming back, a sweeping arc that would cleave him in two if allowed to run its course, but he had fought for many years and wasn't about to let a wide open swing like that end his days and send him to the Shadowland.

He blocked the blade with his shield, ignoring the force of the blow as it travelled along his arm and hacked down with his own sword trying to make his opponent bring his shield up in defence and so leaving him open. The two fought hard and fast, both knowing they didn't have the stamina of the younger warriors, but neither lacking in strength or experience, this had to be fought hard and won quickly. There was a deafening roar surrounding the fighters as warriors from both sides screamed their encouragement and advice. Several warriors slipped down the bank or were pushed and had to be dragged out of the combatants' way. Sir Ector could see that the Duc was tiring. The man was strong and also fast, but years away from any serious combat had left him in a condition that meant he should soon fade. If he could keep the Duc from overpowering him for a little longer, then it would all be over, the Duc would collapse from exhaustion, and all of this would be ended.

But the Duc wasn't finished yet, he lunged, snaking his sword down so that Sir Ector had to jump to the side, yet he managed to knock the sword down in the process, but then only just missed the shield as it knocked into him once more. The Duc kept coming, like a rampaging bullock, but then slipped in the mud under foot and went down onto one knee and Sir Ector sliced his sword down aiming at the base of the Duc's neck. A chorus of cries and shouts erupted as the onlookers sensed the end may be close, but the Duc blocked the blow once more and forced himself up to send Sir Ector into retreat yet again.

'Let us end this, Gerlois, this is madness even for you. Bend your knee to Uther, give up, or I will be forced to kill you in front of all your people.'

'Never!' Gerlois swung his sword onto Sir Ector's shield, and the two exchanged a flurry of blows until Gerlois tripped over a fallen warrior. He regained his footing just in time to deflect a hammering blow from Sir Ector. The two fought savagely back and forth and then stood panting, glaring at each other for a moment as they each re-gained a little breath.

'We are old men, both of us. We lack the youth, the energy to give this conflict true justice.' Sir Ector straightened and eased his back. 'However, I have the greater stamina. I have remained a Lord of war while you have turned to being a Lord of trade. Duc Gerlois, this is the last time I will ask you to yield, to join us once again as a united force against those who invade our country.'

'There is no room for me to yield, you fool. Uther mocks me to the last. He does not call me forth and allow me to capitulate with any grace. He sends you in his stead, sends his dog to break me. Why does he not call me out himself? Allow me to submit to my King or die upon his famed sword. Where is the King? Where is...?' Gerlois' eyes widened as the truth finally registered, anger consumed him, and he lunged at Sir Ector screaming.

'Yaaaaahhhh.' He swung his sword wildly in a flurry of violent blows and then just as suddenly stood panting, sword tip dropped to the mud. His chest heaved and spittle drooled from the side of his mouth, the attack having momentarily sapped him of strength. He glared his hatred and fury; warriors stepped back anticipating his next explosion of wild violence. 'So he goes to Tintagel. Slinks off to meet my cheating, bitch of a wife. Well, he will find more than he bargains for when he gets there. But I ask you, is this the action of a King I should follow? A King whom I should bend my knee to and stand beside in battle? No, I think not. I shall kill you and then my warriors will follow me as I go to Tintagel and kill them both. I shall make a far better King of the tribes than the Pendragon.' Once said, Gerlois drew a deep breath and then dragged his sword from the mud and attacked in a fury of renewed energy that forced Sir Ector back, tripping and falling in the mud desperately trying to regain his footing.

'You cannot run from me, Uther Pendragon, you cannot hide in these woods.' The soft voice floated through the dead still air of the darkness as if carried upon the wisps of mist that flowed through the dank, decaying undergrowth and wrapped around the trees in silent embrace.

'You have evaded the Saxons for now, but I can summon them whenever I wish. For now, I will allow you to hide in whatever dark, rotting hole that you think protects you. You are close; I can smell you... smell your fear.'

As the voice drifted away, the sound of flapping wings replaced it. Uther tried to imagine where the bird could be now. The voice was Morgana's without a doubt; she must be standing on the path, quite close, while the bird was doing the searching for her. Maude moved slowly beside him, and he heard the soft hiss as she slid her knife free of its scabbard.

'I'm coming to find you, Uther... coming to take all your pains away. No more stories, no more lies and no more dreams to trouble you...' The sound of a twig snapping beneath a softly placed foot came close, the other side of the tree. Maude rose and crouched beside him without a sound. Whereas all Uther could do was try to stem his beating heart which sounded so loud in his ears. Sweat beaded upon his brow, and the dank air of the forest was becoming difficult to breathe.

'I have your confession, King of all the tribes. You are responsible for the murder of my father, the bewitching of my mother and the subsequent deaths of thousands.' The voice was coming from all around as if filling the air. The mist rising higher until, looking down, Uther realised only his head was above it. It threatened to rise and rather than feeling he should drop lower and hide within it, he had the awful foreboding that if he did he would drown and be lost forever. As he pushed himself into a higher sitting position against the tree, his jerkin rasped against the bark.

'On behalf of all the many whom you have wronged, King Uther Pendragon, I shall pronounce your sentence... which is, of course, death...' - a flutter of wings - '... and carry out your execution... which shall be... now!'

Chapter 26

Lord of the Storm

The brief stroll through the village of Tintagel had given Uther the opportunity to practice and refine his walk, so that now although he felt foolish pretending to be another man, he also felt confident that if his features did resemble the overweight Duc, then his bearing should come close to matching him as was possible. So far, he had very little confirmation that Merlyn's magic was anything other than a cold, tingling smudge of mud on his forehead and he began doubting that he had seen Gerlois in the Roman glass. It would be just like the old Druid to do nothing more than smear him with slime and expect Uther's boldness and daring to carry him through. It tickled and he was tempted to scratch at it, but he knew that was probably not the best idea.

It was starting to snow again as he splashed through the muddy centre of the village. The wind was gusting in from the sea through the small collection of huts and buildings, and rather disappointingly, there had been no real contact with anyone to confirm or deny his disguise. He shivered, pulled up the edge of his cloak and wished his feet weren't feeling so wet and cold. Two peasants emerged from a hut about twenty paces away, glanced over at him, and then scuttled out of his way. Neither had addressed him, but he supposed they may have moved out of anybody's way who was dressed in a lordly way, not necessarily because he appeared to be Duc Gerlois.

He stopped and looked all about him; the huts seemed to be in a good state of repair. He knew Tintagel was a bustling trading village at any other time of year. The villagers apparently made a good profit from the trade, but right now, except for a rather sad looking goat tethered to a post, which was also ignoring him, there was nobody about. The snow was beginning to fall harder in big fluffy lumps; the villagers would all be inside their huts keeping warm, he was tempted to join them, but no. There was nothing for it but to continue on to the footbridge over to the isle itself.

He hurried and tripped his way down the path towards the cliffs as the wind, blowing quite fiercely now, lashed him with stinging wet snow. It was getting darker too, another storm coming by the feel of it. He shivered and moved on down the slippery trail, leaving the settlement behind, then out onto the clifftop where the path took a steep drop down. Spirits it was cold. He stood for a moment in the shelter of a group of rocks, stamped his feet and blew hot breath on his hands to warm them. The sound of waves pounding on the cliffs could be heard now, the booming sound and rush of water mixing with the howl of the wind as it battered the coastline. He shuffled on; the path levelled and he held his cloak tightly, glancing up into the bite of the wind to see the wooden bridge stretching out ahead of him. A shiver of cold, or was it trepidation, ran through him, and he had to force his foot to move up onto the bridge. After that, it was easier just to put his head down against the gale and make his way across to an uncertain reception.

He counted twenty-five bouncing paces as he walked, head down, fully exposed to the blast of the storm, and then he was stepping from the bridge and moving quickly towards where three warriors leant over a flickering fire. They glanced round towards him, and one took up a spear as he approached.

'Stand by your fire,' Uther called, then pushed between two of the warriors and held out his hands to the blaze, the heat extremely welcome.

'A filthy day turning to a filthy night. May the spirits be with you.' With a wave of his hand, he turned and walked up the path to where he could see it rounded a rocky outcrop and headed upwards onto the isle; he heard no challenge from behind and counted the spirits in his favour, but his relief was short-lived.

The wind and driven snow attacked him the moment he emerged from the protection of the lower part of the path. It hit him with full force, driving, frozen needles that rocked him on his feet, almost forcing him stumbling down the dark slope to where he knew the waves were waiting to drag him to a cold, wet grave, almost, but not quite. Were the Gods and spirits against him? Regaining his feet and raising an arm to protect his face he staggered on. It took him some time to cover what was probably just a few hundred paces, and it was almost dark now, but he could still see the foot-worn trail leading ahead. He tried to remember how far the fortress had been from the bridge when he had studied it from the clifftop just a short while earlier; surely it couldn't be much further. As he squinted ahead he saw two shadowy figures coming towards him, he tensed and readied for the confrontation, but they simply passed him by saying nothing, more intent on their own descent of the hill.

This whole venture was madness. He took a breath and forced himself on almost blindly, counting two hundred paces lest he become lost, and then he saw the light of another fire flickering, not twenty paces away. Relief and fear washed through him at the same moment; he had made it to the fortress.

Close to the fire, sheltering from the direct blast of the elements, two warriors leant against the palisade beside a large door. They were watching him approach but weren't making any move away from the comfort of the fire in his direction. He muttered an appeal to the spirits to aid Merlyn's magic and bless his endeavours.

'Oh spirits, help me now to pass into the warmth of the fortress and make it that the Druid hasn't sent me chasing sheep in a storm with only a smudge of mud for protection.' He drew himself up and marched forward as he imagined a wet and bedraggled Duc Gerlois might.

'A terrible night, I thank you for guarding my family.' Uther looked from one guard to the other and smiled his thanks. He watched as the two warriors, each wrapped in furs to keep the cold at bay, studied him and then looked at each other, and then at the same time threw their furs to the side and reached for their spears.

Uther reacted immediately, but only just managed to draw Excalibur from its sheath in time to deflect the first spear thrust. He was soaking wet, almost frozen stiff and therefore slow in his movements, but thankfully so were they.

'*Attack, we are attacked!*' Uther's blade silenced the warrior by slipping past his spear to slide into his neck. From the side of his vision, Uther saw the other warrior's spear stab towards him and only just managed to move his head out of the way in time. The shaft burned along his cheekbone as he raised his arm and deflected it. He felt the warrior draw the spear back for the next lunge and then spun, bringing Excalibur around in a cut that sliced into the man's midsection almost cutting him in two. His gurgling cry was snatched away on the wind. Uther stood panting, glancing around lest the scuffle had been heard, yet no other threat loomed out of the night, and the door remained closed. He picked up one of the discarded furs and cleaned Excalibur with it before returning the blade to its scabbard. He was shaking after the exertion, wondering what had gone wrong, why had they cried attack? Was his disguise still in place? Had it been cleansed from his forehead in the storm or was there no real disguise, after all, just another of Merlyn's tricks? He held his hands out to the warmth of the fire then looked down at the fallen men. It took just a few moments to drag them some distance out into the darkness, away from the light of the fire, then after another few moments warming himself he lifted the heavy bar on the door and pushed it inwards.

The storm arrived without warning. The day had been cold, but during a battle, the cold is the last thing anyone noticed. Nobody had been looking up at the weather. The seasons and elements were the business of Druids, and with Merlyn away those Druids that remained were of little interest to the warriors making war. A covering of clouds had been moving high above them, much the same as any other winter day, but there had certainly been no indication a storm was coming until it did.

The shield walls of the two Celtic forces had first clashed around mid-morning and now, late in the afternoon they still fought at several points around the hill fortress. Those that still battled were mostly unaware of the contest that was taking place between the two men commanding either side. However, by far the greater number of warriors had stopped fighting and had swarmed forward so that they might witness the struggle between two of the oldest tribesmen on the battlefield. They pushed and vied for position as the fighters moved to observe more clearly a mighty battle that all present knew would be sung in the halls for years to come by bards throughout the tribal lands. The first indication that a storm was coming were just a few dancing snowflakes drifting softly on the breeze. These at first went unobserved. However, within just a few short moments some began to notice that the breeze had become stronger and that snow was falling, with flakes becoming larger and more numerous. The sky had also taken on a more ominous darker shade.

Sir Ector was the first of the fighters to notice, although he gave it little heed having far more important matters at hand. They had stopped fighting and had drawn apart once more to regain some breath and take the other's measure. They were panting, wishing for the energy of their youth, weary beyond the reason to raise their swords yet again, but both knew the other would and therefore so would they. Neither had managed to make a killing blow. Both fighters bled from countless small wounds, nothing serious enough to end the contest and so both were still equally determined to continue and finish the other.

Now the weather had worsened to make their efforts even more challenging. Snow, driven by the increasing wind, beat against the exposed skin of their arms and faces, making them feel as if they were suddenly being attacked with a thousand stinging spears. Squinting his eyes, Sir Ector glanced up and saw clouds sweeping past overhead, darkening as they became lost in the now increasingly heavy snow. He glanced across at Gerlois. The big man was beginning to stand, ready to continue the fight, apparently unaware of the worsening weather. The Duc was bleeding from cuts on both arms and his flesh beneath his left eye hung in a gaping wound, blood soaked through his beard and drenched his tunic on the same side, yet he seemed in no mood to stop fighting.

'Do you still think me a coward, Ector? Think me a man who will not pick up a sword?' He swung his blade, and Sir Ector blocked the cut upon the ragged remains of his shield and sent a swinging blow in return. The sound of screaming warriors had been joined by the howling cry of the wind. As Sir Ector beat blow after blow upon Gerlois shield and they moved up the slope towards the more exposed heights of the last defensive mound it became darker, the wind and driving snow ferocious, the storm had arrived.

Falling and sliding in the freezing mud, forcing himself up after the retreating Duc, Sir Ector pushed himself on determined to kill his opponent. The faces of warriors loomed into his vision beside him, cheering him, goading him on as he hacked and swung, kicked and pushed his opponent, driving him back and back, desperate to finish yet still unable to find room to make the stabbing thrust, the killing blow that was necessary.

Thunder boomed, echoing around them. They had climbed the slope and reached the white plastered side of the fortress and were now on level ground. Gerlois staggered back a few steps. He bent over, gasping for breath, staring through his wet hair at Sir Ector with malevolent hatred. As Sir Ector closed once more, Gerlois threw his shield to the side, grasped his sword in two hands, and ran at Sir Ector, sword drawn back ready to swing a savage killing stroke.

'*Gahhhhh...*' The sword swung, singing through the air. It was a last desperate attack by a man spending the very last of his energy, the Duc demanding one final effort from his muscles.

Sir Ector's body was old and exhausted, but it remembered thirty years of battles. Dropping below the flashing metal, he lunged upwards, immediately feeling his blade enter the Duc's chest. The momentary grating resistance as it met ribs and then the bones snapping and the metal sinking unhindered into the large body as the Duc's weight and momentum drove him on to impale himself.

Letting go of his sword, Sir Ector pushed himself away and watched as Duc Gerlois dropped to his knees beside him, eyes wide open in shock, the blade protruding from his back, twitching as blood pumped out around it. About them, the warriors gradually stopped their yelling and screaming as word was passed back that the Duc had fallen. The Duc coughed, vomited a gout of blood and collapsed upon the blade. His head turned to the side with blood bubbling from his mouth, his eyes vacant and staring. Sir Ector pulled away, forced himself to stand, and gazed down at the beaten man taking no joy from his victory. Gerlois leg shuddered as the last of his life bled out, pooling dark against the snow.

Lifting the bar, Uther slipped past the door and into the hall, instantly feeling the warmth of the large room; he could smell the fragrant aromas of food cooking reminding him that he was hungry. It was meat and bread and... a blow hit him on the back of his head sending him stumbling forward towards the ground, which came rushing up to meet him.

He must have lost consciousness for a moment or two, for the next thing he was aware of was lying face down upon the fortress floor, breathing in the dusty smell of old floor reeds and hay. His head hurt, and he couldn't see properly, pushing against the ground he tried to rise, but soon realised it wasn't the best idea.

'Who are you?'

Uther tried to turn his head and look up, but it wasn't going to happen, he managed to roll onto his side.

'I'm sorry... I didn't mean to hit you so hard... Uther? Oh, spirits...Uther, it's you...'

Someone was crouching beside him, hands upon his face, as he tried to wipe his eyes.

'I thought you were Gerlois, Oh, Uther. How could I have thought... oh, spirits, we have to move you, someone will come.'

'Igraine, is that you?' He tried to focus on her face.

'Please, you have to get up. What are you doing here? Quick, we have to hide you.' She pulled him to his feet and helped him as they moved past the crackling central fire to an area that was curtained off from the rest of the hall.

'Where is everyone? I thought your daughters were here, servants... others?' Uther looked around the room, his eyes slowly focusing.

'I sent them away to one of the other halls so that I might... Well, I thought Gerlois was coming to visit and...'

'And you thought you should give him a proper welcome?' Uther smiled and stood without the need for her support as his vision cleared.

'I was worried he had come. I saw chariots, and I was worried that we would be called to join him, at Isca or Dimilioc... I don't think I could do that. This place is like another world, a place where nothing can intrude, nothing can reach me here, or so I had thought until you tumbled in.'

'I had to come, Igraine, I had...' she put a finger to his lips and rose up to kiss him, her lips lingering softly upon his.' Uther closed his eyes and felt his whole body tense and his mind open in a way that he had never felt before, his heart pounded wildly in his chest. It felt unreal. Without breaking the kiss, he gazed down at her. Her eyes were closed, her body achingly close to his, the sound of her breathing softly filling his world. She drew away and took his hands, pulling him towards a pile of sleeping furs.

'Will the others be returning? Igraine, we should leave… or hide until the storm passes. I fear for your safety; we should…' But she kissed him again and drew him down upon the warm, soft furs and without doubt there was no other place he wanted to be as she smelt of spice and herbs and all things good, her skin was soft and perfect, and the furs they retired to were so comfortable. He gazed into her eyes, such a perfect blue.

'Gerlois' time is over; he will never hurt you again. I shall make you my Queen, Igraine. I shall honour you and love you and do my very best to make you happy… will you leave with me, Igraine?'

'Shhh.' She smoothed the damp hair from his temple and stroked his face exploring every curve and contour before kissing him again. If I am to be your Queen, Uther, I need to know how we would live, if I would be allowed my freedom. I have so little as the bought and paid for wife of Gerlois, who demands I am always within his sight. This is why I enjoy my time here upon Tintagel, away from him.' She smiled. 'But most important, King Uther Pendragon, I want to know if we will dance? Gerlois would never allow me to dance. He said it was beneath a lady of my ranking, but I think I would like to dance. I think I would like it very much.'

Uther smiled and kissed her. 'We shall dance, Igraine, I will dance with you on our wedding night and every other possible night that we can. And you shall have your freedom; I ask only that you love me and allow me to love you in return.' They sank into the sleeping furs and lost themselves in one never-ending moment that war and storms could never tear away.

It was some time later when he was roused from an exhausted sleep by sounds coming from outside the hall. Opening his eyes, he saw Igraine was still sleeping, a fur wrapped around her naked body, her long dark hair spread out across the fur, framing her incredibly beautiful face, so lost in sleep. He reached out to brush a stray lock aside, but stopped as he heard the door pushed open, it was accompanied by a cold gust of air that rushed around the hall billowing the curtains to the sleeping area. Uther hurriedly searched for his clothes and managed to pull a few things on to cover his dignity before the sound of footsteps stopped the other side of the curtain.

'My Lady, are you there, is all well?'

Igraine awoke with a start, glanced at Uther and sat up clutching the furs to her chest. She was about to answer, but it was too late, the curtain was pulled roughly aside. There was a moment of hesitation on both sides, and then the warrior standing there stabbed his spear down towards Uther and cried out in alarm.

'*He is here! The intruder is here!*'

From out of the darkness a blade flashed in the moonlight before plunging towards Uther's heart accompanied by a hiss of expelled breath. Maude lunged forward and caught the wrist just as the point touched Uther's cloak, and punched the darkness where she suspected whatever had become of the Abbess was concealed. It was difficult in the near blackness to see where to hit, but to her satisfaction, her fist connected with something solid. There was a terrible screech of in-human anger and then whatever it was, retreated into the gloom, the wrist dissolving within Maude's grip, the knife dropping to the forest floor with a small thud.

'She isn't human. Whatever that is, it isn't human,' hissed Maude. 'I never liked her, I told you she was poisoning you, but that thing is more than just the Abbess.' She glanced down to Uther, who had slumped again but was trying to get up. She helped him stand. 'We have to keep going, Lord. I think we're on the path to the settlement of Somerton. If we can keep moving, we will reach there before daybreak, and we'll be safe. Can you walk, Sire?'

'Yes. I am feeling surprisingly well considering I just cheated death once again thanks to you.' Uther crouched stiffly and felt about in the mist for the fallen knife. After a few moments, he found it. 'Hah!' He smiled in the darkness. 'Well, if she comes back she faces two able and armed warriors, she doesn't stand a chance.'

'Yes, Lord, let's hope that's enough.' Maude took Uther's arm and guided him back towards the path, stumbling and tripping on unseen branches and brambles, until the vague outline of the path was revealed. They walked a few steps, listening intently to the sounds of the forest around them. The soft movement of the branches rustling overhead in the breeze, their footsteps crunching underfoot sounding unnaturally loud. An owl hooted in the distance and the sounds of small animals scurrying amongst the undergrowth were much closer, and all the time they were expecting something to leap out of the darkness towards them.

'She's watching us, from somewhere up in those trees,' whispered Uther. He had stopped and was looking up at the dark canopy of the forest overhead. 'Morgana,' he called, 'why don't you come talk with me.' Uther gazed around into the darkness, seeing nothing. 'Morgana. I rescued your mother from a brutal, terrible man. I know he was your father, but he was not a good man. Let me finish telling you my story. It's what you wanted from me after all; I have a need to finish.'

'Let's keep walking, Lord,' whispered Maude. She pulled on Uther's arm, and he allowed himself to be drawn along beside her whilst still gazing up into the trees.

'I told you how I entered Tintagel. I suppose I was a fool believing that Merlyn had disguised me, I was lucky that the storm had arrived to hide my entrance. It wasn't me who killed your father, but of course, it was my man who did, and I would have done so in his place if I'd had the chance. Your mother and your sisters joined me and lived happily as part of my household; we did not know where you had gone. I saw you last upon the wall at Isca, when I returned our token, this token.' Uther held up the stone first given to him on the beach by Morgana as a little girl before they had departed on Merlyn's quest. 'You returned it to me when last I left your Abbey.' What happened to you, Morgana? Where did you learn to hate with such passion?'

A loud *'caaawww'* filled the air, and then a voice screamed down at them. *'You all deserted me. My father took me and gave me to the sisters at Laherne. You stole my mother, had my father murdered, took my family from me, you took it all.'* A small shower of leaves and branches fell a few steps in front of them, and they stopped walking.

The shrill voice, much closer in the gloom this time, screamed out, *'I told you where I went.'* The voice continued more softly, tinged with a deep sadness. 'I told you of the sisters and their harsh new ways of the nailed God. Of how I longed to escape. Of my finally meeting the Morrigan and the Fey, who gave me hope, they taught me the old ways and of how things are and shall ever be. You forget so quickly. For a man about to die your senses are still rather dim.'

Uther began to walk again, shuffling along, knife held out in front of him, and Maude started after him, unwilling to be too far apart. She had her sword drawn and was turning so she might catch any sign of movement from the sides or behind them.

'I need to finish my tale,' called Uther, 'and so I shall keep on with the telling. I had managed to enter the fortress upon the Isle of Tintagel, under the cover of the storm without being seen, but they eventually found the bodies of the warriors set to watch the door and then found me rather quickly.'

More twigs and old leaves fell around them as the creature followed them through the branches above.

Her voice was now harsh again, dripping scorn and hatred. 'They found you because you are stupid. Like all men, even Kings are ruled by that which hangs between their legs; they knew you would be humping my mother.' More twigs fell, accompanied by a fluttering of wings, and both Uther and Maude jumped back as a large indistinct shadow landed in front of them then sprang up screeching loudly. They could see enough of it in the gloom to notice it bore what could be conceived as a parody of Morgana's face, twisted and animal in some unnatural way. Its lips drew back in a high-pitched scream, and the face thrust forward, contorted with anger and hatred, spraying both Uther and Maude in splatters of thick, slimy phlegm and breath so foul it made them recoil. The darkness seemed to gather around the creature forming into a cloak that pulsed and flowed in iridescent waves, and then a claw-like hand tipped with sharp talons snapped out and raked across Maude's face. The warrior shrieked and fell in agony, lost to the dark mist of the forest floor where she lay whimpering, unseen and forgotten.

Uther stared at what had become of Morgana, his mind trying to reason with what he was seeing. Whatever it was, its eyes weren't even close to being human. They shone from above a nose, long, black and sharp like a bird's beak, eyes glowing red with small coal-black pupils stared back at him with an evil that was palpable.

'Time to die, Pendragon.' The claw snapped out again with frightening speed, and Uther felt the skin of his cheek raked and split open, but his hand was still holding the knife, and it also moved, striking up into the darkness even as he fell back, more reflex than conscious effort to stab it. He felt the blade strike into something solid, and the creature screamed in anger and pain, and then the eyes drew back and whatever it was folded in on itself, the darkness becoming a small black indistinct creature that fell to writhe upon the ground, hissing, before lifting up and flapping away through the trees screeching one final, *'caaawwww.'*

Uther gazed about him as he staggered a step or so, he noticed with the creature gone it wasn't so dark. The night was receding, and dawn was offering more light to the forest. The darkness, like the creature, was almost gone, the mist between the trees less ominous than it had seemed only moments before. He reached down and helped Maude to her feet, and they inspected each other's wounds. Tearing the sleeve from her chemise, they each took a bundle of cloth to staunch the bleeding before limping on their way through the trees.

After a while, Maude asked, 'How did you escape from Tintagel, Lord? They found you, and I can only guess that they would likely have killed you soon as they could after finding you in the sleeping area of the lady in their charge.'

'They weren't too happy to find me there, no, but in those days I was, even more, abler than I am now, thank the spirits. Getting onto the island was a mixture of believing in Merlyn and blind luck, leaving was a little different, the storm had passed, but it still wasn't as easy as it could have been to get away from Tintagel.'

'You still seemed quite able a few moments ago, Lord. I think you might have saved us both back there; I don't think she will be back anytime soon. Why don't you just finish your tale and tell me what happened? I'll keep looking out in case that thing comes back.'

'All right, why not,' said Uther, pulling his cloak tighter around himself. 'It will pass the time as we get out of these awful woods, but as you say, just keep an eye open for it returning. My first problem was to deal with the warriors who had found me.'

Chapter 27

A Long and Interesting Life

Uther rolled and stabbed out with Excalibur, taking the first warrior in the centre of his chest just as he stepped through the curtains. The man's eyes bulged and he dropped his spear, his hands wrapping around Excalibur's blade as blood spurted from his wound. Uther pulled the blade free; the warrior fell to his knees, Uther kicked him backwards and Igraine screamed. Two other warriors were coming, shouting, screaming their anger as they ran to join their fallen comrade and protect their charge. The first was a female wearing the yellow and red of Dimilioc. She was screeching a high pitched war cry as she ran in to thrust her spear at Uther. He stepped to the side, his footing unstable upon the sleeping furs and dropped Excalibur, then drew the spear alongside him and pulled the girl off balance.

'Don't kill her!'

He heard Igraine shout, so twisted the spear out of the girl's hands and spun, sweeping her legs from under her. She fell with a crash to the floor beside him and he spared her a quick glance as he snatched up his sword, saw she was groaning and not leaping up so no immediate threat, and then faced the last warrior. He was a big, angry-looking man, a blue swirling tattoo covering much of his face and a huge axe that he was swinging down towards Uther's head.

'*Agghhh.*'

Stepping to the side, Uther blocked the axe with Excalibur then moved in and lashed his head forward, butting the man's nose, feeling bone and cartilage break with a crunch against his forehead. The warrior went down, still clutching the wooden shaft as the axe head fell to the floor with a thud. The blow had hurt Uther's forehead, but not as much as it had hurt the warrior who was groaning, blood pouring from his broken nose. Shaking his head, trying to clear it, Uther strode past towards the door and struck the man with Excalibur's hilt knocking him unconscious as he passed.

'Uther, you have to leave, to get out of here,' called Igraine. 'There are too many warriors, you cannot fight them all and many are my friends, they are good people, your people.' She ran to Uther and held him as he turned from placing the locking shaft across the door. 'Go back to your people, kill Gerlois and then come back for me. Only then can we truly be together. There is nothing left for you to fight for here, you already have my heart.'

Uther held her and knew she was right. This wasn't the place to wage a personal war; he needed to end it elsewhere.

'I will come back for you, Igraine, be ready. Make your family ready.' He ran over to the sleeping area that he had so recently shared with her and found his cloak and boots. Both still retained the wet and cold from the previous evening. As he pulled on the boots he wished he had thought to place them closer to the fire to dry, but that had been the last thing on his mind when he had taken them off he recalled, and smiled.

Igraine picked up his cloak. 'When you leave, don't take the main path, the bridge to the mainland will be well guarded, especially now that they know any number of intruders are here. There is a shepherd's track that can take you to the bay. I'll point you in the right direction. It's a little steep, but it will surely be light soon and the storm blew itself out in the night. Just pray the track isn't covered in snow or is too icy.'

'It sounds like it will give me a better chance than fighting through at the bridge,' said Uther standing to tie his sword belt in place, 'Thank you, my love. Don't worry for me. I'll be back for you as soon as I can.

Do not fear.' He took the cloak from Igraine and wrapped it around himself, pulling the hood up over his head.

'The shepherd's track will take you below the bridge. It will be low tide at sunrise, and you can make your way across to the coast through the rocks and find a route up. Go my wild King and come back for me soon.' She fell into his arms once more, he kissed her and then they were parting and he was lifting the locking bar from the door. Dragging it open, he peaked out just as a cold draught of air blew in making them both shiver. Thankfully, there were no more warriors guarding the door; the storm had indeed passed in the night and the sky was just showing signs that it was getting light.

Igraine pointed. 'There... past the water trough, you will see the path there is only one. May the spirits guide you, my love.' They kissed one final time and he ran across the courtyard towards where he hoped his path to freedom might lie.

It was mid-morning when he pulled his cold, wet and very weary body over the top of the hill and lay panting on top of the cliff. The first thing he noticed, was a sheep searching for what little grass it might find. It had stopped chewing and was looking at him curiously, and then he noticed Merlyn sitting on a rock clutching his staff, grinning, white hair and beard blowing about his face by the soft sea breeze.

'Did you have a successful visit, King Uther? Make any princes while you were there?' Before Uther could reply, Merlyn's attention was distracted by a few gulls floating, beaks into the wind, moving effortlessly with small movements of their wings to keep in position. 'Oh, I do wish I could do that,' he mused. 'It's not quite the same when you take over their minds and join them, but more interesting than mice I suppose.'

Uther got up and stretched, then walked across to the old Druid. 'You never did disguise me, did you, Merlyn? You made me strut in there thinking I looked like Duc Gerlois when all you did was make a fool of me. Is my life so trivial to you old man?'

'Oh really, didn't it work? You were disguised when you walked off. You must have rubbed at the rune and spread it all over your face; it's no wonder she rejected you, turning up with a dirty face like you did.'

'Merlyn, you are exasperating, I could have been killed. I suppose I'll never know if you tricked me or not, I will have to give in to the possibility that it was indeed the storm that removed your little bit of magic.'

Merlyn raised his bushy eyebrows. 'Little bit of magic? That was no small trick, please give me a little more credit than that, Uther, but was it all worth it?'

'Indeed it was. We can talk on the way. We need to return to Dimilioc and finish what we started; there is no time to waste.'

Merlyn thrust out his staff to stop Uther walking off and Uther looked questioningly at him.

'Gerlois is dead,' said Merlyn. He stood and placed his hands on Uther's shoulders. 'Riders came this morning, before first light, sent by Sir Ector. Duc Gerlois died late yesterday, probably about the same time you were rubbing my rune all over your face in the storm. After that, the Dumnonii and Cornovii were apparently quick to capitulate and have all sworn oaths to you again; we have won. If you had only known, you could have walked out of Tintagel the same way you walked in. Only this time the warriors at the gate would have bowed down before you, but I'm sure you enjoyed your climb, didn't you?' Merlyn walked to the edge of the cliff and peered over at the steep rocky face, the waves breaking far below against the rocks in explosions of white spray and foam. 'Must have been quite bracing. Come, let's be off, it's a little too chilly here for my liking.'

Uther followed behind shaking his head.

'And did you go find Igraine and rescue her from the fortress on Tintagel?' Maude asked as she and Uther emerged from the forest. The sun had indeed risen, but clouds had come in before dawn because it was a gloomy, bleak winter's day that faced them. A frost covered everything making the ground crunchy underfoot and spiders' webs in the hedgerows were decorated in shimmering winter jewels. The smell of wood smoke was in the air so they knew they must be close to the village.

Uther looked up at the clouds moving overhead. 'I think it may snow.'

'Indeed it might, Lord, but did you ride in and rescue Igraine?' Maude repeated.

'She didn't need rescuing. Igraine and her daughters were well cared for on Tintagel, it was her home, but yes, we rode down into Tintagel and were welcomed onto the Isle. Merlyn then insisted we all accompany him to Stanenges to witness the Druid rites and celebrations to sanctify the stone circle. To be honest, it was all a little cold and tedious. Lots of fires and chanting, but they had managed to set them in place as a circle of sorts. If I hadn't seen them floating across the sea, I would have called them ordinary, but we all knew they were anything but ordinary.'

'And you gave over Arthur, your son, to the Druids. That can't have been easy.'

Uther stopped walking and turned to look at Maude. 'It was the single hardest thing I ever had to do, and of course, Igraine didn't speak to me properly for weeks... months even. I saw him from time to time, mind, but I never really forgave Merlyn for taking him at birth. He had me handing him over the same day he was born; he wouldn't wait. Said he couldn't delay, that the spirits demanded it upon the day of his birth, or the future would be changed.'

Ahead of them a small collection of huts appeared, smoke drifting up through the thatch of most of them. Ducks and geese ran wild amongst the buildings; a goat was tethered to the closest hut, and a few sheep were fenced in an adjacent field. Maude led them towards a larger central construction explaining it was the meeting hall of the community and also where the village reeve lived.

'I met someone who lives on the other side of the village, said there was a hut we could stay in for some time,' said Maude, taking Uther's arm. 'I think it best if I leave you with the reeve while I go ahead and make sure all is well. Lord, I've been thinking, I don't think it's a good idea to introduce you as King Uther Pendragon, you had best come up with another name. I had a cousin named Borin... maybe we could call you that. What do you think, Lord, do you feel like a Borin?'

Uther smiled. 'Not really, no, introduce me as Usher. I've used that name before, and it suited me very well at the time.'

As they walked further into the village of Somerton, they passed several people who welcomed them with a smile and a greeting. They were told a band of Saxons had been seen passing through before first light, but they hadn't returned. Uther was received into the reeve's home where a comfortable seat was found for him by the big crackling fire, and a girl sent for linen and salve for the wounds to his face. As Maude went off to find her friend and arrange a place they might rest and recover, Uther smiled around at the reeve, his family and the assortment of curious villagers who had followed them in.

'You have a cosy home and the fire is most welcome after a night spent in the forest.' Two children came over and sat at his feet, he smiled at them. 'Hail there, what are you two doing in here on a fine day like this?'

'The animals are fed, and it's too cold to be out. Father says it will snow soon, maybe a storm coming. Can you tell us a story, do you know any? We love stories.'

'Children, leave him alone, don't you go bothering him with your nonsense,' said an old woman as she flattened barley cakes and laid them to cook by the fire.

'Oh please, not to worry, it isn't nonsense. I like stories too,' said Uther with a smile. 'I've been telling a long one lately, but it's finished now. I'm sure I have one or two more though and I will happily swap you a story for a barley cake or two when they're cooked, they look delicious.'

'They weren't really for eating now, but I suppose some cakes for a story is a good bargain on a cold winter's day. They're supposed to be for tonight's celebration, being the celebration of Alban Arthan, midwinter's eve an all, but never mind. What story will you be telling us then?' She smiled a gap-toothed smile and dusted her hands on her apron.

'Well… I'm no Druid bard myself, but I was once close to a very good one, and I do love to tell a story… but which one?' said Uther scratching his head. 'Perhaps I could also trouble you for a mug of ale if you have some around here, just to wet my throat. Now let me think what story to tell.' And then his face brightened. 'I have it, gather around. Who else will hear my one true tale? For I am not a man to make things up, I shall only give you the truth of my life, although you will hear that it has certainly been a very strange life.'

The old lady smiled her thanks and passed him a mug of foaming ale dipped from a barrel to the side of the fire as the other villagers present, came across to make themselves comfortable, eager for a tale, a bright moment in an otherwise cold and dreary day.

'My name,' began Uther, 'is Usher Vance, and mine has been a long and interesting life… or so I've been told in company such as this.' Brushing back a strand of hair, Usher gazed about at the small audience of expectant faces and settled himself more comfortably.

'So many years I have lived and so many things I have done and seen…'

The old lady walked over and put another log on the fire, and it crackled and spat as the villagers drew closer to the warmth. Outside, the wind howled, rustling through the thatch above, the first sign of the storm approaching. Usher Vance settled and took a sip from his leather cup, happy to be sheltered, warm and in good company.

'This shall be a story the likes of which you will no doubt never have heard before. Many years ago in a village not so far from here, there was once a young man, I shall not say who, but he fell in love with a girl of the most uncommon beauty. So in love were they, that they flew to the moon in a boat made of petticoats and kisses… and this is true I tell you, not so easy to find enough petticoats of course… but the kisses, well… they came so very, very easily.'

Author's Note

I hope you enjoyed The Shadow of a King, if you haven't already read it, the first Uther book Shadowland is also available as both paperback, e-book and is also now an audio book narrated by the awesome Ioan Hefin.

I also have another series that you can read, either in paperback or ebook, the first in the series is The Flight of the Griffin, its pure fun fantasy following the quest of four young adventurers who live on a boat named *The Griffin*.

I really appreciate any reviews you might post on Amazon and Goodreads, and love to hear from readers via my website, twitter feed or by email.

Happy reading!

C.M.Gray

Email – cgray129@gmail.com
Website – http://www.author-cmgray.com

Printed by Amazon Italia Logistica S.r.l.
Torrazza Piemonte (TO), Italy

16552568R00192